THE CUTLASS TRILOGY

CUTLASS

Praise for CUTLASS

"I love how as a reader, I thought I knew all the secrets until a new one popped up right in my face taking me by surprise. These little surprises kept me on my toes, and made me love Cutlass even more." – *Chandra Haun, Unabridged Bookshelf*

"CUTLASS didn't disappoint. It's a rollicking, adventurous tale, centered around young pirate extraordinaire Barren Reed and his kidnappee (aka daughter of an important lord, aka his brother's fiancée, aka his eventual love interest-of course!) Larkin Lee." – *Nicole Singer at Write Me a World*

"I thought the use of elves, magic in a story centered around a pirates was unique and clever, and the myth of the bloodstone was intriguing. And yes I admit it, I was totally in love with Barren by the end of the book." – *Lipsyy Lost & Found*

"This really was a true epic adventure. It had every element to keep you glued to such a novel, if you enjoy this sort of plot. From sword fights, to romance, and even a few quite comedic moments, it was difficult to put down, and even more difficult not to enjoy." – *Lily at Bookluvrs Haven*

"Cutlass is the sort of book where you can never tell who all the bad guys are and betrayal, politics, and revealed secrets are constantly shaking the plot and causing problems for our hero and heroine." – *Ryan at Book Marks the Spot*

"I thoroughly enjoyed this pirate and elf tale! With brilliant sword fighting, a few adventures that drew out the tension, betrayal on all sides, and a story that finally comes together showing what a tangled web was woven, this was a wonderful, thoroughly enjoyable read." – *Tiffany at A TiffyFit's Reading Corner*

"I could scream out the window to the neighbors, I also want to stop people on the street and tell them to read this book. I honestly think it was that good. – *Michelle at Because Reading is Better Than Real Life*

"I would highly recommend this book to everyone who's looking for a great YA fantasy read. I can't wait till the next book in this series gets released!" – *Elien from So Bookalicious!*

"I freaking loved it! I'll definitely be reading the next book in this series!" – *Kendall at BookCrazy*

The story had me flipping the pages and wondering what was going to happen next! – *Erin at I Think I'm Obsessed*

Summary: A young pirate seeks revenge for the murder of his father, only to be swept up in a battle to save the Orient.

ISBN: 978-0-9911323-0-0 (paperback)
978-0-9911323-1-7 (e-book)

www.ashley-nixon.com

STARSEED PRESS

DEDICATION

For my Daddy and Momma—
the best gift you ever gave
me was the knowledge that
I could do anything.

Mariana

Silvercrest

Conn

Occident

Arcarum

Estrellas

Ore Mines

Oro Isle

Maris

The Cliffs

D'Almar

Maritime

The Orient

Aurum

Orion

The Octent

N

Chapter One
THE ENGAGEMENT

"A ship has dispatched from the harbor," said Leaf.

Barren had seen the white sails seconds before the Elf spoke. It had been two weeks since anyone left the coast of Maris. Barren watched the ship carefully from their position among the Cliffs. It was bigger than the *Kendrick*, but nothing he hadn't taken on before. The ship entered the Cliffs, and slowly began its tedious navigation toward clearer sea.

The problem with Maris was the route one had to navigate in order to get to and from the island. A set of giant rocks emerged from the Orient's waters and cradled the coast. Any ship that passed through them had to maneuver carefully, otherwise the hull might strike something, and the ship would sink.

"Let's set out—we'll intercept them just ahead," said Barren.

With his crew already in position, they prepared to attack. Barren wondered what the ship carried—what was so important that they would break their embargo?

Barren watched as the tall, reddish brown rocks passed. In his location at the head of the ship, he could reach out and brush them with his hand. Barren looked back at his helmsman, Sam Taylor. His eyes were set on their target, and he kept his hands on the spindles of the wheel. One wrong move left or right, and they would be immobile. Barren trusted Sam's skills—he had expertly steered them through this dangerous area multiple times. In fact, of the twenty-five ships they had targeted for attack, twenty-three of them had successfully been intercepted.

Because of this, Barren was known as a terror. Mostly, he thrived on humiliating those who sailed out to meet him. Sometimes, the fight would turn bloody and that was when Barren's reputation as a murderer spread across Mariana. Barren never wanted to be known as having killed anyone, other than his father's murderer. Indeed, he dreaded when crews did not surrender easily to him because the fight that followed always ended with casualties.

It was a pity Barren had to resort to this. He would prefer sailing the open waters of the Orient to navigating the claustrophobic Cliffs, but he had a duty to avenge his father's death. In fact, all of this was for one purpose—to draw his brother, William, the Ambassador of Maris, from the safety of his home and force him to face punishment for his crimes. It would be so much more than a simple duel. Despite the fact that Barren's attacks ruptured trade in Maris, and made many starve, William refused to meet him. It must be comforting to the people of Maris, Barren thought, that even their Ambassador would not sacrifice his life to help those he'd sworn to protect.

"Slack the sails," Barren ordered. "Drop the anchor."

The twins, Datherious and Natherious, did as instructed, dropping the white sails from their holds. Barren heard them fill with wind. With Leaf's help, Seamus dropped anchor. Barren removed his jacket and the guns from their holsters. Last, he pulled his daggers from his boots, then yanked them off one-by-one.

"Are you sure you want to board first?" asked Leaf. "Remember what happened last time?"

Barren smirked. The Elf was worried about him. Though he was Barren's best friend, he often acted like his father, and he could be both encouraging and critical.

"It was just a flesh wound, Leaf. Nothing you can't fix."

The Elf was also a healer, which was lucky for Barren, as his body seemed to attract all types of wounds from all types of weapons. He had the scars to prove it.

Leaf rolled his eyes. "You are never one for the easy route."

"There's no fun in firing a cannon at their mast. What's fun is to see the surprise on their faces when I board their ship."

"It's fun for an eighteen-year-old, but not so entertaining for a one-hundred year old Elf."

Barren shrugged. "My ship, my rules."

"If you want to keep your ship, you'll get going—they've spotted us." The Elf's gaze was narrowed upon their target. Barren turned and climbed up on the rail of the ship. Holding tight to his daggers, and not looking back at his crew, he dove into the Orient. The water felt fresh and clean against his heated skin, and he moved beneath the surface with speed. He knew if he surfaced before reaching the enemy ship, they would spot him and kill him. Growing up around water had given him many skills; perhaps the best of these was his ability to hold his breath for longer than a few minutes.

Barren surfaced near the hull of the enemy ship. He paused, looking back. He could see his own ship between the tall walls of the Cliffs, its sails standing out against the brightness of the red rock and azure water. The ship itself wasn't an easy target, but it didn't need to be. If this cargo ship managed to release its cannons, they would likely bury his vessel beneath rubble and dust.

Barren dove one last time beneath the water of the Orient, and broke the surface on the opposite side of the ship. The hull was wooden, and though the slats were too close for water to slip through, they were perfect for a knife. Barren raised his dagger, and inserted one knife into the slats, lifting himself out of the water. Placing the other knife higher up, he stabbed the blade through another crack and then began his climb to the deck. Once he was at the top of the railing, he paused to listen.

"Ready! Aim! Fi—"

Barren scrambled to pull himself over the rail. The thud of his feet caused the man releasing the command to pause, and Barren's voice rose in the silence that followed.

"I would reconsider if I were you."

Barren watched as a man dressed in a red coat and black pants turned to face him. He was about as tall as Barren, but not as young. He had curly, graying hair, and gray eyes. His features were hard, and a snarl crossed his lips when he saw the young captain of the *Kendrick*.

"Tell your men to stand down," Barren ordered.

No one moved to listen, and Barren suspected they did not imagine him to be the notorious Barren Reed. He probably didn't look the part of the murderer he was professed to be—after all, he was only eighteen.

"You're one man with two knives, what can you do against all of us?" asked the man standing beside the captain. Barren guessed this was his quartermaster. The other men standing on deck bristled in agreement.

There was always one man who gave the rest hope. Barren twisted his daggers in his hands and smiled. "How do you know I am alone?"

In answer, an arrow whizzed past Barren and into the shoulder of the man who had raised the challenge. He screamed and writhed in pain. In response, the rest of the crew scrambled away from him, even the captain, fearing another arrow. All eyes shifted to Barren's ship, whose great sails now urged it toward their own.

"When one has the skill of an Elf aboard his vessel, he is never alone," Barren said, a dangerous smirk upon his lips. He leveled his eyes with the captain's. "Now, tell your men to stand down."

The captain glared at Barren. "Stand down!" he snarled at his crew.

"Now, have all your men come on deck." Barren waited while a crewmate hurried to the hatch and called for the men to come out. Slowly they filed onto the hot deck. Barren smiled at them. "Come on out, boys, there's nothing to be afraid of."

He could tell by the looks on their faces they weren't so sure. Some stared at him with wide eyes, others avoided eye contact altogether. They'd all heard the stories. No one sails from Maris without knowing their life might be ended by Barren Reed.

Luckily, the cries of the quartermaster kept anyone from protesting against Barren's next command.

"Now, you can all be cooperative and drop your weapons in a pile at the center of the ship and move toward the helm or die a bit sooner."

Without pause, the sound of metal crashing upon metal rang out against the deck as all the men followed Barren's orders. He turned his attention back to the captain, who had not moved to follow Barren's command. The pirate approached him and watched as the captain's eyes grew a shade darker.

"Do you want me to make an example out of you?" Barren lifted his knife to the captain's throat.

In response, the captain unbuckled his holster and removed his weapons.

"Take off your jacket," Barren commanded. The pirate watched, amused, as the captain roughly pulled his arms from the coat and threw it on the ground. "Now, on your knees!"

The captain hesitated, and Barren became impatient. He kicked the back of the captain's legs, and he landed on his knees hard. "Hands behind your head!" This time, the captain didn't pause. Barren pulled a piece of rope from his pocket and secured the man's wrists.

"Give me your name," Barren demanded.

"Captain Jay Nelson," the man managed to sputter—fear finally present.

"Jay Nelson," Barren repeated. "You will forgive me—there can only be one captain aboard this ship."

Barren's lips moved into a thin smile when he saw the man's jaw tighten. "You are brave to leave Maris. Your task must be of high importance."

Jay did not respond to him, and by now the *Kendrick* rested before Maris's cargo ship. A plank connected the two, and Barren's crew filed on board. The twins came first, Natherious and Datherious, the most recognizable of the crew aside from Barren, because of their status as the Princes of the Orient. They were King Tetherion's sons, and consequently Barren's cousins. They had joined Barren's crew only months before. Next, there was Slay the dwarf, unmistakable for his height and frizzy beard. In contrast to the short stature of Slay, Sam Taylor was tall and bulky, a dark man with dark eyes and black hair, twisted into long braids. Then there was Seamus, the oldest of Barren's crew, marked by his shoulder-length gray hair. Finally, the rebel Prince of Aurum, the Elf, Leaf Tinavin, arrived at Barren's side with his captain's sheathed sword.

"Boys, you know what to do," Barren's instructions were simple, and he did not look away from the captain as he spoke. His crew set to work—inspecting barrels, opening wooden crates and confiscating weapons. All around them was the sound of shattering glass, metal weapons piling on metal weapons, and the crash of debris breaking the water.

"So, what special occasion has brought you to sea? I've seen no ships leave Maris for two weeks," Barren asked the captain again.

"Spare us and we will tell no one we saw you," Jay begged, but the words sounded forced.

"Spare you? Cowardly words, Jay. I don't care that anyone knows you saw me—in fact, it is better that they know. I care that my brother still lives. A murderer unpunished for his crime. Do you think what my brother did was right, Jay?"

Barren watched Jay consider his words, and he was right not to answer quickly as so many had before him. The men who met the end of Barren's blade had all been quick to denounce his father, Jess, proclaiming his death was deserved and that William was a hero.

"Do you?" demanded Barren.

"He-he was a pirate—"

"All pirates deserve death, is that right?"

It was then Jay set his jaw and met Barren's gaze directly. "Jess Reed paid for his sins. As will you."

Barren raised both his brows, observing Jay's anger for a moment. Then his eyes went cold, and he drew his sword. Barren pointed the blade at Jay's neck, handing the sheath to Leaf.

"You are not my judge," Barren's voice was quiet, and he aimed to strike.

"Barren, look what we found!"

Interrupted, Barren turned to see a couple of his mates clamber from the hatch at the center of the ship. They threw a leather bag at his feet, stuffed full of white envelopes.

Barren drove his sword into the deck of the ship, and stooped to pick one up. He studied it—this one was addressed to a woman from Arcarum, and the lettering was a beautiful, flowing script. The seal on the back was a wax circle with an "L" stamped into it—he broke it, and pulled out a white card with the same flowing script:

> *"The honorable Ambassador William Reed and Lady Larkin Lee request your presence Friday, 8:00pm at the Castle of Maris to celebrate their engagement."*

"An engagement party," Barren muttered to himself. He did his best to smother the surprise and announced much louder, "My brother is getting married! And I wasn't invited? I am hurt. Looks like I'll be inviting myself then."

Barren heard Jay chuckle. "You are a fool—they will be looking for you. You won't have a chance!"

"You underestimate me." Barren placed the invitation back in its envelope. "As is clear by your current predicament."

"The lady is the daughter of Lord Christopher Lee—he's very wealthy and powerful. You would do well to leave her alone."

"I do not care whose daughter she is, nor do I care for her happiness. Besides, what happiness does my brother deserve when he destroyed all of mine?" Barren handed the invitation to Leaf, facing the Captain. "Now, you have two options: I will send you back to Maris, stripped of your clothing, or you can find your dignity at the end of my sword—your choice."

This was the ultimatum offered to everyone Barren intercepted. Some chose the former and returned to Maris unscathed, but Barren never knew their fate once they left his hands. Some also chose the latter, believing they could take Barren and his crew easily, for he was young and his crew small.

Barren would much rather send them stripped of their pride...it was far less messy and more entertaining.

"Why, you insufferable scoundrel!" Jay said through his teeth. Clearly, he didn't think either option was favorable.

"That was not an answer," Barren chided. "Let's see what your crew thinks."

As he turned to head for the crew, Jay made his move. Tearing a sword from the hand of one of Barren's unsuspecting crewmen, he attacked the young captain.

"Barren!" Leaf warned.

Barren turned quickly, blocking Jay's blow. Their swords clashed, and suddenly, Jay's crewmen found hope, as they charged for their weapons, crying for victory.

Barren fought fast and hard against the man who had

challenged him. As with the others, Barren noted the man fought as if this battle would save his life—he fought with determination, with anger.

"I gave you a chance to live!" Barren cried. "What more could you have wanted?"

"Do you think those who return from your clutches live?" Jay scoffed. "If we are given a choice, we are to choose death!"

Now that was something Barren had not heard, and at those words, Jay fought harder. Barren blocked more blows than he delivered, for Jay did not relent, but Barren knew he would soon grow tired, and when he did, Barren took over. He might be young, but he was strong, and his father had taught him how to fight with a mixture of skill and ruthlessness.

Barren's sword clashed with Jay's and it loosened from his grip. Another blow, and it flew from his hands.

"You will answer for your sins!" Jay cried, just as Barren twisted and thrust his blade through the man's stomach.

"This was your choice," Barren whispered in his ear, pulling the blade from the captain's stomach and pushing him away. He fell, blood trickling from his mouth.

Once the captain fell, the others seemed to lose their momentum, and fearing death themselves, surrendered.

"What do we do with the others?" Leaf asked.

"Set the sails ablaze and leave the rest. Let's go."

Barren's crew set to work quickly, moving supplies to the *Kendrick*. The sails of the cargo ship were doused in oil and set ablaze. It would be no time before the flames were seen at the castle of Maris. Rescue ships would be sent out and search the area looking for Barren, but he and his crew would already be gone, hiding in the Cliffs, waiting for their next victim.

***

Barren stood on the deck of his ship, unable to tear his eyes from the billowing smoke in the distance. He was very troubled by this raid. If the words of the captain were to be believed, no one who encountered Barren Reed ever lived—even if he didn't kill them himself.

And then the news that his brother was getting married had been very unexpected. Barren felt a deep sense of injustice. Why was everyone who had wronged him finding happiness? Why, when they deserved no such gift?

An icy feeling encased his heart as he remembered the day his father died. William, mad with hate, had rushed at their father after his back was turned, driving a long sword through his stomach. Jess had fallen and died where he landed. Barren never heard his voice again. He had no last words to hold onto, just the image of his father's face, pale in death.

Leaf crossed the expanse of deck separating him from Barren, the invitation to the engagement party in his hand. He was as tall as his captain, and his blond hair fell in straight lengths over his shoulders. Despite all the time he spent in the sun, his skin was still ivory white.

"You want to attend your brother's engagement party?" Barren glanced at the Elf—above his sea-green eyes, a pale brow was raised in question. He held out the invitation and Barren took it, leaning against the railing of the ship, his eyes tracing the outline of the letters.

"I would like to see what poor girl has been forced to marry William," said Barren.

"I'm surprised they would consider having a party with you patrolling their coast," said Leaf. "Doesn't it seem suspicious?"

"Suspicious? It seems arrogant."

"You can't honestly think they don't suspect you'll make an appearance?"

"Not at the party. They're going to expect me to attack ships—that is what I do."

"And when you don't? What then?"

Barren chuckled darkly. "My brother will think I am afraid."

Leaf's eyes narrowed. "But you obviously aren't smart enough to leave them alone, so what aren't you telling me?"

"If I had a plan, I would tell you," said Barren. Leaf gave him a dull look and Barren gave in, letting out a short breath. "I am going to kidnap my brother's fiancée."

"Why do you deliberately search for trouble, Barren Reed?" Leaf folded his arms across his chest in disapproval. "Kidnapping is very serious and she is the daughter of a lord. You think you are invincible because people fear you, but I can guarantee if you take her, you will meet resistance."

"I expect resistance," said Barren. "I will hold her for ransom, this Larkin Lee, in exchange for a duel! I will finally have William in my grasp."

"What makes you think William will agree to a duel in

exchange for his fiancée?"

"Well he won't just leave her with me, and he will be humiliated that I succeeded in kidnapping her," said Barren. "He would come after me then—he would fight me."

Leaf shook his head. "But he won't fight you at sea. We all know that. Where does that leave the girl?"

Barren shrugged. "With the realization that she would have married a coward."

"Her marriage to William is not about his cowardice, it is about marrying power with power. You should be careful of the enemies you collect."

"Are you suggesting this girl could pose a threat?" Barren laughed, but Leaf was completely serious.

"You aren't going to change your mind, are you?" Barren shook his head and Leaf sighed. "I will tell you that I don't agree with this, and if you are to go through with it, you must follow the code. No harm can come to that girl unless she gives you reason."

"I know what the code says, Leaf. I can handle this."

"And your uncle will not be pleased," he reminded Barren quickly after.

"No, but I never promised to make my family proud."

Barren knew his uncle better than the public understood. After Jess's death, Tetherion had sought Barren out before he'd turned to terrorizing Maris' coast. Teth had tried comforting him and had given Barren two options: he could remain at Silver Crest and pursue his life as a pirate, or come to Maris and be taken in by the king, himself. Even then Barren had chosen his freedom as a pirate. It was at this point Tetherion had to explain how things would be from then on—that Tetherion would not be able to see him, that he may have to let William rise in ranks, even if what he had done was wrong.

"Very well," Leaf sighed and gave him a hard look. "And how do you plan to *handle this?*"

"I'm not sure yet, I haven't thought the rest out."

Leaf shook his head. "I still think you are foolish, but if you really believe this will get you what you want, I will be glad to do something other than raid ships from Maris."

Barren smiled. "Looks like this jacket will be more useful than I thought," he held up what used to be Jay Nelson's coat—it was red with gold buttons and threading.

"The notorious opponent of Maris, dressed as his enemy," said Leaf. "You have reached a new low."

Barren smirked.

Chapter Two
SILK AND LACE

Over the next week, Barren watched as ships from all over Mariana traversed the Cliffs, intent on reaching Maris for his brother's engagement party. The ships that passed were massive and sailed, one right after the other, as far East as possible. They chose the safest paths, clinging to the places where the Cliffs weren't as close and the waters were easier to navigate. Obviously, they were hoping to avoid Barren. If luck was with any of them, Barren thought, he would have his revenge soon and they wouldn't have to worry about the dangers of sailing to and from Maris ever again.

Barren and Leaf decided they would attend the engagement

party while the others prepared for the kidnapping of Lady Larkin. Barren's plan was to hold her hostage until William agreed to a duel.

"Yer gonna get yerself killed," Slay rasped as he fixed his hat on his head. Between Leaf's disappointed glances and the crew's vocal disapproval, Barren felt like a small child being scolded.

"Look at it this way," said Barren. "If I am killed, you are all free to do as you please."

"We're pirates," Sam scoffed. "We are already free to do as we please, and this is what we choose."

"Well," said Barren, putting on his jacket and preparing the dinghy for departure. "You can all continue to do exactly this…as long as you promise to avenge my death."

"Better keep him alive then," said Datherious. "None of us wants to fight William."

"We don't even know who we're looking for," said Leaf. "There's a good possibility we'll come back empty-handed, so let's get this over with."

The sun was setting on the horizon when Barren and Leaf made it to the port. As they climbed out of their dinghy and set foot on solid ground, they realized just how ridiculous they looked. A number of five-mast galleons lined each dock, carrying equally gallant men and women who were now sashaying through the crowd—the pirates were obviously out of place here in the markets where men and women were adorned in lace and gold, not dirt and grime.

Barren observed his surroundings. The ports were crowded

today. Traders and peasants weaved in and out of the throng, carrying merchandise: scarves, hats and figurines, eager to talk to anyone who would spare them a glance. Now and then, Barren saw a nobleman stop his mighty procession toward the castle and glance over something a peasant offered. They never bought from them, however. The most the nobles did was tease the peasants with hope, like a boy teasing his first love—they believed it to be harmless, but in reality, the disappointment took root and sprouted blossoms of hostility.

Barren had heard of small revolts erupting all over Maris because of the embargo placed upon the island. There were demands for William to meet Barren at sea, and demands that the king send ships to destroy this single pirate crew. Neither had happened—the first because William was a coward, and the second because the king's sons sailed with Barren, and to destroy Barren's ship meant killing the only two children of King Tetherion.

While Barren felt a little guilty that his choices had led to so many people's unease, he knew without a doubt that if any one of them discovered him here, they would turn him over in exchange for the bounty upon his head.

"Are you ready?" Leaf asked.

Barren looked down at himself. He hoped he would be hidden enough. Not only was he at a disadvantage because of who he was, he was also half-Elf. Depending on who you ran into, being half-Elf could either be a good thing or a bad thing. Sometimes, you were just ignored, other times you were hanged.

Barren had witnessed both. The hatred humans and full-blood Elves felt for half-bloods truly sprang from ignorance—the humans feared Elves and believed they would destroy all of Mariana with their magic, while the Elves believed humans to be dull and dangerous with their lustful wishes for power. Barren never understood the hatred. He knew very well that no matter a person's heritage, everyone's blood was red.

To avoid being noticed, Barren pulled his hair into a tight ponytail, careful to hide his pointed ears. A hat he had stolen months ago kept most of his head hidden, and placed a shadow over his eyes. Luckily, he filled Jay Nelson's red jacket up nicely and thought he looked quite regal for a pirate.

Then Barren turned to the Elf. He had successfully hidden his long blond hair and pointed ears under his hat, but he still looked Elvish. It was in his build, and with unnaturally ivory skin, bright eyes, and chiseled features, he looked more supernatural than most humans. More than his own heritage, Barren hoped no one noticed Leaf's, as Elves weren't guests of the royal court. Ever since Tetherion's wife, a full-blood Elf, had run away, they had not been welcomed. While no one knew exactly what happened, it seemed the general population believed she'd fallen in love with one of her own kind and left Tetherion to raise his two children by himself. Most of Maris also blamed her for the twins' choice to take up piracy.

On top of this, Lord Alder, the King of Aurum, did not care for the human race in the least. As an immortal, Lord Alder had gone from seeing his race thrive, to seeing it bleed out into the mortal world. More and more, half-Elves dotted the world of Mariana, and Alder grew to despise them. Then when King Cathmor, Barren's grandfather, began vying for land across Mariana—islands in both the Orient and the Octent—Lord Alder had to fight for his right to remain ruler of his people. The deal was settled with a treaty—of which only one detail is known: that Lord Alder could keep his land and rule the Elves—but what he gave in exchange, no one knows.

"I'm ready," Barren took a deep breath.

"Just remember, this was your idea."

"How could I forget?" Barren rolled his eyes. Pulling his hat as far down as it would go, and lifting the collar of his jacket, he and Leaf merged with the crowd, following the stream of people toward the markets of Maris.

The markets at port were a colorful affair. Tents rose in maroon, orange, yellow, and purple. With the sun setting, the sheen of jewel-toned fabric glimmered like gems. The merchandise ranged from weapons to wind chimes, strange trinkets of the sea, even diamonds. And everything was peddled furiously. Women painted with gold danced in what little space they had, musicians worked their instruments until their fingers went numb, men in tattered shirts and dirty pants called out the prices of useless objects, attempting to lure in customers. The market was a loud and tireless place—but this was what Maris thrived on.

Among this rabble, Barren spotted his own face. Wanted posters seemed to punctuate the area. At least he was worth ten thousand pieces, he thought.

The roar of the markets faded as they entered the slums of Maris. Despite their name, the buildings beyond the markets had a certain charm. Most of them were covered in mosaics of reds and teals and oranges. Some buildings had tall columns that rose in support of awnings, laced with scarves. Arches perforated with tiny designs allowed the sun to cast patterned shadows on the walls. The charm, however, ended there. These were the dwellings of those who worked the port. The slums were crowded and smelled of urine. Beggars roamed about, exposing deformed feet with crooked and curled toes or missing limbs, displaying talents in hopes of earning extra gold. The buildings were various sizes, built close together to accommodate the influx of people. Since Maris was the largest island of the Orient and the center for trade for Mariana, it attracted all sorts—sailors, Elves, Dwarves, and even traders from the Octent (the adjoining sea), though they were not well liked in the Orient.

It was through these causeways that Barren and Leaf traveled toward the castle of Maris. While it would have been less suspicious for them to take the main road, all their enemies would also take that route, and Barren preferred to lessen his chances of getting caught.

At some point, the castle appeared before them. Perched upon the highest cliff, it was foreboding as it loomed like a dark cloud over Maris. It was accessed by a wide set of stairs composed of big pieces of flat rock. It was laborious to reach because of the height of the steps and the length of the path. Most rode on horseback, but access to horses was difficult for two pirates who lived at sea.

They made the arduous climb on foot, huffing for breath, and wishing to shed some of their heavy clothing. Another nobleman moved past them, staring as if they had grown two heads. As Barren feared, they were probably eyeing Leaf.

By the time they reached the castle, it was dark. Bright lanterns hung on black rods on either side of the path that led from the stairs to the gates of the wall. Barren and Leaf followed them, and soon came to stand in a crowded line at the entrance of the castle. At first Barren thought this to be bad luck, but when they displayed their invitation, the guard hastily looked over the card, and admitted them.

They moved down a cobbled path. A courtyard extended on their left, exposed to the night. To their right, a garden composed of hedges and roses surrounded a large fountain where water rose forth and burst, falling like rain into the pool. The pirates walked farther and found another courtyard, though this one was covered in stone. Doors could be accessed from here and Barren wasn't sure where they led. He guessed these were rooms for guests, because extravagantly dressed people filed out of random doorways, heading through an archway at the back of the yard.

He heard Leaf chuckle to himself, though it was not out of humor.

"What did you hear?"

Because Leaf was a full-blood Elf, his hearing was

exceptional—something he often complained about.

"Our Lady Larkin is half-Elf," he said, then he nodded toward the courtyard they had just passed. "Seems the men fancy her, and the women despise her."

Barren did not respond, though he found himself wondering what sort of troubles she'd encountered with her mixed blood, or perhaps her rich father had been able to shelter her from such crudeness. Money, quite literally, almost always made others more attractive. William was a perfect example of this. Being both the son of Jess Reed and a half-Elf should have made his possession of the title of Ambassador impossible, but he had been given sponsorship after the murder and rose to power.

The pirates continued through an open gate and into the biggest courtyard yet, located at the back of the castle. Pale lanterns hung from an invisible line, crisscrossing in the sky, and red and gold fabric unfurled over tall stone walls, adding a richness to the otherwise unsavory gray stone. There were round tables clustered at the edges of the lawn, decorated with white linens, gold and red runners, and candle centerpieces. Zipping in and out of the crowd were servants dressed in white, bearing trays of champagne, wine, and various foods—imported meats and cheeses Barren had only seen in the Octent—fruits that were so fragrant, they made Barren's mouth water, and decadent desserts smelling strongly of cocoa. Music lilted softly in the background while the murmur of voices rose above it. People gathered in circles, laughing. Others moved through the throngs, seeking companions. Men of various ranks were decorated with medals or sashes, and some had capes clasped over their left shoulders. The women wore ridiculously layered dresses, composed of silk and lace that created a barrier between them and anything within their reach. Diamonds and pearls acted as accessories, and feathers and flowers adorned curled hair. Barren almost feared seeing what Larkin looked like—he might not be able to reach her for all the fabric.

So, this is how William had been living for five years. No murderer Barren knew had such luxuries.

"This is a little excessive, don't you think?" asked Barren. He peered around the courtyard, taking in all the finery. It had been a long time since either pirate had experienced these things. "We don't even know what Larkin looks like without all this added fluff, much less with it."

"It helps that she is half-Elf," said Leaf. "And she is probably dressed for the occasion, as she is the bride-to-be."

"What does that even mean?"

"Look for something frilly."

"*Everything* is frilly!" Barren mocked.

Barren gazed at the crowd, sifting through the faces. While he wasn't sure who he was looking for, he could only imagine what sort of wife William would need. A woman who was slight and meek, someone who didn't like to stand out in the crowd, or speak up—obviously—or she would not have agreed to marry William. Then again, perhaps Barren was not giving this mystery woman enough credit. Perhaps she saw William as a way out of a situation. Either way, he felt sorry for her.

Barren heard Leaf chuckle and he looked at the Elf. "I think you have no idea who you are dealing with."

Leaf pointed toward a circle of people. Barren's eyes shifted there, and his breath caught. What he had expected was a fragile girl—someone slight, doll-like, and silent. This girl was not so. The first thing he took in was her strength. It radiated from her like warmth from a hearth. She stood straight with her shoulders back, an observing eye upon everyone. Then he drank in the features composing her beauty. Almond-shaped eyes gleamed with emerald irises that shone like sun on the green sea. Her smile, while charming and beautiful, had something mischievous about it. She had high cheekbones, blushed with pink and long, dark curls decorated with white flowers falling down her back and over her shoulders. Her dress, crimson in color, was unlike the others, hugging her hourglass figure like it was made on her. Barren could not have thought up a more beautiful girl, and no one around her compared.

A smug smirk crossed Leaf's thin lips.

"What am I supposed to do with *her*?" asked Barren. His thoughts were all muddled. He had forgotten why he was here, or how he had intended to attract this girl's attention. Could he even do that?

Leaf laughed. "Oh, you silly boy, we won't make it out of this one alive, will we?"

Barren glared at the Elf. "Don't tell me you expected her! How could she ever agree to marry *my* brother?"

Leaf shrugged, still smirking. "Ask her."

Barren froze. He watched her again. She seemed content; he could hear her laughter—full of love, of affection for life. His stomach flipped and a knot formed in his throat. He shook his head.

"I'll wait," he said.

Leaf rolled his eyes. "We'll be here forever."

"Well, you didn't expect me to just walk in and take her, did you?"

"Yes, actually. You're Barren Reed, you do stupid things all the time and it somehow always works out."

Barren said nothing as he watched Larkin, afraid to look away for fear he'd lose her. He wondered if she would ever be alone tonight. Surely she would tire of so many people gawking at her. He watched the men around her. Despite having ladies on their arms, they still cast her yearning, hopeful looks. The women, though they smiled and seemed enthusiastic, gazed at her with jealousy, always checking their hair against hers, their dresses, even the way they spoke. Leaf had definitely heard right. Did she know she had no friends among these people?

In that moment, she turned her head and her eyes met Barren's. The mischievous smile that pulled at her lips faded and she seemed very serious, but Barren tilted his head to the side, holding her gaze and the corners of his mouth turned up. She seemed lost in that moment, unaware of what she was doing. Someone touched her arm and she turned. Barren looked away before he could tell who had disturbed her.

He turned around. "Come on, Leaf," he said and retreated

through the crowd of people and into the shadows of the courtyard.

As they did, a roar of clapping sounded and the music ceased. Barren turned to see Lady Larkin arm in arm with his brother.

William.

A fire ignited in Barren's belly and climbed to his limbs, urging him to pick up his sword and fight. He stood firmly, his hands clenched tightly as he observed the man who murdered his father. He and William had always favored each other, though William wore a more cynical expression. His hair was cut short and his dress expressed his status—gold buttons, a gold pocket watch, and a decorated coat of medals. Barren wasn't sure what the metals were for, but had a suspicion most of them were granted after Jess's murder.

The couple glided into the center of the courtyard, and Barren could see why they were together—their mere presence spoke of their power. It made his teeth clench. William pulled Larkin closer, one hand threaded through hers, the other on her hip, as they prepared for their dance. The music began—a slow fanciful tune that made Barren's stomach tighten. Soon the guests began dancing. Everyone broke into pairs and trotted around to the music, but Barren kept his eyes on his brother and his wife-to-be.

While Barren was more of an expert when it came to sword fighting, he had definitely seen better dances. Larkin moved mechanically alongside William. They twisted and turned, the distance between them formal. Barren couldn't be sure, but he sensed they were a good match in all but love, and it relieved him to see their disconnect because, had William, the merciless kin-slayer, found happiness and love reciprocated, the pirate would not have been as calm as he was at that moment.

"Aren't they a lovely couple?" a voice sighed dramatically beside him. Barren froze and glanced askance quickly. An older woman stood beside him, her dress seemed to billow around her like a cloud, and she held a fan in her hand, adorned with lace and jewels. He decided it was best that he nod.

"And look, Lord Lee standing there admiring them. He must be proud!"

Barren's eyes shifted to Lord Christopher Lee. He emanated power, though he was old and walked with a black cane. He was a tall, broad man, dressed in blue. He had short gray hair and a beard that came to a point at his chin. The only thing he and Larkin shared was that they radiated power and confidence, otherwise they were stark opposites—one cold and frightening, the other warm and inviting.

"I am going to raid the buffet," Leaf leaned over to say. "Since all you are going to do is stare at the lady."

Barren glared at the Elf, but watched him as he disappeared from sight. He returned his gaze to his brother and fiancée. Barren gulped wine from a glass he'd snatched off a servant's tray. Twisting the stem between his fingers, he meandered through the dancers, edging his way toward the couple. He wasn't sure what he hoped to accomplish. Surely this would only lead to exposure, but he wanted to see them close up—watch Larkin's face as he passed, look into his brother's eyes…and then kill him.

The closer he got, the more he noticed William stumbling over his own feet, his distant, glazed stare—he must be drunk. Though Barren could feel people weaving around him, he suddenly felt like no others existed but his brother and him. This was his chance. He had a knife in his belt. It would be simple: take the knife and jam it through William's back. He would fall and Barren could escape over the edge of the courtyard. He knew that water; it only looked dangerous. His fingers remained on the stem of his glass, while his other hand clasped the blade at his side. His chest tightened, he was trembling with adrenaline, but he could do this—hadn't it been this easy for William to kill their father?

Something hit Barren's elbow, throwing his glass of wine from his hand and onto William's back. The glass fell into the grass, and William whipped around to face Barren. All went quiet. Suddenly, it was like Barren's entire body was coated in ice. He could only think to clutch his knife and drop his head as his heart pounded frantically in his chest. Barren was sure not a single eye strayed from him.

"What do you think you're doing?" William growled. It had been a long time since Barren had heard his brother's voice. He kept his eyes on his feet so William could not see his face.

"Sorry, sir. I didn't mean to…sir." Barren's teeth hurt from clenching his jaw so tightly. It unnerved him to use courteous words with the murderer of his father.

"Imbecile! How dare you ruin *my* night!"

William raised his hand and Barren's grip tightened on his

knife. "You'll only ruin the rest of *your* night if you hurt him," Larkin stepped in front of Barren, shielding him with her slight form. "Leave him be, it was a mistake."

William hesitated a moment, clenching his fist. Barren watched as his brother's fiancée bent to pick up the empty glass. She handed it to him, smiling, though Barren barely lifted his gaze. "Perhaps you should take a stroll *around* the dancers next time."

Barren swallowed and nodded in agreement.

William scowled and grabbed Larkin's arm, pulling her away from Barren and out of the crowd. Barren stood there for a moment, staring at his empty glass—if only his hands had been empty, then maybe there would be blood in the grass, instead of red wine. He slinked toward the shadows. The music began again, and slowly everyone stopped looking at him.

He kept near the wall, one hand on his knife, the other clutching the glass at his side. He knew Leaf had seen that little display, and he probably knew Barren's intentions, too. While it would have been easy to end everything right here, this was not the place to fight William. There were too many others who could intervene. No, Barren needed to wait. The sea would be a much better place.

Barren allowed himself to relax a little. He took a deep breath as the wind washed over him, causing the fabric draping the walls to rustle. He dropped the empty glass to the ground, and let his fingers loosen their hold on his knife. He still felt eyes following him. He had drawn too much attention. Now people would ask who he was, where he came from. Did anyone recognize him? Just as hysteria began to creep back into his mind, he spotted the figure of Larkin Lee retreating from the courtyard. She seemed in a hurry, and just before she slipped out, she looked around to see if anyone noticed her.

Barren wasn't sure where she might be headed, but he felt he needed to follow her. Perhaps she was wandering off alone to escape this crowd. Just as he prepared to cross the lawn, Leaf reappeared.

"And where do you think you're going?" he asked, his mouth full of food.

"Larkin's left the party," said Barren. "I need to follow her! She's alone!"

Leaf dropped the grapes in his hand. No," said the Elf. "What if she's *not* alone?"

"I'm sure if she is meeting her lover, I can take him down easily," Barren argued.

"Or she could be luring you into a trap. You don't know her! And she could have recognized you. Don't think I don't know what you were doing!"

"Leaf, it flatters me that you worry about me so, but you have to let me do this."

The Elf's features hardened, and he raised his head a little. "Mocking me for my concern is a little foolish, don't you think?"

"Look, you said you were tired of chasing cargo ships. I'm just trying to remedy your boredom."

"Do what you want, but when it all goes south, I'm going to

remind you of my words. And by south, I don't mean what happens tonight, tomorrow or the next day. But I swear by Saorise, you will regret toying with Larkin Lee."

***

Though the moon was full, it was hard for Barren to navigate the terrain outside of the castle, as he didn't take the steps back down to the port—he followed Larkin down the side of an uneven hill. She held a lantern in her hands that bobbed about as she moved ahead of him. Now and then she'd stop to pull her dress free from brambles that caught it, but her determination kept her moving forward. He couldn't help but be curious as to what she was hurrying toward.

He sent Leaf to the ship to inform the others that they would be sailing soon, though the words the Elf had said before Barren's trek were ever-present in his mind. *You will regret toying with Larkin Lee.* Even he couldn't ignore the feeling of dread in the pit of his stomach. So why was he going through with this?

As he came to the end of the hill, he saw Larkin's shadow disappear into the darkness of the embankment below where the shore met the ocean. Barren followed in a less than graceful manner, as the moonlight didn't reach every crevice, or illuminate every rock. As Barren stumbled into the sand, Larkin's voice rang out, alarmed.

"Who's there?" she turned, holding the lantern up and gripping at the scarf draped around her shoulders like a weapon.

"S-sorry to startle you," Barren said, holding up his hands.

The girl regarded him for a moment, and he saw her eyes

narrow. "You're the man who poured wine on the Ambassador. You've been watching me all night."

Barren's heart beat a little faster—maybe she *was* onto him.

"You must forgive me. I suppose I let my shock get the best of me."

"Shock?"

"Yes," Barren nodded, walking toward her. "I had come to see what woman would take William Reed as a husband, and did not expect...you."

He didn't feel like he needed to explain *what* he'd expected, exactly.

"I am rather uncertain of how I should feel about that," Larkin replied.

"It is no insult, Lady."

"Perhaps not to me, but to my fiancé, it is."

Barren couldn't stifle his laugh in time, and Larkin didn't seem pleased with his reaction.

"You seem very out of place in the company you just left," said Larkin. "William didn't seem to recognize you, and everyone in attendance was a guest of his."

"How unfair that seems," Barren mused.

"Well, as he made it so perfectly clear, it was *his* night," she said sarcastically.

Barren tried not to meet her gaze. He felt the less she saw of his face, the better chance he'd have of kidnapping her.

"Do you come here often?" asked Barren after a moment.

The rush of waves was a pleasant sound to Barren. The smell

of salt hit his nose and he longed to rush into the water and swim away from Maris. He longed to forget the intentions he came here with, to forget that his brother was here, that his father was gone. But he hesitated—remembering that the blood of his victims also swam in that water. He shuddered.

Larkin laughed a little. "I try to come here when I feel overwhelmed. I suppose tonight is one of those times. The sea is...calming, but after I am married I will come less often. My fiancé thinks I will be kidnapped by pirates."

Barren laughed. "Let me guess—the notorious Barren Reed will seek you out?"

"Yes. William thinks Barren to be a coward and a nuisance and all he can talk about is his death...though he will do nothing to be accountable for it."

Barren did not respond.

"You look a lot like William, you know."

Barren chuckled. "I am insulted, Lady. Me, favor William Reed?"

"Yes...almost too much," she said.

Then something happened Barren did not expect. Larkin flung the lantern she held toward Barren. The pirate dodged the blow—moving back, his feet automatically taking up battle stance, and he withdrew a short blade from a hidden holster attached to his back—one couldn't expect Barren to march among his enemies without weapons. From the folds of her scarf, Larkin withdrew a similar blade. She looked like a warrior, her eyes ablaze in the night.

"You are either brave or foolish for coming here," she said. "I haven't yet figured out which one."

"And you are not what I expected." Barren was still a little shaken and all his previous notions about the girl vanished.

"What? You didn't expect me to fight?"

"Not so suddenly, no," said Barren. "So you did recognize me in the courtyard. I wonder...why did you not expose me when you had the chance?"

"It is not for me to be responsible for anyone's death, even someone as foul as you," Larkin's hand tightened visibly on her blade, then she smiled. "Are you going to fight me?"

"If that is your wish," Barren replied. "But answer me one question—why William? Why a murderer? I know you do not love him, so why?"

"You do not know me, sir," she said evenly.

"I do not need to know you to understand you. There are a lot of girls like you, and since you're not marrying for money or power, you must be marrying to appease someone."

Larkin attacked, and it was like a dance, strong and graceful. Her blows made Barren's teeth clench as metal struck metal. He recognized this fury; it was the way you fought when you hated someone.

Either because they were both half-Elf or for some other reason entirely, she was completely in tune with his movements. If he stepped backward, forward, or side-stepped, he was met with her counter attack, and her strikes held a force that shocked him. He could kick himself. He had all the clues before him. She had recognized him from the moment their eyes had met, and when she stopped William from hitting him, she had done it to protect her fiancé, knowing Barren's intentions, and yet he still let himself think she was harmless. He was stupid.

"I think you only fight so viciously because you know I am right," said Barren as he parried another blow.

"How do you live with yourself?" She cried harshly. "Murdering all those people—do you feel that is right?"

"Do you think your husband was right to murder my father?"

"He. Is. Not. My. Husband!" Her words were punctuated by the strike of the sword against Barren's. On the last word, Barren misdirected his blade. He felt a burning sensation down his arm and knew he was cut. He didn't let her blow vex him; he didn't have time. Her attacks seemed to grow stronger with every strike. Barren was getting angrier by the second—the men he encountered at sea hardly gave him this much of a battle. His blade nicked her fingers, and she dropped her sword. Barren moved quickly, grabbing her weapon and throwing it into the ocean.

He turned to laugh at her, but Larkin had more surprises up her sleeve—she bent and picked up a handful of sand, throwing it at Barren's face. The sand stung his eyes and he lost focus as he tried to rub it out. Larkin made her move, pushing him to the ground, grabbing his sword as he fell. She held the tip of his blade inches from his nose.

"Cheater," she accused breathlessly.

"You're the one who threw sand in his face," Leaf called from the darkness beyond, and Barren felt relief flood his body. "But if you were referring to his misuse of his blade, he's a pirate, Lady. What did you expect?"

Barren was relieved when he saw the blade against her neck. Larkin went rigid and straightened slowly. Leaf pried the short sword from her hand, tossing the blade at Barren's feet. The young pirate stood, still rubbing his eyes. He glared at Larkin whose gaze was narrow, her jaw tightened in defeat.

"I thought she killed you," said Leaf. He pulled Larkin's hands behind her back and tied them tightly with rope. "It would have been a pity—I would never have been able to tell you how right I really was."

"You could have gotten here a little sooner."

"Oh, I was here," replied Leaf with a smile. "I just enjoyed watching you struggle."

"Some friend you are."

As Barren rubbed his eyes free of sand, he noticed a long chain around Larkin's neck. Barren reached forward with his blade and strung the chain along the tip, lifting it from her chest. Now he saw what was at the end—a silver circle, the top encrusted with diamonds. Her engagement ring. Barren hadn't even thought to check her finger for the stone, but there it was, dangling and forgotten. Barren's gaze met her menacing stare, and he withdrew his blade and let his arm fall to his side.

Then, using Leaf for support, Larkin leaned into him, kicking up her legs, her heeled feet smashing into Barren's chest. He fell backward into the sand, and was then met with Larkin's ridicule—as if the pain that shot through him wasn't enough.

"You're a bloody bastard!" she seethed. Leaf pulled her back, holding her in his tight grasp so she couldn't maneuver again.

"I didn't think ladies spoke with such crudeness," Leaf laughed, which annoyed Barren even more, considering what had just happened.

Barren got to his feet, resisting the urge to put his knife at her throat and said, "I had no wish to kill you, but if you have any belief in the stories you hear about me, you better think twice before you *ever* do that again."

His threat didn't seem to sway her, because she glared just as fiercely as before. Barren stood back and met Leaf's eyes. He didn't have to speak for the Elf to know what he was thinking. As Leaf fitted the gag over Larkin's mouth, she tried to scream and lurched violently away from him, but Barren was there to hold her tightly against him as she struggled, earning more than his fair share of profanity-laden curses.

When the gag was in place, Barren pushed her toward Leaf so he could lead her to the ship—he'd had enough of her.

"Come on. I can hear them searching for her," said Leaf. "They'll come here first. We should be on our way."

Barren followed behind them, feeling humiliated and defeated. As they left the shore, he noticed Larkin's scarf on the ground. He kicked it where it lay. Tonight he had met his equal.

Chapter Three
SAIL HO!

As they headed toward the ship, Barren could hear Leaf chuckle now and then. He ground his teeth. He knew the Elf wouldn't let him forget his near-defeat at the hands of a girl. He wondered where Larkin had learned to fight like that. What use were those skills to a lady of Maris? Perhaps her father had wanted her to be well-prepared, just in case she was hauled off by pirates. But Larkin wouldn't have been a target until she decided to marry William, and those skills weren't from a few weeks of instruction—no, they, like Barren's, had come from a lifetime of training.

The *Kendrick* sat behind several large rocks on the other side of the port. It was a hard task moving through the brackish water and mud that plagued the shore on the way there, but the three fared well enough and ended up safely on the ship, and as far as they knew, unseen by anyone. Barren's crew didn't manage to do much other than stare at the girl he had kidnapped.

"That's William's fiancée?" asked Sam as Barren approached him. Sam towered over the helm. He was broad and bulky and when he stood with his arms crossed, everyone around him felt intimidated.

Barren turned and watched as Leaf helped Larkin kneel down and then sit on the deck; her hands remained tied behind her back. Then the Elf moved toward the helm where he kept a bag of supplies for treating wounds and other illnesses caused by the sea.

"Don't be fooled," Barren said to Sam, and his hand tightened around his shoulder, keeping pressure on his wound. "She's not all pretty and sweet."

"Don't let *him* fool you," said Leaf. "He's just angry because he found himself in a little trap. That's what he gets for underestimating his opponent."

"I certainly overestimated our friendship, considering you chose entertainment over my life."

"You're still here. Quit being dramatic." Leaf rolled his eyes.

"Fix this," said Barren, taking off his jacket and moving his injured arm in Leaf's face. The Elf scrunched up his nose in disgust, but Leaf was a healer; he had seen worse. Shoving Barren's shoulder out of his face, he said, "You can wait. Ladies first."

Leaf walked over to Larkin whose eyes were so fierce, they almost looked glassy. He spoke to her quietly for a moment, and then Barren watched as the Elf removed her gag and cut the ropes that held her wrists captive. He cleansed her wound, smeared a clear slave on her fingers, and bandaged her hand. When he was finished, he secured her wrists in the ropes again, only now her hands rested comfortably in her lap.

"Oh yes," Barren said as Leaf approached. "Leave her tied up like that, see if she escapes by morning."

"She'll be fine."

"I think you revel in defying me," Leaf chuckled, and Barren knew that technically, as quartermaster, Leaf had the ability to override any orders Barren gave—that was part of the code.

The Elf poured the herb mixture he used on Larkin's hand into the ocean. Sitting on one of the steps leading to the helm, he patted the space next to him. Barren sat. The Elf poured water from his canteen into the wooden bowl and sprinkled more herbs into it. All of his actions were slow and precise, right down to dipping a rag into the mixture, so when Leaf jammed the soaked poultice into his arm, Barren didn't react well.

"Dammit, Leaf! What did I do to you?" He cowered away from the Elf, holding his arm, as the gash started bleeding profusely.

"That's for making yet another stupid decision that almost got you killed!"

"Leaf, I'm far from death, don't you think? I've been closer than this before."

"The fact that your veins are filled with immortal blood does not make you invincible. You'll do well to remember that, Barren Reed." Leaf said nothing more and focused on his work—smearing salve on the pirate's arm, and bandaging it tightly. He left without another word.

For Barren, it wouldn't be a normal day if he didn't do something to get on the Elf's nerves. Sometimes he felt like everything he did was stupid, because that's what Leaf always said. He cast his gaze over to Larkin. She was examining her binds. Barren wouldn't be surprised if he found her gnawing on them later in an attempt to break free.

He unbuttoned his shirt and surveyed his chest where Larkin had kicked him. Broken skin and a little bit of blood marked two places on either side of his sternum where her heels had hit him. The wounds weren't nearly as bad as they had felt. When he looked up, he caught Larkin's eyes on him, and he buttoned his shirt quickly. He didn't want her to know she'd harmed him any more than was already visible.

Barren stood and moved up the helm. Seamus was standing there beside Sam. He was a thin man with gray hair that swept his shoulders and he knew weapons better than anyone in the Orient—which was why Barren had chosen him as his Weapons Master. There was an odd brightness to his eyes and he was laughing. Barren could just imagine why—it wasn't every day Barren was beaten by a girl.

"Didn't think you'd snag such a beauty," said Seamus.

"She'll be more trouble than she's worth," grunted Slay as he plopped down on the deck, having been up in the crow's nest. The dwarf took his place beside Seamus and crossed thick arms over his chest. "I say ye had a bad idea."

"I'm aware that it wasn't one of my best." Barren folded his arms over his chest and glared at Larkin, almost mimicking Slay. Then he watched as Larkin drew her legs up and managed to rest her head on her knees, turning away from the pirates. She seemed almost a child then, perhaps sick with the reality of her situation. Barren felt the angry tension in his face give way to a frown.

"Go find her a blanket, Slay," Barren ordered.

"But...but she's a prisoner!"

Barren glared at the dwarf. Slay exhaled sharply, and stomped away, diving into the hatch to find a blanket. Seamus glanced at Barren, his old eyes permanently squinted and watery.

"You know, you have time. You can change your mind. Take her back."

Barren wasn't sure why, but the notion angered him. "No." he said resolutely. In the end, Barren had kidnapped Larkin for one reason, and if her disappearance didn't bring William right to him, nothing would.

Seamus shook his head. Barren expected him to say something, but the old man turned and hobbled away. A loud crash came from below. After a moment, Slay climbed out of the hatch, a blanket in hand. He walked up to Larkin and stuck out his hand to give her the blanket. She stared at him, looking both curious and confused. Slay grew impatient and dropped the blanket at her feet, turning swiftly. He walked away grumbling, and went back to his post in the crow's nest.

"Where to, Barren?" asked Sam, hands on the helm. Though it was dark, they all knew they couldn't sit here so close to Maris. They would at least have to retreat to the Cliffs.

"We will return to the Cliffs for the night. If no one is searching for her by daybreak, we leave altogether."

Sam shrugged. "You're the captain."

***

Larkin had a hard time trudging through the mushy path of water, rocks and mud wearing a ball gown. She tripped several times on the too long skirt, only to be caught up in the ever-present arms of her kidnapper. It was infuriating. She would prefer being covered in mud, rather than allowing Barren's constant attempts to keep her on her feet.

She couldn't really figure out how to feel—she was scared, yes, but also strangely intrigued. She knew why they'd taken her: as bait to lure William to sea. Her father had warned her that she might be targeted, and she felt stupid having been taken. Every time she looked at Barren, anger flared in her chest.

She'd decided to leave the engagement party after spotting Barren. She'd gone through her options—returning home meant signaling a carriage and drawing attention, and while the castle might offer safety, it didn't offer her peace. That's why she'd chosen to head to shore—why would a pirate ever suspect she'd go there? She was a lady, after all. She'd thought she had been discreet on her way out, even escaping Barren Reed's notice…but, instead, she'd drawn it.

She fell again and jerked away when she felt his hand on her arm.

"I am perfectly capable of standing on my own," she spat.

Barren gave a short laugh. "Really? Because you've been stumbling all over since we left the ship."

Larkin reached down and gathered her dress up as much as she could and continued forward. "If it is too bothersome for you, we can cut the skirt away."

Larkin twisted, almost slipping as she did. Her eyes fell upon Barren, narrow and unkind.

"You will *not* touch me."

Barren held up his hands. "I was just offering an option to ease your struggling."

"I'm not struggling!"

She turned around and to her great annoyance, fell again as the rocks and mud gave way beneath her feet. This time, Barren stood aside as she got to her feet again. She refused to look at him, her face burning with embarrassment.

Soon, the large mouth of a cave appeared before them, an endless hole in one of the many cliffs. It rested before the water silently. Larkin gazed behind her—no sign of Maris lingered there—no outline of the port, no castle, not even lantern lights. Barren gave her a little push and they were engulfed by the darkness.

The crew filed into the cave, one by one. Barren steered

Larkin toward a wall, leaving her in the muggy, dank atmosphere.

"Start a fire, Leaf," Barren's voice rose in the darkness.

Larkin scoffed. "And draw your enemies to you…good idea."

As she spoke, blue fire sparked at the center of the cave, and Leaf's face was illuminated over the glow. "It's not a normal fire, Lady," said the Elf. "It will only provide us with a soft glow so that you may eat and, most unfortunately, see our faces."

Larkin stared at the fire apprehensively. Despite being half-Elf, Larkin had been taught to believe that Elves shouldn't be trusted—that they were mischievous folk, devious and unkind and their magic was worse. Her governess had said that during Cathmor's reign as king, the people of the Orient endlessly feared attacks by magic. Even now, there were rumors that the Elves hid a powerful magic that had the potential to destroy the whole of Mariana. It was for this reason only that Lord Alder was still allowed to rule his kingdom, which was technically within the bounds of the Orient and should be ruled by the King of the Orient.

"Is that magic?" she asked.

Leaf laughed, clearly amused. "No," he said and extended his palm to her—tiny seeds were stuck to his hand. "Unless you count seeds and herbs as magic."

Larkin didn't say anything. Instead, she looked around, observing the cave they were in. The place looked much like a storage room with pots and pans stacked in the corner, a few sacks of potatoes, and even more sacks of apples. Several barrels filled the back of the cave; she imagined they were full of ale or wine. Then there were fragments of everyday life that made her think this was where Barren and his crew stayed when they weren't sailing before Maris, awaiting the chance to attack ships and kill William Reed. Makeshift beds were scattered about, composed of hay, a blanket and a pillow, and even some clothes hung above her head on a frayed rope. The light from Leaf's magic fire did not make for a warming glow; instead, it cast bluish shadows on the wall, and gave everyone's skin a pallid flush.

Her head shot toward the entrance as a laugh filled the cave. It was deep and strangely rough and it emanated from Barren. Larkin felt chills prick her arms. She found it strange that Barren and his crew ambled about this cave doing completely normal things like laughing. She always imagined them plotting to kill, constantly lusting for blood, and using especially crude manners. While she had experienced the crude manners, the other two things had yet to be seen, and she wondered when they would transform into the monstrous men she knew them to be.

"Where are the twins?" Larkin asked suddenly. The twins were Natherious and Datherious—the king's sons—and she didn't see them anywhere.

Barren chuckled. "You already admire members of my crew? Now, that did not take long."

"I do not admire them," Larkin protested. "They are traitors to their crown—"

"Watch yer tongue," Slay snapped. "The twins won't like what yer saying. Like it or not, they're still yer princes."

Larkin glared at the dwarf.

"They are keeping watch, Lady," said Barren, his back was to her as he and Sam unrolled a blanket composed of twigs and leafy branches over the mouth of the cave. Now the opening that once overlooked the moonlit ocean was gone, hidden from unwanted eyes. "We must have someone watching out for your saviors." Barren brushed his hands together, removing dust and bits of grime.

"If you are thinking William will save me, you are wrong." She sat before the enchanted fire.

"After the evening I had with you, I wouldn't save you either." Barren pushed a stick into the fire and sparks exploded above it. Then he took a seat opposite Larkin.

"But your hope in capturing me was to lure your brother out to sea. He will not follow."

"And why are you so sure? He does love you, doesn't he?" Barren questioned with sarcasm.

Larkin's features were frigid. "My father will be the one to find you, and he does not fear you."

Barren laughed deeply. "You think my brother fears me?"

"If he does not face you, then he must fear you."

"So you think he is a coward?" Barren raised a brow.

Larkin's expression was cold, and she refused to speak further. She didn't owe Barren any explanation for how she felt about her fiancé.

"I often call him a coward," Barren continued instead. "But I know his fear—he does not want to meet me on my own turf. I am master here. And I would not want to meet him on his. So you are my only option, unfortunately for me."

Larkin raised a brow. "By the end of this, Barren Reed, you will wish you never met me."

"I already do, trust me."

Silence fell and Leaf sat next to Barren near the fire. The Elf handed him bread, and he pulled at it with his teeth. Larkin watched him quietly, pressing her lips together. Earlier, she had compared Barren to William, but really, they didn't look all that much alike. Barren's skin was bronzed, his hair was lighter, almost blond in places, from exposure to the sun's rays. He had a strong jaw, and he had higher cheekbones. Now and then, he moved his long hair behind his ears when it fell in his face. He had the boyish charm William lacked, and though the passion that lit his eyes was motivated by the death of another, it was strangely inviting. In the few minutes she had spoken with him, she'd seen both the depth of his pain, and the spirit of his will. It was fascinating, and she wondered what those desperate feelings would produce if used for good.

She was drawn from her thoughts when Leaf uttered a very impish laugh. "You know, she hasn't actually asked you to take her back. I wonder why?"

"What good is it? You won't," said Larkin.

"You're right—I haven't got what I want yet," said Barren. "But I'd think a lady would miss the warmth of her soft bed and her feather pillow."

She pressed her lips together and attempted to suppress the anger his assumption ignited within her.

"I don't intend to be in your care long, Barren Reed."

"So you really do think your father will be the one to rescue you?"

"My father hates everything you stand for," Larkin said evenly. "He hated your father, and he will detest that you have me."

"I can't imagine what my father could have done to yours other than exist." Barren spoke with as much vigor as she. "Tell me, did you get all your ideas about the kind of person I am from your father?"

"I don't need to gather ideas from anyone. You're a pirate—by default that makes you a terrible man," she replied.

"Terrible? What have I done? I did not capture you to hurt you, or ask for ransom."

"You did not do those things because you do not desire gold, and my pain would not ease your pain. Only one thing will, and that would be William's death. That has been your only goal."

"If I wanted to, though, I could hurt you. I could break your heart."

It was Larkin's turn to laugh. "By killing William?"

"I suppose that all depends on who has your heart," said Barren. He gazed at her for a moment, and then he smirked, moving away from the fire toward a pallet on the rocky ground. As he prepared his bed, Larkin's voice rose behind him.

"Aren't you going to remove my binds?"

"No."

"How am I to sleep?"

"How do you normally sleep?"

"Not tied up."

"Surprising. Then this will be a first for you. Good night."

Larkin looked at Leaf who still sat at the fire, his legs drawn up. He smirked and then blew on the fire, and all went dark.

***

Any other time, Barren would be able to sleep easily on the cold floor of the cave, but not tonight. Tonight, the rocks dug into his back, the blanket was too thin, and every small noise put him on edge. He expected two things to happen: either they would be discovered, or Larkin would try to flee. So far, Larkin was quietly leaning against the wall of the cave. In the darkness, he couldn't tell if she was sleeping, though she shifted a lot, probably trying to find a comfortable position. He laughed to himself a little. This girl had probably never slept on the floor in her life. She was used to feather beds, warmth, and linens.

It was then Barren finally heard it—an explosion erupted, and a cracking sound filled the air as a cannon ripped into the Cliffs. Barren shot to his feet.

"Everyone up!" he yelled in the darkness, though it was probably unnecessary considering the terrible sound the cannon had made. "Get to the ship!"

The crew followed quickly. They were all calm and very thorough, making sure to gather as much food, artillery, and whatever other belongings they needed before heading out of the cave. They had prepared for this.

Barren hurried to pull on his sword belt and boots, then headed for Larkin. He pulled her to her feet, and she stumbled and fell, hitting the rocky ground. Barren helped her up gently, despite the chaos surrounding them.

Outside, the night was cool and misty, the air smelled of smoke, metal and dust. Barren led Larkin through the mud and water as the sounds of war riddled the air.

"If they were trying to save you, this wasn't the way to do it. This will only get you killed." Barren's voice was steady and serious. He was angry. This was exactly the opposite of what he expected William to do. Not only would this attack drive them farther from Maris, it left Barren no opportunity to take Larkin back to Maris if he wanted to.

Keeping his hand on Larkin's back, he led her toward the ship. He wondered what she was feeling at this moment—did this attack come as a surprise to her as well? If she was afraid, she was good at hiding it.

As they boarded the ship, a cannon ball crashed into the cave that had been their refuge, a deafening crack shattering the air. A section of the Cliffs collapsed; pieces of rock broke apart and fell into the ocean, causing water to rise up and accost the air.

Barren moved Larkin to the center of the ship and left her there as he and the others prepared to sail. Barren knew his men were skilled at working under pressure, and the ship was moving in no time: anchor lifted, sails drawn, weapons prepared, just in case things went south. After part of the Cliffs collapsed, the firing stopped momentarily—whoever was attacking them was waiting for them to flee.

Leaf peered through the curtain of darkness, searching for the source of the cannons.

"Who are they?"

"I can't tell," the Elf's brows came together. "The ship bears no mark of Maris, nor that of a pirate."

Barren was silent. He turned to look at their old refuge. What was once a massive wall of rock in the center of the Orient was now a pile of rubble.

"Did they not think about this?" asked Leaf. "They could have killed her. And how will they know they haven't?"

"Perhaps the only intention was to lure us out," suggested Barren. If they were careful and headed in the opposite direction, the attacking ship would never see them and they could escape—it was too dark for human eyes to catch them. "Tread carefully, Sam. The Orient will protect us if we take the hard way out to sea."

"Where are we headed?" Sam called from the helm.

"Silver Crest," said Barren without thinking. He wasn't sure what made him choose that island, but when he did, the decision felt right. "Let's go to Silver Crest."

The Elf and Sam exchanged a look. "Really? You want to take her there?"

Barren nodded, and Leaf raised his brows, shrugging. "You're the captain."

Silver Crest would be the safest place they could go with

Larkin, mostly because it was the pirate haven of the Orient, and Barren would be welcome there. It was also nearly impossible to find if you didn't know how to navigate the sea; especially since the Orient was very particular about whom she let through. Another reason Barren wanted to go there was that he didn't expect William to come with one ship to reclaim his bride. He would send a fleet. Barren did not have a fleet, but he guessed there were several pirates in Silver Crest ready to go to war against Jess Reed's murderer.

Chapter Four
SETTING THE STAGE

The steady tick-tock of the grandfather clock was the only noise in the study. Outside, the occasional rumble threatened rain. Sleepless and angry, Christopher Lee and William Reed were still up, contemplating their next move. William looked around him, trying to rest his eyes on anything other than Lee himself. The man had not stopped glaring at him since his daughter disappeared. On a regular basis, Lee and Reed really didn't get along, and this situation had done little to alleviate the tension between them.

After a moment, the lord stood and walked toward the window—gray light streamed in from the moist morning air.

"So, do I understand you correctly? Let me repeat the news you have for me—the Cliffs were destroyed on your order, the rubble was searched, and there was no sign of my daughter or the pirates. Is that correct?"

William swallowed hard. "Yes, Lord." William, sitting tensely in his seat, gripped Larkin's crimson scarf.

"And you made this decision without the king's orders? And without consideration of my daughter's safety?"

When William didn't say anything, Christopher turned around. His presence seemed to swell and fill the room. His ice-blue eyes chilled him to the core.

"So, you will not take responsibility for your careless actions?" the lord's tone was biting.

"We both know the king would not have approved of destroying the Cliffs with his sons aboard Barren's ship, even if he were here to make that decision."

"But *I* did not approve of destroying the Cliffs with my daughter aboard Barren's ship!"

"The rubble was searched, and there were no signs of the pirates. They must have fled before we got there. Larkin is alive."

"Alive? She's alive for now," Christopher's voice rose in anger. "Considering your engagement to my daughter was my arrangement, I think I must reconsider, since you are so willing to put her life in danger for your own gain. Pray, tell me again what you gained from destroying the Cliffs?"

If Christopher did call off the engagement, it would leave one of them happy—Larkin had made it perfectly clear that she was only agreeing to the marriage to satisfy her father. She had also made it clear that she could never learn to love him, even if he learned to love her. William ground his teeth together, recalling those words. She would learn to love him or he would see to it that she never loved another.

"Everyone knew Barren's strength came from his ability to move in and out of those Cliffs, hiding in the shadows. They should have been destroyed long ago to prevent him from wreaking havoc on our island."

"Yes, and you should have met him at sea long ago! Yet here you sit, stewing in your anger as I lecture you about your rash decisions!"

William pressed his lips together. "Ensuring her safety at the party was not my responsibility, alone."

"Are you attempting to blame me for my daughter's disappearance?" Christopher stepped behind his desk again.

William averted his eyes. While he couldn't completely blame Christopher, he knew he was part of the problem. Christopher always seemed lost in his own thoughts and consumed with his own agenda, which left Larkin to fight for his attention in any way she saw fit. This normally added up to her inappropriate behavior in society—meaning she often voiced her sonorous opinions about politics in the Orient and relations with the Octent, not to mention she had habit of sneaking off to the shore late at night. She remedied this by doing anything Christopher asked—like marrying William.

Christopher leaned across his desk. "Do you think I

arranged this marriage because I'm fond of you?" His voice was low and gruff. "I agreed because you are the king's nephew and may someday become king, especially since Tetherion's sons have gone rogue. But if you defy Tetherion's rule, how do you expect to become king?"

"With force," William replied simply.

"Force? This is politics, William. Plain and simple—your job is to show them you're king material, not act the part of an ex-pirate."

"If King Tetherion hasn't removed his sons from succession by now, what makes you think he will? I will have no choice but to take the throne by force, and Larkin's disappearance is just the beginning of that."

"And how is that?" Christopher wasn't hiding the fact that he felt William was an imbecile, but William knew the old man by now. If he weren't intrigued, he wouldn't have asked.

"The king can easily be blamed for Larkin's disappearance," said William at last. "His orders have stopped any attempt to destroy that ship. Now, with the embargo and Larkin missing—well, the public will only take so much. Maris has already stomped several revolts because of Barren."

Christopher's brows perked, and he sat back in his chair. "What are you suggesting?"

He had had a lot of time to consider what he was about to propose to Christopher Lee. Through the night, he'd sat on the shore near the ocean, fighting the anger that welled within him at the realization that Barren had gotten the best of him, but perhaps that was not so…perhaps this was the perfect situation to accomplish an even greater goal.

"This situation has put us in the perfect position." William finally met Christopher's gaze, and with a shrug he said, "What if we say Larkin has been killed? And blame Tetherion for not taking care of Barren when he became a nuisance? For not dealing with pirates properly?"

"But she is not dead," said Christopher.

"Barren will not return her until I meet him at sea. Who's to say we are lying?"

"The people will want proof."

"Is it enough that I cannot prove she is alive." William held up the scarf. "I am a grieving lover, do I need proof?"

Lee was quiet for a long moment. He tapped his fingers together as he considered what William was saying. "And you think this will be enough to shake the foundation upon which Tetherion stands?"

"I do," William replied. "Would you not agree it is the perfect storm?"

"Perfect storm, perhaps—but you would incite rebellion. You realize this is treason?" Christopher raised his brow in question, as if William were stupid. The Ambassador wiped his sweaty palms on Larkin's scarf. They'd waited for this opportunity for a long time. Here it had presented itself in the strangest of situations, enabled by his brother, and he wasn't about to let it slip away from fear of prosecution.

"We barely have a king," said William. "Once we go

public with our grief, it is only a matter of time before the people of Maris are revolting in the streets, demanding that King Tetherion be removed and I put in his place. What does Tetherion think he can do? Ignore Barren until the public forgets that he has murdered half our population? Before they forget his sons joined in on Barren's cause? I think not."

Lee shrugged. "They have before."

"But Barren has never crossed over to the boarders of Maris. This is different."

"What happens when the people of Maris discover Larkin is not dead?"

William shrugged. "It will merely be a happy ending."

"You risk death," Christopher reminded William, and then he was silent for a long moment, reclining in his chair, fingers steepled. "Tetherion could return and crush you easily. You do not have the support Tetherion has. The nobles would turn against you...unless you possessed power greater than Tetherion's title."

"What has more power than the title of king?"

Christopher smirked, and it made William feel uncomfortable. "Why, the stone that binds your blood to the throne."

"You've gone senile in your old age," William said. "The bloodstone is just a legend."

"Legends bear some truth," said Christopher. "And I can assure you, the bloodstone is real. It has only been stolen."

The legend Christopher was referring to was known as

The Elder King and the Bloodstone. In it, the Elder King, Eadred, fought against Gesalec the Defeated for the kingdom of the Orient. Eadred was given a bloodstone by the Elves, and was able to defeat Gesalec, winning the throne of the Orient. No one was really sure how Gesalec was defeated, and the legend only claimed that the stone tied the Reed line to the throne, making it impossible for any other to lay claim. The legend was one of the reasons the people of Mariana still believed the Elves were hiding powerful magic in their realm.

"Who took it?"

"Your father," Christopher replied. "He, of all people, despised its existence. He believed that nothing entitled a man to the throne. He has hidden the stone somewhere in Mariana, I am sure of it. If you really want to become king without opposition, you'd do well to find it."

"But if it truly exists, then it is of no use in my hands. It would only mean I am entitled to the throne, as I share Eadred's blood."

"On the contrary, at this moment, the bloodstone is not in any one person's possession, which means it is protecting the whole of the Reed line, but if you were to possess it, it would recognize you as king and do anything in its power to protect *you*. You would be...invincible."

All his threats would be eliminated. A chill spread down his spine.

"Where do we begin searching?"

"I have a few ideas," said Christopher. "But first, I want

my daughter. If we are to hold up this charade, she cannot come here, and I'll be damned if she remains in Barren's hands."

"We can send our privateers for her," said William. "She'll be as safe with them as she is with us."

"Well, then, let's get to grieving."

Chapter Five
SINK ME!

The next morning, Barren emerged from his cabin, a stale roll in his hand—breakfast. He tore at it absently, chewing on small pieces. The sun was abnormally bright, and almost blinded him as he left the shadow of his shelter. He moved up the stairs to the helm where Sam and Leaf stood. The Elf clutched a compass, and he and Sam were discussing navigation. Though they were both used to sailing to Silver Crest, there was always that chance that they'd make one wrong turn and miss the island entirely.

Barren stared out at the deck of his ship. Datherious and Natherious were gathering supplies to repair a sail the violent wind had torn in the night. Seamus was inspecting several swivel cannons resting on the gunwales of the deck, and Slay sat perched in the crow's nest, cutting away at a piece of wood: the shavings fell like rain, landing on the deck below. Barren thought about telling him to stop, but he guessed after having the pirate go after a blanket for Larkin, it was probably best to let him chop away at the stick, or he might find the knife in his back.

"Anyone following us yet?" Barren asked Leaf.

"Not that I can tell," replied the Elf. He gazed around him one last time, not needing the aid of a spyglass. His Elvish sight was far superior to anything manmade.

"Has she said anything?" Barren nodded toward Larkin. She remained against the wall of the ship where Barren had left her after the attack on the Cliffs. Remnants from the previous day still adorned her. Bits of flowers were tangled in her hair. Loose curls fell around her face, and black smudges beneath her eyes. Her dress, dirty and tattered, was spread out before her, and the jewel-toned fabric shimmered in the sun. To his annoyance, Barren still thought she was beautiful.

"Not a word," said Leaf. "She's barely moved, and more surprisingly, she hasn't complained. If I couldn't hear her breathing, I would assume she was dead. You might want to feed her, though. She is looking pale."

Barren watched her again; she didn't look up. It was as if she were deliberately trying to stay focused on anything but the pirates. Barren took another bite of his roll.

"I still marvel at how my brother managed to become engaged to her."

"I am surprised, too," replied Leaf. "But only because she would not let him have his way so easily. Perhaps she will be good for William...she might put him in his place."

"Blasphemous words, Leaf," said Barren. "Suggesting that anyone can be happy with William Reed. Besides, if she is so independent in thought, how did she let herself be directed into a marriage she did not want?"

"You are not a part of their world, Barren. The only aspect of her life she has no control over is who she marries. Who she loves, well, that is a different story entirely."

"To marry William would be a waste."

"I must remind you that Larkin is half-Elf," Leaf's sea-green eyes were on her now. "And she can hear every word we are saying. Now...the bread?"

Barren looked down at his roll again. He grabbed the canteen of water sitting next to the helm, and moved away from Leaf. His boots thudded against the deck but even then, Larkin didn't look up. Barren stood before her for a moment, waiting to see if she would acknowledge him, and yet again, she didn't move. So the pirate knelt to meet her gaze—her eyes seemed to simmer, and despite the fury aimed at him, he smiled.

"Here," he held out a piece of bread for her. "Eat."

She hesitated for a moment and then took a bite of the bread as he held it to her mouth, chewing slowly. After she swallowed, she met his gaze.

"You can untie me. I'm not going anywhere."

"How can I trust you when you attacked me so viciously last

night?"

She smiled cynically. "I can't swim."

He didn't want to believe her, but he remembered her saying that her father refused to let her go to the shore for fear pirates might abduct her. If that were true, why then wouldn't he teach her how to swim? He took a knife from his boot, and, placing a finger through the ropes around her wrists, he lifted her hands to him. He studied her face for a moment before slicing the ropes and letting her hands fall into her lap, hoping she wouldn't slap him. "Here," he handed her the bread. "Eat, then."

Larkin still stared at him fiercely, nibbling at the bread. Barren laughed at her. "It's not poisoned, I was eating it."

When she took a bigger bite from the roll, Barren was satisfied. He rocked back on his heels. "So where did *you* learn to fight like that? Seems strange that someone like you would have such skill."

"What do you mean someone like me?" Larkin snapped.

"Don't pretend you don't know what I mean," Barren said blandly. "You were born with a silver spoon in your mouth. You've never wanted for anything—so why would you require swordsmanship skills?"

"I require them because people like you exist," she said. "My father wanted me to be well-prepared."

"So it was your father? And where did he obtain such skill?"

"He was a commander during the Ore Wars," she replied sharply. "Tasked with destroying your father's ship, the *Imperial*."

Recognition settled on Barren—so that was where Lord Lee's

hatred of Jess Reed came from. The Ore Wars had occurred during Cathmor's reign and had begun over an unnamed island that contained an Ore Mine. The island bordered both the Orient and the Octent. The people had gone to battle for it, and Jess had undermined the king's attempts to conquer more territory by destroying battleships. What most did not understand was that Jess also destroyed ships from the Octent. The public believed that Jess did this out of jealousy of his brother, Tetherion, who was first-born, and to inherit the crown, but Barren knew his father never wanted such a restraining position. No, his father had destroyed those ships out of his belief in Saoirse—in freedom.

In the silence, Larkin spoke up, changing the subject. "Where did you learn to fight? Your brother does not fight like that."

"My father taught me," replied Barren, taking a gulp of water. He wiped his lips and handed the canteen to her. "William had no desire to learn from my father. Do not make the mistake of thinking he isn't a good swordsman, though. He is playing dumb. He is superior to anyone in the Orient. *My* equal, in fact."

"You still think he will come."

"Your knight in shining armor? Yes."

"You may be waiting a while," said Larkin, taking a gulp from the canteen. "People only rescue the ones they love."

"Ah, I see," said Barren. He pressed a finger to his lips. "Even if William does not love you, he will loathe that I have you in my possession....even if it wasn't as easy as I anticipated."

"You speak of me as an object," she sounded disgusted. "I

belong to no one—not to William and not to you."

Barren laughed humorlessly. "It's not I who says you belong to anyone—that's what society says. Once you marry William, you are his to tame."

She ground her teeth together and crushed the roll in her hand. "I don't want to listen to you anymore. My father will come for me."

"Oh no, the terrifying Lord Christopher Lee," Barren said colorlessly. While Barren wasn't afraid of him, he had no wish to meet a man who felt his father was better off dead.

"Do not mock him; he is not to be trifled with."

"If you're trying to scare me, it won't work," said Barren. "I do not fear what men can do to me."

"What about women?" Larkin raised a brow.

Barren smirked and lifted the sleeve of his shirt. "You did manage to get a hit on me, but I could take you, given that there's no sand."

Barren noticed her lips twitch. It was the first time he'd seen her smile since she'd tried to kill him.

"You should think of this as a peaceful break," said Barren. "You didn't actually want to marry my brother, did you?"

"You make it sound like I won't marry him now."

"Will you?" Barren nodded to the chain around her neck that held her ring. "You do not wear the ring he gave you."

She was silent before she responded—if anything, that answered Barren's question quite directly.

"I don't want to marry him, but it is not my choice," she

replied evenly. Barren could tell she was forcing herself to sound resigned.

"How isn't it your choice?" he asked, confused.

"You are a pirate and abide by no law—moral or societal. You would not understand loyalty," her voice cut through Barren like a knife.

"You misread me, Lady." Barren's voice was surprisingly steady for how angry he felt. He watched her squirm under his gaze. "I am a pirate, I always follow my heart. It is the only thing I am loyal to."

With that, he moved away from her, heading to the helm.

***

Larkin wasn't sure how she should feel about Barren Reed. She expected to be dead by now, actually. In fact, she was still waiting to discover the bread had been poisoned. But the longer she waited for her throat to close up, the more she realized Barren really wasn't out to kill her. All he wanted was William. Larkin knew the reality of this situation: one would kill the other someday, and she couldn't be sure who would win. But if Barren did not succeed, she would marry William. Only one thing overrode any desire of her heart, and that was her father's wishes. She would do what she could to make him proud.

Since Larkin's bonds had been removed, she rose from her place against the rail and walked along the deck, rubbing her wrists. It felt nice to stretch her legs, and she loved being in the middle of the ocean. It was the one place her father had always hoped she'd never find comfort because of his experiences fighting Jess Reed. Her father's hatred of the notorious pirate brought William to Maris after the murder—he knew the prestigious landlord would keep him safe. Her father had taken Will under his wing and bought him a place among the nobles. Only weeks ago, her father had come to her with the proposal. She had been appalled at first. She hated everything William stood for. He had no virtue she admired, and all the vices she disliked. He talked constantly about one thing only—Barren Reed's abominable behavior.

After their engagement, he spoke of one additional thing: the prospect of becoming king. There was no luster to being a queen in Larkin's eyes. She saw the position as frightening and restraining. Since learning of her impending marriage to William, she had felt an overwhelming urge to flee from the duty to her father and William. Her heart only gave her one option: the open sea. Though now she was thinking she should have been more careful about what she'd wished for.

"Excuse me, Lady," came a voice from behind her. Larkin turned to see the young Datherious Reed. "Hand me that rope there, will you?"

She hesitated for a moment, finding it strange to be in the presence of the prince once again. It had been a long time since she'd seen his face.

She did as he asked, bending to scoop up the rope and handing it to him. "You are one of the rogue princes."

Datherious smiled, though she found it a little unpleasant. He was a handsome man, but had an air of darkness about him.

Perhaps it was all in his features—dark hair, cut short, and two very dark brows arched above his deep grayish-blue eyes. His face was brushed with facial hair, and his lips a little too red for the color of his skin. She hadn't seen him in a couple of years, and he had changed.

"One of two," he said with a smirk.

"Where is your brother?" She had seen him once while boarding the ship in the night and then he had disappeared. He couldn't have gone far; they were on a ship.

Dath pointed upward. A man sat on one of the branches of the mast, his legs wrapped together to hold him in place as he threaded another rope through one of the sails and secured it against the breeze. It was Natherious, his brother.

"You sure left Maris in quite a state," she said, looking up at Nath who was more pleasant to behold. Perhaps it was because his eyes were lighter, and he smiled brightly.

Dath chuckled. "What do you mean by that?"

"Well, Tetherion has no heirs now that you've joined with Barren," she said. She remembered Slay had warned her against talking to the princes as if they were traitors. By definition, they were and she was all too curious to see how they viewed the situation.

"Of course he does," said Datherious, moving toward the mast. He threw the rope up to Natherious. "Nath and I are his sons."

"You are not his only kin," said Larkin. "William is your cousin, and nephew to the king. He is also not a pirate and more likely to take the throne."

Datherious laughed darkly, and Larkin heard Natherious chuckle as well. Her cheeks colored crimson though she didn't understand what was so funny about the situation; it was perfectly plausible that William could be king. Why else would he carry on the way he did? Nath finished threading the last piece of rope through one of the chains on the mast and climbed down, hitting the ground with a soft thud.

"Did I hear that correctly? Did you just insinuate that William would be king?" Natherious chuckled and then he motioned to both himself and his brother. "Over us?"

"Now that is something I have not yet heard," said Barren, he turned to look at Datherious and Larkin. "William wants to be king?"

"I don't understand how this is a surprise to anyone," Larkin faced all of them, confusion written all over her face. "You two are traitors to your crown, and William is the only one of your family who isn't a pirate."

Datherious's face was frightening as he looked at her. She shuddered, hating the way he seemed to demean her.

"First, we are not traitors to our crown." Larkin felt frustrated by their constant denial of their treason. The twins were now pirates; they ran against the law set forth by Tetherion. How were they not traitors? "Tetherion never removed us from the succession, Lady Larkin. We are still the rightful heirs to the throne of the Orient."

"They're right," said Barren. He paused for a moment, his

brows furrowed. "What concerns me more is the fact that William seems very convinced that he could be king in the event of Tetherion's death."

"Yes, he has very easily cast us aside," said Natherious. "I wonder what he is planning."

"He is planning nothing," said Larkin. "William doesn't mean to become king through subversion. It is merely logical that the nephew of Tetherion would be king when his sons are busy committing acts of piracy at sea."

"Your logic would be sound if the twins weren't still entitled to the crown," said Barren. "If he has told you he wants the crown, he is contriving a plan to make that happen. Which means he intends to sabotage Tetherion."

"Why would William dare take the crown with all of us defending the king?" asked Datherious. "It is a dangerous task. This is not good. We must let our father know of the danger William poses. He could plan to kill him."

"Kill?" Larkin swallowed. Though she shouldn't be all that surprised. She knew William had already killed one man to gain a title. It was one of many reasons she had not wished to marry him. Now she wondered if he would kill another to get the crown of the Orient.

"Something you must understand if you are to marry that scum," said Natherious, and the tone of his voice made Larkin flinch. She hadn't expected Nath to sound so hateful. "You are dealing with a man who lived with pirates for fifteen years. No matter how disgusting and brutal you think we are, William's roots are also in piracy. He knows more about the Orient than he'll ever let *you* know. If he's been talking about the prospect of being king, he has a plan to get that crown."

"And you thought we were the traitors," Datherious's eyes were like coals as he stared at her, arms crossed over his chest.

She felt guilty in a way—yes, she had considered the princes traitors, but if it turned out that William really was going to kill the king…well, that was far worse than the twins' decision to sail with Barren Reed.

"Aye! We got trouble!" Slay's voice came from above them. He was leaning against the edge of the crow's nest, peering north.

Chapter Six
JONATHAN KINGSLEY

Barren and Leaf turned their gaze in that direction. They knew immediately the trouble was not from Maris—Maris was east. A ship was on the horizon, fighting the waves of the Orient, heading straight for them.

"Who would be on this route other than pirates?" asked Barren. He watched the Elf's features. A crease appeared between his brows as he stared intently at the vessel. He was trying to figure out who was on the ship.

Leaf shrugged. "I cannot tell who they are. Privateers, perhaps? Unfortunately, we can't be too careful. They are moving fast and we did just capture the fiancée of William Reed."

Privateers were groups of men hired by various islands to sail the Orient. They carried letters of the marquee, granted by the government, which kept them from getting in trouble for piracy. To the public, their only purpose was to fight pirates, however most abused the power they'd been granted by attacking any and all ships, plundering for their respective islands. If they left survivors, they always claimed pirates from Silver Crest had attacked them. Privateers were toxic, and any time pirates of Silver Crest encountered them, the privateers were destroyed, as it was against the code to keep them alive.

Without another word, Barren turned to his crew.

"Prepare for attack!" Barren moved from the helm and headed toward the hatch to gather more weapons. Larkin was right behind him.

"What? Why?"

"Because we do not know if they are friend or foe—self-interest, *Lady*," said Barren. He was not looking at her.

"So you would kill them before knowing anything about them?"

"No, not kill—scare, maybe. The trick is to be the first to attack."

Barren descended the stairs into the hatch; he wasn't surprised to hear Larkin's feet on the steps behind him.

"You are barbaric!"

"Heard that before." Barren rolled his eyes. "You obviously don't understand our situation."

"I don't understand *your* situation?" she sounded exasperated.

"You care for no one but yourself!"

Barren turned to face her. She flinched, nearly running into him. His face was only inches from hers and she was forced to focus on his eyes. While his anger melted into concern, his eyes remained lit with passion. He spoke through clenched teeth. "What I care about is the safety of my crew, Lady. If you would open your eyes, you'd see that."

"But those people have not hurt you!"

A loud boom shook the ship. Larkin stumbled back, grabbing Barren's shirt as she fell, but Barren's feet weren't stable either, and he collapsed on top of her.

"You spoke too soon."

Barren could feel Larkin tense beneath him. He pushed himself up so he wasn't pressed against her, but he didn't move to stand. He watched her carefully as she examined his features. She seemed to be assessing him, or perhaps comparing him to William. The last thought made him angry, and then he watched her blush and look away.

"It may be hard for you to trust me, but do me one favor and don't make assumptions about my character," he said quietly. "I did not bring you here to make you suffer, and I have no wish to make you miserable." Barren pushed himself to his feet and held out his hand for Larkin. She refused, and made it to her feet on her own. Barren chuckled. "It doesn't hurt to accept help now and then."

She opened her mouth to respond when she was interrupted. "You two can stare at each other all day tomorrow, but at this moment, we have a crisis on deck," said Leaf.

Barren left Larkin and hurried upstairs. On deck, he was not surprised to see that the mast of his ship was broken. Chunks of debris were scattered all over the place. The ship that had done the damage was already lined up with them. Everyone stood, tense and ready for their attackers to board.

"Damn it Leaf," complained Barren. "You didn't mention it was an *Elvish* ship!"

One of the ways Elves gained a little favor in the Orient was by selling their ships. Pirates and governments alike had an advantage if they had Elvish ships. They were light, fast, and, of course, beautiful.

"I told you it was fast, didn't I?"

"What happens now?" asked Larkin.

Barren looked at her, his eyes held a warning. "If you get involved, I swear by Saoirse, you're going in the ocean and you will either learn to swim or drown."

Her eyes narrowed and she crossed her arms over her chest. A glance from Barren to Leaf told the Elf to move next to her, just in case she tried anything.

Five men from the Elvish ship boarded Barren's *Kendrick*. They were quick, swords drawn, ready to fight. The tallest one was a man with dark brown hair that came to his shoulders. Whiskers covered his chin. He was dressed in brown pants and a white airy shirt. He smiled and said, "Barren Reed, I never expected to find you so far from Maris."

"I guess it is unfortunate for you." The pirate sounded

bored—as if he already had this situation under control, though he had never expected to be found so far away from Maris while William was still alive.

"I don't know about that. It seems as if I have the advantage."

"So you think."

Barren raised his sword, and as he did, he heard his crew unsheathe their weapons. Leaf withdrew an arrow from his quiver, and fitted it to the string of his bow. The twins had double swords, and they moved them against each other, hungry to fight. Slay had a cutlass, Sam a long knife, and Seamus opted for a long black chain. In response to Barren and his crew, the five men behind their attacker moved into battle stances.

"What is your purpose?" Barren asked.

"I came to find you," the man replied simply.

"I have no dealings with privateers," Barren said, accusing him outright.

"I am not a privateer, but I will fight you if I have too. Will you speak to me otherwise?"

"If you were a friend, you would not have destroyed my ship so decidedly."

And without another word, Barren attacked—their swords clashed and moved against each other in a harsh clank of steel.

Barren recognized formal training when he saw it—and this man was skilled. He had fluid, but mechanical movements. It didn't make him an easy target by any means, but it was even more evidence against him. Barren fought hard, the impact of his blows caused his attacker to slow.

The crews remained behind their respective captain; they would only become involved if one drew blood, and in that instance, a battle would ensue. Despite the common idea that pirates did not play by rules, they respected their own code of conduct.

The attacker's sword reverberated against Barren's, catching between the blade and the hilt. Barren pushed him, and he stumbled and fell, landing on his back. Barren didn't move to assault, he stayed where he was, waiting for his opponent to get up and begin fighting again. The attacker smiled at Barren, breathing hard.

"Give up?" Barren questioned with a raised brow. He didn't expect him to surrender. Privateers never surrendered.

The attacker shook his head, still trying to catch his breath. Barren swung his sword, and the attacker barely had time to block. He deflected the blow, but Barren was already preparing for another one. The clash of metal was fierce...clank, clank, *clank*...and the sword the attacker desperately tried to hold on to flew from his hands, landing across the deck. Barren's sword was at the man's neck.

"Down," he ordered.

The man went to his knees. As was his custom, Barren pulled a piece of rope from his pocket and tied the man's hands. Then he pointed to the rest of the attacker's crew.

"Drop your weapons and move over there," he gestured toward the helm where Sam was standing. The attacker's crew obeyed and metal clanged to the ground.

Barren turned his attention back to his prisoner, but as he moved to make a circle around him, he heard the attacker call out to one of his crew—the only one who didn't actually belong.

"Lady Larkin?"

Barren looked up at her questioningly, he could tell by the look on her face that she knew him.

"Jonathan? What are you doing here?"

She stepped forward, but Barren held his sword out. "What did I tell you?" His voice was dark. Leaf stepped in and moved Larkin back. Barren blocked Jonathan from her view.

Any other time, Barren wouldn't have had a second thought about taking a privateer's life, especially if they attacked his ship—it was part of the code. These men had endangered him and the lives of his crew; what other price was there to pay? But he felt anxiety creeping over him as he stood, poised for the kill. Larkin already thought he was a terrible person, and if he went through with this, it would only confirm it.

"It is required by the code that I kill any privateers I come into contact with—a waste, really. You were brave."

Barren moved his arm back and thrust the blade toward the young lord. Larkin moved quickly, snatching Leaf's cutlass from his hand, she deflected Barren's sword and stood between the two.

"No!" she cried fiercely. "You will spare him!"

"You do not command me!" Barren's voice was deadly.

"What would you gain from his death?"

"He cannot be trusted!"

"You've spent all your life killing the wrong people! How many more lives will you take to pay for one?"

Barren let his blade fall to his side. His gaze seared her, and he could tell she was afraid. Her eyes were wide, and she breathed heavily, but her hands tightened on the hilt of Leaf's blade. For a moment, he wanted to end her life. Then he would have no more interferences, but he knew he couldn't. He took a step toward her, eyes narrowing.

"Move," he commanded. Larkin glared up at him and shook her head. Barren tightened his jaw.

"It's okay, Larkin," she heard Jonathan's voice. "Move."

Barren watched as she turned to face Jonathan. Because she was distracted, Leaf was able to reach forward and pull her away from the scene, ripping the blade from her hands. Barren stepped forward, repositioned himself before the man and pointed the sword at Jonathan's neck. All Barren had to do was push ever so slightly and blood would pool on the ground, a terrible gurgling sound that would fill the air. Larkin would scream—scream that he was a monster. Only now, she would see it, she would really know it.

Barren moved his sword back a little and thrust the blade toward Jonathan.

"A-Albatross sent me!" Jonathan cried.

Barren's blade froze in his hands. "Albatross?" He narrowed his eyes and then used his sword to pull back the fabric of the man's shirt. A black 'X' covered his heart: it was a sign of his loyalty to the code of Silver Crest. The mark was newly made as it was still raised and the skin around it red. Barren moved his sword away.

"He must speak with you. It is urgent," Jonathan continued, speaking quickly.

Barren sheathed his sword and pulled a dagger from his boot to cut the ropes he had knotted around Jonathan's wrists.

"Where is he?" Barren asked.

"Silver Crest."

"And you had to destroy my ship to tell me that?"

"He said it was for the best you left your ship behind," said Jonathan, as he stole a gaze at Larkin. "And now I understand what he meant. If anyone following you finds this ship, well, they won't very well know where you went, will they?"

"And why not tell me earlier that Albatross had sent you?"

Jonathan looked embarrassed as he turned his gaze from the pirate and spoke quietly. "Well...it was a bet. I thought I could capture you first. You know, make it fun."

Barren surveyed the man for a moment, and then laughed. "You are very new to this whole pirate gig?"

"A little, yes."

Barren stuck out his hand and helped Jonathan to his feet.

"What do you mean, you're new to this? You cannot be a pirate too," said Larkin. "That's treason."

Jonathan turned his gaze to her. "By what law? Pirates have a different code, and by their code, I am not committing treason."

"You cannot just make your own code to justify the wrongs you commit!"

"Please...someone...make her stop!" Barren pleaded. "If you weren't so determined to hate us, you might find you fit in better here than you did in Maris!"

Jonathan laughed. "I agree—it's about time you joined this crowd. I never cared much for the other company you kept."

Larkin was speechless. "But you've been to every state dinner since I have attended. You are the son of a Senator in Arcarum. You've mingled with the company of Christopher Lee and William Reed, even King Tetherion, and here you are on the open sea, talking to Barren Reed as if he were your equal? That doesn't make sense!" Larkin threw her arms up in the air.

Jonathan chuckled, amused, but when he spoke next, there was a certain warning in his voice. "You may not want things to start making sense, Larkin."

"Albatross said nothing of what he wishes to speak to me about?" asked Barren.

Jonathan shook his head. "It may have something to do with Lady Larkin. She complicates things a bit."

"She was a mistake." His words were harsh. He glanced at her, seeing the shock and anger on her face. He was still fuming from her interference.

"It was not my decision to come here! You were the one who kidnapped me."

"And if I had known you'd be so difficult, I wouldn't have bothered!"

With that, Barren turned from everyone and stalked toward his cabin. Before he closed the door behind him, he turned to give orders. "Gather only the belongings you need. Everything else must stay."

Chapter Seven
LIGHTS AND LUNGS

Barren sat on the steps leading to the helm of Jonathan's ship the *Slayer*. His sword lay over his knees. Upon the blade, a leather journal rested and on the leaves of those pages, Barren began to sketch the image of a face. Every now and then he would pause to watch the outline of Larkin and Jonathan before him. Perhaps he had been wrong...maybe she didn't want to marry William because she loved another. As Larkin's laughter rose, Barren felt the acid in his stomach react. It was sickening really, her girlish reaction to someone who had just proven to be a liar and a pirate—that which she hated most of all.

He turned his thoughts to even less pleasant things. Most of the time he tried forgetting the day his father died, but recently, he couldn't get the image out of his head. It had only been five years ago. Barren had been thirteen years old, William sixteen. William had agreed to play a game of hide-and-seek. Barren was to seek. He hid behind a huge coil of rope as he counted loudly, waiting for William to retreat into some shadowy corner and hide. When he counted to ten, he turned and beheld the murder of his father.

At first he thought he had stumbled into a nightmare, but reality shook him as William moved toward the turned back of their father. He was packing supplies, unaware that his son would skewer him at any second. Barren wanted to scream, but words went dry in his mouth. His body told him to run for his father, but fright paralyzed him. He was unable to do anything. Jess turned at the very moment William was upon him and...he didn't move. He had plenty of time to defend himself, but didn't. William stuck the sword through him.

Barren stepped out of the shelter of the rope, and Will turned to face him, his eyes full of bewilderment. It was not the gaze of triumph, but a lost expression, one that had no comprehension of what had just happened. For a moment, Barren thought William would come after him, but he didn't. He dropped the sword and ran. Barren had approached the body of his father cautiously, but there was no movement. The crew found them soon after, Barren crying over his father's dead body.

Barren watched the blade beneath his sketchbook shine under the moonlight. It was the one William had used to kill his father. Barren had washed away all the blood himself, tears plaguing his face all the while. He couldn't help thinking that if he had called out to his father, maybe he would have been alive today. But there was something in Jess's eyes...a resolution that made the pirate wonder if it really would have mattered.

Leaf approached and peered down at Barren's sketchbook. His fist rested over his drawing, and the pencil poised in his hand was still. "Nice drawing...Larkin, is it?" asked the Elf, taking a seat next to Barren. "Interesting, considering you look as though you might stick that blade through those two."

"I *might* stick the girl," replied Barren coldly.

"She's done nothing to earn your punishment, and no— undermining your authority doesn't qualify. Though, they have been carrying on for *ages*," Leaf rolled his eyes and covered his ears. "None of you have respect for the Elf—I can hear *everything*. For once, someone should sympathize with me."

Barren smiled, but he didn't say anything. Leaf waited a moment before he continued.

"She sure did test your nerves today." A smirk played across his lips. "I will say that I am proud of you. You'd have killed anyone else who dared to do what she did."

"No, I wouldn't," Barren said in protest, closing his sketchbook.

Leaf gave the pirate a dull look. "You are used to being obeyed. It's nice to have someone who can order you around."

Barren frowned.

"She won't be doing that much longer. I intend to put her on a ship and send her back home."

"Well now, this whole thing would seem a little pointless then, wouldn't it?"

"You were right. I shouldn't have kidnapped her."

Leaf smiled, and Barren saw all the mischievousness of his Elvish heritage in that one look. "Did you ever think that you weren't the one who kidnapped her? Maybe she kidnapped us?"

Barren's brows came together for a moment, then he shook his head. "She doesn't even know what she wants..."

"Sounds familiar," mused Leaf, resting his chin in his hands.

"I mean, look, she says she'll marry William, but she finds Mr. Pirate-Politician over there a charming substitute! How does that even make sense?"

"You sound jealous," said Leaf.

"I'm not jealous," Barren averted his eyes and toyed with the worn leather binding on his book.

Leaf stared at him and his eyes glazed over as if he didn't care to hear Barren deny how he felt. So what if he were jealous? What was it to the Elf? It was one thing to know Larkin hated him for what he was. It was another thing to witness her girlish affection for a man who was no different from him.

"Look, Leaf," he said with a sigh. "While I've not made the best decisions in the world, all I've ever tried to do is right a wrong."

Leaf's features softened at Barren's confusion. "Barren," he said quietly. "We are all here because we believe what you are doing is right. Granted, not all of what you do is particularly good, but your goal is what keeps us all together. Never forget that. All of us here—we are loyal to you and your father's memory."

Barren had nothing to say, but he nodded his head, suddenly overcome with exhaustion.

"Now, go lie down. With the way these Elvish ships ride, we'll be at Silver Crest in no time."

Barren stood without another word and walked to the corner of the ship where blankets were piled for him and his crew. He sheathed his sword, keeping it close to him as he lay down and fell into a deep sleep.

***

"Who is Albatross?" Larkin thought he sounded rather unpleasant. She imagined a dirty sort of man—old, maybe missing his teeth. "Are you really a pirate, Jonathan? You can tell me—I won't expose you." Words poured out of Larkin's mouth as she attempted to register what was going on with the man before her. She couldn't believe someone she'd known for years, someone who had seemed so loyal to the crown, was now a pirate.

Jonathan smiled. "Albatross is a good friend, Lady, and I am sorry to disappoint you, but I joined the code of Silver Crest not three days ago."

Larkin frowned. "But why?"

"Because I believe in a free world."

"But...how did you get involved in this, when you, of all people, have been freer than most?"

"Well that's exactly it. How fair is it that no others in this world are allowed the opportunities I have been given just because of my parentage? I daresay, Lady Larkin, haven't you always been the rebellious type? Does this life not seem to suit you more than the one you were born into?"

"I cannot answer that in fairness," Larkin said, "as I don't know what it means to be a pirate."

"Ah, but what it means to be a pirate is simple. A pirate loves the sea and revels in his freedom."

Larkin glanced over her shoulder; she watched as Barren lay down to sleep. She did not miss the exhaustion tearing at his features or the distress in his eyes. As he pulled the covers over his body and laid his arm over his sword, she let out a low breath, feeling overwhelmed. Jonathan caught her gaze and smirked.

"How do you like him?" he asked.

She looked away from Barren quickly, gazing out at the ocean. The waves were silver under the moon. "Like? There is nothing to like. He is mean and barbaric," she shook her head. There was nothing she could like about a man who found her to be a mistake. "He is stubborn and immature…"

"And it sounds like you're reading from a list you've made of things to hate about him."

Larkin frowned. "He's a bad man, Jonathan."

"Oh? How so?"

"I need not enlighten you. He was a second away from killing you before you opened your mouth about *Albatross*—whoever that is," she said, surprised that she even had to explain herself. It was that one little act that made all her assumptions about

Barren's character seem completely true. "And I know you've heard the stories. He stakes out the coast of Maris, intent to kill any who leaves the shore. He thinks it will somehow convince William to fight him, when all he does is damn himself."

"You are very unreasonable, Lady," he said. "Barren has seen things no child should see. You know he watched William murder his father in cold blood, and your father is to blame for that."

A lump rose in Larkin's throat. "What do you mean?"

"Well, I'm sure you've heard your father talk about how Jess was one of his greatest enemies. Your father is the one responsible for sowing the seed of power in William. Your father bribed William to get what he wanted. All it took was Lord Lee promising William status, wealth…and his daughter to convince him to kill Jess."

Larkin shook her head. "That cannot be true."

But the look on Jonathan's face told her it was. "I'm afraid so. Your father planned your engagement long ago. Much more than three weeks ago, I assure you. Your future was determined when Jess Reed's ended."

Nothing in the world could have prepared Larkin for this news. She had been more prepared for Barren's kidnapping than this. Her chest felt tight and her heart pounded painfully against her ribcage, driving home the realization that, not only had part of her been responsible for what Barren had become, but her father had used her as a puppet to achieve his greatest wish—the death of Jess Reed. Though Larkin did not agree with piracy, the means her father took to accomplish his goal shocked her. If there was truth to this—any truth at all—it meant her father was partly responsible for leaving Barren fatherless.

"It was not your fault, what happened to Barren," Jonathan reminded her gently.

"So I was a tool?" she questioned quietly. "I was…an *object*."

Larkin constantly attempted to please her father, to get his attention. He was always so busy, locking himself in his study all hours of the night. Sometimes, she would hear objects slamming against the wall or glass breaking, as if hurled by a man in a state of rage. Once she'd tried to see if he was okay, but he had ordered her away.

"If you knew, why didn't you tell me?"

Jonathan was quiet for a moment. She could tell he was choosing his words carefully. He was hiding something.

"We all have reasons for our secrets, Larkin." She was surprised by his answer—she expected him to talk his way around her question. Instead he was doing something worse, acknowledging that this was just the beginning.

"That's not answering my question."

"Enough questions will be answered once we're in Silver Crest," he said. "By then you'll regret asking just one."

Larkin didn't like the sound of that. "Did Barren know? Is that why he targeted me?"

"I'm not certain what Barren knows about you," said Jonathan. "My guess would be he merely saw you as an easy way to lure William to sea."

Larkin grasped the rails of the ship until her knuckles were white. She didn't like that at all, and it deepened her animosity toward Barren. He had also seen her as a way to get what he wanted, just something he could cast aside as soon as he was finished. Well, she wouldn't be that easy to get rid of; she would make sure of that.

She could feel Jonathan's gaze on her, and she glanced at him. Seeing his sympathetic stare made her blush. Now self-conscious, she released the rails, her fingers tight with pain.

"Get some sleep. We're still a ways from Silver Crest and we haven't reached the hardest part of the sea yet."

Larkin reluctantly moved toward the captain's cabin— Jonathan had given up his quarters earlier in the day, and though Larkin attempted to refuse, he would not hear of it. She was thankful for a bed. She had slept slumped over the night before and now her muscles were knotted.

As she approached the cabin, her eyes fell on Barren. His sleeping figure seemed to be lost in peaceful slumber, but as she got closer, she could tell he was having a nightmare. His brows were furrowed deeply and his jaw set tight. She was conscious that Jonathan was watching her, so she swept through the doors of the cabin as quickly as she could, taking in Barren's pained expression. As she lay down to sleep, she decided one day she would ask him what he had been dreaming.

***

Sometime in the night, Larkin was startled out of her sleep by furious shouts. Her blankets were so warm and her sleep so deep, she thought she was back in her own bed in Maris, but reality hit her as she opened her eyes and remembered she was on a ship. She listened for a moment: rain tapped against the windows, feet pounded on the deck outside, and the ship itself moaned as it charged against the water. She guessed they were closer to Silver Crest.

Curious, she crawled out of bed and hurried outside, only to be met with chaos. The wind blew hard; the rain came down in horizontal sheets, falling upon her in waves of coldness. She was instantly drenched and chilled to the bone, but she couldn't allow herself to go inside. The battle between the ship and the elements was too fascinating. Lightning flashed so often it was easy to see the men on deck running around, some securing weapons, others tangled in the sails, trying to collapse them before the wind ripped them from their place. The ship itself rose with the hectic waves, stumbling over the harshness of the Orient. Larkin suddenly wondered how it was so easy for pirates to love something this vicious.

"Lady Larkin! You should not be out here!"

She heard Jonathan's voice from across the deck. She could see his outline, a rope in hand, trying to help the others with the sails. Larkin ignored him and turned to see Barren at the helm— his eyes dead set in front of him, as if he could peel back the darkness and see the route ahead. He had no aid of a map or compass, and it seemed like every slight turn of the wheel was an intuitive decision. Were these the skills of a pirate or a result of his half-Elf heritage? She stared out at the sea and in that moment, she could see beyond the curtain of water, into the churning ocean. It was dark and endless, but she had the sense that she was not in danger. She turned to look at Barren again—perhaps this was his thought?

His eyes met hers and she gripped the rail beneath her hands tighter as the sea thrashed about. Barren's gaze was untouched by anger, and she found it hard to look away—water beaded off of him and his hair stuck to his face. He had shed his usual jacket in favor of a white shirt. The fabric clung to his body, muscles rippling beneath. He was fascinating, beautiful in a terrifying and rough way. Barren smirked and she looked away quickly, wondering what he had seen.

The ship lurched violently, and Larkin lost her balance near the rail. She tumbled over and screamed. It felt as if her heart was going to burst out of her chest even before she hit the water. When she did, fear froze her. She hadn't had time to hold her breath, no time to close her mouth. Water filled her lungs, and she panicked. She moved her arms in tireless circles in an attempt to break the surface.

When she broke through, she gasped for air. "Someone help me!" she screamed. But who would help her? To leave the ship was asking for death, she thought helplessly. All around her was dark water, except for the violent flashes of lightning striking the sky. Her body ricocheted between the waves.

"Larkin!" she heard her name called and she cried out in reaction.

"I'm over here!" her voice was raw. She continued to move her arms to stay above the water, but she was tired. She could only do so much to keep her body afloat as the waves thrashed her about in nauseating circles. Another wave barreled toward her, and she was plunged into the water. This time, she wasn't sure she could make it to the surface, though she fought with all her might. She moved her arms desperately, but they were like lead. She opened her eyes and closed them quickly. All was dark.

She had never imagined such a horrific way to die. Her lungs felt like they were going to burst, her chest ached; her heart beat so erratically, she was sure it would explode. What would happen to her body? Would she float away to some foreign shore? Would she ever be discovered? Would her father ever know that Barren had, indeed, not killed her?

It was time—she couldn't hold her breath any longer, and the more she tried to return to the top, the more the waves resolutely pulled her down. She opened her lips and felt the bubbles escape her mouth…

Something brushed her fingers and then crushed them—her body was jerked forward into something hard, but…very much human. She was only half-conscious, but aware that at some point, she no longer felt the sea around her. She clung to her savior, resting her head on his shoulder, and then all went dark.

***

Her eyes flew open and she lurched to her side. Salt water spewed upon the deck, burning her throat and her lungs. She coughed violently, her entire body shaking. Then she collapsed, feeling light-headed as exhaustion consumed her. She drew in a haggard breath and didn't want to move. She moaned when strong arms picked her up and carried her back into the cabin where she had slept. She leaned into the man, wanting the pain in her chest to go away.

"Can you stand?" Barren's voice was low and strangely gentle. Larkin nodded her head, but when her feet touched the ground, she found that all she wanted to do was sleep. Barren's arms wrapped around her again and he sighed. "You said you could stand."

"I can..."

Barren didn't let her go, even though she shoved against him weakly. Instead, he directed her to the bed. "Don't go to sleep yet. You need to change or you'll catch a cold, and Leaf doesn't like healing colds."

Larkin didn't manage to stay upright for long. She landed against the covers, the soft folds welcomed sleep. Her throat hurt and she wanted nothing more than to close her eyes and forget the frigid feeling within her. She still shook inside, consumed with the fear that she would die.

She watched as Barren moved somewhere in the darkness. For a moment he fumbled around, trying to locate something. It wasn't until a candle's warm glow filled the cabin that she knew what he had been looking for. Without glancing her way, the pirate moved toward a trunk in the corner and began sifting through clothes. He pulled out a white shirt and a pair of brown pants.

"This is all I could find," he said, laying the clothes next to her on the bed. Larkin looked up at him in the faded light. Her eyes still stung from the salt water. Barren observed her for a moment, his gaze heavy with worry.

"I...I didn't think you would save me," her voice rasped and she coughed. The pain brought tears to her eyes. She couldn't understand why he would save her—he had a chance to be rid of his *mistake.*

Barren frowned, and though there was no hesitation in his eyes, Larkin knew he didn't like what she had said. "If the sea had wanted you, I wouldn't have been able to save you."

Barren was about to leave when Larkin reached out and grabbed his hand. His skin was rough, and his fingers tense, but he didn't move away. Larkin pulled herself into a sitting position and then stood to meet the pirate's gaze.

"Thank you," she whispered.

Barren raised his brows, studying her for a moment; the flame of the candle flickered, reacting to the battle the ship still waged.

"Get some rest, Larkin," his voice was barely a whisper. He stepped back, pulling his hand from hers.

With that, he was gone. Larkin managed to peel her wet clothes off her body, and shrugged into the dry ones Barren had found for her. Then she climbed into bed and closed her eyes, but whether from the fright of the night or the electric sensation present on her hand from Barren's touch, she could not fall asleep. Dawn broke through the small round window before her eyes were heavy enough to send her into sleep.

Chapter Eight
OLD SALT

"Lady Larkin, wake up," the voice was soft and familiar, but not the one she had expected to hear. Her eyes opened into slits and her head pounded with fatigue. Jonathan's face loomed above hers.

"What time is it?"

"It is late afternoon," he replied. "Silver Crest is in our sight."

She sat up, but the rush made her head spin and she fell back onto her pillow. Jonathan frowned and helped her into a sitting position.

"Last night must have been terrifying for you, Lady."

Larkin was quiet for a moment. Yes, it had been terrifying. It was still terrifying. She looked down at herself, observing what she wore, and remembered Barren made her change out of her wet clothes—strangely considerate, she thought.

"Barren saved me," her voice was low. She tried combing her fingers through her hair, but they got stuck in matted clumps of salt. "Why did he save me?"

An amused look crossed Jonathan's face. "You think he would let you die?"

"I am more trouble to him than he wants," she said. "What care has he if I die?"

"He has several reasons to care. But most importantly, if any harm does come to you, it would be a violation of our code of piracy. Barren would face marooning, even death."

"So he keeps me alive out of fear of his own death?"

"Barren does not fear death. He honors the code because he's loyal to the sea."

"It doesn't matter. I will be around so long as I prove valuable to him." She recalled the conversation they had the night before, and it still angered her. "He is no better than William."

"You see such terrible things in a very pained man," observed Jonathan. "It might help for you to put aside what you've been told about him, and look at the man you've been presented with."

Jonathan stood, but Larkin remained sitting, staring up at him, still wanting answers.

"There is nothing to put aside. Murder is murder...even I cannot forgive William for his sin."

"Yes, murder is murder, but that boy saved your life. Do you think it was for his own gain? Indeed, if he were as ruthless as you say, he would have let the Orient take you. Trust me, it would have been easier." His face was cold, and though it unnerved Larkin to see him angry, she still glared at him. She wasn't used to Jonathan the pirate, and it still irked her that he defended Barren.

"How can you take his side after all that he has done?"

"After twenty-five attacks, Larkin, you would have to wonder why no one was trying to stop Barren."

"We did try to stop him! We sent ships to meet him—"

"Do you know that for sure?" Jonathan raised a brow. "Or did your father and William tell you that? Or wait...perhaps the king?"

"What are you saying?"

"I am saying that one simple order from the king for William to sail out and meet his brother in battle might have silenced what you find so appalling about Barren."

Larkin was quiet. She had never been sure if she liked King Tetherion. He seemed nice enough, the few times she had spoken with him, but there was always something about him that made her uneasy. Perhaps it was his relatives: they were all pirates. Or maybe it was his false ignorance when it came to Barren attacking ships off the coast of Maris. Even keeping those things in mind, she had never considered how involved the king was or should have been in the endeavors of his nephews. Now that she thought about it, why wasn't he more conscious of what was going on? Or was he? Did he enjoy what was happening to his people?

"Come, we will be arriving soon. Leaf has prepared some medicine for you. It will make you feel better." Jonathan held out his hand. Larkin took it and let him help her out of the cabin. The day seemed far too bright, even though it was late afternoon. She felt dizzy and nauseated, and she forced down the bile rising in her throat.

"There you are," said Leaf.

He and Barren were above them, standing next to Sam at the helm. Barren's features were perfectly cold. It was then Larkin realized Jonathan was still holding her hand, making sure she didn't fall. Though she wasn't sure what made Barren angry, his gaze made her feel self-conscious. She let go of Jonathan's hand quickly and ascended the stairs leading to the helm.

"Gave us all a fright last night," the Elf continued. He produced a cup filled with a warm liquid smelling of herbs and handed it to her.

"What is it and how did you make it warm?" asked Larkin suspicious of the drink. As far as she knew, there was no way to heat water in the middle of the ocean.

Leaf smirked. "The warmth comes from the herbs—it's medicine. Drink it, it's like tea."

Larkin hesitated for a moment, but placed the cup to her lips and drank the mixture. She instantly felt warmth running through her veins, relaxing every pain and subduing her pounding headache.

"Amazing," she said, still eyeing the drink with concern.

"You are very skeptical of Elvish things, even though you are one." Leaf pressed a finger against his cheek and observed her with amusement.

Larkin touched her ears self-consciously and Leaf chuckled. "Oh, that's not your only Elvish feature, Lady."

And it wasn't—as Leaf had observed before, her almond-shaped eyes and high cheekbones were signs of her heritage. "My mother was Elvish…" she said quietly.

"Barren's mother was Elvish, too."

Larkin knew that because William had the same pointed ears as she did. He never talked about his mother, and she never asked. She guessed she wasn't used to having a mother to talk about, so it didn't seem like something to mention. She wasn't sure what prompted her to ask her next question.

"What was her name?" Larkin asked.

Barren shrugged, still refusing to look at her. "Her name was Sysara."

"Do you miss her?"

To that, Barren didn't respond immediately, and when he did, he just said, "I never knew her. I don't need to chase another memory."

There were few she found who had also lost their mother, and perhaps that's what made her say what she did.

"My mother's name was Kenna. Father says she was killed by pirates."

Leaf looked perplexed and Barren even inclined his head toward them.

"Do you happen to know the name of the pirates responsible?" asked Leaf.

"No," Larkin shook her head.

"Do you know if they are dead?"

"I don't know," she admitted. "Father never said," then she narrowed her eyes. "Why? What do you know?"

"It's just…more than likely we would know the name of your mother's killer. It's against the code for us to kill women or children, and those who do, hang."

***

Silver Crest came into view. Gold lingered on the horizon, bathing the Orient in richness, and casting things in shadow. Larkin watched the island grow as they came closer. She wasn't sure why, but her stomach formed knots and she wondered how the people there would react to her. Would they know her name? Everyone she had come into contact with seemed to know her, and she sort of resented it. Would they hate her because of her name? And would Barren protect her if they did?

Lights ignited in the distance and glimmered like welcoming beacons, awaiting the sunset. Larkin felt someone beside her. She glanced to her right and saw Barren. There was something commanding about his presence. She took a deliberate breath, her heartbeat speeding up as she watched him. His eyes were on Silver Crest too, and the air between them filled with apprehension. She wondered if he was hesitant to return to this place, or to speak with her.

"How do you feel about going to Silver Crest—the center of

everything you hate?"

Larkin wasn't sure how she felt about that. Did she hate everything piracy stood for? She had before Barren kidnapped her, but now she couldn't be sure. This was freedom. "I don't know how I feel." Her voice sounded small and she cleared her throat, hating how uncertain she sounded.

"Jonathan would be more than happy to escort you back to Maris. In fact, I would prefer it. He will take you as a diplomat from Arcarum, as long as you swear to keep his secret."

Larkin pressed her lips together. If anything, she should agree to this—she did not belong here, and to head into Silver Crest was probably a death sentence. Instead, she hated that he suggested she return to Maris, that he really hadn't found her valuable.

"You did not ask me if that is what I want," she said, her voice shook a little.

"Do you know what you want?" It wasn't about knowing what she wanted; it was about knowing what was right and what was wrong. If given the choice, she *should* go back to Maris. That was the right choice. She heard Barren sigh impatiently. "I will *ask* that you decide before I let you see Silver Crest. Once you enter…the way you view the Orient will change."

She wondered if he was joking with her. She stared, captivated by his gaze. There was something missing—his eyes were sort of lack-luster, not bright and passionate like they usually were when he was kidding. She found herself wondering what it would take to bring that look back.

"I will go with you to Silver Crest," she said quickly, stopping her thoughts from exploring the subject further. Barren raised his brows in surprise, and the corners of his lips turned upward in amusement. He probably thought she was making a bad decision—one that would be entertaining to him, but there were too many things Larkin had been told and had seen now; she wouldn't allow herself to ignore them. While William and her father kept things from her, Barren was offering answers and she wanted them.

"Then I will ask you to put aside your prejudice because what you see and hear will shock you."

Larkin gave him a hard look; he was trying to frighten her. She looked away from him, watching Silver Crest as the lights grew bigger and brighter. She wished she knew what she was getting into, but part of her was excited about this new adventure.

"Jonathan said something...that you are loyal to a code...of *piracy?*" She emphasized the last word, like she didn't expect the thing to be real.

"You laugh, but we went to battle for our code, and we believe in it strongly." Barren said. "All pirates of Silver Crest abide by a code set forth by our elders. Our agreement is binding and set in ink over our hearts."

"And this is enforced?"

"Yes, strictly. If anyone is found to have hidden an offense, that is also punishable."

"But how would they know if it wasn't followed? You could

easily lie."

Barren laughed. "Yes, you could easily lie...but the Orient does not lie. It seems that bad luck follows those who breach the code. If they are not punished by those who enforce the code, the sea will have her way with them."

"It's surprising—that you would have your own code when you do your best to ignore the laws set forth by the king."

"It's only surprising because you think we choose to sail the sea based on a wish to do evil. Do not judge other pirates by what I have done. Most are not murderers—thieves, yes, but assigning them a terrible sin because of my infamy is wrong."

"And why do they thieve?" she challenged.

"Because other options are far less appealing. Being a peasant means you work hard to see the rich thrive. Being a solider to the king binds us to be enslaved—which is against the very nature of a pirate."

"*Your nature?* What is your nature?"

"To protect a basic right, freedom—Saoirse."

"Saoirse? That's what you swear by."

"What is more binding than a pirate swearing by his freedom?"

Larkin pressed her lips together. "You act as if King Tetherion hasn't been good to his subjects."

"You mean the ones in the castle?" Barren questioned quickly, sarcastically. "Or maybe the ones who own land? The statesmen in Arcarum? What about the poor? The traders? Has the king allowed them the right to climb your caste system? I don't think so. Monarchy is a ridiculous tool. What in this world gives one mortal man the right to rule over another? Our blood is no different."

"Yes, but we share this world with others, not just mortal men. Others who have magic and would wish to destroy us with it."

"Who?" Barren questioned with a raised brow. "Yes, there is magic in this world, but it is not a force that can be easily wielded."

"As far as we know. There has always been a fear that someone would figure out how to harness the magic in this world, Barren Reed. The Elves know those secrets. Don't let them fool you."

"The Elves do know those secrets," Leaf's voice rose from behind them and caused Larkin to twist on her heels. She met the Elf's severe gaze. She had forgotten he could hear everything within a two-mile radius. "Or rather, one Elf, the King of Aurum, Lord Alder. He's also very aware of the harm magic can do. Do you question his wisdom, Lady?"

Larkin couldn't say yes or no—she didn't know Lord Alder, but he didn't seem all that civil. He kept to his own territory and never mingled with humans.

Barren chuckled, and she turned her gaze to him. "Before you speak ill of the Elves, perhaps it is best to remember their prince sails with my crew."

***

Silver Crest didn't try to hide very much from the view of

outsiders. The coastline was crowded with several ships. The skyline was dotted with flags of all natures, representing each ship. Some were white, some were black, others bore a skull and crossbones, and some bore crossed cutlasses. Others were Elvish ships, light wood and light green sails were a trademark, while still others seemed to be especially made by the pirates themselves, polished to a shine with hand-stitched sails. Here, ships were a point of pride, and it was not favorable to keep them in disarray or leave them damaged.

Larkin studied the ships with amazement as the pirates finished settling their vessel at port. She wasn't sure why she found them so fascinating. She had seen several ships in the past, but none of them seemed to possess such...personality.

She heard someone chuckle behind her and she turned to see Jonathan watching her.

"You are...amazed?" he questioned with a furrowed brow. He seemed confused by the look of awe on her face.

"I've just never seen so many ships before," she said. "Doesn't it seem a little extravagant?"

She heard Barren choke with laughter. "Extravagant? You think this is extravagant?"

Larkin rolled her eyes and turned, placing her hands on her hips. "Yes, having hundreds of ships crowding your shore is a little extravagant."

"This coming from Miss Poofy Dress, flowery hair, and diamond jewelry?" Barren crossed his arms.

"I do not choose what I wear to balls," she countered.

"Just like you don't choose your husbands?"

Larkin narrowed her emerald eyes, but Barren only stared back with an equal amount of intensity. He seemed amused by her frustration, and she could feel her anger building in the air between them. He really didn't seem to think her situation was difficult at all—he should imagine himself in the position of having to marry a woman he did not love, then he would understand. Finally, she moved past the pirate, pushing him aside as she went.

Jonathan looked at Barren. "You are not smooth."

"I wasn't trying to be smooth."

As Larkin walked away, she was surprised to encounter a man moving toward her, holding up a lantern. He hadn't noticed her yet because he was focusing on his legs, as he only had one. The other was a wooden peg, which got stuck in the ground every time he tried to move. He supported himself with a cane that helped him wade through the sand, but he was still slow. When he looked up and met Larkin's gaze, he began to yell.

"Now! You stop there! Don't come any further! State yer name and yer purpose! Oh!"

The man fell face first to the sandy ground. Larkin hurried to him and tried to help him to his feet, but the man snarled at her when her hands touched his arm.

"I can do it m'self!"

She stood aside while he tried to pick himself up again. He rolled over, pushed himself into a sitting position and then thrust his cane into the sand.

"Alex?" Barren's voice was heard in the darkness. "Alex McCloud?"

It was now nearly too dark to see anything, and the old man turned his head in all directions, trying to locate the voice, though he knew it well.

"Barren Reed?" he laughed, and Larkin was struck by the sound. He had seemed so hostile before, but now he was excited. "Is that you?"

In no time, Barren was beside Alex, helping him to his feet. The old man embraced him, patting him loudly on the back. "Oh, m'boy! Never thought I'd see ya this soon!"

The amount of joy in Alex's voice was hard to ignore, and Barren's was equal. "What're you doin' 'ere?"

"Well, we were intercepted by Mr. Kingsley here. A...diplomat from Arcarum, it seems."

Alex looked at Jonathan and nodded. Larkin guessed they had met before.

"That whole gang is 'ere! Albatross'll want ta see ya. Just didn't expect ya to be 'ere so soon. Thought Jonathan would 'ave a whole lot of trouble catchin' you, really."

"He might have, had I not had a little...setback," said Barren. He glanced back at Larkin and Alex's eyes followed. While Barren's only swept her frame, Alex kept his gaze on her, cold and mistrusting.

"Lady Larkin," he said. She was surprised this old man knew her, and she shuddered at his tone. Had he recognized her before he fell? She looked down at her clothing, her skin...anything to see what would make him observe her as if she were the grim reaper. She was dirty, yes, and she probably smelled, but she was still the same Larkin she remembered. "Not sure you were expected."

"She will be my problem while we are in Silver Crest, Alex," said Barren, and this time his burning brown eyes were on her. Even in the darkness, she knew it was a warning—as if she were a child that had to be watched and punished. "No harm will come of it."

Larkin couldn't imagine what harm her presence would inflict.

Alex nodded. "If ya say so," he paused and turned, pulling his peg leg out of the sand. "Well, let's get you away from this shore! Everyone's at the Bloodshed. Ya know, we 'aven't seen much of ya since yer father died."

Barren rubbed the back of his head guiltily. "It's been a little busy, Alex."

"Busy?" Leaf scoffed. "More like boring—all we did for months was sit off the coast of Maris and eat stale bread."

"That's not all we did!" Barren snapped.

Leaf crossed his arms and gave Barren a hard look. Larkin would definitely have to agree with the Elf. She knew all too well how he'd spent the last months. Barren had done nothing other than stalk the coast of Maris, waiting for ships to depart from the harbors. Barren had been obsessed with watching their every move—if they moved port and tried to sail from a different area of Maris, he knew about it and met them head on. Usually he dealt an even greater punishment for their attempts to elude him.

"Well, it's no matter, I'm glad yer 'ere."

Larkin couldn't imagine anyone being happy to see Barren Reed. His sails usually meant death—though she had been waiting for her own demise since he had captured her and she was still breathing. Barren even saved her. She was beginning to believe Barren wasn't the bad person everyone in Maris made him out to be, but he had still tried to kill Jonathan. She needed to keep in mind that everything Barren did was for his own gain.

Silver Crest was very quiet for the most part. There were a few lanterns here and there that illuminated a long dirt road snaking its way down the small island, directing traffic to different shops and some houses. Everything was composed of weathered wood and thatched roofs. On this night, there was a heavy breeze and the fresh smell of salt and foam hit her nose. It reminded Larkin that she hadn't been on land in a few days.

She watched everything; she wasn't sure if it was because she was curious or because she was afraid someone would jump out and stick her with a sword. She didn't let her guard down—the town might be quiet, but she expected some sort of brutal activity.

She watched the crew she sailed with—they were all casual, making small talk with Alex as they headed to this...Bloodshed Pub. She was a little frightened by the name, and when they approached the two-story building, she swallowed hard. All the windows were lit with yellow lights. Men stood on the terrace outside of the pub, smoking long pipes, and making rings of smoke dance above them. There were more people on the balcony above, most leaning over languidly, staring droopy-eyed at passersby.

Larkin stared at the rundown building and felt a knot rise in her throat. She didn't want to go in—she would be surrounded by pirates: people who hated her for no reason, people who hated her father. She wasn't sure why she wanted them to like her, a pirate's approval meant nothing...but when they didn't, when Alex glared at her like a criminal, she felt hurt and confused. She didn't want to feel judged by all of these people, by people who didn't know her.

As they headed up the stairs, she was surprised when Barren moved out of the way, pushing her before him. He kept his hand on the small of her back for a moment, steering her beneath the golden lights of the Bloodshed. Inside, music, smoke and liquor hit her nose like a whip. She was a little stunned by the mix, and staggered for a moment, having never smelled anything like it before. Clanking glasses, out of tune singing and laughter rose as part of the melody of the pub, and no one looked their way, too consumed in their own stories and ale. Larkin felt relieved, but when she realized they were passing through the main part of the pub into a darker, smaller area in the back, she got a little more nervous. Barren moved his hand to her shoulder, steering her along in the darkness. He was all too familiar with this place, which eased her mind, but only slightly.

After the dark hall ended, an inviting and warm room opened up to them. It was round with a fireplace full of burning embers.

The air was cleaner, and the walls were sheeted with ebony wood. There were no windows in the room, but tarnished sconces decorated the walls, lit with waning candles. There was furniture, too—one red couch and one cream couch faced each other, and a table divided them.

The room itself was already occupied by several people. At first, Larkin recognized no one in the strange, new atmosphere, but after a moment of surveying her surroundings, she noticed one man, thin and willowy, perched upon the arm of the couch. He was dressed in a familiar black suit and had dark, glossy hair that came to his shoulders.

"Ambassador Rowell," Larkin's voice seemed to carry across the room and slowly murmurs died down, silence enveloped all, and she felt everyone's eyes on her. She sensed she had said something wrong, but she wasn't sure what.

The man she called *Ambassador* moved his dark eyes to her, cool yet caring. He smiled the same charming smile she was used to and pushed himself off the couch. He bent his willow frame in half, bowing deeply to her as he did at all formal gatherings. For a moment, she wondered if he was mocking her, but as he rose, he spoke and there was nothing in his voice that suggested he was making fun.

"Lady Larkin, a pleasure."

Then it hit her: Alex had said they were going to see Albatross, a man who had sent Jonathan, an apprentice from Arcarum, to retrieve Barren.

"Y-you're Albatross?" Larkin stuttered, suddenly realizing that the man she'd thought was fearsome and ugly was exactly the opposite. He was the educated and kind Ambassador of Arcarum.

Cove Rowell gave a sweet smile, and he seemed to pity her. "That is what they call me at sea."

"But...but you're a good man!"

He laughed. "Yes, and I am still a good man, though I sail the sea."

Larkin scoffed. "Surely you know a good man and a pirate cannot be the same thing."

A snickering laugh escaped from the corner, a laugh she recognized also. Larkin spun and saw the pale face of Senator Hallow Dallon. Bright blonde hair made his eyes seem blacker. He leaned lazily against the hearth, white arms folded over each other.

"You look like you've seen a ghost," he observed when her eyes fell upon him.

Larkin pressed her lips together. "None of you are pirates."

She knew them: they had gone to state dinners, balls, and coronations. They had sat in the dining hall with the king. How could they also sit in the middle of Silver Crest? Or embrace Barren as a friend?

"We are not pirates in your world," corrected Cove.

"There is one world and it is Mariana," she said evenly. "And in it, you are either loyal to your crown, or a traitor."

Barren rolled his eyes and sighed heavily. "You think *everyone* is a pirate if they sail the sea and disagree with you. Don't get her started, Cove." He pushed past her, moving into the room. "She'll lecture us all on how we're traitors to our crown and barbaric men. Although, she's somehow still breathing."

"Barren Reed," said Cove with a laugh, and it was evident in his glittering eyes that he was both happy and relieved to see the pirate. "It is very good to see you here, and surprising that the Lady Larkin is in one piece."

Barren swiped a glass of wine from the table. "She's been my headache ever since I picked her up in Maris."

Larkin clenched her fists as Barren's gaze landed on her, but he smirked, eyes taking on an amused glean.

"You had your chance to let me drown."

"And be responsible for your death?" Barren laughed at the idea, and took a drink from his glass. "No."

A tense silence fell between them. Cove cleared his throat and Larkin moved her gaze to the Ambassador.

"It is actually very good Barren didn't let you die, no matter how tempting. It will be easier to clear up this situation and merely return you to Maris. I will escort you, if you'd like."

"No," she said defiantly and Cove raised both brows, surprised by her response. "No."

"I already tried that," said Barren.

"I'm surprised—you seem so appalled by us. It would be better for you to be with your kind."

For some reason, those words stung Larkin, and she wanted more than ever to be seen as their equals. Why, here, was she treated as if she didn't belong? As if she were something to step upon? These men were pirates. As she looked around, however, her thoughts produced acid in her mouth. She knew these people—they were all senators and lords from Arcarum; they were kind, gracious, and known for their good deeds. These were not the people of horror she had learned about. Perhaps her first mistake was thinking pirates were beneath her.

"I want the truth," she said, her face felt hot. "My father won't give it and neither will William. So my only option is you."

Cove stared at her for a long moment and then nodded. "What do you want to know?"

"Who are you?"

"I am Ambassador Cove Rowell...when I am in Arcarum."

"And now?"

"I am captain of a crew of what you would consider to be pirates."

"Why?" her voice sounded harsh and angry, but she felt betrayed. "Why be like him?" she pointed at Barren angrily, though he was still smiling.

"What exactly are you accusing us of, Larkin?" asked Cove darkly. She did not miss how he disregarded her title. It was no matter, did it really have any significance here?

"You take what does not belong to you," she said. "And murder those who protest. You, who are supposed to abide by the laws of your king."

"You are just like your father—you hear and see only what you want," Cove's voice was biting and his eyes became slits of ink. "For what it is worth, Larkin, I was born into this life, I did not begin it."

"Born into this life?" she questioned. "Your father was killed by pirates—that should be enough reason for you to reconsider what you are doing!"

Cove's eyes blazed. She guessed she had unlocked all the anger and hurt associated with his father's untimely death. She had to admit, the grief was still fresh—she had only attended the funeral about two months before.

"My father betrayed me. His death was due," Cove spoke harshly.

Larkin flinched. "What do you mean?"

"My father began this—sailing to fight those who threatened us at sea. He, too, corrupted his purpose and hoarded riches, and his greed overpowered him. My father was giving information to Christopher Lee regarding his crew. Only he claimed I led the Arcarum Pirates, when it was his creation and still his crew. On the day he was to expose us, the crew he led rose up and murdered him. He cared nothing for us, and he cared nothing for me." Cove was silent for a moment, and then he leveled his gaze on Larkin. "Though I have a different title on land and another at sea, it does not make me a thief or a murderer. Reconsider your words."

Silence followed and Larkin found that she could not meet Cove's gaze anymore. She was both angry and embarrassed by her assumptions, and being compared to her father in this situation seemed very much an insult, especially coming from the pirates.

"Cove is not like me," Barren spoke up in the silence, and Larkin looked at him. He was standing with his arms crossed, leaning against the dark walls. There, the light from one of the sconces poured over him, illuminating his cheekbones, but keeping his eyes in shadow. His body seemed broad and strong, and a lump rose in her throat as she studied him. "His crew is not like me, and my crew is not like me. What I have done, all that I have done, has always been my decision, and I never want my actions to speak for all pirates, because they do not. Cove fights privateers—men you would say do good for their islands, but men we would say have corrupted their purpose."

"What do you mean they have corrupted their purpose?"

"Privateers are glorified scoundrels. They are men with letters of the marque which make them exempt from facing punishment for their deeds at sea," said Cove. "King Cathmor, Barren's grandfather, wanted a force to combat his son, Jess, after he betrayed his title and his blood to sail the sea. For a while, their only purpose was to seek pirate ships and fight them. They did little good, really. It is difficult for a group of rogue men to fight skilled pirates, but they soon found that they could attack any innocent sailors—traders, refugees, and even government ships— and plunder if they posed as pirates. They would bring a percentage of the goods they stole to their respective islands and seem like heroes, when, in truth, they were just giving pirates a bad name and hurting innocent people. My purpose is to fight them, and I do, just as other pirates of Silver Crest do."

"But that would not make you a pirate."

"It does," said Cove. "I am caught in a very ironic situation. Because I fight privateers, men who are hired by the government—your father and your fiancé, to be exact—I am committing a crime against the government and would be considered a pirate."

"My father is responsible for this?"

"It should be of little surprise. Your father has always hated pirates," said Cove. "His goal is to wipe piracy off the face of Mariana."

It was hard to believe that her father would be so careless as to allow people who were meant to combat an evil, to instead conduct such malicious acts.

"He cannot know what the privateers do," Larkin said at last. "He fights for the innocent lives Barren destroys!"

Barren chuckled. "Does he fight for them? Or does he just send more into my hands?"

Larkin glared at Barren. How could he be laughing?

"He has a point," said Cove.

"It is sweet to wish that your father is a good man," said Barren, though his tone mocked her naivety. "But in many ways, he is just as bad as me."

"What does the king think of this?"

"I can do nothing against your father," said Tetherion. Larkin jumped and whirled around to see the king's outline in the doorway. He loomed above them, tall, powerful, filling the space with his greatness. He had salt and pepper hair, brown eyes, and his jaw, like Barren's, was strong and defined. He was dressed as if he had been traveling—black boots crusted with mud, brown pants, a black shirt, and a brown cloak. Nothing on his person hinted that he was a king, except he had that same prideful grace that also surrounded Barren.

Datherious and Natherious entered the room on either side of him, melding with the crowd as if they weren't Princes of the Orient. Larkin had the urge to curtsy before him, because every other time she had seen him, it was customary, but in this crowded room of pirates, not one person moved to honor him, and so she stood still and instead questioned him.

"But you are not a pirate." She felt like she had been saying that a lot lately. As it was turning out, it seemed that everyone in the government was a pirate.

"Not in the way you would think."

"But you supported Jess's death."

He glared at her for a moment, and she knew she had overstepped her boundaries.

"Uncle, what a surprise to see you," said Barren quickly. He moved past Larkin. "In Silver Crest, of all places."

Teth's eyes shifted to his nephew. "It is safest. Come, I must speak with you."

Larkin's gaze passed between the two. She never expected to see this encounter. She wasn't sure what relationships existed between them, but she had imagined it wasn't very good. Tetherion seemed to support William and his rise in status in public. Even so, Teth had never openly condemned Barren for his deeds, and every action taken against the pirate had been the result of her father's or William's order.

She watched as Teth turned from the doorway, but before he took another step, he paused and turned slightly, glancing askance at Larkin.

"You, too, Lady Larkin."

Barren followed without hesitation, but Larkin stayed behind. Even she didn't understand where the sudden doubt came from. She had trusted Tetherion up until this point. Perhaps it was the environment that made her stay—everyone in the room was looking at them now. Barren turned to her. "Come, don't keep him waiting."

Chapter Nine
CHANGING TIDES

Barren and Larkin followed the shadow of Tetherion up the stairs. Once at the top, he turned to the left and entered a room. Barren held the door open for Larkin and she slipped past, avoiding his gaze. They were in a study where most of the walls were lined with books. A fireplace protruded from the far wall, and windows interrupted the rows of shelves behind a desk. Amid the various colored spines, were pieces of treasure from the Orient—gems and jewels that shone beneath the lantern light, gold statues with glittering eyes, and navigation pieces—compasses, spyglasses, and sextants.

Tetherion moved behind the desk, and Barren closed the door

loudly before making his way to the fireplace and leaning against the mantle. It was his way of telling Teth he didn't intend to stay long. Teth didn't sit either, moving instead, to close the curtains behind him. Only then did he look at Larkin. His eyes no longer possessed the darkness they had before; now they just looked worn.

"I did not expect you to have the Lady Larkin with you, Barren," said Teth at last, then his gaze met Barren's. The pirate raised a brow.

"I didn't expect to have her, either, but she refused to go home."

In a swift movement, Barren took out his sword. He didn't miss the way Larkin watched him—she was guarded. He sat down beside her, and lay the weapon across his knees.

"Well, I am glad to hear the rumors are false, then," said Teth. His voice taking on the tone of his eyes—grave and tired. He sat down.

"What do you mean?"

"I heard you had murdered her."

Barren chuckled, but Larkin was in disbelief.

"Believe me, I wanted to kill her more than once."

Larkin scowled. "Barren wouldn't have captured me if Leaf had stayed out of it!"

For a brief moment, Tetherion looked amused, but that was soon replaced with seriousness. "Neither of you realize what you've gotten me into, do you?"

"Me? Being kidnapped was hardly *my* fault!" Larkin crossed

her arms over her chest. "And I am obviously *not* dead!"

"No," the king answered and Larkin was under his eyes again. "You are not."

"What are you talking about?" Barren demanded.

"You were sent for because your brother announced Larkin's death, and, as a result, a revolt has begun in Maris. I cannot be certain if Christopher Lee was involved, however, it is my belief that he either believes you are dead as well, or is conspiring with William. If the former, Barren will be met with war, if the latter, I will be forced to deliver justice."

"It wasn't meant to go this far," Barren said quickly. "I only kidnapped her to lure William to me, but once they attacked the Cliffs, I could not return her."

Tetherion clamped a hand over his mouth and then dragged it down his beard.

"What if I went back? My father would see that I am alive. The revolt would cease," Larkin suggested, and she moved toward the end of her seat. Barren didn't miss that she'd already assumed her father's innocence.

"It goes deeper than that, I am afraid," Tetherion's voice sounded so grim. "This is about easing fear. They feel I am not doing enough to protect them from Barren. You've never crossed the shore of Maris to capture one of their own until now. They are afraid. How am I to ease their fear, Barren? I warned you our relationship would not be easy the day you chose piracy. Now do you see why?"

At first Barren felt guilty. He didn't mean to cause more

trouble for his uncle, but then again, William had lived at peace in Maris for the past five years. He'd lived a comfortable life, ignoring Barren's calls to meet him off shore. Larkin's situation was just as much Tetherion's fault as it was William's. If Tetherion had not wanted this to happen, he should have ordered William to meet Barren.

"You owe me the chance to kill him," Barren said evenly.

"No one owes you a life," Larkin interjected.

"You made a selfish decision." Judgment and anger ran through Tetherion's voice. "But I should not have expected more from someone so young."

For a moment Barren felt overwhelmed by their scrutiny, and then it quickly turned to anger.

"You realize William has wanted the crown for some time—"

"You really thought he would succeed in his attempts?" countered Tetherion powerfully. "Do you think I am a fool? I know what William wants!"

"Has he not proven he would do anything to get what he wants? He could have killed you!"

"And if he did?" Tetherion was on his feet, voice rising. Barren stood, sword in hand. "Datherious or Natherious would have been there to defend the throne. Now you have given those people someone else to look to—a false leader! What is worse? His living as a mere Ambassador? Or his succession as king?"

"I did not know William's intentions! Had I known he was waiting for a precise moment to move against you, I would have reconsidered my plans!"

"Would you? Barren, part of growing up is realizing limits. Realizing that there is a whole world that has suffered just as you, and you are not entitled to any sort of revenge!"

Barren looked away from his uncle, his throat worked. He might not be entitled to revenge, but he would have it. His eyes fell on Larkin who was staring intently at her hands.

"Did you know?" he demanded, turning toward her. She met his stare with unkind eyes.

"No I did not know! It was my understanding William assumed he was the natural heir to the throne. However, it's clear that is not the case."

"It seems you both provided a proper arrangement for William's success," Tetherion said.

Barren slammed his fists against the oak table, and the silence that followed was deafening. He sat down in his chair again. Barren hated to think William had gotten the best of him. What was worse was not knowing his next move.

"Where is William now?" asked Barren. "Do we know what he is planning next?"

"I do," Tetherion paused for a long moment, and Barren and Larkin suddenly had the feeling that Teth dreaded this conversation. He rubbed his eyes as he sat in silence, deciding how he would proceed. "Your brother has left Maris in search of the bloodstone."

Barren laughed. "But that's a myth, why would he go after something that's not real?"

Tetherion lifted his eyes to Barren, as if admitting to guilt.

"Because it is real, and it was stolen…by your father."

"You're lying!" Barren wasn't sure if he thought Tetherion was lying about everything, or the accusation against his father. Either way, he had heard about the bloodstone from the time he was a child. The stone was said to bind the Reed line to the throne. Barren just assumed the legend was created by those in Mariana who felt the Reeds had come into power unfairly. If there was any truth to the tale, it meant that the stone bound the Reed line to the throne by dark magic.

"There are many secrets the throne must keep from the public. Some are too dangerous to let loose, others would create imbalance in the world. The bloodstone is both of those."

"So all the rumors are true," Larkin sat higher in her seat. "The Elves are hiding magic."

"They are not hiding it," said Tetherion, crushing that assumption quickly. "Not all Elves can control magic. Only Elves born with Lyric blood, and there have been none of those born for years, and those who were in existence are dead. So yes, at one point, the Elves were hiding magic, but they learned their lesson with the bloodstone."

"What do you mean?"

"The bloodstone was offered to Eadred during the First War by Lord Alder in exchange for a promise that the two kingdoms would rule together in peace within the Orient. Eadred was to give the stone back once he won his crown, but when the time came to release it, Eadred refused. There was nothing Lord Alder could do, as the stone would protect Eadred no matter what."

That would explain why Lord Alder hates mortals so much.

"And why would my father steal such a stone?"

"Well, if it was in his possession, then he would be untouchable." Barren felt his eyes darken, and anger rose in his chest. Tetherion continued. "The stone was stolen around the time of the Ore Wars. Jess was fighting our fathers' soldiers.

"You want me to believe my father stole a bloodstone in order to make himself invincible? He was a pirate! He had a sense of honor!"

"And your father's wish for Saoirse triumphed over that," Tetherion countered. "But do not think his decision wasn't met with deep regret in the end."

"What do you mean by that?"

Tetherion took a deliberate breath, and Barren knew he wasn't going to like what his uncle was about to say. "You never knew your mother, but she was perhaps the most powerful Lyric in Mariana. When she discovered what your father intended to do with the bloodstone, she sought to destroy it, but the bloodstone is composed of dark magic, and over time, it strengthened. The stone drained her life-force, and she died."

Barren was silent. Part of him couldn't wrap his mind around any feelings he should probably have, and the other part of him was angry. He wasn't sure what to say. Sysara. Sysara had been a Lyric. Even now the thought made him uncomfortable. He never liked to hear about his mother because he didn't remember her. For all he knew, she had never been around or loved him. It was easier to think she didn't exist than to wonder *why* she didn't exist.

"Why tell me this now?" Barren asked slowly. "Why now when you've had five years?"

Tetherion seemed confused for a moment, and when he spoke, it was sincere. "I could not add to the pain of your father's death."

"So you choose to now? As if it would be easier?"

"It is now a necessity," Tetherion's voice was stern. "William is after the stone, which means when he finds it, he will be unstoppable—against me, my army, and you. I am asking you to stop him, to find the stone."

"And what would I do with such a thing once I had it?"

"Destroy it," Larkin interrupted. "Nothing like that should be in existence."

"We would all be better off if it were not in existence," agreed Tetherion. "But dark magic cannot be destroyed, unless you are ready to surrender your life to the otherworld."

"So you want it?" Barren's question sounded more like an accusation.

"It is better, is it not, to have such a device in the hands of someone who will not exploit it?"

"But you will not be the only king. There will be others who are not as wise." Barren argued.

"Can you not trust your cousins, Datherious and Natherious, who so ardently believe in Saoirse, that they joined your crew? Believe me, Barren, the hope is that this stone will be returned to the crown's vault and not looked upon again. It has no power so long as it is in none of our hands."

Barren shivered hearing the promise in Tetherion's tone. He was very quiet. He did not like the idea of this stone being in existence. Even if he trusted the king, and even if the twins believed in Saoirse, it still left the potential for the throne to be unopposed, and while that was convenient for any king, what if the world no longer wished for a king? What if that king was a terrible ruler? That stone had the ability to lay waste to many. To hand over such a stone felt like treason to Barren since he upheld the right to Saoirse and the code.

"I would go after it myself, but I have a rebellion to quash in Maris. I believe I should stay put for a spell, since this isn't the first." Tetherion added more guilt to Barren's shoulders. "Barren, I am offering you a chance to have your revenge. Do this for me, and whatever happens to William along the way will be no one's fault but his own."

"What?" Larkin stood immediately. "A life is not yours to offer up in exchange for anything, not even for something as dangerous as this stone."

"I am not handing over a life, Lady Larkin. Barren has to catch William first."

Barren understood what Tetherion was offering. William would be at sea in search of this stone. He would be vulnerable, and he could take advantage of that by seeking out the bloodstone for Tetherion.

"Don't you trust me?" Tetherion added, as if he could read Barren's mind.

The pirate was at a loss—he did trust Tetherion…with his life. The king had done nothing to harm him, always remaining blind to Barren's antics, despite the fact that he allowed William to move up in the ranks. At any point, he could have sent Barren to the noose, and now, as Tetherion's dark eyes surveyed the pirate, that truth was all the more evident. Not only that, but Tetherion was offering Barren an open invitation to pursue his wish for revenge.

"I don't even know where to start looking," said Barren.

"Your brother will begin by seeking members of your father's crew who were with him at the time."

"Members like Alex?"

"Alex's injuries kept him here in Silver Crest during the time your father took the bloodstone, but it is Alex who will take you to Conn and there you can begin your search. He says he knows someone." Barren was a little irritated that his uncle had already taken the liberty of discussing this with everyone else before he ever agreed to do it.

"But William has known about the stone longer, how do we know he hasn't already found it?"

"You will know when he comes into possession of the bloodstone. He will begin to destroy what he hates most in the world—pirates. The most frightening thing about the bloodstone is that it is dark magic—the power of evil, of selfishness, and it cares for no living thing. It will corrupt in whatever way it feels necessary—through famine, disease, or natural disaster."

Barren stood quickly, and Larkin jumped. "Is that all you

needed of us?

Tetherion nodded. Barren extended his hand, motioning for Larkin to leave. She brushed past him and hurried for the exit. Barren was right behind her, but before he could escape, Tetherion called to him again.

"I will be gone by morning," he said. "I must return to Maris and clean up the mess your brother has made. Promise me you will bring the bloodstone."

Barren only held his uncle's gaze for a moment, then he closed the door behind him. Turning to face the cool air of the hallway, he hadn't realized how hot it had been in the study. He let out a low breath.

"What are we going to do?" Larkin asked, waiting for Barren to speak.

"Stop William and find the bloodstone," said Barren simply, not missing that Larkin had suddenly involved herself in his expedition to destroy her fiancé.

"You mean kill him?"

Surprisingly, Barren felt more concerned with the knowledge that his mother was a Lyric, and his father had been the reason for her death. If anything, he felt motivated to attempt this quest to find the truth.

Barren leveled his gaze with hers. He didn't want it to seem that his wish for revenge had lessened during the course of their conversation, because it hadn't. The thought of an unstoppable William Reed was not favorable to Barren in the least. So he asked, "Are you going to protect him as you protected Jonathan?"

"And if I did, would you kill me?"

"No one gets in the way of my revenge."

The look she gave him challenged that statement. "Do you trust your uncle?"

"I have no reason not to trust my uncle," Barren said, scratching his prickly chin. "I may not always like him, but he has done me no wrong."

The two headed downstairs and out of the Bloodshed Pub. He imagined Larkin was more than happy to leave the pub. She kept her pace with Barren as he headed toward a white, two-story house at the end of the road. It was a charming home with a wrap-around porch, warmly-lit windows, and delicious aromas.

As they approached, they found Alex on the porch, rocking in a chair. He had a knife and was whittling away at a piece of wood. When he spotted them, he stood and held the door open for them.

"Mary's got some food saved for ya. She wouldn't go to bed 'til she knew you'd all eaten," he said, leading them into the kitchen.

Mary was Alex's wife. She was a round woman with a round face and flush cheeks. She kept her hair in a bun, though wisps of it escaped and flew in a frenzy around her face. When she saw Barren enter, she hugged him tightly. She pulled away, and placed her hands on either side of the pirate's face.

"You're such a good boy," she said. "A good, kind-hearted boy."

Then Mary's eyes fell on Larkin, and it was as if she'd known her all her life.

"What a doll you are!" she said, spreading her arms wide and embracing her. Larkin seemed surprised but accepted the welcome with a smile as she returned the hug. "Barren, where did you get such a pretty girl?"

Mary pulled away, but managed to grasp Larkin's hand as she did.

Barren smiled and rubbed the back of his neck, not meeting Mary's gaze. "That's complicated, Mary…"

"I'm from Maris," Larkin interrupted. Barren watched her as she spoke, relieved that he didn't have to explain to his only mother-like figure that he'd kidnapped a girl. "You could say I stowed away on Barren's ship. Not my best idea."

"I'd say," he muttered.

"Well, you better be nice to her," Mary placed her hands on her hips. "A man's only as good as he treats his lady."

Barren buried his face in his hand. He would have attempted to correct Mary—tell her Larkin was most certainly not *his* lady, but he had learned long ago it did no good to right her.

The rest of Barren's company had already eaten in the time it had taken for him and Larkin to speak with Tetherion and had now retired to their rooms. Mary gave Barren and Larkin their supper. They ate between questions from Mary, which were both entertaining and awkward. Barren had the strangest feeling of ease as they all sat around the table, laughing together—he would never have guessed this would be happening. Larkin was *actually* enjoying herself, and Barren found that he liked watching her smile more than he should.

When they were finished, Mary ushered Larkin down the hall, offering a hot bath, new clothes, and grooming. Larkin was more than happy to concede, but gave Barren a worried look as he was left alone in the dining room.

He didn't stay there long, however. He grabbed a bottle of wine from the cabinet and moved through the double-doors into the kitchen and then out the back door. He made his way down the rocky path to a small marker—a cross carved out of wood. It wasn't really the place Jess was buried, but when Barren was in Silver Crest, he liked to imagine it was. He sat down on a slab of rock next to the cross. He rested his elbows on his knees and leaned forward. Pulling the cork out of the bottle, he took a long drink, ignoring the bitterness as he swallowed.

He watched the ocean for a moment. It was calm. The light of the moon drifted over it like a ghost. Then he looked at the cross as if it had spoken to him. "I thought I would have avenged you by now. I hope you will forgive my neglect. Things haven't gone my way."

Then he laughed at himself. This piece of wood wasn't going to respond to him, and even though he knew that, he was struck with sadness. Rubbing his face vigorously, he stood and left the silent cross.

Chapter Ten
LESSONS

The rain was cold and harsh. Barren stood knee-deep in the water. He wasn't sure where he was. Everything was dark, but as he began wading through the water toward the shore, he heard his name cutting through the air like a knife.

"Barren! Help me, Barren!"

It was Larkin. He spun around; the water fought him, rising up in giant waves to wash over him. He pushed forward into the dark blue-black of the ocean, searching for her.

"Larkin! Larkin! Where are you?" he cried desperately—his tone sounded foreign to him. He felt anxiety and fear overpower him as he searched for her in the impossible darkness. The panic spread through his chest and pulled tightly.

"Barren!" her voice was a distant echo, but he turned in the direction from which it came and finally saw her lithe frame. She fought the brutal waves of the Orient.

"Larkin!" Barren moved toward her as fast as he could, diving into the Orient's resentful waters. He propelled himself forward, his arms and legs hurt from the force of the waves, and the pressure against his ears made his head pound. His chest burned from holding his breath. Finally, he broke the surface, taking in a deep breath. Larkin was before him, fighting to stay above the water.

"Larkin! Take my hand!" He reached for her, and their fingertips touched.

"Barren," she breathed, helplessly, exhausted. Her eyes shimmered dully. With a final push from the Orient, he grabbed her arm and pulled her to him. Her breath was weak, and her body limp. The Orient seemed to react by pushing them to the dark shore. He stumbled out of shallow water, staring down at her white face.

"Larkin," he whispered. "Larkin, don't let go...stay with me."

Her eyes were slits now; the only life left in them was a dull glow. Barren fell to his knees with her, holding her head in his lap. He pressed his hand to the side of her face. "Don't let go!" he ordered, but she just smiled faintly.

Then a thick dark streak ran from her mouth. He moved his thumb over it, wiping it away, realizing it was blood. It was only then he noticed his shirt was soaked with a warm substance.

"Larkin!" he cried desperately, as he saw the blood pool at a hole in her abdomen—she had been shot. "No, please...please don't leave me!"

She still smiled, and placed her ivory hand upon his face. She moved his hair behind his ear. "I am sorry."

Her hand left his face, leaving a streak of warmth. Her body went limp in his hands. Numbness overtook him, and pain spread through his limbs as he lifted her against him, and buried his face in the hollow of her neck.

***

Barren opened his eyes and sat up quickly. Light blinded him and he fell back, hitting his head against the wall. "Ouch!" he placed his hands behind his head, as the pain burned beneath his fingers. Lying there for a moment, he gathered his thoughts. He was relieved that he had been having a dream, but he couldn't shake the feelings he had experienced—they were so strong, so real and all for someone who had given him hell since the moment they'd met.

He had proven, however, that he would save Larkin no matter the danger, when he jumped into the Orient to pull her to safety. Part of it was the fact that he could not be responsible for her death, but there was another reason. There had to be...Barren didn't simply disregard his own life for anyone. Now he was having dreams about Larkin's death. This had to stop. Either Larkin was going to have to return to Maris, or Barren would never sleep again.

He stood up, rubbing the back of his head. Grabbing his shirt from the chair he'd left it on the night before, he pulled it on, and splashed his face with cool water. The smells of breakfast—freshly baked bread, eggs, and sausage—came to his nose, and his stomach growled, angry at its emptiness. He had forgotten how much he missed real food after having only eaten stale bread and potatoes for the past several months. Barren hurried out of his room and headed for the stairs.

"Hungry, are ye?" laughed Slay. Barren turned to see him and Leaf.

"Better get there before the dwarf, or there'll be no food left."

Slay grumbled and glared at the Elf.

"Sleep well?" asked Leaf, observing the purplish bags under Barren's eyes.

"It was a rough night." Barren turned from the two pirates and headed down the stairs.

"Tetherion was pretty hard on ye, eh?" asked Slay. "Cause you took Lord Lee's daughter?"

"Not hardly...although that probably didn't help," said Barren. "It was another matter entirely, but I'd prefer to tell you after I've had some food."

The three entered the dining room. It was a large red room with a huge bay window overlooking the road outside. One of the windows was open, allowing a cool breeze to circulate. Chairs crowded the dining table, enough to seat Cove and Barren's crew. Silverware and white china lay before everyone, and plates of food sat at the center, filled with eggs, meat, and breads. There were also glass pitchers of juice and water, and a ceramic pot of coffee. The aromas made Barren's mouth water.

Alex was already there, sitting at the head of the table, helping himself to several heaping spoons full of eggs and sausage. He smirked when he saw them enter and patted the space beside him.

"Come! Sit and eat with me!" He looked so jolly that Barren wondered what had him in such a good mood. Maybe the prospect of having to sail to Conn was exciting for him. It had been a while since Alex had sailed. His injuries and obligations to Silver Crest usually kept him inland.

Cove, Hollow and the others filed in shortly after Barren. They all looked refreshed and were in very good spirits. It had been a few years since Barren sat at a table with his friends. Barren had known Cove since Alex introduced them five years ago. The Ambassador expressed his sorrow at hearing of Jess's death. Aside from the pirates of Silver Crest, he had been the first to give Barren his sympathy and he understood Barren's wish for revenge. They had been secret allies ever since. It was one of several reasons Barren had been free this long. That, and the fact that Tetherion had kept anyone from declaring war upon him.

As he looked around the table, he noticed Larkin was missing. He didn't like how his eyes had suddenly gone in search of her, but he chalked it up to the nightmare he had last night. His gaze landed on her as she stepped through the doorway; her hair streamed over one shoulder in curls. Her face was refreshed and radiant: a slight blush pressed over her cheeks, and a smirk threatened her lips. She exchanged the clothes Barren had given her for something more fitting—a brown cotton dress and a red corset that hugged her waist. He smiled, though he wished he hadn't because Leaf caught his gaze and the look in his eyes told Barren he'd hear about this later.

"Larkin!" exclaimed Leaf. "Come! Sit!"

She laughed as she walked toward Leaf, taking a seat next to him—right across from Barren. Their eyes met as she picked up a fork and began scooping food onto her plate.

"Tetherion left early this morning. Seems his favoritism landed him in hot water…it only took twenty-five ships and one kidnapping," said Cove. His dark eyes were on Barren as he took a drink from his mug.

Barren met the Ambassador's gaze. "How is it you know everything before anyone else, Albatross?"

Cove smiled. "I did not spend the last few years doing nothing. You know my network reaches far and moves quickly."

Cove's network was often referred to as *The Network* and consisted of a web of pirates dispersed all over the Orient. They were basically spies, and exchanged messages constantly, but it was not only for the Ambassador's private use—any pirate could use it to get a message to another and in this way it acted as a sort of postal service.

"Yes, if only it could tell us where the bloodstone is."

"*The* bloodstone?" asked Leaf. "You mean the one that's not real?"

"Oh no, apparently it's quite real—a royal family secret." Barren's eyes landed on the twins. "You two didn't know about this, did you?"

The two exchanged a glance. "We knew it was missing," said Datherious, "but father always seemed okay with its absence."

"So what's changed?" Cove's dark eyes were on the twins first, then they settled on Barren.

"William is after it," said Barren. "And Tetherion wants me to stop him, and find the bloodstone. He seems to think it is best kept under his care."

"Is it not?" questioned Datherious. "You know father would protect it."

"It's not about who would protect it best," said Larkin. "That stone is composed of Barren's blood—"

"Our blood," said the twins in unison.

"*William's* blood," Barren reminded them sternly. "And if he has it, he will, essentially, be invincible. You've all heard the legends—Eadred was able to destroy the whole of Gesalec's army with that device. Imagine what William would do to the pirates of Silver Crest—worse, the rest of the Mariana."

"How did something as important as the bloodstone slip out from under the king's nose in the first place?" asked Hollow.

"I am unsure," replied Barren. "All I know is that my father was responsible for stealing it. Tetherion said he wished to possess it in order to defeat Cathmor's army during the Ore Wars."

Barren cringed as he spoke—he still didn't believe his father capable of such a motive.

"You sound unconvinced," observed Cove.

"If you were informed that your father's decision led to your mother's death, you'd probably be skeptical, too."

"Wait," Leaf interrupted. "Tetherion had information about your mother?"

"Apparently he's had it for quite some time." Barren ran his hand over his face. "He said my mother was a Lyric. She tried to destroy the bloodstone, and died."

"Well, things make a little more sense now," said Leaf.

"How so?"

"There are few things I know about the Lyrics—one was that they were supposed to remain pure, and their relationships with mortals would have surely been forbidden. Your mother would not have been allowed the privilege of a family, so you would not have known her."

That didn't make Barren feel any better. "Was that a rule of your father's?"

Leaf stiffened. "The Lyrics knew the rules that bound their magic, and they betrayed those rules."

"What more do you know of the Lyrics?"

Leaf shook his head. "Not much. I know they were exiled, and in Aurum, it is forbidden to speak of them. Their memory is more of a…disgrace."

Barren set his teeth. He might not remember his mother, but hearing those words used to describe her made him angry. She was a disgrace because she'd met his father. She was a disgrace because her children were half-Elf. Maybe the hardest part of all of this was trying to accept the selfishness of his father, and the selflessness of his mother.

"Whatever happened in the past does not matter now," said Barren, his voice steady. "We're dealing with the present, and we must keep William from finding the bloodstone." Barren's eyes turned to Alex. "I was informed you would take us to Conn?"

Alex nodded, taking a drink of his coffee and wiping his mouth. "Tomorrow," he said as he cleared his throat. "We must be on the move quickly. We don't know 'ow much information William 'as. He could be leagues ahead of us, even now."

"Would it not be easier to go straight to Lord Alder? I am sure he remembers the Lyrics and their choices well. Perhaps he knows where the stone is hidden."

"The only thing Lord Alder despises more than a mortal is a half-Elf," said Leaf. "That would be a bad idea."

"Not if you were asking for it," Barren countered.

"We will stick with searching for members of Jess's crew," said Alex. "If we can get to them first, then we may save their lives. It isn't likely any of your father's crew will willingly help William."

"You will need help," said Cove.

Barren's eyes shifted to the Ambassador. "I cannot ask it of you," said the pirate. "We don't know what we're getting into. I could not allow you to face the same uncertainty, not when you have an obligation to your position as Ambassador."

"I am not giving you a choice," said Cove. His eyes were serious but his smile warm.

"We'll need yer 'elp, Albatross. Thank ya," said Alex. He gave Barren a hard look. "I suggest we all prepare today, ya won't have time tonight—folks wanna have a dance. We'll leave at daybreak tomorrow."

Barren was the first to excuse himself from the table, feeling full and suddenly sick at the smell of food. He walked out onto the McCloud's porch in the late morning. It was a pleasant day— the sun was out, and a light breeze stirred the air. In the distance he could hear the pounding of a hammer upon an anvil, children laughing, playing...things he had not heard in a very long time. It was normal, and unfortunately made him feel very uncomfortable. He felt guilty almost—here he could have a home. Mary and Alex had been his mother and father after Jess died, but land—even land that served as a pirate haven—just didn't feel right.

Barren could feel eyes on him, even as he leaned against the porch rail. People stared at him from the windows of their shops, shot glances from the street as they passed. Everyone knew who he was—the infamous Barren Reed, greatest enemy of William Reed. Barren had heard some wild stories about himself—things he had never done, like destroy the dreaded Kraken of Nymph Isle and fight giant Octopuses' in the Octent. It was as if he had been sculpted into this legendary hero, but he felt like a fraud. He had done nothing but wait for his opportunity to kill, never once seeking to do anything great. He was far from a hero, far from a legend. Now, as he stood in the middle of Silver Crest, he was ashamed.

The screen door opened and closed behind him. He didn't turn to see who it was—he had a feeling he already knew.

"You seem a little troubled."

Larkin appeared beside Barren, mimicking the way he stood, leaning against the rail. He watched her, but she didn't look at him. She seemed so relaxed here—a strange contrast to how she'd been last night in the Pub.

"Will you walk with me?" He decided not to acknowledge how he was feeling, and didn't look at her, either. Maybe he was afraid she'd say no, but it wasn't as if Barren planned on letting her get out of it. He needed her to learn an important skill if she was to stay with them at sea.

"Sure."

Larkin followed Barren from the porch and down the road. Now that it was daylight, Silver Crest was bathed in its true color. It was a little worn, a little old, but not terrifying. When most people thought about Silver Crest, they often thought of it as a barbaric place with no rules or order, but it was exactly the opposite. People raised families here, and called it home. It was the one place all pirates of the Orient could come and not be judged as heathens.

They walked among men and women moving about in their daily routines, carrying water, working on small, overgrown gardens, and cleaning. Some were mending sails, others fashioning the hull of ships with bent pieces of wood. Some sat beneath thatched roofs in rocking chairs, others sharpened swords, but no matter their tasks, they still nodded and waved as the two passed.

"I thought pirates had to answer the call of the Orient," said

Larkin, looking about. "If that's so, why does this place exist?"

Barren laughed. "Think of it as a meeting place. Alex told me that his men happened upon the island. They took it as a sign the Orient wanted them to use it, and so they did. When nobles in Maris and surrounding islands started to see pirates as a nuisance, this became the only place they could go."

"You speak as if pirates have never been a nuisance."

"Pirates love the sea, Larkin, and they believe freedom is a right we're born with. That is only a nuisance to a government who wishes to control its people."

"You know, not all law and order is terrible."

"No," he agreed. "But it should never be up to a few to decide the fate of many."

She had nothing to say to that.

They walked slowly and in silence for a long time after that, neither sure of what to say to the other. The ports came into view—masts, chains and ropes hindered the horizon. In the night, the scene had been quite breathtaking, but in the daylight, the ships crowding the shore looked frightening, as if the whole of Silver Crest was being overrun. Barren took Larkin farther down shore, to a narrow strip of sand where there were no ships, only the rush of the sea coming toward them. A peace settled between them. It was strange how easily the sea could bring such comfort.

Without looking at each other, they both began to speak. "I'm sorry—"

There was a pause and they gazed at each other.

Barren chuckled and ran a hand through his hair. "I'll go first," he said, taking a deep breath. "I am sorry for what has happened to you and what will happen beyond this point. I had no inkling of my brother's intentions, and no idea he would use your disappearance to his advantage."

"Well, it definitely did not produce the results you wanted, though I can say I am grateful for that," she smiled a little, pausing as the sounds of the sea filled the air. "And I owe *you* an apology. All my life I have only been told one side of your story, and to have yours...well, it doesn't make accepting the murders any easier, but it helps."

He smiled ruefully, shaking his head. "You don't have to apologize for your morals. What I have done is not good, and despite Cove's attempted excuse, I have killed for only one purpose—to avenge my father's death."

In his voice, there was a tremor of regret, but his face remained emotionless and blank.

"Why are you so focused on that task?" she asked. "For five years it has been your one goal...and now you are wavering from it."

Barren stared down at his hands, running his fingers along the calluses marring them. "I feel as though I am betraying him. I feel like my revenge should have been fast and sweet. Instead, it is burdensome and bitter."

"Then why do you continue like this?"

He looked at her, his eyes burning with longing; he wished she understood. "I am waiting to feel...right again. You have never lost anyone dear to you, Larkin. You don't know what it's like...and I watched him die. I still have nightmares about that day. If ever I succeed in my wish to kill William, you still would not know my pain."

She pulled at her curled strands guiltily. Barren's eyes flickered to the chain around her neck—her engagement ring.

"You've seemed convinced of my detachment since you met me," she said.

Barren nodded. "It's because you weren't wearing your ring. If you loved him, wouldn't you wear it?"

"I don't understand why it bothers you."

"Because you don't even have affection for him," said Barren with a shrug. "And you are going to marry him. Why? So you can betray your marriage and love another?"

Larkin frowned. "My father said he didn't care who I loved, he cared who I married. I never really considered the situation—I just assumed I would love one day—married to William or not."

Barren kept his eyes on the sand, hearing her speak. If there was one thing he disagreed with, it was not honoring the institution of marriage. When he looked up, he saw Larkin smirking at him.

"What?" Barren asked, his brows came together.

"Nothing..." she said. Barren gave her a guarded look, and was about to say something when Leaf appeared.

"I hear Larkin will be with us for a little longer," said the Elf. "I think it would be a good time for you to learn how to swim...you know, just in case the Orient decides to test your skills again."

"No," Larkin said immediately, and her eyes blazed.

Barren chuckled. "We're not going to throw you into the middle of the ocean and let you drown. You can take baby steps—shallow water first?"

She shook her head and crossed her arms defiantly.

"Oh, I see," said Barren and he moved his body to face her, drawing his sword. "Then we'll fight for it—I if I win, you have to learn. If I don't...then you can drown the next time you manage to get thrown into the Orient."

"I don't have a weapon," she said.

"Then I win," said Barren, he sheathed his sword. "You should always be prepared if you are going to be around us. We are everyone's targets."

Barren headed for the ocean. Larkin narrowed her eyes. "But I have nothing to swim in."

Barren turned, but didn't look at Larkin. He was looking at Leaf. The Elf shrugged. "Just jump in. It's only water. It will dry."

Teaching Larkin how to swim was very hard for Barren. It was as if she expected the Orient to rise up and consume her, despite how calm the water was. Getting her to wade into the water was a task in itself. When she finally joined him, he taught her how to float, as that would probably be her best option if she ever ventured too far from the ship. That was the easy part....getting her into the deeper, colder parts of the ocean where she couldn't touch the sea bottom was the difficult part.

"You're never going to learn if you don't get out here," complained Barren. He smacked his forehead in annoyance.

"I don't like this."

"I saved you once, I can save you again. Trust me," he said.

"At this rate, he'll push your head under and drown you himself. Barren isn't patient," said the Elf. He was sitting on the deck, his feet dangling in the water, amused.

"That's exactly why I don't want to go out there," said Larkin. She crossed her arms over her chest.

Barren glared at the Elf. "You're not helping." He turned his attention to the girl again, "Please..." She shook her head. Barren sighed and dove under water, appeared behind her, and pushed her into the deep.

"No!" she turned on him, grabbed his shoulders and wrapped her legs around his waist. "Barren Reed, I *will* kill you!"

"You'll never learn to swim like this." His hands were planted firmly on her shoulders.

"Take me back!" she demanded.

Barren rolled his eyes and began moving back. Larkin released her grip on Barren, but just as she did, he pushed her further into the water. She reached out for him, but missed. Her head went under and she forced herself above the surface, spewing water and flailing her arms. Barren blocked the splashes attacking his face.

"Bastard!"

Barren laughed. "Kick your feet and move your arms!"

She wasn't listening. "Help me!"

"Not until you listen. What did I say to do?" He heard the Elf chuckle at his teacher-like tone.

Barren moved back even more to show he wasn't going to help her. With more determination than he'd ever seen on her face, Larkin dove into the water, and began splashing like a maniac, but she moved her arms and kicked her feet like Barren had told her. It took her a while, but she was finally within Barren's reach. He caught her arm and forced her to stop.

"You're okay," he said, but he couldn't help but laugh. "You can touch the floor now."

Larkin stopped finally and stood. The water was above her waist when she ceased kicking. Without much warning, Larkin splashed him with water. "You! I will never forgive you for this!"

Barren hurried away from her as she pushed more water toward him. "You swam!" he called. "My lessons were a success!"

"Bastard!"

Leaf was laughing in the background. "You'll never win with her, Barren. If you had failed, you would have gotten a better reaction."

Barren charged at Larkin as she continued to pelt him with water, he grabbed her wrists and as he pushed his body into hers, she glared at him fiercely.

"You swam, so stop calling me names," he said. He let go of her and walked out of the water. Larkin followed, behind, ringing out the fabric of her dress, and her hair.

"It's a good thing I was here to witness this fiasco," said Leaf, raising a brow. "Or others might find you both a little suspicious."

"Maybe you should take a swim," suggested Larkin. "Then it won't be so *suspicious*."

The Elf's gaze was suddenly dull. "I am in the water enough for both of you...I think I'll stay dry this time."

As the three made their way back to the McCloud house, they noticed poles had been driven into the ground and a black line ran the length of them, following the edges of the road. The blacksmith was down the road, driving the last of the poles into the dirt. A woman with a black scarf tied around her head was walking the length, hanging lanterns from the line with hooks. She smiled at the trio.

"Must get ready for the dance tonight," she said. "It's gonna be a fun one."

Leaf continued inside. Barren paused at the door, holding it open for Larkin. Perhaps he felt like they were getting along better, or maybe as an apology for his do-it-or-die swimming lessons, but something made him say, "You owe me a dance...you refused last time, remember?"

"Yes, I remember. I chose to fight you," she said, as water dripped from her body onto the porch. "Which was more fun, I might add."

"You wouldn't find favor here if you fought me," said Barren.

"Then I'll dance with you...but only because I still owe you for saving my life."

She smiled and moved past him, hurrying upstairs to change before Mary saw her soaked gown.

Chapter Eleven
CONSTELLATIONS

Barren sat behind Alex's desk, a map of the Orient spread before him. It was a treasured possession of the old pirate's—the ocean was colored in various shades of blue, the islands bore colors of green and gold, and the mountains were a range of browns and purples. Alex stood at the window, a pipe poised in his hand, and every now and then he would place it to his mouth, suck in a breath, and smoke would fill the air. He was watching the commotion below as the pirates prepared for the dance.

The lanterns the blacksmith and his wife had put up earlier were all lit, casting a silver glow on the ground. Tables and chairs were pulled from the Bloodshed and set up around the ring of lights. People were already gathering outside—women, men, and children alike were all dressed in their cleanest and best clothing.

"Have you been to Conn recently?" asked Barren.

"No," the old man shook his head and leaned heavily on his cane, moving to the front of his desk. "But what're ya so worried about? I know who I am lookin' for."

"I'm not worried about you," said Barren. "I'm just wondering what precautions I need to take. Are the people of Conn going to hate me just like those of Maris do?"

"Yer father considered settlin' there after yer mother died," said Alex with a shrug. "But considerin' yer crimes against Maris and yer recent decision to kidnap Larkin, it's better ta assume they'll be lookin' for you. Small islands like Conn need the bounty on yer head."

Barren pursed his lips. He felt strange sitting in this chair, so far from the future he imagined when he kidnapped Larkin.

"I know it'll be 'ard fur ya, but we have ta do this. It's either this or William gets the crown."

"I know," Barren said quietly. "I'm more afraid of what I'm going to find out along the way. I thought I knew my father."

"Ya do know yer father," said Alex. "And don't let anythin' ya discover on this journey change what ye thought 'bout 'em."

"Did you even know?" Barren met Alex's watery, blue-eyed gaze. "Did you know about the bloodstone? About my mother?"

"There were always rumors 'bout yer father's dealings with the Elvish folk, but nothing grew into solidity," said Alex. "Well, until William and you came along, but then I just assumed yer mother was Elvish…I'd 'ave never thought she was a Lyric."

Barren could feel Alex's eyes on him as the pirate stared down at the map. He was marking coordinates down on a blank sheet of parchment to give to Sam tomorrow morning. When he heard the old man let out a ragged breath, he spoke up.

"I noticed you did not tell me who we are traveling to Conn to see."

Alex chuckled and took the pipe out of his mouth. "Ya would not know 'em, so what's the need in namin' 'em?"

"It's nice to have a name."

"Do ya not trust me?"

"I trust you," said Barren. "But Tetherion said that this man was once part of Jess's crew. Maybe I'd remember him."

Alex was quiet for a moment, and then he let out a low sigh. "'E's name is Devon Kennings. 'E wasn't around much. 'E was…a spy for Jess."

"A spy?" Barren stared up at the old man.

"'E was Chancellor of Maris, specifically, 'e was in charge of foreign affairs. 'E…kept your father updated on all of Cathmor's thoughts and actions. That's 'ow Jess always knew where to attack."

"Was he caught?"

Devon laughed, as if the result was obvious. "Yes, and Cathmor's best assassins were sent to annihilate 'em…but that didn't go as planned. Thankfully for us, 'e's still alive, and I believe 'e might have information on the bloodstone."

"If he's considered a traitor to the crown, he could be

anywhere. What makes you think he's still in Conn?"

"It's the last place the Network saw 'em. We 'ave to start somewhere in any case."

A knock sounded on the door and Mary poked her head in. "The dance has begun! You must come down!"

Even Mary had dressed up for it. In place of her usual work clothes—a red button-down dress and white apron—she wore a blue gown with puffy sleeves that swept the floor. The color toned down the red tinge of her cheeks. She had also taken her hair out of its normal bun, and braided it so that it fell down her back.

Alex grumbled. "Must we?"

"Yes," she huffed. "We didn't spend all evening getting ready for nothing!"

"Barren and I didn't 'ave ta do anythin'," said Alex, though he was heading to the door as he spoke.

"And it shows!" said Mary as they walked out the door and down the steps. Barren remained in his seat for a moment, but when the music floated through the window, he pushed his seat back and peered outside. It seemed the whole of Silver Crest was gathered together for this event. They had formed a line and were dancing, exchanging places and laughing. Barren felt a sense of comfort at seeing this again.

He searched the crowd, unsure of who he was looking for until his eyes fell upon Larkin. She was dancing with Jonathan Kingsley, a smile spread wide on her face. Her dress was simple—a white chemise and a black corset hugged her waist, and yet her silhouette was just as graceful against the silver of the lantern light. Barren groaned inwardly—he didn't want to find his brother's fiancée attractive. What was worse, he recognized that pang of jealousy welling up inside him—it was time for a drink.

Barren headed downstairs and into the cool night. The music seemed to drift around him, and a breeze tousled his already wild hair. He pushed his hands into his pockets and gazed out at the merry setting for a moment. As a child, this place had been his home—he felt safe here, enveloped in the knowledge that these people did not hate him, but he also felt sadness because many of his days spent here were days wondering when his father would return to see him. He took a deep breath and then descended the steps, hearing his name called after stepping beyond the shadowed porch.

"There he is! Barren!"

The pirate craned his neck in the direction of the voice and saw a table where Alex, Leaf, Cove, Hollow, and Slay sat. He smiled at them.

"Come and sit, my boy!" Alex called. "Mary won't let ya rest if ya don't dance, though!"

Barren chuckled as he approached. "I'm not a very good dancer."

"That's not what you told Larkin," said Leaf. Barren glowered at him—damn Elvish hearing. Leaf shrugged. "Well, it isn't."

Slay pushed the pitcher of ale toward the pirate. "Drink," he said. "If you won't dance."

"Thanks, Slay," Barren poured himself a cup of ale and drank it slowly. The clear liquid was cool in his mouth and made his tense nerves relax just a little.

"Have fun this night," Alex advised, a mug of ale resting on his stomach. "You won't have many of these nights in the near future."

"I know," Barren said quietly, and he took an even bigger gulp of ale.

"We've sent word to Arcarum that we will be detained at sea a little longer than we expected," said Cove. "All is in order for us to sail with you."

Barren nodded his head, and was silent for a moment, but words formed in his thoughts and forced their way off his tongue. "I don't like it. Fighting privateers is one thing, but helping me? That is treason of the highest kind. You could lose everything."

Hollow chuckled, his dark eyes were like hot coals in the night, and he sat with his back straight, a cigar between his fingers, smoke rose in the air. "It is not your decision. Besides," he said as he sucked on the end of his cigar, blasting smoke between his lips. "We've no blood to hold us to Arcarum. What have we to return to but politics and money?"

Barren's gaze passed between the two, and while Hollow's eyes remained on Barren, Cove let his gaze fall, and he stared at the table, his eyes running along the grain of the wood. He wondered what the Ambassador wasn't telling them—what blood did he have in Arcarum to return to?

"If you keep drinking, you won't be able to dance." Larkin's voice startled him, and he choked on his ale, spitting what was in his mouth back into his cup and coughing as the rest went down wrong.

"Or I'll be dead!" he said, trying to catch his breath.

Leaf laughed. "Lady, you'll have to try not to choke our captain to death. We do really need him, despite his stupidity."

Larkin smirked. "Considering he is a pirate, I expect him to always be prepared for what I have up my sleeve."

"Enough amusement at my expense," said Barren, and he stood. "Let's get this over with."

"Oh, now you act as if I'm burdensome?" questioned Larkin as they walked away. "You were the one who wanted to dance."

Leaf shook his head. "They are going to make me an old man...and that's very hard to do because I'm an Elf. Do you know how many years they would have to age me?"

"Yer already almost a-hundred years old," said Slay. "Ye are an old man."

"Take it easy on the aged," warned Alex. "Before you *is* an old man."

The music began: a slow tune—sweet and melodious. Barren rolled his eyes.

"I know it's torture," said Larkin with a laugh. "Would you prefer fighting?"

"Is that not what we were doing?" asked Barren.

"What? No...that was bickering. There is a difference."

"Really? Isn't bickering just another word for fighting?"

Barren smirked and Larkin punched him in the shoulder. He

smiled as he took her hand and pulled her toward him, placing his other hand around her waist. He kept his gaze on her, watching to see how she reacted to his touch. It was strange for his hands to hold something so fragile when he thought of how often he carried steel.

"You know, you've thrown more insults my way since I met you than Leaf has in our entire friendship."

"I doubt I could claim such a feat," Larkin looked up at him as they moved about, and though her voice held an edge of sarcasm, she was grinning.

"So," said Barren after a moment, he raised a brow. "Jonathan Kingsley?"

"What?" For a moment she seemed confused, and then realization settled in. "What? No! Why would you think that?"

"He just seems to have taken a liking to you," said Barren.

"No," she shook her head. "Jonathan is merely a friend. And to make matters worse, he has lied to me for years."

"Well, I surely would never have told you I was a pirate. You are the fiancée of William Reed, remember?"

"I don't think I would have reacted badly."

Barren raised a brow, as if to say *whatever*.

"You always think the worst of me."

"Hardly, My Lady! In fact, I would say it's the other way around."

She only stared at him, her lips clamped tight.

"By the time you do return to William, you will be so much of a pirate, he might not want you."

"What do you mean?"

Barren smirked, and for a moment, he wasn't sure he should tell her what he meant. "Well…you have opinions. Can't imagine that goes over well in your previous company."

"It doesn't go over well in my current company, either."

Barren chuckled. "What I mean is…Saoirse seems to fit you very well. It's okay to admit you want freedom."

Larkin was silent. Barren knew she would not see piracy as freedom. She saw it as breaking the rules; it would mean she was a traitor.

"I know where your opinion on pirates comes from, and I just want to say I'm sorry about your mother. It probably doesn't mean much coming from me, but I do know how you feel."

Larkin's eyes fell from Barren's, and while he expected some answer in return—an insult, at the least a thank you—what he got was much different. She rested her head on Barren's shoulder, which caused his arm to tighten around her waist. He thought back to the night of the engagement party when he had watched Larkin dance with William—they had not seemed so in tune with each other, and William could not move without stepping all over Larkin's gown. He looked down at her as they swayed back and forth, wondering if she was aware that she was in the arms of a murderer.

The music stopped and the two froze, Barren stepped away from her, and their eyes finally met again. He only nodded his head as he departed, making his way toward the table where his crew sat. He took up his mug of ale and drank deeply.

The evening wore on after that with more dancing and more drinking. The pirates never seemed to lose their energy. Larkin had been to several balls in the past, but none were as exciting or as exhausting as this. After Barren had taken his turn as her dance partner, others rose to the occasion, even the twins jumped in to whirl her around the makeshift dance floor.

At some point in the night, Larkin found herself resting her head against the post of the steps to the McCloud house, sleepy and a little tipsy. She was alone, watching figures move in the distance. They were all blurry images—beautiful and happy. She watched as two came into focus. One was Mary, the other was Alex—he leaned heavily on his wife and his cane, face sweaty and red. He let out an exhaustive huff as he plopped down in a chair near the porch. He began unbuckling the latches that held his wooden leg on. Mary disappeared to find water.

Larkin wondered what happened to Alex—how he had been wounded so terribly. Had he lost his leg and eye all in the same day? What other scars had he endured from his life as a pirate? Did he think it was worth it?

The slender figure of Leaf Tinavin approached. The Elf looked as if he were enjoying himself, and bore a smug smirk upon his thin lips.

"My Lady," Leaf bowed his head, and he took a seat next to her. She kept her eyes focused on Alex, and she must have had a rather pitiful look on her face, because after a moment, Leaf leaned over and said, "You can quit feeling pity for him, he's not sad he doesn't have a leg. He was also paid handsomely for his loss—eight hundred pieces per limb…probably more." Larkin seemed appalled and Leaf laughed. "At least we're a little bit remorseful about the whole thing."

"Is *that* according to pirate code?" Larkin meant that to be sarcastic, but Leaf nodded. "What happened to his leg?"

Leaf chuckled, and then did something that made Larkin want to hide her face for eternity. "Hey Alex! Larkin wants to know what happened to your leg."

Alex looked up and laughed. "This thing? Ah, it was during an ambush. Man came up to me and sliced right through my leg beneath the knee. Had no chance of savin' it. Just had to sear it and keep goin."

Larkin looked horrified. "Sear it?"

"Yeah, burn it. You know, with fire."

The look on her face made Alex laugh harder. "Better quit laughing, Alex, she'll think you're joking."

"He's not?"

Finally, Leaf looked a little sympathetic. "We've limited ways to treat wounds out on the open sea. I'm a healer, but even my knowledge is limited. Alex would have bled to death had his wound not been cauterized. That's life as a pirate."

There was a lull in conversation. Larkin pressed the palms of her hands to her cheeks as the redness drained from her face. She'd never been so embarrassed and so appalled in all her life.

"I hope my young captain has been good to you tonight," Leaf said, pulling at the skin around his nails. Larkin smiled at the statement—it was like Leaf was checking up on Barren.

"Your captain does not always like me," she replied. "But he will tolerate me."

"Barren tolerates no one. In case you didn't realize that during his encounter with Jonathan. So he must like you. A little."

Larkin shuddered. She would rather not think about what would have happened had Jonathan not spoken up about his purpose. That was the closest she had actually come to seeing Barren kill anyone, and she honestly hoped she never had to witness him commit murder. She wasn't sure what she would think. Being told stories of his deeds was one thing, but actually seeing it—that was another matter entirely.

"How do you do it?" asked Larkin after a moment.

"What?"

"Follow him. He's so much younger than you, and here you are, letting him make rash decisions that lead you into situations you would never have gotten yourself into without him."

Leaf smirked. He studied her for a moment, and then let his gaze fall to his feet. "I know you'd like to forget we have rules because it's so much easier to think we're evil, but," he leaned in before finishing his sentence, *"it's part of the code.* Barren *created* this crew, and we agreed to follow. That made him our captain, but it is more than that. He believes in us, cares for us. He's passionate about Saoirse and upholds the code with loyalty. The second thing you must understand is that we do not follow him unwillingly. We swore our loyalty to him, and we protect him, just like he protects us. Now, you won't ever see it the same way—you see Barren and you think he is a monster. You think he is...rash and childish, but Barren has never played a child's game, unfortunately. Not since he was twelve. He watched his father die and he lost everything in mere moments. Now, who do you know that walks around with such a burden?"

"Only him," she whispered, and was silent for a moment. "But he will let no one share that burden."

Leaf shook his head. "No, and that is why he pursues it so diligently, so obsessively. He has nothing else to turn his attention to, nothing else he wants."

Larkin frowned. She wanted to help Barren in some way, though she wasn't sure why or how. Maybe it was because Barren had actually shown her compassion—he had saved her, even if it was because of some stupid code...but that code kept Barren loyal, and if he was such a bad person, would he really follow it?

Leaf chuckled and Larkin snapped her head in his direction. He had a look on his face and a smirk on his lips that suggested he was reading her mind.

"What?" she asked defensively.

Leaf stood. "Stick around, Lady. Just stick around."

Larkin watched the Elf as he disappeared behind a crowd of pirates. She'd have to remember to ask Barren later if he could read minds.

***

The events of the night were waning; some pirates had broken away from the crowd and gone home, others still sat in chairs from the Bloodshed, talking in low, sleepy voices, or snoring.

Most of the lanterns had burned into nothing but fine smoke, and the only light was from the perfectly round moon. Barren appeared and took a seat next to her. He leaned back against the steps, supporting himself with his elbows so the drink in his hand would not spill.

"Do you like stars?" Barren asked, staring up at the vast sky.

Larkin looked at him. "I haven't thought much about them in a long time. I wasn't allowed outside after dark."

"That is a shame."

"When I was younger, I had a governess who told me I could navigate using the stars. She said that's how pirates found their way at sea." Larkin paused for a moment. "She wasn't my governess for very long after that."

Barren chuckled. "You told your father she mentioned pirates?"

"Not on purpose. I just told my father what I learned that day. I remember being excited about it. After that, I wasn't allowed to learn about the stars."

"That is an unfortunate thing."

Larkin glanced at Barren. "So it is true? Can you navigate using the stars?"

Barren looked at her and laughed again.

"Yes, I can. When I was young, my father and I would lie on the beach and watch the stars. That's how I learned about constellations."

"Show me," she said.

Barren smirked, and then peered up at the sky. "By our

location, you automatically know that you will only be able to see certain constellations. We'll look for Navis." Barren was quiet as he gazed up at the stars. After a moment he stuck his arm out, pointing at one of the brighter stars in the sky. "See it? Follow that bigger star downward a little way, and then see how it follows a curve upward?"

Larkin stared at where he was pointing. For a moment, she didn't see anything.

"It's a sail," he added, and as if her vision reacted to the word, she could suddenly make out the sail of a ship. It was strangely connected to a hull that was composed of six points in the sky.

"It's a bit of a stretch, but I see it," commented Larkin.

Barren chuckled. "Well, if you can see it, you should be able to see the bow sticking out from the right?"

"Yes," she nodded.

"It's pointing south," said Barren. "So from Silver Crest, you could reach Arcarum if you could find Navis in the sky."

"Do you use constellations often?"

"No," said Barren. "I don't really need to, but it's nice to know if you are a beginner. Sometimes the Orient likes to teach you a thing or two. Before I was an experienced sailor, she sent me far into the Octent, south of the Orient. I'd never been there before, never had a map, only what my father taught me about the stars. I used Circinus to find my way home. Depending on how you look at it, it points east or west—meaning you can also find north and south if you spot it."

"Circinus?"

"The drafting compass," said Barren.

Larkin returned her gaze to the sky. Barren laughed a little. "You probably think this is silly," she heard Barren say. "But my father always told me that stars ensure all that is lost is found."

"No, your father taught you survival," she replied. "My father didn't even teach me how to swim."

"Your father did not raise you to be a pirate, either," Barren pointed out.

"Do you think your father raised you to be the man you are today?"

For a moment, Barren thought that was an easy question, and he almost said yes, but he hesitated, and thought of all the ways he would be different had his father not died. Everything he was today—the murderer, the angry hunter, was a result of what his brother William had made him, not his father.

"Not the man I am at this moment," he said. "The man my father created is buried deep—but if he were ever to surface, he would be wise, understanding, and happy."

"Why can't you be that man?"

"Who is there to bring those traits out in me?" asked Barren. "My father is dead."

"You do not believe your crew can do the same?"

"They make me better," he agreed. "But they have not changed me."

There were times when Barren did want to change. Times when he wanted to be more like his father. Jess had been a man who fought for Saoirse. He fought for everything it meant to be a pirate and sail the seas. While Barren felt it was important to avenge his death, he sometimes wondered if his father was disappointed in the path he took.

Chapter Twelve
PRIVATEERS

The commotion started suddenly—one moment, Larkin was sleeping deeply, and the next she was jolted awake by Barren, who had stood suddenly from their place on the porch swing. Several pirates who had fallen asleep at the table and chairs taken from the Bloodshed were also on their feet. A bell was ringing steadily from somewhere on the island.

Larkin rose to her feet immediately, her heart pounding. Whatever was happening, she knew it wasn't good. "What's going on?"

"Someone's threatening our shores," said Barren. He turned to head inside, but was met by Leaf, who threw open the door to the McCloud house. The Elf handed Barren his sword. Leaf's quiver was already on his back, and his bow in hand.

"Privateers," he said.

Behind him, the remainder of Barren and Cove's crew filled the door. Barren took his sword. It seemed the bell had grown louder and the ring more consistent.

"Stay here," Barren warned Larkin.

"Do not tell me what to do!"

"You'll want to listen to him this time," said Cove.

"Why?"

"Because they're here for you," Barren said.

Larkin's eyes widened.

She watched as the pirates hurried from the McCloud house. Before Barren ran too far, he turned, and it was as if the look he gave Larkin was supposed to weld her to the spot. Instead, she set her teeth and threw off her blanket. She took off running for the shore. The bell hadn't ceased, and a crowd of pirates hurried from their homes, weapons drawn. They ran for the beach.

Amid the ringing and the shouts from the pirates, several explosions sounded, rocking the entire island. As Larkin came to the edge of the shore, she saw the damage. The beautiful, magnificent ships that had once crowded the coastline of Silver Crest, were now reduced to ash and fire. Smoke rose and filled the air, and it was suddenly the perfect backdrop for battle.

Though it was chaotic, and their precious ships destroyed, the pirates stood in ranks by weapon, ready to attack an enemy Larkin had never beheld before. Her eyes shifted to the dark dots that spotted the water. The privateers were grizzly, with tangled hair, unwashed skin, and lustful gazes. They were what she'd imagined Barren to be before she had met him. Behind them, sitting on the Orient's waters, were two massive galleons, which had brought these men to Silver Crest's shores.

Why were these men here? Barren had said they wanted her, but how could he be sure? If the privateers had found Silver Crest, surely they were here to battle with the pirates. Perhaps this was her father's way of rescuing her. But why would he send these men? Why would he not come himself?

"You do not listen," Barren's voice came from behind her. She whirled around and faced him.

"What if my father sent these men for me?" Larkin asked. "You could prevent bloodshed if you handed me over."

"Your father might have sent privateers for you," said Barren. "But that will not prevent bloodshed. Besides, do you think these men intend to return you to Maris? Didn't you hear what Tetherion said?"

Larkin narrowed her eyes. "Do you want proof?" Barren asked with a raised brow. She hesitated, glancing at the privateers, and Barren seemed to take that as a yes. "Let's go ask them, then."

He grabbed her wrist and pulled her along with him. He walked fast, so it was hard for Larkin to keep up at first. They were walking toward a man who looked ten times bigger than Barren. Larkin could only assume he was the captain of the privateers who now littered the sandy shore. He had frizzy hair and a black beard. His body was weighed down by excess clothing and holsters which supported various weapons. Larkin wondered if he really could use all of those in a fight.

"Well! It is Barren Reed!" he exclaimed, and laughed deeply. He clearly thought he already had this victory in hand. "And Larkin Lee, too! Come to hand her over, have you?"

"Not exactly," Barren replied, glancing at her. "Just to be clear—you have invaded my shores for the purpose of reclaiming Lady Larkin, correct?"

"What's with the diplomacy?" The man was still amused. "Tryin' to impress the lady?"

"More like...proving a point," Barren clarified. "Who instructed you to come here?"

"We've orders to reclaim her for her father—wants her taken some place safe."

"That doesn't sound too promising," said Barren. "Let me guess—some place safe doesn't mean her home in Maris, does it?"

The privateer laughed and looked at his mates on either side of him.

"Doin' that would ruin some very important plans, don't ya think, boys? I think we'll take her for a little cruise across the Orient. There's places she's not yet seen, things she's not experienced."

Larkin cringed hearing that. She didn't think her father would approve of their language, and suddenly felt she'd be better off with the pirates than these privateers.

Barren raised a brow and looked at Larkin. "You might want

to take this." He handed her a knife from his belt, and then charged the burly privateer. He was unprepared and stumbled back to miss Barren's blow. The men who stood on either side of their leader, drew their weapons, but were distracted by the twins, who had drawn their double blades.

Suddenly, the pirates and privateers converged in a fierce rage that sounded of clashing metal and cries of hatred. Larkin stumbled back with her knife in hand. Perhaps this would have been a great time to listen to Barren, but she had expected these men to take her home. Instead, she'd discovered her father's plans fell in line with William's, and going home to Maris wasn't going to happen as long as they needed the people of Maris to believe her to be dead. That meant Tetherion's assumption that her father was a traitor rang true.

"This would be a good time for you to run!" Barren yelled.

But Larkin didn't want to leave. Where would she go? Everyone around her was fighting, but that wouldn't stop the privateers from going into town where women and children were hiding. She held up her knife, ready for a fight, but as she showed signs of staying and defending herself, privateers moved to encircle her. She stood tense but ready. She would fight them—she was skilled with a sword. How different could a knife be?

One of the men chuckled. "Feelin' scared?"

Larkin narrowed her eyes, trying to appear as collected as possible. "Never," she said. Her eyes shifted to Barren who was still engaged with the frizzy-haired leader of the privateers. It seemed the problem was that there were more privateers than pirates. With four men surrounding her, she had a few options that might keep them at bay.

One man reached for her, and she struck. The knife hit him. He drew back quickly, holding his bloodied hand to his chest, and after that, there was no time to lose—the other three men moved for her. She twisted, her knife brandished.

"Come now, love, don't you wanna go home? What'd your father think if he heard you were fightin' to stay at Barren Reed's side?"

"He shouldn't have sent a bunch of ragged privateers to claim me," Larkin replied. An arm wound its way around her neck, and another hand pried the knife from her fingers. Within seconds, she was pressed against a privateer's chest, her own knife to her throat. He began pulling her away. She had allowed herself to be distracted. She struggled against the man, and found that the privateer wasn't afraid to press the knife into her skin further. She relented a little.

"Gone soft for the pirate now?" the man said against her ear. "Well that's certainly a tale for your father. Though, I might be willin' to keep it a secret for a price."

"I'd rather you told!" Larkin's nails dug into his arm, but his grip only grew tighter.

"Oh, I'll tell all right," the man's breath was on her neck and she cringed. "And I'll have my way with you, too."

Larkin moved to elbow the man, but the blade at her neck cut into her skin.

"Now, now—we are playing nice. Just ease back and no harm will come to you." Larkin remained tense. The three men who surrounded her before now formed a barrier, and all fought pirates who were trying to come to her rescue. Larkin's eyes found Barren and she watched him fight. His muscles rippled as his blade crashed with his enemy's. She had fought with him, but never observed him before. She expected his fighting style to be brutal, almost unfair—instead she found that he was precise, calculated, and fast. It was because of this, that he was finally able to take down the leader of the privateers. When Barren turned to face Larkin and her captor, she felt the man's arm tighten around her neck in fear, and he began dragging her quickly away.

The barrier meant to protect Larkin and her captor from Barren failed, as each person was engaged in battle with another pirate. Barren rushed around them, only to be met with another privateer who had come to the captor's rescue. With her abductor distracted by Barren's attempts to gain ground, Larkin was able to grasp the man's sweaty arm tightly, and relieve the pressure of the knife from her neck. She jammed her foot into the man's leg. He hollered in pain, and released Larkin enough so that she could pull away from him, twist his arm, and take possession of her knife once again. She raised the blade at the greasy privateer and he snarled. "Now what're you gonna do with that?"

"What I meant to do before," she replied.

He rushed at Larkin, and she jumped out of the way, slicing the man's arm. He howled in pain. Whipping around, he pressed a hand to the wound, blood seeping from between his fingers. He glared at her, breathing harshly. "I'm gonna kill—" his voice was cut short and he fell, an arrow in his back.

Larkin stared at the lifeless body before her. She wasn't sure she could have killed him. She tossed the blade into the sand as a bloodied Barren approached her.

"Larkin," he was breathless. "Are you okay?" The privateers were retreating, hurrying to their ship, and leaving their ruins behind. The pirates weren't finished with them, however, because a few had produced hand cannons—they were smaller, and anchored into the ground by a piece of wood. Shots rang out and crashed into the privateer's ships.

Larkin stared at Barren; she was unable to think clearly. He grasped her shoulders, but only for a moment. As she looked at him, a crease appeared between his brows and his eyes grew wide. Larkin hit the sand as two gunshots rang out. She saw Barren fall. He was on the ground, his voice rose in painful gasps.

"Barren!" Larkin crawled to him. Blood pooled from a wound at his shoulder and one at his side. Barren's hands dug into the sand as his breathing grew heavier and heavier. Larkin gathered the fabric of her skirt in both hands, pressing it to his wound.

All she could think to do was scream; she was afraid. "Someone help me!"

Leaf pulled her away and she fell into the sand. "Nath! Dath! Help me!"

They picked him up and carried him toward town. Larkin trailed quickly behind. The trek to the McCloud's house seemed to take forever as they hurried through the small town of Silver

Crest, sad eyes following them. They entered through the front door and hurried Barren upstairs. His head fell back and she caught his gaze.

"Don't die," she whispered, standing in the doorway of the house, Barren's blood dripping from the hem of her gown.

Chapter Thirteen
RECOVERY

Barren woke up on a cold table. Darkness surrounded him. He shivered, not remembering how he had gotten here. After a moment, he sat up, studying the air. He wasn't sure what he was expecting—maybe a light to blaze, or someone to say his name, but silence filled the space. He moved off the slab, his feet touched the ground. Pushing his hands out, he ran them over a cold wall—it was smooth like marble. With the guide of the wall, he inched forward, stumbling into a set of stairs. He found, however, as he tried to climb them, that they only led to a thick set of doors—he could feel the cool handles beneath his skin. He struggled against them—their weight on his shoulders. Pausing, he rested for a moment, before taking a deep breath and pushing against them again.

The doors flew open with force, and he stumbled through, attacked by light. He fell, unaware that there were steps leading down from the place he had been. As he lay in the grass, his eyes adjusted, and he could see a figure above him—Larkin, but she was not paying attention to him. Her gaze was on something else. He followed it. A great mausoleum rose up before them— marble and magnificent. He realized it was the room he had just stumbled from, only now the doors were closed, and above them was a name, etched in black: "Barren Reed."

Barren shook his head, "No," he stood, reaching for Larkin, but his fingers only produced a chill. She didn't even look his way. Then he noticed something different about her: a gown of deep purple was wrapped around her body. She wore a cloak of the same color, a gem clasped tight at her neck. The engagement ring that once hung there was on her finger. Upon her head was a crown of gold and diamonds, but all the wealth she wore could not hide her unhappiness. Her face was pale and drawn with loss. What had happened here? Why was she this person?

She wasn't meant to be this person.

But how did Barren know that? He had taken her from her home, from her life. How did he know she didn't belong?

Because it didn't feel right. Because no matter how stubborn Larkin was, she did not deserve William's inattention.

As if on cue, the bulky form of his brother appeared. He was happy—a stark contrast to his bride. He placed an arm around her and pulled her to him. He was dressed in a rich red shirt with gold clasps, black pants, and a fur-lined cloak, but the one thing Barren couldn't take his eyes off of was the crown on his head. It was a gold circle of fleur-de-lis, and at the very front, a bright red gem glowed. Barren could only assume it was the bloodstone. But if William was king...where was Tetherion? Nath and Dath...everyone else? Barren slowly moved beyond his mausoleum and horror met him. The graves of his crew stretched before him. He felt sick. All he ever wanted was for them to be safe.

He ripped his eyes open, sitting up with a start. Overwhelmed with pain, he fell against the pillows, breathing hard. He reached for his chest, where the sting was worse, but someone stopped him, moving his hand to rest against his stomach. Larkin appeared above him, worry written all over her face. She sat down on the bed, smoothing his hair away from his face and laying a wet towel on his heated skin.

"Larkin," he breathed.

She smiled faintly. The worry in her eyes receded a little.

"What happened?"

He remembered fighting privateers, but everything after that was a blur.

"You were shot," she whispered. "The bullets didn't exit. You almost died."

Barren swallowed. His body felt clammy and he shook with cold, though somehow he knew he was probably feverish—his body was covered in sweat. He was trying to think clearly, but his mind was muddled with pain.

"Jonathan is dead," Larkin's voice shook as she spoke, and her eyes were red. "There were privateers...they came to kidnap me so I could not return to Maris and ruin my father and William's plans."

Barren was quiet for a long moment. Larkin's gaze fell as tears threatened her eyes. "I should tell Leaf you are awake. He will want to know."

Before she could move away, Barren grabbed her hand. "Don't leave yet...please."

She stared at him for a moment and then relaxed, sitting back down on the bed.

"It was not your fault that Jonathan died," he tried to comfort her, but he knew nothing he said would work. People had been trying to tell him his father's death wasn't his fault for years and he still blamed himself.

"I could have exposed you in the courtyard," Larkin said quietly. "Or stayed where I was supposed to...now look what's happened."

A pang of sadness shot through Barren.

"Life has happened, Larkin. Your regret will not change Jonathan's fate."

"You should have handed me over. What good am I to you, anyway?"

"Why are you suddenly treating yourself as an object?" Barren narrowed his eyes.

"It's just...I don't have a place here."

"How do you know that?" Barren paused so she could answer, but silence filled the room. "Larkin, it's not shameful to run from responsibility. Sometimes we do what our heart tells us because reason isn't worth listening to."

"But that is how you justify avenging your father's death," said Larkin. "And it doesn't make sense!"

Barren's eyes grew dark. "What do you want me to say?" She didn't respond. "Why are you fighting me?"

"I have to!" she cried angrily. "I have to because if I don't, I'll never go back! Don't you understand? I don't want to go back!"

Larkin was suddenly overwhelmed with tears. Barren wasn't sure why, but he instinctively reached out and pulled her to him. She didn't resist him, instead she rested against his bandaged chest, weeping. Her body shivered against his, and he had no words of comfort. It wasn't up to him to decide whether or not this life suited her best—that was her decision. Even if she did not marry his brother, her undying loyalty to her father would keep her in Maris.

He buried his head in her hair, taking a deep breath.

"Well, this wasn't unexpected at all," came a voice from the door.

Leaf stared at the two, his eyes bright with amusement and a smirk lingering on his lips. Larkin moved away from Barren quickly, brushing tears from her face. She stood. "I will leave you two."

Neither Leaf nor Barren objected, but even if they had, she would have been out the door before they could utter a word of protest.

After she left, Leaf raised a brow. "You are going to be in trouble."

Barren ran his fingers through his hair and sighed, letting his head fall into the pillows.

"No, she will not be separated from William," said Barren. He looked away from the Elf, not feeling like being lectured.

"I think she already is," said Leaf.

Leaf handed Barren a cup that smelled of mint.

"Have you decided what Larkin will do while you are searching for this bloodstone?"

Barren took a slow drink of the mixture. It was bitter, but warmed him instantly and the clamminess left his body. "I cannot take her back to Maris, and her presence here has already proven to be detrimental. She's a liability either way."

"Well you are still responsible for her well-being," said Leaf. "If you take her with you, you have to make sure she behaves in a way that doesn't expose your crew."

That might turn out to be harder than it sounded, considering Larkin did everything in her power to defy every order Barren gave—it started with Jonathan Kingsley, and continued during the attack on Silver Crest. Searching for the bloodstone was bound to offer more conflict between them.

"I worry those privateers will return," Barren said.

"If they do, at least the pirates will be prepared. Since the attack, they have worked to rebuild their ships, and the blacksmith has set to fashioning more weapons."

Barren was still concerned. He knew the pirates would fight, but this was their home—there were women and children here, and privateers would only see pirates.

"My ship was left abandoned, you know," Barren said. "There is little chance those privateers could have found us so easily."

"Are you saying someone has betrayed you?" Leaf asked, and he paused, though Barren knew he had thought the same thing. "Larkin, perhaps?"

"It has put me on my guard," said Barren. "As far as Larkin being responsible, I do not believe so. She could not live with herself if she had been the cause of Jonathan's death."

"Speaking of Jonathan, now that you are awake, we can bury him," said Leaf. "Alex wants to leave as soon as you're well."

"When will I be well?"

"Soon," the Elf said with a smile. "You've been sleeping for about two days."

Barren gulped the rest of the mixture down. "How long was Larkin here?"

"She slept in here," said Leaf. "She wouldn't leave your side. She was very worried about you, and I think she felt bad because this is the second time you have risked your life to save her. Interesting that you would sacrifice so much for a woman you fight with all the time."

"If she dies, the blood is on my hands," said Barren. "People already think I killed her and look how they are reacting."

"Well, you didn't know Tetherion had a revolt on his hands the first time you saved her and with all this fighting, I would have thought you would have been glad to be rid of her."

Barren glared at the Elf.

"I'm just saying…if your interest doesn't lie with her, you are doing more harm than good." Leaf moved toward the door. "You'll feel sleepy soon. Don't fight it."

With that, the Elf left, and Barren leaned back, looking up at the ceiling. He hated when Leaf slipped him sleeping draughts. It seemed counter-productive for him to have to sleep since he had just awakened from a two-day coma, but Barren knew sleep was the only thing that would heal him. Instead of feeling angry, he closed his eyes and accepted the drowsiness.

***

The pirates stood on the rocky hill behind the McCloud house. The rush of the Orient against the base of the hill created a harmonious backdrop for the funeral—it was what Jonathan would have wanted.

"Jon was a good man and a dedicated crewman," Cove's voice was deep, and when he spoke, he kept his head up; he wasn't afraid to let everyone see his grief. "I took him in, introduced him to this world—something I do not regret, despite his end."

Those words rang with bitterness in Larkin's ears. How could Cove say such a thing? What had Jonathan fought for that was worth his life? Larkin tried to keep her tears at bay, but a man she'd known all her life was now buried deep, lifeless and cold.

Everyone crowded around a freshly stacked mound of rocks. Larkin had watched from the window as Cove, Leaf, and the twins dug the grave, settled Jonathan's body in the bed, and piled dirt and rocks upon him. It had been raining the whole time—and even now the clouds above were thick and threatening. Thunder rumbled deep within them.

Cove walked to the head of Jonathan's grave, a sword between his hands. He drove it into the ground—in place of a cross, he would have his blade. The Ambassador kept his hand on the hilt; he bowed his head and closed his eyes in a silent memorial of his lost comrade. After a moment, he stepped away from the mound and left silently. The others soon followed suit, until all who remained were Larkin and Barren.

Larkin stepped forward and kneeled on the wet ground. A thin mist was all around her, shrouding her body. She could feel Barren watching her closely. She wasn't sure why he stayed behind. Maybe Jonathan's death had frightened him; maybe he realized how close he had come to this—because he had been close, and Larkin had been so frightened for Barren's life, it never occurred to her that anyone else might have perished in that moment of terror.

But Jonathan had, and without any final words. And worse yet, was that Jonathan had lost his life at the hands of men her father had sent to reclaim her, all so he could carry out his plans with William. Perhaps the best thing that had come out of Barren's kidnapping was the truth about her fiancé and father.

"What will they tell his family?"

"That he was lost at sea," said Barren. He stood solemnly behind her, his arm in a sling.

"Is that fair to his family?"

"Life isn't fair," said Barren. "It's the best comfort we can give."

She turned to look at him; raindrops ran down her face, and in the dullness of the day, her eyes were bright. She wore a grey cloak, the hood covering her head. "You've done this before?"

Barren nodded. Many other men had died far from their homes, and many families never knew the truth—that their husband or father was a pirate who had fought to keep the sea free from privateers. Died because the government they worked for killed them.

"Jonathan wouldn't have wanted to die in Arcarum. He died for something he believed in. We all want that."

"But what good did his death produce? The privateers are still out there."

"You must not think he died in vain merely because you do not understand the world he was a part of."

"I understand it!" Larkin's cheeks were red with anger, but Barren smiled at her sympathetically.

"Then understand this: pirates will always have an enemy. If not privateers, something worse. Our world is the sea, and we only fight to protect our right to sail it. We all hope to die fighting to protect what we love. Jonathan was no different."

Barren chuckled. "But until I die, I won't stop fighting for it. Why do you think I so ardently want your fiancé dead? I owe it to my father to avenge his death, but I also owe it to the people of Silver Crest."

It was as if he mentioned William deliberately—an attempt to remind her she didn't belong, or maybe that she belonged to another. But no matter how much she resented her engagement, she would never want Barren to take William's life.

The look in Barren's eyes told her he knew what she was thinking. He turned to leave her.

"Barren!" she called, and he paused stiffly. For a moment she wasn't sure he would turn around, but he did and she scrambled to her feet. "Can we agree to something?"

He was guarded for a moment. "I won't promise anything."

"Don't mention William. Do not mention him as my fiancé, or your wish to kill him. Nothing."

"He wants to be king, Larkin, and we're setting out to fight him, how am I supposed to do that?"

"I just don't want you to call him my fiancé. I don't want to hear how adamantly you want him dead. Please. I can take it from anyone else, but I can't stand it from you. All William ever did was talk about how he wanted you dead. Don't be like him, Barren."

She knew he was angry—she could see it in his eyes, but he didn't turn away. At last he nodded. "Fine," he said. "But you must also do me a favor."

"What is that?"

"Trust me."

Barren's gaze was serious, but Larkin smiled. "I trust you now. You did save my life twice."

"Oh, you'd think once would be enough!"

Larkin laughed a little. "You are a pirate! What am I to trust about that?"

"You are only to trust in that," he said. "It is the one thing I will always be loyal to."

They stared at each other for a long moment, the wind picked up, making raindrops crash into them. The temperature was dropping steadily.

"Come," said Barren. "We need to get inside before we catch colds. That's all we need—Leaf scolding us for something like that."

"I think you're more afraid of colds than dying."

Barren chuckled, but remained silent, and together they walked back to the McCloud house.

Chapter Fourteen
CONN

It was early morning. The day was getting lighter, but the sun had not risen yet. Larkin sat on the floor of her room with her legs crossed, packing clothes Mary had given her. Now that Jonathan was buried and Barren healed enough to rise, they would begin their journey to the bloodstone. Cove had tried unsuccessfully to determine William's whereabouts through the Network. Barren said that meant he hadn't actually come to port yet.

In the three days of quiet, there had been a lot of turmoil for Larkin. She had attempted to come to terms with the fact that her father had agreed to let privateers come after her, wrestled with the loss of Jonathan and a tense fear of losing Barren. The last one was still surprising to her, but she chalked the feeling up to the fact that she'd come to learn a lot about Barren in the past week—not only from his words, but from his crewmates, and even the people he interacted with in Silver Crest. Slowly, she was stringing together the story of Barren Reed, but that was only complicating her feelings.

Larkin jumped when a knock sounded at her door.

"Come in!"

Barren opened the door. His right arm still in a sling, he held a sword in his left.

"Can you fight left handed?" She suddenly realized if they ran into trouble, Barren might not be able to help.

The pirate smirked. "We'll see. Here, take this."

He extended the blade to her. She stared at it and then at Barren. He was giving her a weapon out of trust; she knew that, even if he didn't say it.

"Are you not afraid I'll kill you?"

Barren laughed. "I'm convinced you couldn't kill anyone, harm maybe." He paused. "I will need your skill if we come into trouble."

Larkin repressed the will to smile. "You realize you just admitted that I am as good as you with a sword, right?"

He shrugged. "You can hold your own. If you would have had a sword against those privateers, maybe this would never have happened to me," he gestured to his injured shoulder and then paused. "And I can blame myself for that, because your sword is in the Orient off the coast of Maris. So here."

She took the blade in her hands, staring down at it in amazement.

"*Where* did you get this?" It was sterling—delicate and beautiful with a green emerald at the top. She looked at Barren as he rubbed the back of his neck, almost too embarrassed to speak.

"I had it made for you." Larkin wasn't sure what to say. "It is a gift...an apology, if you will."

"Thank you," she said softly.

"Oh, there's one more thing." Barren pulled from his pocket the crimson scarf she had worn the night of the engagement party. "It washed up on shore. One of the twins found it."

Larkin grasped the fabric, shuddering as she did. It seemed so long ago since the night she'd worn it. It was a reminder of the life that was waiting for her when this whirlwind adventure was over, and surprisingly, she didn't know how to feel about that.

Barren cleared his throat. "We will depart soon, make sure you are downstairs within the next hour." He closed the door behind him.

***

Mary was a mess, seeing everyone leave. She wasn't very good at hiding her emotions—her red face and eyes told everyone she had been crying. She packed nearly everything in her pantry for the pirates and prepared their water canteens. The blacksmith gave them several new swords, all of which they were thankful for. Because most of the ships, including Jonathan's *Slayer*, had been destroyed by Christopher and William's men, Cove had sent for one of his vessels from Arcarum, and it arrived sometime in the night. The *Vasa* now graced the shoreline of Silver Crest— its massive white sails were a bright beacon against the dull gray of the horizon.

The pirates moved supplies up the boarding ramp quickly. Barren stood on the dock, staring at the ship. It was a beautiful creation—intricate in its woodwork with detailed spirals carved along the rail, awash in gold. The cabin and main hold were all lined in ebony wood, which caused the white sails to stand out like stars against the night. In contrast to the black, the hull of the ship was a rich rosewood. It was unbelievably fancy, and Barren almost mourned what would become of it on this journey.

"We've got to leave sometime, you know," said Cove from behind him. "You can't just stand here forever."

Barren looked at the Ambassador. He wasn't sure how Cove managed to be both pirate and politician, but he was highly respected in both worlds. Perhaps it was because he never took advantage of his power—he was always kind and generous, but also deadly. No one ever messed with Cove without reaping what they sowed.

"I know," said the pirate quietly. He still didn't move. He cleared his throat. "It's just so nice."

Cove chuckled. "Come on." He took the bag of clothes and food Barren was holding. "Let me show you to your quarters."

A crease appeared between Barren's brows. "This is your ship, Albatross. You are captain."

The Ambassador shook his head. "No, I gave this ship to

you—treat her well. She is the best I have."

As was Cove's nature, he did not let Barren protest. He turned away from him immediately. Barren followed, knowing it would be rude not to, and that he'd have to board soon anyway. They made their way up the plank and onto the deck of the ship. Their crews were busy organizing the cargo. Sam was already at the helm, his hands on the spindles of the wheel—he was excited to steer this vessel. Seamus set to work inspecting the cannons below deck. It would take him a good hour to get around to all of them. Datherious and Natherious were up in the sails, and Slay was making his way to the crow's nest.

Cove opened the door to the captain's cabin and stepped aside for Barren to enter. He couldn't move any further into the room—his jaw was on the floor. These were the nicest quarters he had ever had, and the biggest. There were three windows on either side of the room. On the left, a desk of solid wood sat. A map of the Orient was already stretched across it. At the center of the room was a large four-poster bed. Rich red fabric made a canopy above it and silk blankets covered the mattress. Barren didn't want to sleep in it—it was much too fancy.

"I don't need this, Cove," Barren moved into the room. "I'm a simple man."

"You can get used to it," said the Ambassador. He dropped Barren's bag on the floor. "Besides, you'll need a comfortable place to sleep to recover from your wounds."

Barren shook his head.

"Or maybe you'll find someone to share your bed," Cove

smirked, then he quickly changed the subject. "I must thank you for allowing my crew and me to come with you. We would not miss this journey for the world."

"I assure you, Cove, it is I who am lucky to have you aboard my ship."

Cove chuckled and gestured to the room. "See? Not so hard to get used to this, is it?"

The Ambassador departed and Barren was left alone in the big, empty room. He picked up his bag and threw it on the bed. There was a trunk in the corner he managed to pack all his clothes into. He tried to make a point of using his injured arm, but the more he did, the more painful it was. Finally, Barren stood behind his new desk; the map upon it was just like the one he had admired in Alex's study. Barren narrowed his eyes, examining it closely—the island of Conn had a small red speck upon it—it had been Alex's. Barren shook his head in disbelief. He would have to find some way to repay them all for their kindness. Then again, he had a feeling this was their way of repaying him. What they were about to set out on was an adventure. It was a quest. This is what they had craved.

The ship set sail when the sun broke over the horizon. It was a slow start, but Conn was not very far from Silver Crest, and all Barren could hope for was an easy voyage there. The pirate left his cabin, and headed to the back of the ship with his leather-bound sketchbook. He took a seat on the deck, leaned against one of the barrels of ale, and positioned himself so his knees were drawn up and his sketchbook rested there. Though his right arm was still in the sling, he managed to move the charcoal between his fingers and begin sketching faint outlines of sails. He wasn't sure when this habit had begun, but it always brought him peace. In these drawings, he could make anything happen—they could be his reality, or his fantasy. Because of that, he felt his sketches should be kept secret. Leaf was really the only one who knew of his talent, and even then the Elf had stumbled upon it one day by accident.

Barren didn't have many memories of his father, but there was one he always cherished, one that never made its presence in his dreams, though he would love to relive it. He and his father sat on the shore of Silver Crest. Jess had taken up a stick and began to draw images in the sand. Barren, then no more than a small child, thought they were magnificent. While drawing, Jess told the story of a very mean king who hated his sons. In retaliation, they fled and joined a pirate's crew. He would make up adventures for the two brothers—encounters with lost treasure, evil sea monsters, and other worlds. Barren hadn't realized how important those moments were. The stories. The time he had with his father.

After a moment, he looked up from his drawing—Cove stood with his hands in his pockets, examining the picture Barren was working on. The pirate quickly shut his book and straightened.

"Albatross," Barren grunted.

"I apologize," said Cove, he bowed his head a little. "I didn't want to disturb you."

Barren smiled, but he wasn't comfortable with the idea of

being watched, especially at something he tried to hide most of the time.

"I....want to talk to you," Cove continued. "About Conn."

Barren waited for Albatross to continue, but before he did, he took a seat next to him.

"I know you'd rather go at this alone, but I think it would be a good idea if Hollow or I came with you into Conn, too, since we can still appear in public as figures of authority. You know, just in case things go wrong."

"That is exactly why you can't come with me. What does it say about you if you are protecting me? You will only be seen as a traitor."

"I don't think it will come to that," said Cove. "But I think it would be beneficial if you'd let us at least get you past the ports. After that, Alex can take the lead.

Barren was silent; he traced the metal clasps of his sketchbook with his finger. He didn't want to agree to this—both he and Cove knew what it meant if he was caught with Barren. No one would excuse his betrayal. The Ambassador would be forced to leave a life of privilege. He didn't know how lucky he was to have a place to call home.

"I have no blood in Arcarum I am bound to."

"You are lying," said Barren quickly, and he met Cove's dark gaze. "I know you are. I saw the look on your face when Hollow made that same statement. There is someone."

Barren had never seen Cove's features turn so cold before. His jaw clenched and his eyes lost a little of their luster. He looked away, attempting to gather himself before he spoke, and when he looked back, Barren saw a very confused man.

"It isn't what you think. The affection I have for her is not shared, and even if I acted upon my wish, I do not think I could bring her into this world. It is too dangerous."

"And I only make that danger more real," said Barren.

"I can control my desires, Barren," said Cove. "What I am helping you with—this is far greater than two people. Besides, even if not my lover, she will always be my friend. I will never lose her."

Barren studied Cove for a long moment. He had known the Ambassador for years now, but he had never heard him speak of affection for anyone—not even his own family. Cove was a private man; he had to be. He carried too much knowledge—he knew about scandal, betrayals, and plans for revenge, both in his political world and the pirate world. Cove was given the nickname Albatross for that very reason. To those who sail the sea, the Albatross symbolizes burdens.

"Very well," he said. "You and Hollow can lead us into Conn."

A smile spread across Cove's face, and he stood quickly. "I knew you'd see it my way."

Barren chuckled, following the Ambassador, and getting to his feet. "If you find yourself in trouble, remember that I did not recommend your coming."

"I will keep that in mind," said Cove, and as he was about to depart, he paused. "By the way—nice drawing."

Barren narrowed his eyes, muttering a thank you as heat

burned his face. The Ambassador smirked, and then turned quickly to leave.

After Cove's request, there came another—from Larkin Lee herself, who made it known she would not stay in the shadows while Barren paraded through the Orient in search of the bloodstone. She was still Barren's responsibility, and he was bound by the code to keep her safe. He hadn't considered her leaving the ship. She was probably the most recognizable of all of them, and once she was spotted, the rest of them were doomed.

No matter how many times he refused her, she fought all the more feverishly for her side.

"You do realize if you are caught, you aren't going back to Maris," said Barren. "They're going to hide you, or worse, let privateers deal with you."

"Then that's just more incentive for me to keep my head low when I'm out and about," said Larkin.

"Or stay on the ship where you won't have to worry about being spotted," Barren pointed out.

"And what if they search the ship? They're going to be looking for you now that everyone in the Orient believes you killed me."

She had a point.

"And how can I trust that you won't tell the entire population who I am?"

Larkin raised a brow and smirked. "You gave me a sword," she said.

"And what does that have to do with what I just asked?"

"You trust me."

Barren opened his mouth to speak, but found that he didn't know how to respond, which angered him even more.

"Well, *Lady*," he mocked. "Do what you prefer, but I am not responsible for anything that happens to you from this point on."

When Barren turned from her, he came face-to-face with Leaf. "Abandoning the code?" he questioned. "Tsk, tsk, tsk."

"Come on, Leaf! She's practically agreed to join us."

"Your uncle said she could not go back to Maris, privateers came for her in Silver Crest—I don't think there was a choice in the matter."

Barren scowled at his quartermaster.

"I'm not letting you out of your responsibility for that girl. You had better watch her close in Conn."

"When you're around, I don't feel like much of a captain."

The Elf was amused, and then his features softened. "You know you'd rather hear it from me than the Elders."

There was truth to that.

The night wore on, and Barren was glad for the silence, despite the fact that it gave him more time to think. They would be at Conn by mid-morning, and he wondered how the island might have changed since the last time he was there. A lump rose in his throat at the thought. Conn bore the stain of his father's blood. It would never be washed away, not until William's death.

***

Barren slept lightly that night and woke early in the morning. Stepping out of his cabin, he relieved Sam from his duty as helmsman for a few hours. As he observed the gray morning and the slow sunrise, he was reminded of how peaceful the Orient really could be—here she was at her best: cool and crisp. As the hours passed, Barren watched his crew rise and begin preparing for the day. It wasn't until the island of Conn came into view that Barren passed the ship's helm to Leaf.

Despite Barren's fear of exposing Cove, Hollow, and the other Arcarum pirates, they had a good disguise—he was on a ship from Arcarum and Cove would present himself as the captain. It would take all the attention away from him and the other members of his crew who would follow him into Conn.

Barren disappeared into his cabin. Walking up to the washbasin, he stared at himself in the mirror. Though he looked tired, he couldn't feel the heaviness of it yet. He splashed cold water on his face, and tied his hair into a ponytail as best he could with his injured shoulder. In exchange for his normal brown pants, he pulled on black ones, and shrugged into a black jacket. As he stepped outside, he appeared much like the other Arcarum senators.

"I don't like it," Larkin said when she saw him. "The way you look."

"Have you ever?" he asked with a smirk. Larkin averted her eyes, but her cheeks colored with pink. "It is your turn now. Everyone in the Orient knows your face."

Larkin frowned, but she must have agreed, because she disappeared into the hatch, appearing later with a darker cloak on, her hood drawn up over her head. It was a simple solution, and it did its job, shadowing her face and hiding her hair.

"That will work," said Barren, observing Leaf in comparison—he had opted to hide his body in a cloak, and keep a hat pulled over his ears. They would draw more attention if anyone could tell they were Elvish.

Conn was a small island, mostly dominated by three-story brick buildings that made the island a maze to travel through. It was not a town focused on the sea, which was one reason Barren never understood his father's favoritism for the island, but it was quiet and peaceful and as they walked off the ship in a pack, eyes did not follow them.

Alex followed Cove in the line-up, waiting for his chance to take over. As they made their way down the dock, they could see that the square before them was crowded with people and tents, stained with mud. A gray light seemed to illuminate everything, and a fine mist was in the air. Barren felt particularly vulnerable, surrounding himself with so many people, but there was no backing out now, and from what he could tell, there was no other way into Conn but forward, for, at the very back of the courtyard, a large wall of rock rose up, enclosing the market. The only way through it was by a dark causeway in the distance.

The pirates moved forward into the crowded market before the town of Conn. The ground was covered in uneven cobbles, and mud and straw. The tents were small, and not everyone had one to protect them from the mist. Some sat crouched down beside wooden carts, heads bowed from the weather. It seemed a miserable place, and because of the obvious poverty, it was easy to pinpoint those of wealth. It was paraded around, evident by their attire—flaunting the privilege that came with a prestigious surname. It was hard for Barren to watch.

The market led into a passage that opened to the rest of the island. It was narrow and shadowed, and now and then haggard men and women passed them, dragging sacks or pushing wheelbarrows full of vegetables or fruits down the narrow way. The moisture covering the walls made the moss stand out against the stone, and the odor in the air was a mixture of decay and filth. Trash lined the crevices where the buildings and cobble met, and fat rats with red eyes munched on leftovers. Barren half-expected Larkin to scream at the sight of the creatures, but she remained quiet, only glancing their way briefly, and hurrying a little faster down the passage.

The causeway ended, and a three-story brick building rose before them. Like the one they had just passed under, its facade was blackened brick, and dark windows lined the front in drab rectangles. It was long and stretched from one end of the island to the other like a giant wall. The only way to get beyond it was through another passageway built into the center of the building.

"This place is set up like a maze," said Larkin. "It doesn't seem convenient. Are these the only passageways people can go through?"

"Yes," said Alex. "Conn is not built for convenience. It is built for survival."

"Survival? From what?"

"Attacks," replied Cove. "Pirate attacks."

"I don't understand," said Larkin. "How do these buildings protect against pirate attacks?"

"Usually, when pirates attack, they send a warning shot—a cannon. Because of the way Conn is fashioned, it is unlikely that pirates would be able to raid. A cannon would destroy the first building, creating a barrier between the attackers and the rest of the island."

Barren looked around uneasily.

"Well, Conn is in one piece...they must not have much trouble with pirates," said Larkin.

"No," agreed Cove. "But then again, pirates are not the only ones with cannons."

The crew continued, forward, entering another causeway. Finally, they came to the end of the island and the last brick building. It was probably the shabbiest of them all—broken windows were scattered randomly across the front. Parts of the building were black from age. Stone stairs, chipped and crumbling, led to a weatherworn door, stripped of paint. The pirates looked up at the building and cringed.

"I don't think anyone lives here at all," said Cove.

"'E's on the third floor," said Alex. He took a step forward.

"Are you sure this is safe?" asked Larkin.

Alex looked back at her. "No, but we look pretty suspicious just standin' out 'ere starin' at this place."

Alex made his way up the stairs, and pushed in the rickety door. As the pirates entered the building, the smell of mildew hit their noses. Furniture still crowded the entryway and living room;

old rugs covered the dusty floor. It looked as if nothing was out of place, even the cobwebs hung undisturbed. Many of the windows were painted black, so the only light that greeted them were the bits that peeked in through the chipped panes. Alex didn't pay attention to the look of the place; he had eyes only for the stairs, and hurried up them. The company followed, only slower, because as they moved over the steps, they creaked beneath their feet, worn and warped.

"I don't think anyone is here," said Larkin.

"People are 'ere," said Alex. "They are just hidin'."

The silence was deafening. If anyone was here, they were dead.

The third floor was just as lifeless as the rest of the building, except that the air was warmer, and the smells were stronger—spice and sweat hit their noses. The hall was filled with dust and cobwebs, and the walls were covered with peeling patterned paper—dark green with pink flowers. Alex hurried to the end of the hall and knocked on one of the many doors. There was no answer.

Barren stepped forward and withdrew a small knife from his boot, jamming it into the lock. The door swung open.

"I bet this isn't what you expected to find," said Barren.

The room had been ransacked. Nothing was left unbroken—wooden pieces from chairs and tables were everywhere, the windows were shattered and glass covered the floor. Barren stepped inside the room, looking around at the mess. Luckily, there was no body or blood—whoever had been here hadn't killed

Devon Kennings.

"Did William find him?" asked Larkin.

"We did lose three days," Alex stated grimly, shifting garbage around with his cane.

"What do we do now?" asked Leaf.

Barren looked at Alex who was about to respond when an elderly man stumbled into the room. He was dressed in a tattered blue coat. A long white beard adorned his face, stained with alcohol.

"Ye lookin' for Devon?" When he spoke, gold teeth were visible beneath his mustache.

"Yes," said Barren, turning to him. "Who are you?"

"No need fer names, but there was some soldiers in 'ere the other day. Took off with the 'ole man. He gave 'em a fight, but they took 'em anyway. Trashed the place."

"Did you recognize the men who took him? Were any of them from Maris?" Cove asked.

"They were all hooded. Didn't fit in well with this crowd, I'd say."

"Where'd they take him?" asked Barren.

"Well, I'd imagine Estrellas," the old man leaned against the door. "That's where they take all those fugitives."

Estrellas was a fugitive island. It was where the islands of the Orient sent their worst criminals. To the pirates, it was known for its brutal forms of punishment.

"What'd they arrest him for?" asked Alex.

"He's involved in piracy. Was part of Jess Reed's crew, he was.

Guess it came back to haunt him." Barren turned again to look at the room. He didn't want to listen to the man anymore—he could tell by the way the old drunk was speaking that his opinion of Jess Reed was not favorable. "What do you need with 'em anyway?"

"That is none of your business," Cove's voice rang with authority, but the older man just looked amused and narrowed his eyes.

"*Yer* from the government...Arcarum, is it?"

"We do not want any trouble," said Cove evenly—it was a warning that the man should leave.

"If yer walking around with Barren Reed, you do."

Cove's quickness surprised everyone. One moment, he was perfectly still, hands clasped behind his back, the next he had the man pushed against the wall, a knife at his throat. "You have two options: you tell no one you saw us, or you die. Which is it? And don't think I won't find out. I have spies everywhere. You speak, you die. Maybe not today, but keep in mind, I make no empty threats."

The man seemed to consider Cove's warning, but when the pressure increased around his neck, he wheezed, "I-I'll tell no one."

Cove relaxed his grip slightly and stood back. The old man glared at the Ambassador, rubbing his neck. "But make no mistake—pirates and politicians don't mix. You're either one or the other."

This time Cove wasn't giving him a chance. He lunged at the

man, stabbing him through the stomach. "You sealed your fate." He said through clenched teeth before pulling the blade out with a jerk.

Barren glanced at Larkin, wondering what she was thinking. She looked bewildered, as if what Cove had just done hadn't quite sunk in yet. Barren had to admit, he was a little surprised himself. Cove could usually keep calm, but when it came to a threat against him or his crew, he wasn't so patient. The Ambassador turned, pulled a white cloth out of his pocket, and cleaned the blood from his blade.

"He would have spoken up the moment we were out of sight," he said, not looking at anyone as he worked.

"How do you know?" Larkin's voice shook a little as she spoke.

"He voiced his opinion on pirates a moment before he fell," said Cove. "He would have met his end sooner or later."

"Why do you hide in that uniform if you're going to act like them?"

"What's that supposed to mean?" Barren demanded.

She ignored him and continued to stare at Cove. He, however, was completely calm and collected. "What would you have done, Larkin? Turned him over to the authorities here? Let him run and tell whomever may be within distance that Barren is in Conn and he is with the Ambassador of Arcarum? In this business, we have to choose whose life is worth saving and whose life is worth ending."

Larkin looked horrified, so Barren stepped in quickly. "We

should leave soon. There is nothing for us here. It would be beneficial if we could figure out whose soldiers took Devon."

The company made their way out of the building and back into the streets. They decided to split up and head for the ship, just in case anyone had noticed them in a pack. Cove and Hollow went one direction, Alex and Leaf disappeared down an alleyway and Barren and Larkin continued toward the markets, hoping to blend in with the sea of people who would be unfamiliar to this territory. The two pushed through the square easily, and with the ships in sight, they thought they were home free.

Larkin pulled on Barren's arm and pushed him behind a tent. Peering out into the market from the shelter, she whispered, "It's William. Looks like he just arrived."

"What?" Barren stared in the direction she was looking and saw his brother in the crowd. He walked casually before carts of fruit—picking up an orange or an apple here and there, judging its quality. He seemed tense as he tried to maintain his composure, as if he were attempting to slow himself down, as if he didn't want to appear suspicious.

Barren set his jaw, and he felt his eyes darken. He pulled off his jacket hurriedly, intending to fight.

"Barren, you cannot fight him," Larkin snapped. "You're injured. What if you can't kill him?"

Barren glared at her. "I'll be fine."

"Barren, please don't fight him!"

He studied her for a moment, repressing the anger he felt boiling in his stomach at seeing her plead for William's life.

"Larkin, the one thing I won't do for you is keep him alive."

Her eyes grew dark. "This isn't about him, it's about you," she snapped.

"I know what I'm capable of," he hissed. "So let me by."

She didn't say anything, but stepped aside so Barren could move past her. This is where Jess's life had ended—why not end William's life here, too? Barren held his sword in his left hand, but it felt awkward and uncomfortable. He had used knives before, but this was different—a sword was heavier, harder to maneuver, but that didn't stop him from calling out to his brother.

"William!"

As his brother whirled around, caught off-guard by the familiar voice, Barren suddenly felt insecure. At any other point in his life, he was the most confident swordsman in the Orient, but seeing his brother's hatred flare at the mere sound of his voice made him wonder how easy it would be to win this fight.

"Brother! I did not expect to see you here. It seems my privateers did a decent job—you still look pale from the bullets."

"It has always been your cowardly way—to send others to face me."

"I am facing you now, brother," William drew his sword, and the zing of the blade sounded against the silence in the market. Until now, Barren hadn't realized how many people were here or how many eyes were on him. He was vulnerable. Any one of these people could step in and take him down, just to gain William's favor. He couldn't worry about them, however—his target was before him. "Do we end this here?"

"Better now than giving you a chance to be king later."

William struck, Barren jumped back, deflecting his brother's attack. Barren's arm already ached from the strength of William's blow. Up until this moment, he had sworn to fight William on his own terms—at sea. So why had he made the exception? Perhaps he felt if he could win this fight, it would end the need for the bloodstone. Then he wouldn't have to go searching through his past, digging up things that might only hurt him more.

"So, how did kidnapping my fiancée work out for you?" he mocked.

"I didn't know I was helping you," said Barren through his teeth. "But she is too good for you."

William laughed. "I suppose you think you're better?"

Barren's arm was growing weaker. The harder he tried to the hold the hilt of his sword, the more his hand shook. He knew William had the advantage. Every strike he made was filled with power and hate.

"No," he growled. "You used her!"

"And you didn't?" William parried Barren's blade and the pirate stumbled forward, catching himself. He glared at his brother. Yes, he supposed he had used Larkin to lure William to him, but she had known that from the beginning. Larkin was Barren's prisoner, what else was expected? Barren forced guilt from his thoughts. He couldn't be concerned with Larkin at this moment.

"I only wanted to fight you."

"And you got your wish." William nicked Barren's fingers and the pirate dropped his sword. He ducked as William's blade flew over his head, throwing out his leg, tripping his brother. Barren reached for his blade, but William was already on his feet, kicking Barren in the stomach. He landed on his side, grunting from the pain. He had no time to recover before William's sword was at his neck, the tip cut into his skin. His arm felt as if hundreds of daggers were stabbing him, and he knew there was blood, but he glared at William, not taking his eyes off his brother, daring him to strike.

"How does this feel?" he yelled. "You have failed brother!"

He raised his blade, intent on cutting off Barren's head.

"No!" Larkin ran out of hiding, pushing back her hood and drawing her sword. Gasps broke from the crowd surrounding them.

"Larkin!" William moved his sword from Barren's neck and held out his arms for her, but she did not embrace him. Her gaze was dead. She moved between the two, standing with her sword aloft. When William saw she was not going to touch him, his gaze burned. "I thought you were dead," he said, sounding disappointed.

"You knew I wasn't dead, bastard!"

William laughed. "I see my brother's language has rubbed off on you. But it is no matter, now that you are safe, you will come home with me, and I will *break* that habit."

Larkin's eyes blazed as William reached for her. "No! I will not come with you!"

William snarled. "Move! Let me finish him!"

"I won't let you hurt him," she did not yell, but there was promise in her voice.

Barren watched her raise the sword he had given her. William laughed. "You realize you are admitting to all these people that you are a traitor."

"I am no traitor. You're the traitor! You are guilty of slander! You will never be my king!"

William eyes flared, and he charged at her with all his strength—their battle began. There was no pause in the clang of the two swords, no break. They would clash and recede, like the ocean, each intent on destroying the other. Larkin had fought Barren, but not with this much intensity, not with this much hatred. Larkin parried two attacks and then spun, her sword met something, and then startling silence followed.

Larkin stood, eyes wide with shock as she watched him. William hugged his abdomen, but blood quickly seeped through his crossed arms, staining his skin and the ground before him. Barren got to his feet at some point during their brawl, and now he was pulling her away from the display.

"Let's go! Run!" he said as he pulled her along, grabbing his sword as he went.

"Get them! Make sure they don't escape!" William commanded.

Barren and Larkin ran. They were already close to the ports and Barren could see his crew working feverishly to get the ship away from the docks as men were running toward it, weapons drawn. Leaf stood on the railing of the ship, bow out, arrows strung, shooting at any who made an attempt to reach them. Barren's sword was still drawn, and despite the weakness in his left arm, he managed to cut down anyone who came after them. When Barren noticed Larkin lagging, he pushed her before him, keeping his hand on her back, and making her hurry toward the ship.

"Go!" he shoved Larkin up the boarding plank as Datherious pulled it away.

Barren braced himself for another fight—a fight he wasn't sure he could win. His left hand and arm were bloody, and he held up his sword shakily. Four men inched toward him, laughing, and a lust for blood glinted in their eyes.

"You don't want to fight me," Barren said.

"You couldn't fight your brother; you cannot fight the four of us."

"My brother has my skill—none of you are my equal."

"We'll see about that!" One of the men ran forward, but Barren parried, and the man fell into the ocean, a wound through his stomach. The other three attacked at once, thinking they would be stronger in numbers, but Barren guessed their plan. He turned, skewering one man through the stomach; he jerked the blade from him and sliced another man's neck, finishing with his blade in the last man's face.

"Retreat," he said, and the man ran away.

The ship was a little way from the dock, and Barren knew he

could make the distance with his injuries, but Natherious tossed a rope in his direction. He grasped it and, holding on tightly, the twins pulled him toward the ship. He landed against the water with a splash, and he could feel the resistance build against his body until he surfaced, scratching the wooden sides of the ship as they pulled him on deck.

Looking back at Conn, a crowd gathered to watch them. William was lost somewhere behind them. They were in trouble now—not only did William know they were all after the bloodstone, it seemed there was now an additional party in search of the gem.

Chapter Fifteen
PROMISE

Barren sat on the steps of the ship while Leaf bandaged his fingers and stitched the cut on his arm. Behind them, Conn was fading into the background. Cove paced before them, and Alex was nearby. He kept looking back at Conn, a troubled expression marring his wrinkled brow. Natherious and Datherious stood with their arms crossed, waiting to hear their next move. Larkin had hurried to the hatch once they were all onboard, and had not yet returned.

"Just for once, couldn't you have considered the importance of this mission over your own wish for revenge?" asked Leaf.

"Part of this was about stopping William," Barren argued.

"And I'm not some lap dog for the king. I'm a pirate. I'm free to do as I please."

"The fact that you are free to do as you please has nothing to do with what is best for our situation. William knows you're after the bloodstone now. We will have to move fast."

"His injuries will delay him," Barren argued. "And the knowledge of Larkin's survival may work against him."

"At this point, Larkin's survival will only work against her. She saved your life. There's little explanation on her part for that," said Cove. "The public will see it as her siding with you."

"Her father can buy back her reputation, just as he bought William's position in government," Barren replied. "I'm not worried about her."

Leaf's hand met the back of Barren's head with a smack. "Ouch! Why'd you do that?" Now Barren had an aching arm, shoulder, and head. He was never going to feel better.

"She sacrificed her reputation to save your life, the least you could do is have some care about her well-being."

That was the hard part. Larkin was *his* prisoner, the only care he needed to have about her well-being was designated by the guidelines of the code, which only included harm to her physical person.

"Be a little more compassionate, Barren," Cove urged. "She's not as horrible as you make her seem."

"In case you hadn't noticed, Larkin Lee can't stand to see anyone hurt. She didn't save my life out of loyalty to me."

"Well, just in case *you* hadn't noticed, it's about morality, not loyalty, for Larkin."

Barren rolled his eyes. "Can we focus on the more pressing issue at hand? If William was not the one who took Devon Kennings from Conn, who did?"

"Well, either 'is past is comin' back ta 'aunt 'em," said Alex. "Or someone else is after tha stone."

"If Devon wouldn't give those soldiers information when they came for him, then they probably felt they could torture it out of him," said Leaf. "That's what they do in Estrellas."

"So what do we do now?"

"There're no others we can turn to for 'elp now," said Alex. "The others are dead."

"We'll have to go to Estrellas then," said Barren.

"Estrellas is a dangerous place, Barren," said Leaf. "You'd do well to stay away from there."

Suddenly, the Elf looked his age—his eyes seemed heavy as he knitted his brows together, and the corners of his mouth turned downward deeply. Leaf was a much more pleasant person when he wasn't trying to be serious.

"We're at a dead end without him," Barren argued.

"Devon is a good friend of mine. I won't let 'em rot in Estrellas."

"So you would rather we all died saving him?" asked Leaf, his sea-green eyes narrowed.

"Not everyone must go; I'll go alone if I must," Alex maintained, but the look on Leaf's face suggested he didn't think the old man would get out alive.

"Then I will go with you," said Barren.

Leaf punched Barren in his wounded arm, and he yelped in pain. "You are both ignorant! How will you get into Estrellas? It's guarded by a ten foot wall and the only way in is on a ship."

"We have one," said Barren. "And it's from Arcarum."

All eyes were on Cove in that moment and the Ambassador looked surprised. "What? I'm not going to be the one to settle this feud."

"Can you retrieve prisoners from Estrellas as Ambassador?"

"Only if they are from my island, and Devon Kennings is not."

"But you've taken fugitives to Estrellas before?"

"Yes, what is your point?" Cove crossed his arms and stood stiffly.

"Only that you can get us into Estrellas...as fugitives."

"That is the most ridiculous idea you've ever had." Leaf stood. "Think about it Barren—you are a pirate, wanted all over the Orient. Wanted, not only because you're a *murderer*, but also because you kidnapped Larkin. They'll torture you to death if they catch you. You are walking into a trap!"

"Then I'll just have to avoid capture."

"It's not that simple!" Leaf cried, and motioned as if he wanted to pull all his hair out. "You've never been there, you don't know!"

"Have you?" Barren countered.

Leaf's gaze was bright with anger. He folded his hands over his chest—he was about to challenge Barren. "As quartermaster, by the code, I have the right to veto any decision you make, Barren Reed. If you decide to go to Estrellas, I will veto."

"Then I'll give it to the crew to vote on," Barren countered. "Need I remind you of your words to me? Consider the importance of this quest. Devon is potentially the only one who can lead us to the bloodstone. If we do not at least attempt to go after him, we leave William an open target."

Leaf's face hardened. "Why is it that this quest is only about the bloodstone when it's convenient for you?"

Barren ignored the Elf and turned to Cove. "Can you get us in?"

"I can," he said with a nod. "But I can't promise you'll be safe when I leave, or that they won't separate you."

"All I need is to get inside those walls, what happens after is not important."

The Ambassador's brows rose as if he knew differently. "I'm going to encourage you to think about what the Elf has said. You really don't know what Estrellas is like. It is a very, very terrible place, and with your track record, they would take much pleasure in seeing that you don't walk out of there alive."

Larkin's humorless laugh suddenly sounded, and all heads turned toward her. At some point during their argument, she'd returned to deck. Parts of her hair were wet around her face, and her eyes looked a little red—perhaps she'd been crying.

"Barren thinks he's invincible, in case you hadn't noticed."

Barren met Leaf's and Cove's gaze. "I have to do this."

"Okay then," said Cove. "I'll help you...but after I deposit you on the island, I can do no more, so decide who you will take and create your plan."

Leaf rolled his eyes and he stuck his finger in Barren's face. "I'll go. You don't know your way around. Even then, I may get the opportunity to tell you I told you so."

"I'm coming," said Larkin, stepping forward.

"No," Cove and Leaf said in unison.

"Barren going into Estrellas is one thing, but a girl? And one like you? No, absolutely not," Cove crossed his arms tightly, as if that finalized everything.

"What do you mean a girl like me?" Larkin demanded angrily. "If anything, it should be you and I who venture into Estrellas. We're nobility, not fugitives!"

"I can only reclaim prisoners sent from my island," said Cove. "And I am sure the people of Estrellas, whether they know of your kidnapping or not, would not take kindly to you being on their island."

"My father is responsible for part of its creation. Those who run Estrellas would do well to do as I say."

"It may benefit them in the long run, but those who run Estrellas do not think that way. If they see a chance at revenge, they will take it."

"What are you talking about? Revenge?"

There was a common belief that Estrellas was just an isolated prison and it seemed Larkin held that belief, too. The governments of Mariana—and pirates—knew differently. Estrellas was a chamber of torture and death.

"Estrellas is a terrifying place, Larkin. Even the idea behind it is morbid. The king, your father, and others rationalized that if they could put like people together—people who were mean and merciless—they would kill each other off. It is a place of torture, and if you survive, you become a member of their community," said Cove. "And you should never assume that being sent to Estrellas will break prisoners of the hatred they have for those who put them there."

Larkin shook her head. "But...my father said..." Her voice faltered, and Barren knew she was having a hard time accepting this. He could only image what her father said—that Estrellas was an island dedicated to the imprisonment of particularly vile beings, that they were lucky to be sent to Estrellas because other options were far less pleasant.

"Even if you were in disguise, we could not risk it," said Cove.

"Besides," Leaf said. "You are still a prisoner on this ship. If we send you into Estrellas, we will breech the code, and then we'll have far more than a bunch of fugitives to worry about."

"You seem to have had personal experience in Estrellas," she accused the Elf. "Care to explain?"

Leaf's features hardened again, and after a long pause, he spoke in a cold, dead voice. "I was a prisoner there once."

This came as a surprise even to Barren. He had not known Leaf spent time in any jail. For some reason, Leaf always seemed incapable of getting caught, and Barren wasn't sure if it was because he was the most level-headed of the group, or because he was an Elf.

"There are few crimes that warrant imprisonment on Estrellas," said Leaf. "One of those is murder. I killed men...several men a long time ago. After, I had no will to live and so I was captured and sentenced to Estrellas. I would have gladly taken the noose over that place."

"How did you escape?"

The Elf laughed bitterly. Barren didn't like this Leaf. This was the merciless, emotionless Leaf. The deadly one. He noticed Larkin hugged herself, and her body instinctively bowed away from the Elf.

"It's not something I remember well. I know I killed a lot of people and once I was over the wall, I swam for days. I made it to Aurum and I was welcome there, so I stayed for a few years...that's how I am the person I am today."

"But you are a prince, how did you end up in this life anyway?" Larkin seemed confused.

The Elf shook his head a little, as if he were disappointed in Larkin. "Crowns are not for everyone, my Lady, and they certainly aren't for me. Besides, when the sea calls you, you have to answer it. It is a force you do not want to come into conflict with."

***

The rest of the day passed slowly. Nighttime fell: the darkness of the sea reflected the sky, and it seemed that they were in a tunnel of stars. Barren let Sam rest and took the helm for the night. He slipped off his sling so he could steer. Leaf would probably advise against this, but Barren was becoming skilled at ignoring the prince's displeasure. Besides, he'd need his arm in shape by the time they reached Estrellas.

Barren was used to having to heal. He had been wounded several times in his life; his body was a map of ugly scars. It was apparent when Leaf had begun healing him—the scars weren't as bad.

"You should rest your shoulder," said Larkin.

Barren jumped at the sound of her voice; he had assumed he was alone. He looked at her and smirked. "Well, if you could navigate, perhaps I would."

She stared at the helm, but didn't move toward it.

"I was surprised to see you at the helm the night I fell overboard," said Larkin. "I didn't think captains did much but bark orders."

Barren chuckled. "Well, if you asked Leaf he would probably say that's all I do."

She smiled, but Barren could see that she was a little detached, as if she were recalling the night she was thrown overboard. It was probably one of the most horrific memories she had. Or maybe she was still a little shocked by her encounter with William. "You seemed very certain of your direction that night in the storm ," she said at length.

He shrugged. "Navigation is probably my best skill. If you let it, the Orient will guide you anywhere you need to go."

Larkin frowned. It was probably hard for her to feel like she could trust the Orient after their last encounter. As Barren observed her contemplation, he laughed to himself and then took a step back, gesturing to the wheel.

"Take it, I'll be right behind you."

She hesitated for a moment, but stepped forward, gingerly taking the spindles. Barren could tell she wasn't certain what to do with the giant wheel; she just held it in place, as if the ship would tumble over if she moved it. Barren reached forward to move the wheel to the left. His hand covered hers for a moment and he noticed that she blushed. Silence fell between them as he moved away.

"How..." she paused, hesitating to ask whatever question she had. "How many people have you killed?"

Barren shifted uneasily. He wasn't sure what brought on this question, but he guessed it had something to do with her fight with William.

"I don't know," said Barren.

"Why do you ask for their names then, if not to remember them?"

He sucked in a breath. "If I call them by their name, it's personal."

Larkin shivered. "Why would you want it to be personal?"

Barren moved to lean against the rail so he could watch her face as he spoke.

"Because my father's death was personal, and every reaction to his death, I took personally—good or bad. When my father died, no one showed sympathy. No one questioned the wrongness of it. A son killing his father? Isn't that barbaric? No one thought of it as murder, but that is how I saw it. I watched it."

Larkin shuddered.

"What you are doing—taking these lives—it's no better than what William did. Worse, you are leaving people to live with the same pain you carry now. Why do you do it?"

"I don't *want* to do it," he said, feeling the sting of her words in his chest. "No matter what *you* think, I didn't start out with the intention of killing anyone. The best way I knew to get William's attention, was to send people back to Maris to let him know I was waiting. What I didn't expect was that those people would fight me. I started to offer a choice: they could die at the end of my sword, or return to Maris, stripped of their clothes and defeated, to inform William I was still there…"

His voice trailed off and he looked up at Larkin. She was shaking her head and her eyes took on a bright shade of green, the way they did when she was mad.

"You saw that it wasn't working, and yet you continued with the same ploy. I don't understand, Barren."

"For my purposes, it worked. I freed far more men than I killed," he said. "I'm not denying that my actions were selfish. Haunting the coast of Maris was a tactic to make me feel better…to make me feel as if I would finally have revenge for my father's death. But the ships we attacked became more hostile, and we ended up fighting for our lives several times. Bloodshed is not something I revel in, Larkin.

"So why did you keep doing it? Attacking ships? You could have found another way."

Barren was silent, and he bit his lip as he thought. He wasn't sure how to answer that. "I don't know."

"Well...shouldn't you have a clear answer if you're going to keep doing it?"

"Why are you asking all these questions?" Barren countered. He didn't like being interrogated, and worse, it felt like she was judging him.

"I'm just trying to understand you."

Barren chuckled. "Any luck?"

"Yes."

"Really? Then what do you understand about me?"

"I know you are in pain...and I know there's something about you worth saving. I risked everything today so that you would be safe."

Barren's eyes grew dark, and his lips twisted into a faint smile. "I was prepared to die," he said. "You had everything before you—a way to return home, wealth..."

"But nothing I want," she said, quietly.

Barren's eyes narrowed. "What do you want?"

Larkin looked away and took a deep breath. "Not the life I had."

"When did you make that decision?"

"When you almost died." She looked at him again and her eyes were bright with emotions Barren's couldn't quite discern.

"Well, we're even now—one for one," he said and walked forward, taking the helm. "You've been going the wrong direction for the past five minutes."

"Sorry," she blushed, stepping away. "And you're wrong—it's

two for one. You saved me from the Orient."

Barren smirked. "Well, you owe me one then, but I'd rather you not have to save my life again."

"Why? Because I am a girl?"

"No," Barren shook his head. "Because I should be able to protect my own crew."

"Then what do I owe you?"

"A chance to prove I am not a bad person."

"I don't think you're a bad person."

Barren smirked. "Yes you do…I can see it in your eyes, hear it in your questions. You speak to me with accusation in your voice."

Larkin's eyes grew dark. "Why do you care about my opinion?"

Barren considered that for a moment. He supposed he only cared to be understood, and yet he was soliciting understanding from a girl who'd been fed realities of the world by her father. She trusted too much in the title of a man, believing that it, not his conscience, gave him honesty.

Her opinion really shouldn't matter, but Barren was confused; if she thought he was such a horrible person, she should have let William kill him.

"You seem to think you are immune to the realities of this life, but if you stay in it long enough, they will corrupt you. It's already begun. You protected me over your fiancé, wounded him even. Am I to believe it is because you felt I was the better man?"

"Truly," Larkin said. "Things are not always as they seem, but if you are insinuating I will become just like you, you're wrong. I have a conscience. I could not live with myself if I hurt anyone."

"Oh, I would never believe you'd be capable of hurting anyone, *Mrs. Reed*."

Larkin slapped him. The sting of her hand made Barren flinch. "That's for breaking your promise!" she said vehemently. After a final furious glare, she stormed away, disappearing in the darkness.

Barren sighed. "I'm an idiot."

Chapter Sixteen
THIEF

It was dark, but the moon was full and bright light poured over the ocean, causing everything to rise in shadow. Larkin crept up the steps from the hatch where she'd slept since leaving Silver Crest with the pirates. She hoped that Leaf was sleeping, because that was the only way she'd get past him and his hearing. She crawled out of the hatch, careful to close the door quietly behind her. For a moment, she stood on deck of the ship, waiting to see if anyone had noticed her. Sam was at the helm, but he was busy talking to Slay and Alex.

She moved through the darkness, stepping carefully. Her destination was the cabin. She froze when laughter rose out of the quiet, crouching before Barren's door. Though her heart was pounding from the sudden sound, she realized this was probably the best time to go inside, considering the sound of the door opening and closing would draw attention. So she slipped inside, careful to close the door behind her. She turned, wishing she could hold her breath, as it sounded loud in her own ears. She turned to observe the still room.

Moonlight streamed through the windows and illuminated parts of the cabin. The desk and all its clutter were completely aglow, and the light reached far enough to the bed, where Barren's sleeping features were highlighted. He had one arm thrown over his forehead, and another resting upon his stomach. Larkin's breath caught when she heard laughter from outside again, and she watched Barren closely, wondering how he could sleep so deeply when his crew was so loud. Then she found what she was looking for—a trunk in the corner.

She moved toward it and tried to pry it open, but found it was locked. She turned and faced the room. Because of the lack of light, the only place she'd have any luck finding a key was the desk. Why would Barren lock his clothes up in a truck? It wasn't like anyone wanted them...unless he was hiding something.

For some reason, that gave Larkin all the more motivation to find a key. The desk was crowded with things she'd become accustomed to seeing while away from Maris—most, she assumed were for navigational purposes. A map took up most of the space on his desk, and it was weighted down by pieces of silver. It was a beautiful map, and looked as if it had been painted—thicker paint made for varying textures in the sea and the mountains. Larkin found herself studying it longer than she expected to. This map portrayed the whole of Mariana—the Orient islands and those of the Octent. Larkin had never been to the Octent, but she recognized the names from the history she'd been taught by her governess. Most in Maris referred to the Octent as a barbaric nation, one consumed with the mystique of magic and deception. Larkin always understood them to be a sort of gypsy culture—one that was so separate from what the Orient tried to be that it seemed archaic and backward.

Larkin's eyes moved from the map to a leather-bound journal. She'd seen Barren with it from time to time, but only when he went off by himself. Thinking it to be filled with writing, she untied the binding and opened it. What she found was very different—drawings. Pictures came to life: there were maps, extending far into the Orient, awash in tones of blues and greens. Landscapes unfolded on the page and she studied them for a long time, having never seen these places before. She wondered if they were even real, or if Barren had seen them, and strangely, if she would ever see them.

Turning the page, a port crowded with ships lingered silently. She recognized it as the port at Silver Crest. As she turned each page, a new image came to life before her eyes—there were portraits of Barren's crew—Leaf, Sam, Seamus, Slay, the twins, and it seemed they were drawn without the knowledge of the model. Soon she came to blank pages. She frowned, continuing to turn them, thinking she would find something in the opaque leaves. She wasn't sure what it was about these drawings, but they made her feel closer to Barren. They made her feel as if she understood him more than anyone in the world because in these drawings, she saw emotion, she saw what he cared for, and his vulnerability.

Just as she was coming to the last page, she ran upon a sheet that was marked by a folded piece of paper. Larkin recognized it as her and William's engagement invitations. She cringed as she picked it up and examined it. This must have been how Barren knew when and where to go to find her. She didn't think too long on the matter, however, because she noticed an unfinished drawing. Enough of the draft was done for her to make out a beautiful young woman's face. It took her a moment to recognize her own stare, but when she did, she couldn't look away. There was such softness to the way she had been portrayed—something she would never expect from Barren. She ran her fingers along the page, feeling the texture of paper and charcoal.

"What are you doing?" the voice shot through her. She dropped the book immediately, and she stumbled away from the desk, the silver light spilling over her.

"Nothing," she said hurriedly. Barren had gotten out of bed without her noticing. He stood before her, the light illuminating the muscles of his chest, and the black 'X' that marked him as a pirate of Silver Crest. He reached for the journal she'd been looking at. She watched him shove it in one of his drawers and turn a set of keys that had already been sticking out of the lock. She could have kicked herself—they were right in front of her eyes and she'd allowed herself to be distracted.

"You're in my room," said Barren. "Where you don't belong. Obviously, you are doing something you're not supposed to, like looking through my stuff."

"I wasn't going through your stuff!"

Barren glared at her. "Then what are you doing in my room?"

"I—" she started, but there wasn't a good reason for her to be in here. She'd come for clothes, and she'd ended up getting distracted. "I—"

"What were you looking for?"

For a moment, Larkin felt embarrassed, but then her stubbornness took over. "What are *you* hiding?" she demanded. "You must be hiding something, or you wouldn't be so upset."

"This is my cabin, I'm not hiding anything!"

"It was out on the desk!" she argued, as if that were a good excuse for her curiosity.

"So that makes it fair game?"

Larkin crossed her arms and glared at him. The keys jingled in Barren's hand and he moved away from his desk. Larkin watched Barren walk away from her with the keys.

"I...uh...do you have a jacket?"

Barren turned to look at her, perplexed. "A jacket?"

"Yes," and her words came out in the next breath. "It's cold...in the hatch. I came in here for a jacket."

For a moment, Barren's brows were still creased, but it smoothed with recognition. "Oh."

He walked over to the trunk, and unlocked it. He searched for a little while through the clothes, and finally pulled out a brown jacket.

"And pants," Larkin added.

Barren narrowed his eyes. "Why?"

"My legs get cold," Larkin added.

"And you don't have a blanket?"

"You don't exactly have the best blankets," she argued, and that wasn't a lie. They were thin, paper. Not at all warm.

She watched as Barren returned to the trunk and searched for a pair of pants suitable for her. She was relieved he didn't question her further—perhaps he wanted her out of here as fast as possible. After a moment, he pulled out a pair of dark brown pants and handed them to her, then he shut his trunk with a loud thud.

"Perhaps you'll mind your own business now that you can stay warm," he said, standing.

"Yeah," Larkin breathed, hugging the clothes to her chest. She turned and hurried away from the pirate, but before she left, she turned. "Why did you start drawing?"

She noticed Barren set his jaw. "I thought you weren't looking through my stuff."

When Barren showed no signs of answering her question, she said, "Well…they are very good," and turned to leave.

"I started drawing because my father did," he said at last. "It's one of the few memories I have of him, and I *don't* like for people to know."

Larkin turned. "Does it ever help you to remember?"

Barren laughed, running his hands through his hair, and bracing his palms against his neck, leaving his muscles bare to the light, which made Larkin's heart stutter in her chest. It was hard for her to really look at Barren and take him all in, mostly because her cheeks warmed every time she tried. There was no shame in being embarrassed by him, she thought to herself.

"No. I think I wouldn't be so desperate for memories if the ones I had were good, but it seems the ones I have retained are all horrific, save for drawing."

Larkin frowned. "And you've no memories of your mother, either? Not a one?"

He shook his head.

"Does William?"

"Would a fiancée not know?"

Larkin set her teeth. "I'm just thinking—he is older than you, perhaps he knew more about her. Perhaps she has more to do with his anger than we know."

"William is kind of like you. He tried all the time to get my father's attention in any way he could. He felt father was not proud. But I'd bet anything father was proud of William. Proud even when he understood his death had come at the end of his son's sword."

"Is that your hope?" Larkin asked quietly. "Do you hope your father was proud of William?"

Barren met her gaze. "I know he was. I always knew better than William how much my father loved him, but you cannot make another see love where they only see hate."

Larkin wasn't sure what to say. She couldn't imagine her father being proud of her now. Not after she'd ruined their plans and publicly defended a pirate by injuring her fiancé.

"I should go," she said, turning for the door again.

"Stay." Barren's voice was rough as he uttered the word, and Larkin froze. Turning toward him, her eyes were wide with shock. Then Barren continued, hurriedly, "You know, if you're cold. You can take my bed. I'll sleep on the floor. This was Cove's ship...I'm still not used to such extravagance."

Larkin shook her head. "What will your crew think?"

"At best? That I am a gentleman who gave up his bed for a lady."

She raised a brow. "And at worse my reputation will be ruined."

"True," he said. "But you've been on a pirate ship for nearly a month now—I'm not sure your reputation is still intact."

She smiled a little, but backed up to the door.

"Good night, Barren," she said quietly.

"Good night," he said.

She retreated to the hatch, and covered her entire body with her thin blankets, rubbing her face until the heat disappeared from her cheeks.

Chapter Seventeen
ESTRELLAS

When black smoke appeared on the horizon, Larkin got a sinking feeling in her stomach. She looked around—there was nothing but ocean and endless sky. While the sight was normally comforting for her, at this moment, it only made her feel as if no one could save them if things got bad. She would have little to worry about if she actually planned on staying on the ship, but that wasn't the case. Even if it were, she couldn't deny she was worried about Barren and Leaf making it out alive.

The pirates were within a couple feet of each other—they looked different, their faces dirtied by coal, clothes tattered, and hair matted. Larkin imagined they wouldn't stop there, even. To be really well-disguised, neither could be recognized from a distance or close up. The only scars that marked them as pirates were the ones over their hearts—the 'X's, and so long as they escaped before they could be stripped, they might make it out alive, or at least, that's what Larkin heard Leaf say.

Cove turned to Larkin. "It might be early, but I think it's best you hide now. If any guard sees you, none of us will be sailing away from Estrellas."

Larkin shivered. Cove had said the *Vasa* couldn't remain within sight of the island. It would be too suspicious. Larkin assumed Barren and Leaf had an escape plan—it probably involved a lot swimming. The thought made her arms ache. She turned and headed for the hatch, but before clambering down the dark stairs, she paused, feeling Barren's eyes on her. When she met his gaze, his eyes were hard and his features tight. She wasn't sure why, but every time he looked at her like that, it was as if he were welding her in place. If only eyes worked that way.

She disappeared beneath the deck, securing the door closed. She hurried to where she slept—toward the back, away from the men. She reached into her hammock and pulled out the pants and jacket Barren had given her, and started to change. She paused now and then when she heard the thud of boots above her, fearing she would be discovered. No one wanted her tagging along into Estrellas, but she really didn't think Barren and Leaf could smuggle Devon out of the towers without her. So she was going in with them, without their knowledge. If she were caught, she didn't believe those who ran Estrellas would harm her—she was Lord Christopher Lee's daughter. Her word overrode any who dwelled within the walls of that island.

She left her corset on, as it would do well for a shirt, and it was all she had. If she'd asked Barren for one of his, he would have been too suspicious. She pulled on Barren's jacket. It was far too big in the shoulders, and she had to roll up the sleeves in order to use her hands. She knotted her hair in a tight ball using her scarf. She imagined she looked ridiculous, but this was the best disguise she could muster. She secured a couple of daggers on her person—one in her boot as she had seen Barren do, and one at her waist, hidden by the jacket. Lastly, she had found an old hat in the back of the main hold. As she was fitting it on her head, she almost lost her footing when the ship groaned to a stop. She hurried to the gunport on the left and peered out.

Below her was a dock, small and slick. A few men stood there, all dressed in black, and all but one had masked faces. At first she thought they were guards, but then she noticed they all had weapons—strange swords with curved ends. She didn't want to know what kind of damage they could do.

Her eyes shifted beyond the port to the rest of the island. There was nothing magnificent about it, except for the horror it seemed to promise. In the dusk of the evening, the place was covered in shadow and orange fire. The walls surrounding Estrellas looked as if they would consume the entire island: black metal spires stuck out from the top of the wall, and curved inward. Two towers rose in the distance, one taller than the other. Both were connected by a covered bridge, illuminated in torchlight. The bottom halves of the towers were obstructed by two large gates, preventing entrance. The smell in the wind was ash, fire, and decay.

"*Get moving, scum!*" Larkin jumped when she heard a terrible voice tear the air. She cringed when she realized it was Hollow's. She hated how disgusted the Senator sounded with his prisoners. She shrunk away from the window a bit when Barren and Leaf filed off the ship and stood below her. She noticed they kept their heads bowed and their shoulder slumped, as if the burden of their sins weighed them down.

"Didn't think we'd get a shipment today, Ambassador."

Larkin shuddered. Shipment. Like they were objects, not people.

"Jail was full, Cas," Larkin heard Cove say. He was speaking to the biggest man of the group—the one without a mask. One side of his face had been burned badly, leaving most of his features to droop. His eye was red pulp. The other side was the shadow of the man he used to be. A knot formed in Larkin's throat as she recalled Cove's words. *It is a place of torture, and if you survive, you become a member of their community.* She didn't need any more proof than what was before her to know Cove's words were true. And she was horrified.

Cove continued his exchange with the man he called Cas. Every word that came from the guard was sharp and gritty—weighed down by the horrors he had experienced, no doubt. Larkin watched as another guard strung Barren's and Leaf's shackles together with a chain. The guard was not gentle, and the two pirates stumbled forward with the first jerk of the chain as they were led toward the tower.

The pull of the ship brought Larkin's attention back to what she was supposed to do. The *Vasa* was leaving and she needed to be off this ship. She rushed to the opposite gunport and squeezed between the window and the cannon. The ship lurched a little, and Larkin hit the side of the gunport hard. The cannon rolled toward her, pinning her in place. She struggled, trying to wriggle her way out of the space. If she didn't get out soon, she wouldn't be able to carry on with her plan. With all her might, she pushed her weight against the cannon and tumbled into the water below.

She was not prepared for its horridness. The water was thick and the smell was worse—it dug into her pores, and burned her nose. She closed her eyes tightly, and pushed herself to the surface. A terrifying growl kept her from taking in a great breath and coughing up the horrible water that managed to slide down her throat. She clung to one of the slimy beams holding up the port to keep from being seen.

"Something ain't right 'bout that," a voice grated, and her skin crawled.

"Rumors are goin' in the Orient. People sayin' Cove Rowell's sailin' with Barren Reed."

"Take 'em to the holdings...we'll hafta rough 'em up a bit. Find out fer ourselves."

Larkin's heart pounded in her chest. Barren and Leaf were sure to be discovered then. She recalled the face of Cas, the guard who had spoken with Cove, and cringed. The idea that they would endure torture made her frantic. She had to reach them before they could be hurt—she was their only hope now. Cove and the others would not return.

Larkin waited a few moments before peering over the deck. She watched two figures move to their posts on either side of the black gates blocking her entrance to the towers. She would never get in that way, and while she considered approaching them, the feeling in her stomach told her not to. If these men already knew that Cove might be in league with Barren, they'd probably know that Barren had kidnapped her, and as backward as it sounded, she needed to rescue Barren and Leaf, not be rescued herself...but how?

The smell of the water pierced her nose with a ferocity it hadn't before and she realized that it was not the Orient which produced such foulness, but the island. Estrellas was responsible for the contamination. The sewage that flooded the normally pristine water had to be coming out through some sort of duct. It would also have to take water in.

Her sudden realization had her heart pounding, but she had a renewed sense of hope. She could do this. Despite the awful water, she dove beneath. She wasn't yet a good enough swimmer to dive too far, so she grasped strange slimy things that erupted from the river's wall, or dug her fingers into the mud in order to keep going down, hoping at some point she'd come to a drainage canal. She squeezed her eyes shut tightly, forcing away every disgusted thought that entered her mind. When her lungs felt as if they were about to burst, she pushed herself to the surface.

Her breath exploded from her mouth, and she inhaled deeply, the thick water beaded off of her, the smell suffocating her. She wasn't above long before she dove under again. This time she was faster, feeling along the wall, using whatever her hands came into contact with to force herself down farther and farther, until her fingers touched a slimy metal grate. Her entire body shuddered with disgust, but her hand grasped the eroded metal and she pulled as hard as she could. The grate didn't budge.

The urgency and anger that overcame her next surprised even her as she began to pull on the grate obsessively. Bubbles escaped from her mouth, and filthy water took its place, sliding down her throat as her lungs begged for air. Finally, she could stand it no longer. She reached the surfaced and retched.

Frustration swirled—the longer she went without the knowledge that Barren and Leaf were okay, the more desperate she felt. She took a deep breath, making it to the grate quicker than before. She strained her arms, jerking it repeatedly. Each time she pulled, she felt it give a little more until finally the grate broke free.

She cast it aside and squeezed into the small circular opening, feeling the slime against her body. She fought the urge to gag. She shut her eyes tightly and pulled herself through the tunnel. If there was anything lucky about dragging herself through this duct, it was that the tunnel had a current as it took in water from the Orient, so she moved easily along, feeling when it veered left or right. At the last minute, it moved downward, sweeping her through the tunnel at a speed so fast, she couldn't stop herself.

Her heart jumped into her throat and she forced herself to keep her mouth shut tightly. Without warning, the tunnel ended, and she tumbled into a pool with a loud splash. She surfaced, gulping for air.

She rolled out of the pool. The stench of the water clung to her. She'd never wished so desperately for a bath in all her life, but that was something far out of her reach at the moment. On her back, she stared up at the ceiling—it was all shadow. Then she sat up and peered around the room—thankfully, it was empty, except for a torch at the door. The pool she'd landed in stretched around the room, and she assumed it carried water to various parts of the tower.

She pulled the small dagger out of her boot as she moved toward the door. She no longer had her hat, so she felt a little exposed. Not that her disguise would do much good while she roamed the halls of this tower.

She pushed the door open as carefully as she could, unsure if anyone stood outside. Fortunately, it opened into a shadowy, vacant corridor. She paused for a moment, listening as horrible sounds reached her ears—high-pitched screams tore her eardrums. She clung to the door to hold herself up. Though they weren't close, it didn't ease her fear any less.

She knew couldn't stay in this place forever. She had to find Barren and Leaf. She took a deep breath and started down the hall, blade poised in her hand, ready for whatever she encountered. The sound of screams rose again in the distance. Larkin hesitated; her heart pounded against her ribcage hard and fast. Other sounds joined the screams now—moans, cries, barely audible whimpering. She knew her former beliefs about Estrellas were far from the truth that was now before her. She would never have believed her father could be responsible for such cruelty, but clearly, something horrible was happening here and Lord Christopher Lee had played a role in it.

Holdings. I have to find holdings, Larkin thought desperately. If she kept her mind focused on Barren, perhaps she could keep her feet moving forward.

She rounded a corner after a long climb up a hall that moved steadily at an incline. She assumed she was somewhere on the bottom floor. All that she could see before her was a hall of rock, illuminated by torches. There were no windows, no doors, and the only things that suggested there was more to this tower, were the screams that consistently interrupted her thoughts. With a churn of her stomach, she realized that moving in the direction of those screams might lead her to Barren. It might also get her captured, but she didn't have any options.

Setting her teeth, she quickened her pace. Part of her wanted to be mad at Barren for this. He'd pushed going to Estrellas, but really, she could only blame herself. She'd made the choice to come. She had believed she could help Barren, ensure his safety in some way. Mostly she wanted to prove the pirates wrong—wrong about her father and this place, and wrong about the way they saw her. Just for once, she wanted to have it right. Time after time, she'd believed in her father's innocence, his goodness, and yet each time, he had proven to be anything but good. He'd gone along with the idea of her death, agreed to have privateers keep her from ruining his plans, and now this treacherous island.

The hall twisted to the right, and continued at an incline. At some point, she'd come to windows, doors, and *guards*. This was a prison, after all, and people kept watch. As she continued, it was like she moved in circles—everything looked the same, and the lights were dim and hurt her eyes. A pounding in her head took half of her attention, so when shadows formed against the wall, her heart jumped into her throat.

Quickly, she moved into the dark as footsteps drew near. She could just hear their conversation over the moans.

"Did ya hear? Cas brought in Barren Reed and his quartermaster. Said Ambassador Rowell deposited him at our doorstep."

"I'd heard they was pals. Seems odd he'd take 'em to his death."

"Maybe 'e betrayed 'em? Never know who Barren Reed'll cheat to get what he wants, or so I've heard. Guess it's good 'e came to us. He won't survive the chambers. He's too young."

"Aye, he might be young, but he's survived a lot in his short life. I'd wager he'll last longer than some of our strongest."

So they had discovered him, but was he in the chambers or holdings? Now Larkin had no way of knowing. It wasn't like she could ask the guards. As she thought that, the two men stopped just a few inches from her. They were like shadows in the hallway—all dressed in black, and faces masked. She held her breath.

"Somethin's not right 'ere," the guard breathed. "The air's all wrong."

Larkin's eyes widened, her hand tightened around the hilt of her blade.

"You've had too much ale," the other guard said.

But he was looking right at Larkin. Desperately, she clung to the wall, willing the darkness to consume her. After what seemed like an eternity, the guard said, "You could be right."

The two took off, and once Larkin was sure they were gone, she stepped out of the shadow. She wanted to run, but what was before her might be worse than what was behind her...or so she thought.

"That's a pretty." A voice stopped her in her tracks. "Told ya I wasn't seein' things."

Larkin turned and saw the two guards who had passed her. They were at the end of the hallway.

"Hello girlie," his voice cracked. "Whatcha doin' 'ere?"

The other one had been quiet and observant. He elbowed his friend. "That's Christopher Lee's daughter. Bet she was on that ship with Barren Reed. What'd you come here for girlie? Lookin' for someone to save ya?"

They both laughed. Larkin took a step back.

"Oh don't be afraid of us! We can't do anythin' to you until Cas sees you. Once he's done with you, that's when we get our turn."

They laughed again and that's when Larkin ran.

"There's no gettin' away from us, girlie! We know every twist and turn of this place!"

She had no doubt that they did. Whatever she might encounter before her, well that was better than surrendering easily to these people. Besides, she'd seen Cas and that had been enough for her.

Just as she feared, a guard ambled toward her. By the way he was walking she wasn't sure he'd spotted her yet. He was staring at his feet, and he stumbled a bit—drunk perhaps? She panicked, and brandishing her weapon, she ran upon him, running her blade along his legs. She knew it wouldn't be enough to hurt him, just sting, but it did its job. The guard fell to the ground, surprised by the sudden attack. His recovery was sloppy, as he had a hard time rising from the floor. Instead, he gave a loud cry that Larkin was sure would bring every guard in the tower right to her.

The hall began to level out as she ran and she saw windows ahead. Outside, against the inky-blue of the sky and the orange glow from the fires, she could see the image of the bridge. It wasn't far from her—only a few windows down, but she was above it. Her eyes shifted to the roof. The only problem was the steepness, but if she could manage to get across it, maybe she could hide in the other tower until things calmed down.

As she came to the window overlooking the bridge's roof, she stuck her legs out the frame. She hesitated for a moment, fearing that she might fall off either edge of the roof. There was nothing there to catch her if she fell—just spikes sticking out on either side that might scratch her. Shouts from inside the hall caused her to move. She focused on the roof and pushed herself off the window's ledge. She landed and wobbled a bit, and then fell forward on her hands and knees.

"Get back 'ere you little wench!"

Larkin got to her feet and, balancing along the top of the roof, she managed to move across with more ease than she anticipated. A bell rang out—harsh and dull—and she knew she was in trouble.

When she neared the end of the bridge, she noticed there was no window to climb through on the other side of the tower—that only left the bridge beneath her as an entrance. She swallowed— if she thought she'd be safe up here, she'd stay, but she knew differently. She inched toward the edge of the bridge, grasping the spikes in hand. They were cold and metal. She tried not to think what would happen if she fell. She just focused on slipping between spikes, and pushing herself onto the bridge.

She landed with a loud thud on her hands and knees, so when she got to her feet, two guards were already coming toward her. She kept her blade brandished, waiting for them to make their move.

"Gonna fight us, girlie?" One of the guards asked as they approached. She couldn't see his face, but it seemed one of his eyes had been sewn shut. She didn't say anything, but grasped her blade tighter as the guard moved toward her. He clearly thought taking her captive would be easy—as he kept his blade at his side and reached for her, intending to grab her wrist. What he got instead was a knife through his hand. The guard's screams filled the air, and Larkin was slammed to the floor. Her breath escaped her. Fear crept into her throat as she struggled to force air into her lungs. She was wrenched to her feet and met yellow eyes.

The sounds of footfalls tramping the ground echoed in her ears, and she knew she was surrounded.

"You are Christopher Lee's daughter," the man she'd stabbed through the hand spat. He lifted his blade and the curve of the end fit perfectly against her neck. "It'd feel so good to have my revenge."

"What's going on here?" a man's voice rang out coldly. A burly guard parted the crowd. Larkin recognized him as Cas. Her eyes fell to his weapons. At his side he carried the same curved sword as the other guards, but it was what he held in his hands that scared her the most: a ball and chain. The spikes gleamed bright silver, as if they'd just been sharpened. Every time she glimpsed his face, she swallowed hard in an attempt to keep from vomiting.

"This girlie here, Cas," said the one who held her. "She's been causin' trouble. Stabbed one of our guards."

Cas's eyes were on her. What Larkin found most frightening was that she couldn't tell what he was thinking—did he want to kill her? Was he angry at her father too? Did he want revenge?

"Causing trouble?" Cas questioned. "She doesn't even belong here."

"Had to come on the ship with Barren Reed," said the other. "Rumors are on the sea that he kidnapped her."

Cas did not say anything. Instead, he stepped forward and his big hand grasped Larkin's shoulder tightly.

"Get to work!" he cried and the guards scurried away—all but the one she'd stabbed. Larkin knew what his gaze meant—he would see her head on a pike if he could.

Cas pulled Larkin roughly. She kept pace with him, not wanting to be dragged by him—already his fingers dug painfully into her skin. The sting brought tears to her eyes, but she gritted her teeth hard, knowing she couldn't show any sign of weakness here. She also knew these men had a reason to hate her father, and that if she had experienced what they had, she would hate him, too.

Cas took her down several halls that twisted and turned until she had no idea where she was in relation to where she'd begun. There were no windows, and she didn't know if they had gone farther up the tower, or into its belly. After much walking, they came to a door. Two guards stood on duty. Without question, one opened the door to allow them entrance. Cas pushed her inside and she was consumed in darkness.

At first she thought he meant to only take her this far—but his presence swelled behind her and he shut the door. Panic filled her, and she began thinking of what she would need to do to get away from him. She still had the dagger at her waist, and if she could manage, she might be able to pull Cas's sword from his sheath. She'd never fought anyone who wielded a ball and chain before, but she would try.

Cas's hand returned to her shoulder. It occurred to her that he underestimated her will to fight—at least she had some advantage.

The hall was dark and long, and she wondered what could be down here. She didn't hear anything—no screams of torture, and at the end of the tunnel, there was a dim light. She decided she would wait until then to attack Cas. She'd have to watch his weapon closely.

Finally they entered the light, and she saw a cell.

"Larkin?" the voice was familiar, and her heart rose a little—until Cas threw her on the ground before the cell.

"What are you doing with her?" Cas demanded, and his voice was like acid raining down on her.

Larkin hit the floor hard. She scrambled away from Cas, her back to cell the pirates were in. She wanted to look at Barren, but knew taking her eyes off Cas was a bad idea.

"You haven't heard?" Barren questioned.

"Let me ask this a different way," Cas said, reaching for Larkin. He grabbed a handful of her hair and yanked her to her feet. She cried out, but didn't have time to focus on the pain, because Cas had withdrawn his sword and had it at her neck.

"What are you here for?" the guard demanded. "Cove Rowell delivered you, and it's rumored you are friends. Next I find this girlie running among my halls. You're up to something. Better tell me or I'll take her head right off."

Larkin met Barren's gaze now. His fists were wrapped tightly around the bars that held him captive. He'd been roughed up. Bruises formed beneath his eyes, and his lip was split. She was relieved he wasn't hurt worse and could actually move. The blade pressed into her neck and a breath escaped between her lips as the pain shot to her head.

"We came to find someone!" Barren called quickly. "A man—he was delivered here a few days ago, maybe."

Cas's arms rested just a little, and it was enough for Larkin to make her move. She withdrew the small knife she had in her belt and plunged it into Cas's side. He let out a cry and she grabbed the sword from his loose fingers. She twisted and faced Cas, who pulled the dagger from his body and tossed it aside. Pressing his fingers into his wound, he looked at them in the light, raising his ball and chain. "So you wanna play that way?"

"Larkin! What in the hell are you doing?" Barren demanded.

"Saving your life," she replied.

Cas laughed, and she saw his teeth were black. She cringed. "Forgive those you've wronged," he said. "Because you are about to take your last breath."

Larkin wasn't sure who was at a disadvantage at the moment. Cas seemed to grow bigger in this small space, but Larkin knew not to underestimate the power of his weapon. Even if he didn't have much range of motion, it could still prove deadly, and she had to remember that Cas himself was a weapon—as he could easily crush her.

He charged, swinging the ball and chain over his head. He brought it down upon her. Larkin ducked to the left and twisted, aiming her sword at the guard's side, but Cas was too fast and stopped the blow with the chain.

She jumped back quickly, her back hitting the cells. They

stood for a moment, staring at each other, attempting to gauge the other's next move. Cas's weapon dangled at his side, and the sound of the chains running against one another made Larkin shiver. A smile broke across the guard's face, and he swung his weapon at her. Larkin ducked again, and the ball and chain crashed into the stone wall, causing pieces of rock to break loose.

As if the ball and chain were feather light, he reared back and swung it again, bringing the weapon down where Larkin landed. She rolled away from him, and the chain hit the ground. She got to her feet in time to counter a blow to her body with her sword; the force was so great, it ripped the blade from her hands.

Cas laughed deeply, and he stood there for a moment, taking in the length of her.

"Such passion when you fight. Let's see if I can break you."

Cas began to swing the ball and chain. Larkin spotted the dagger Cas had cast aside—it lay in the corner, bloodied. She reached for it, having no other weapon handy. The ball and chain flew from his hands and barreled toward her. She moved just in time and it crashed into the wall behind her. It wasn't until Cas was upon her that she realized it had only been a distraction. His impact sent her stumbling into the wall, but the contact was enough for her to push the dagger into his tough skin. It lodged in his stomach, and Cas just stood still for a moment, staring at the hilt of her blade. He growled.

"You were lucky before. I was going to go easy on you," he said. "But now I think you deserve a punishment fitting of your nature." He cracked his knuckles into his bloody hand. "Perhaps we will brand you with the stigma of the Estrellas fugitives. We can break your fingers, or cut an ear off...or burn your skin and peel it off ever so slowly. Whatever punishment might break you of your *unruly* behavior. Would it not be grand for the daughter of Christopher Lee to favor those prisoners he ensnared?"

She shook, and she knew she had to end this now. She caught a glimpse of her blade. If she was fast, she could grab it. She made her move, lunging for her sword, but just as her fingers grasped the hilt and she managed to point it at Cas, he clasped the blade. It was as if he felt no pain as he inched his way toward her hands. He laughed at her shock.

"What do you take me for? A weakling? I did terrible things to get here. See my face?" he yelled.

Maybe it was the thought of what Cas would do to her if she was captured, or the knowledge that she was the only one who could free Barren and Leaf, or blatant fear, but something gave her strength. She pushed against the sword with all her might. The blade slipped through Cas's hands and through his stomach. He fell to his knees and then onto his side, taking in haggard breaths. Larkin hurried to him, kicking him onto his back. She took the hilt of her sword and drove the blade into him over and over again.

When she was sure he was dead, she reached for his keys and rushed to the cell where Barren and Leaf remained, watching the entire spectacle. Her hands shook so badly, she had a hard time fitting each key into the lock to test it, and the longer it took her to find the right key, the more frustrated she became.

Barren took the keys from Larkin's shaking hands and she collapsed against the wall before the cell. With a click, Barren found the right key and the door groaned as it opened. She wasn't paying attention anymore—her eyes were focused on Cas's body.

Barren's rough hand clasped her face, and she met his gaze. Of all the times she'd looked into his eyes, they had never been as dark as they were now. "Are you okay?"

She nodded, but Barren set his teeth, and she knew he didn't believe her.

"Why are you here? Did I not beg you to stay?"

"I...I thought I could help and I had to know," was all she could say.

Barren seemed disappointed, but his hands left her face, and when they did, she felt even more exhausted.

"Leaf, help me."

They moved Cas's body into the cell. "We have to hurry and find Devon. Leaf, do you know where he might be?"

The Elf was busy as he pulled Cas's cloak from his body and folded it over his arm. He straightened, shaking his head. "I'm not sure. We can check the chambers."

"*Check*? We don't have time to just check the chambers!"

"Remember this was your stupid idea," said Leaf. "So don't get angry with me when it doesn't go like you planned."

"I didn't have a plan."

"Maybe that was your first mistake."

Larkin didn't understand how they could be bickering at a

time like this. A guard was dead. And not just any guard—Cas was someone the others would look for.

Leaf moved past her and Barren and headed down the dark hall. She wasn't sure she could move right now. Her body was shaking, and she couldn't take her eyes off the man in the cell. He was lifeless, but somehow, she felt as if he just might rise up and slay her.

"Hey," she heard Barren say gently. "We have to go."

Larkin looked at him. His face was close to hers, and now she could see a gash at the top of his brow. "You're hurt."

Barren laughed a little. "Odd time to be concerned about me."

Barren helped her to her feet and they moved down the hall, following Leaf.

Chapter Eighteen
THE ASSASSIN

Leaf was dragging a body through the door.

"Leaf! What are you doing?" Barren scowled. "The more of them you kill, the worse off we'll be."

"Should have thought about that before you decided to come here."

"Are you trying to teach me a lesson?"

"No," Leaf handed Barren a mask and a cloak he had pulled from one of the dead guards. "I'm teaching you survival."

Barren understood what the Elf was doing—disguises, and while they weren't the best, they would at least not be recognized immediately.

Leaf disappeared again and came back through the door dragging another body. From it, he seized another cloak and a mask and handed them to Larkin.

"Put these on."

She didn't question him, but she turned from the dead men on the floor as she pulled on the mask. Barren did the same, shuddering as he thought about the face that had once worn it.

Leaf picked up one of the guard's swords and examined the blade in the dim light. They would all need one—their weapons had been taken. "These aren't meant for killing," he said. "They're meant to make their victim suffer...to bleed out."

Chills ran to Barren's core. He knew Leaf was trying to make a point—Barren understood, this was both stupid and dangerous, but what else were they supposed to do? They needed Devon. How else were they going to find the bloodstone?

After they were dressed, and each of them had a weapon, they left the holding cell, making sure to secure the door behind them. The longer everyone went without knowing Cas and two other guards were dead, the better.

They stood in the shadows for a moment while Leaf found his bearings. Either the Elf was having a hard time telling where they were, or he was listening for things, because he kept peering down the hall, left and right. The Leaf who stood before Barren at this moment was different in some way. He was tense, and his features were harder—his eyes had darkened, snuffing out the mischievous glean that always made them inviting. It was unsettling.

Barren knew it came from whatever had befallen him while he stayed in this tower. Places like these were horrible to experience for anyone, but in particular, for Elves because their senses were so heightened—the guards took great pleasure in that. Barren was only half-Elf, yet had already noticed an increased awareness after passing into this tower. His eyes caught creatures scurrying in the shadows—rats with plump bellies, strange worm-like things with thousands of legs crawling the walls, even dried blood on the floor. The smells were a mixture of death and mold, and of course there were screams, begging, and harsh laughter, all rising together from somewhere in the tower. All these things, Barren could hear, which meant Leaf experienced them at an even greater level.

Finally, the Elf led them left—whatever he'd heard down the hall to his right must have driven him away. They moved with a certain amount of tension, sticking to the shadows. Barren kept his hand on the wall. It was gritty and wet in places, as if water were leaking through the cracks. It made him wonder how far below sea level they were, and where the drainage tunnels were located. Larkin might know—she'd obviously used them to gain entrance to the tower, as her hair was wet and her clothes—*his* clothes, the clothes he'd unknowingly given her for this very event—held the stench of the water. If they could locate those drains, maybe they would provide the best escape. It wasn't like they were going to be able to walk out the front doors, and the jagged rocks he'd seen upon entering made a barrier around the tower. So windows were also off-limits.

He considered their escape routes as he watched Larkin. She hugged herself, and her head darted around at every tiny noise. Watching her fight Cas was both amazing and terrifying and she should never have had to do it. This day, Larkin had fought for her life, she had fought for her innocence, and she'd fought to hold onto the morals she cherished. And she'd lost. She had just killed a man—brutally. What bothered Barren most was the fact that she'd fought for his life, too. While he was grateful, he had questions for her—most pressing: why did she risk her life for him?

Pain registered with Barren—it was slight, but stinging. He looked down at his hand and released his fist—crescent shapes were indented into his palm, some bled. As the blood pooled, he felt weak. What was he becoming? He was noticing things about Larkin, worrying about her—it wasn't long ago that he'd wanted to throw her overboard.

Shouts rang out in the hallway. "Get them!"

"Run!" Leaf commanded.

Behind them, heavy footfalls sounded, and before them, growls erupted angrily—they were surrounded. They stopped in their tracks and backed into a circle as more and more guards encircled them. They were clearly human—for their flesh was like Barren's, but what they'd experienced had taken them far beyond human comprehension, so that as they moved around them, Barren felt he was being watched by wild animals.

"You have few options. You fight here and die sooner, or you surrender and die later," a guard's voice rose above the cries of the crowd.

"Then I suppose it makes no difference whether or not we start now," said Leaf.

And the fight began. Barren knew there were too many of them, and Larkin was weak from her earlier encounter with Cas. The only advantage they had was that it was hard for all of them to fight at once, and even then, the crowd did not allow for much movement.

Barren and Leaf fought, taking down guards as best they could, but Larkin struggled, and the more Barren became distracted with her distress, the less focus he had on himself. Pain shot up his arm, and he noticed his hand had been hit by a blade. He ground his teeth and looked up, thrusting his blade through the guard's gut. Pulling it out, he went after another, cutting him down where he stood with a blow to the shoulder and head, but it seemed the guards thickened. They'd drawn every man in Estrellas to their spot. Their biggest mistake had been coming here, the second biggest had been killing Cas.

From the darkness above, a figure fell. For a moment, Barren thought it was a guard, and that they were done for, but when the figure landed—perfectly on its feet, clad in a hooded cloak— it twisted and cut down guards as if they put up no fight. There was grace and skill in each movement, and fast and deadly precision. That fighting style could only come from one kind of person, an assassin—a woman assassin if Barren had to guess by her stature and slight build.

Soon, more guards riddled the floor than stood, and they fell back, calling for reinforcements.

"Follow me!" the hooded figure demanded.

And they did.

They followed, running as quickly as they could. The figure rounded a hall in the darkness and then crouched before a grate in the wall. Working it free, their savior slid into the opening without a word. Leaf followed, and Barren turned to Larkin.

"I'll help you down once I'm inside."

She nodded in agreement. Barren squeezed through the opening and then reached for Larkin, catching her long legs, and guiding her safely to the floor beside him. Leaf reached up and moved the grate over the opening.

The group held their breath as feet shuffled past. Curses were whispered and weapons clanked. Soon there was silence again.

"You can let go of me now," Larkin said quietly.

He looked down at her, surprised. Barren hadn't realized he was still holding her. One arm was on her waist, the other positioned on her back protectively. Both of her hands were pressed to his chest, as if this closeness bothered her. He continued to stare at her. He'd forgotten how small she was, and having only held her once before, he found himself amazed that someone so delicate could kill someone as massive as Cas.

"Barren," Larkin's voice was even. He shook his head, snapping out of his stupor. He released her, clearing his throat as he stepped away. He turned to observe his surroundings. There was light up ahead, but where they had landed, it was dark. Barren could hear water moving close to them.

"Let's go," an unfamiliar voice said.

"Wait," Barren demanded. "We don't even know who you are."

"Do you need to know who I am? I just saved your lives."

"And by the looks of things, you're an assassin," said Barren. "So I'd very much like to know why you're here and why you saved us."

A sigh escaped from her mouth and a light flashed in the darkness. The woman held up a small torch she must have been carrying under the cloak. "You're like your father," she said and the assassin threw back her hood. "Suspicious, even of old women."

She was older. She had long, silver-blonde hair pulled back into a braid, and blue eyes as bright as a youth's. Her cheekbones were high, which made her seem aristocratic. And the voice she spoke with—it was warm, like honey…like a mother's voice.

"You knew my father?"

"I helped Jessdia out many times when he was in need," said the woman. "If he were still alive, I am sure he would owe me many a debt."

"Not many called my father by his full name, even close friends."

"You're right," she agreed. "I was the only one of his friends to call him Jessdia, but then again, I was not always his friend."

"So…are you or are you not here to kill us?" Leaf stepped in. "Because I can't tell whose side you're on."

"That all depends on why you're here," she said, and suddenly that warm voice was cold and frightening. Barren's hand wrapped around the hilt of his sword, but her eyes narrowed. "Are you sure you want to attempt to fight me?"

Barren didn't want to fight her—she could probably take him down in a second, but he was tired of stalling. "Tell us who you are."

The woman considered it for a moment, and then began. "You do not know me, or rather, you don't remember me, so my name will bring you no comfort. I am Emmalyn. You can call me Em. Like your father, I prefer my nickname."

"Wait," Leaf interrupted. "You knew Jess, and you say you were his friend, which means you could only be here for Devon Kennings."

The woman's lips twitched. "Now what I need to know is why three pirates are searching for an old man?"

"Perhaps we are here for the same reasons you are," said Barren. "Unless you're the one who placed him here."

The woman scoffed. "I was not the one who placed him here, and it is unlikely we are here for the same reasons, as you do not love the man you're seeking."

Barren felt stunned. He certainly hadn't expected that. He cleared his throat. "Well, you'd be right about that."

"We believe Devon has some valuable information concerning the bloodstone," said Leaf.

Em's features became hard, and it was evident she knew exactly what the Elf was talking about. "Devon would be of no use to you in matters concerning the bloodstone."

"What makes you so sure?" asked Barren.

"If you are doing anything that involves its recovery, you'd do well to leave him out of it. He will not help you."

"Then will you?" Barren was becoming impatient with this woman. "Because you seem to know a lot about it."

"I did not come here to relive my past," said Em. "I came to find Devon."

Em turned and headed down the tunnel.

"It is not *my* wish to see the bloodstone recovered," said Barren quickly. "Please, I…I just need answers."

There was truth in what he said: it really wasn't his wish to actually find the bloodstone, but to stop his brother, and he really did want answers. It hadn't been long ago that he discovered his mother's identity as a Lyric, and his father's supposed involvement in her death. There had to be someone who could give him clarity, someone who could tell them where the bloodstone was.

Em froze at his words and turned slowly to face Barren. He almost wished he couldn't see her features in the torchlight—while she seemed angry, she also seemed to pity him and if there was one thing Barren hated most, it was that.

"If you're going to ask him anything, we have to find him first. Let's go."

Barren felt triumphant, though he wondered why Em seemed so resolute that Devon would not help. He had a lot of questions, but they could wait until after they found Devon.

Barren realized they were now roaming the duct system of the tower. This tunnel would lead outside the tower walls. The smell around them was rancid, and Barren pulled his cloak over his nose and mouth to muffle it. There were torches interspersed along the walls. They were far enough apart, though, to force them to follow only the light of Em's torch for long intervals.

For a while, Barren didn't want to speak—but the silence in the duct grew to be too much for him, especially since they were following a woman they'd just met in the tower of Estrellas.

"So were you a member of my father's crew?"

"Yes, but only after I tried to kill him," she replied, her voice so warm, Barren knew it was a part of her disguise. "I was once a royal assassin."

"A position as a royal assassin isn't easy to come by," said Leaf. "You must have been good."

"I was," she agreed. "But Devon was better."

"But...I thought Devon was a Chancellor," said Barren.

"Yes, he was...but he was also a killer. You can be two things at once—after all, isn't that what Albatross does?"

Barren clenched his jaw—he decided not to acknowledge that last part.

"I worked closely with Devon before I knew of his betrayal to the king. That was how Devon was able to protect your father, which I should say I am grateful for now. It wasn't until after he was exposed, and I was sent to kill him and Jess that I realized I might love him."

"Why were you sent to kill my father?"

"Because Cathmor was desperate for him to cease his

involvement in the Ore Wars," said Em. "Apparently whatever there was to gain from that battle was far more important than his son's life."

Barren let that last sentence settle into the silence. There were few things he actually knew about the time of the Ore Wars. Most of it involved his father fighting to prevent Cathmor from gaining more territory. Jess had been an advocate for freedom, an advocate for islands whose wish was to remain immersed in their own culture. There was so much to love about that, and Barren hated the thought that his grandfather had attempted to destroy it.

"Where are we going?" Larkin's voice quaked in the stillness. Barren wondered if it was from fear or cold. His fingers ached for her in a way he didn't really understand. He just wanted to touch her, believing it might comfort her—but what comfort came from the hands of a killer?

"We're heading for the cells," Em replied. "I checked the chambers—where men are tortured, and thankfully Devon was not there. However, the cells are for men who are held for a purpose...held because someone expected them. It's much more dangerous to go there."

Again there was silence.

They walked on until Em found another grate. She pulled herself up and looked through for a long moment—Barren figured she was listening. Then, she slowly pushed the grate aside and soundlessly climbed out of the duct. Leaf followed next, and Barren lifted Larkin to the opening, while Leaf helped her to her feet. Barren was the last out, and he looked at their surroundings, finding them similar to the place they'd entered—dark, plain, and cold.

They continued down the hallway, stopping every so often as the sound of shuffling feet and the clank of weapons reverberated off the walls. Barren kept a close eye on Larkin—she watched everything with unveiled fear. He started to reach out to her, but when her gaze met his, his hand faltered.

"They won't harm you," he said.

"You can't promise that."

Maybe not, but he'd like to think he could.

They continued down the hall. Barren found himself wondering exactly how Em knew her way around here...and how did she know to look for Devon? Had she been watching him? And if so, why?

Em paused at the end of a hall and peered around the corner. She motioned for everyone to stay where they were and disappeared. The three heard a faint crack and shuffling. There was a click, and more snapping and shuffling. Barren assumed that was the sound of necks breaking. When Em returned, she motioned for them to follow. As he suspected, there was no one guarding the cells and the door stood wide-open. Barren looked around in the shadows, trying to guess where she might have hidden the bodies, but he saw no evidence of where she'd disposed of them. He swallowed thickly.

She motioned for them to hurry inside the cells. Once there, she closed the door behind them. Like the rest of the tower, this place was dimly lit by torchlight. From here, Barren could see several halls twist before him. This place was hot, and when he breathed the air he felt as if it were full of toxins.

"These are the cells," said Em, she peered around, sword aloft. "Devon may be in here somewhere. The cells are like mazes, so be sure you are aware of your surroundings, and kill any guard you encounter. Let's split up into pairs."

Em charged forward into the labyrinth without another word, and Leaf followed her. Barren took a step forward, taking one of the torches from the wall. He hesitated, turning to Larkin. "Are you coming?"

"I'll be fine here."

Her arms were crossed over her chest, and she leaned against the wall, as if she willed the shadows to consume her. He knew she was exhausted and shaken. He hated that he wanted to help her so much.

"What's wrong?"

She looked at him and shook her head slowly. "I don't want to be here. I was wrong to come. *You* were wrong to come."

Barren swallowed, his teeth set tight. "Don't sound like Leaf. You know I had to do this. And *no one* told you it was a good idea to come here."

Larkin pressed her lips together, and her eyes got brighter, but she didn't say anything. Barren turned from her and made his way into an adjoining hallway. Several passages branched off to his left. Each one was lined with barred cells. Some were lit by torchlight, and others were left in shadow. As he managed his way down this hall, he moved slowly, listening carefully for any signs of life. What he found so frightening was that there were none: he heard no breaths, no cries—*nothing*. If anyone was here, they were all dead.

That thought didn't sit well with Barren, not that much in Estrellas did.

He was halfway down the hall when an odor accosted his nose and he gagged.

"Oh, God," he grabbed a handful of his cloak and put it to his face. "What is this place?"

He moved farther down the hallway, and the passages to his right were all darkened. The farther he went, the stronger the smell became. Bile rose in this throat, and his eyes watered. He knew what it was—it was the smell of death, but he moved toward it. What if it was Devon? How would he know? He only had a description from Alex, and by the looks of things, men who entered Estrellas didn't come out resembling who they once were.

He came to the last row and pushed his light into the shadow. The first cell had three bodies in it. Barren could only assume they were dead. They hung by their hands, suspended by chains. Their heads rested against their chests, and blood colored their faces. A lump rose in his throat, and he moved on to the next, but he did not approach it with the torch—the odor came from here. All he could see was a hand twisted around the base of the bars holding the corpse inside. He could no longer hold the bile down. Tossing the torch aside, Barren hurried away, vomiting in the hall. The acid burned his throat and nose, and the smell of death seemed to cling to him, making everything worse. He would never forget this nightmare.

He rose with his sword, wiping his mouth. Suddenly, panic filled him: they had to get out of here. Devon might be their only link to the bloodstone, but surely their sanity, surely their lives were far more important than that stone. Larkin was right. Leaf was right.

Barren made his way back to where he had left Larkin, but the passage was empty.

"Damn it!" He ran his fingers through his hair, pulling at the strands. He moved down the hallway in the direction Leaf and Em had gone. "Larkin, where are you?" he whispered hurriedly.

Barren rounded the corner, and there he found Larkin—her hands were tied behind her back, and she was on her knees. Behind her stood her father, Lord Christopher Lee.

"Barren Reed. Nice to finally meet you."

Pain spread through the back of Barren's head, and all went dark.

***

Barren was only half-conscious, but he knew something was wrong. As he opened his eyes, the first thing he noticed was the pain in his wrists. The feeling was intense, and he realized it was what had awakened him from his sleep. He hung suspended by iron chains, and now the metal was biting into his skin. As if that wasn't bad enough, the back of his head began to pulse violently. Barren struggled for a moment, but as his vision cleared, he stopped, realizing that Larkin was lying on the ground before him, motionless.

"Larkin! Larkin!" Barren thrashed in his chains, causing the metal to bite into his wrists, but he didn't notice, because Larkin still wasn't moving.

His desperate cries were met with laughter.

"She isn't going to answer you...not yet, at least," William's voice came from the darkness.

"What did you do?" Barren demanded. William came into view; his dark eyes were full of hatred. He hadn't changed much since Barren saw him last, but it was evident he hadn't been inland in a while. William's features were haggard and whiskers covered a portion of his chin. He had exchanged his noble suits for clothes more fitting of a sailor—a white shirt, brown pants and black boots. In his hand he held a long black whip. He didn't seem to be bothered by the wound Larkin had left him with back in Conn.

"She tried to fight for you. While it was noble, it was foolish," said William, his tone mocking Barren. "And she fell. Not to worry, she is still alive."

William unleashed the long whip. Its tail landed on the floor and Barren cringed. The pirate had been stabbed, cut and shot, but he had never been whipped, and he dreaded the feeling.

"Hold now," Christopher Lee said as he entered the cell. He approached the still form of his daughter. Refusing to favor pirates, he opted to wear a blue suit, decorated with gold buttons and tailored cords. In his hand he held a metal bucket. "I have to see this for myself."

Taking the bucket, he aimed the contents at Larkin. Water washed over her and she woke, coughing and breathing as if she had been drowning. Christopher was beside her instantly, and he held her face between his hands, forcing her to look at Barren.

"Father," for a moment, she was confused. Then, she realized what was happening, and she became more frantic. "Father, no!"

Christopher's eyes were dark and thoughtless. William cracked his whip and the sound made Barren flinch. He gritted his teeth together in preparation for the blow. But nothing could have prepared him for the sting of the leather against his flesh. He could feel his skin split. Warm blood seeped from his burning flesh, running in rivers down his chest. The sound he made was one he had never heard escape his lips.

"No!" Larkin tried to yell, but her voice was raspy and weak. Tears slid down her face, unchecked and forgotten as the whip sounded again. Barren struggled in the grasp of the iron.

"Stop!" Larkin was desperate, she tried to pry her father's hands from her face, but the harder she tried, the tighter he held. Every time Larkin begged, the violence of William's lash grew, as if to match her grief.

"The more you beg for him, the more he will hurt!" yelled William, whirling around to face her. The whip dripped with Barren's blood, unforgiving and morbid. Christopher let go of his daughter. Larkin moved into the corner, away from her father.

"Leave her alone!" Barren growled through his pain.

"What are you going to do?" mocked William. "Kill him?"

"You betrayed me!" Lee's voice resonated through the cell.

"You...you ran off with this pirate, chose him over your fiancé and now I find you begging for his life. What do you take me for?"

"You're a monster!" she said through her teeth. "You went along with the lie of my death....all so *he* could be king!" She jabbed a finger in William's direction. "What kind of father are you?"

"If a daughter's manners are the judge, a very bad one," replied Christopher evenly.

"Manners?" Larkin piqued. "You used me! *Used* me! And I am to blame for my anger?"

"I did not *use* you for anything. This is how the world works: it is not your place to choose your husband," said Lee evenly.

"I won't marry him. I will not be his wife or his queen!"

In retaliation for those words, William's whip bit into Barren's skin over and over again. The louder Larkin begged for his freedom, the harder William seemed to swing his whip. Barren had no energy left to fight the pain, or even react to it.

"Stop!" Lee ordered. "Stop!"

William stumbled back, and threw his whip in the corner, disgusted by it. Barren wanted to be dead. He would have relished in that numbness. Instead, his body was alive with shock.

Someone unlocked his shackles one-by-one and he fell to the hard, cobble floor.

"Barren!"

He opened his eyes to see Christopher holding Larkin back. He had seen Larkin afraid, but this fear was deeper, and it was for him. To ease her panic a little, he tried to raise himself up on his hands and knees, but his limbs shook so violently, he collapsed. Lying there, he heard William and Christopher speak.

"We are wasting time here, leave him to die," said Lee. William didn't say anything. He only glared at the old man. "We must search for Devon Kennings. We've been delayed far too long. Take the girl with you." He sounded disgusted as he pushed her forward. "We will head to Cape Oceaniana after this."

William and Larkin left, and Lee crouched down beside Barren. He could see every line of the old man's face. He placed something around Barren's neck—something red. As he looped the ends around, Barren realized it was Larkin's scarf. Then the fabric tightened around his neck. The pressure increased, and Barren clawed at Lee's hands, but it was of no use—for someone so old, he was strong and full of hate.

"You think you can kidnap my daughter and seduce her? Break her?" The words were cold and each syllable lingered like frost. Lee let go of the scarf, and Barren gasped for breath, his body heaved. Lee placed his knee on Barren's chest before he could recover, and produced a needle. Barren could tell something about it was strange—it was black and thick, tapered at the end. He reached for Barren's hand and touched the needle to his finger.

"The effects will be slow, but once they take hold, they will never let go."

Barren watched as Christopher straightened and moved out of his line of vision. Barren felt as though Lee's knee was on his chest again—the pressure was heavy and uncomfortable. Then, his heart rate began to slow, though the beats were like explosions, painfully pumping the poison through his chest.

"Leaf!" He pushed himself up and began to crawl toward the door, but an acidic taste in his mouth caused him to heave. His limbs were weak, and numbing quickly. He collapsed by the doorway. His last effort was a scream—it was deep, gurgling, and frightening for those who heard it. It was the sound of the pain of defeat...of fear.

"Don't let them take her!"

"Barren!" The pirate could no longer see, but he knew Leaf's voice.

"Barren, give me some sign you are alive," the Elf's hand was on his face, checking his forehead for fever. Automatically, the Elf picked up his hand and examined the needle-sized wound. "This is not good."

Barren wanted to say something, but he could feel the words being sucked out of him, muddled together in a mind riddled with poison. There was nothing else for him to do but sleep.

Chapter Nineteen
HEMLOCK

Barren was on a beach he didn't recognize. The sand beneath his feet was pale and like velvet. He had never felt such soft sand. He glanced around: before him were trees. They were thick and dark but above them rose tall mountains, their peaks shrouded in clouds. It was beautiful but foreboding. Barren shivered. He turned and his heart dropped into his stomach. Before him in the ocean were several ships, all broken and beaten. They littered the coastline, as if an invisible line destroyed all things daring to come its way. There was one that had made it, and it stood still next to the only port. It was a massive ship with huge white sails and it was the only thing Barren recognized—his father's ship.

A figure walked slowly off the boarding plank and onto the dock. He was lordly, but dressed as a pirate. His jacket was brown, a white shirt beneath. He wore brown pants and black boots. A leather hat covered his head, but hair hung at his shoulders, bleached by the sun, and his skin was bronzed, too. It was Barren's father, and all he could do was run to him.

"Father!"

Jess laughed when he saw Barren, a wide smile on his face. He stooped to one knee, holding out his arms to embrace him. Barren hurried to his father, hugging him around the neck.

"Father!" behind him a younger William ran toward them— about the age of thirteen. He embraced his brother and his father, and Jess laughed deeply.

"I see my boys are growing." His eyes shone with life Barren didn't remember. "Come." Jess stood, the hands of his sons in each of his.

"Father, you must fight me," said William. "I will show you I have improved. I will beat you."

"Oh? And who has been giving you lessons?"

"I have been teaching myself in your absence. I fight with mother."

Barren's heart began to race when William spoke of their mother. Did he remember her?

"Well then," said Jess as they reached the shore. "Let's fight."

Jess unsheathed his sword and William did the same. Will was shorter than Jess, but only by a few inches, and he had been practicing daily, sometimes for hours straight. Barren was too young to understand Will's wish to fight better, or his determination to prove to their father he could fight just as well as him, but he knew it had started at a young age. Now Jess and William stood opposite one another, swords poised, ready to fight. William charged at Jess, but all he did was move aside and hit the top of William's sword. The pirate laughed as William stumbled forward.

"You're too passionate a fighter," said Jess and William whirled around. The young man growled and charged after his father again. This time his sword met Jess's and the clash of metal was fierce and powerful.

"You act as if I am your enemy."

"I will be fighting enemies, won't I?" countered Will quickly, trying to deflect Jess's easy movements.

Jess sighed and hit Will's blade with all his strength. The blade flew from the young boy's hands and into the sand, too far for him to reach. He was left to stare into his father's eyes. "You fight with hatred," said the pirate. "Why?"

"I fight to win!"

"But you didn't win," said Jess. "You fight without a goal, only anger." Jess stuck his sword in the ground. "When you can fight with a goal, I will fight you again."

Barren and William watched the image of their father head to the dark forest before them.

"I will never be good enough," said William, staring at the sand.

Barren looked up at his brother.

"Father loves you...you should listen to him."

William turned his gaze on Barren. It was filled with anger and disappointment. "Father will never be proud of me because I am not like him. You are like him, Barren. You will always be his advocate, and he yours."

A crease formed between Barren's brows. "I don't understand."

"You will one day...we are not alike, you and I."

"We're brothers."

"Yes," William nodded. "But we will never be the same."

Suddenly, their surroundings changed, and the image before Barren was that of Conn. Barren hid behind a coil of rope and peered out at the scene of his brother sneaking up on Jess. It was the same fear that paralyzed him before—he was shocked, and wanted to cry out, but he couldn't speak. He stared, wide-eyed, watching his father's death again—Jess, jerking in pain, falling to the ground and William running from his father's dead body— and he was reminded of William's words.

We will never be the same...and they weren't.

***

Barren opened his eyes. Pure, white light flooded his room. The covers, like silk against his skin, were pale green; the walls were made of earthy-stone and gleamed with gold as the sunlight washed over them. He was not on a ship.

He sat up rigidly, his body stiff. The memory of what had happened flooded his mind: He had made a mistake. It was a mistake to enter Estrellas, and while it might not be his fault that

Larkin was taken, guilt pierced him like a knife. His chest tightened, and unchecked shivers ran down his arms when he recalled her cries as she begged William and her father to leave him alone. He wasn't sure what punishment she would face for her betrayal, but they would attempt to break her of her favoritism.

Barren had to save her. This time, it wasn't about the code.

He pushed his legs out from under the covers and onto the cool floor. His body felt rigid and little shocks of pain shot through him. As he looked up, he caught his reflection in a mirror that ran from floor to ceiling—it was one of several along the walls, breaking apart the windows. It was the first time he had seen himself since arriving in Estrellas. He was bandaged up—arms, chest, abdomen—and some of the white stripes were stained with blood. His face was pale and haggard, his eye still bruised slightly. He never remembered looking so rough, even after some of his worst fights.

As he was about to stand, he noticed only two things rested on his side table—a wooden cup filled with a brown liquid that still steamed vigorously, and a crimson scarf...Larkin's scarf. It had come to represent many things for him. Carefully, Barren gathered the piece of fabric into his hands. It was soft to the touch, vibrant, and...bloody. Barren cringed and crushed the fabric between his hands. Horrific flashes of that black whip curling around his body jolted him. He could hear Larkin's screams echoing in his ears. He had never been as helpless as that night.

As Barren stood, he heard a clear voice behind him.

"Drink," it said. He turned and saw Cove sitting in a chair in the corner. He was dressed all in black; a very strange contrast to the brightness of the room, though it seemed to make his eyes all the more vibrant.

Barren reached for the cup slowly. The wood was warm against his skin, and as he placed the drink to his lips, he was overwhelmed with the scent of mint and sandalwood. He drank, and the liquid burned, but only for a moment. Suddenly, all the stiffness that paralyzed his joints was gone.

"Where are we?" he asked, putting the cup down. He kept the crimson scarf in his hands, running it through his fingers.

"In Aurum," replied the Ambassador. "Leaf thought it was best since you were near death when we found you."

"Found me?"

"Yes, Leaf found you...in the cells of the tower." Barren struggled to remember. Everything after Lee's little trick with the needle was a blur. "Leaf said only the Elves could heal you then. He didn't have enough supplies to deal with your wounds or that poison."

"Where is he now?"

"With his father," said Cove. "He has been for some time. I am not sure we are welcome here, but because you were near death, Lord Alder didn't refuse."

Silence settled like a cold breeze in the room. Barren would never have expected to be welcome here in Aurum, mostly because of his tainted blood. Now that he knew more about his mother, however, he imagined Lord Alder saw his stay as a threat. The Elfin Lord had worked hard to banish any memory of the Lyrics, and Barren's presence threatened to unearth those memories.

The pirate swallowed hard and moved away from the bed toward a wall of arched, glassless windows. He walked slowly. Though his legs didn't cause him pain now that he had drunk the Elvish medicine, they still didn't want to move properly.

Barren studied the courtyard outside his window. It was beautiful and bright, like his room. Several willow trees kept it secluded and personal. A statue of pure white stone stood at the center of the courtyard in the shape of a beautiful woman. She was clad in robes that seemed to flutter around her, and long white hair rose in tangled disarray like a halo. Graceful hands covered her heart...and indeed, it did seem like she was sad, for her eyes were downcast, and her mouth pulled into a solemn frown.

"They tortured you." Cove stated and Barren cringed visibly. He didn't want to talk about what they did to him. That wasn't important.

"She begged for my life, Cove." Barren shook his head; he glanced briefly at the Ambassador, and then stared into the bright courtyard again. "I must find her," he twisted the scarf around his hands. "They will hurt her."

"That's what they want you to think," said Cove. "Christopher would never hurt Larkin."

"I can't believe that," said Barren. "He is a cruel man."

"Barren." Cove stood, his black cloak unfolded behind him, and he was frightening, though Barren knew he was only desperate for him to listen and understand. "You showed Reed and Lee that you had a weakness. You know not to underestimate those two—and here you are, doing exactly that! They know they can lure you wherever they go if they have Larkin."

Cove was quiet for a moment. He ran his fingers through his hair and let out a low breath.

"What I'm trying to tell you is that you're forgetting she was your prisoner. She's home now, and we're after the bloodstone, nothing more, nothing less. "

"I didn't ask you to come!"

His shouting gave way to tension and silence. All of Barren's strength seemed to be in the words he had spoken, and suddenly he felt weak: his shoulders fell, and a heaviness settled in his chest. Maybe part of it was the realization that he would never be able to continue forward against his brother or Christopher Lee without help. Cove also had a point—Larkin wasn't his to rescue. Technically, she was home.

"Do you even know where she is?" Cove's voice was low when he spoke, almost as if he were afraid to ask, knowing Barren would probably have an answer.

"They were meeting someone…at Cape Oceaniana, possibly handing Larkin over so she would not ruin their plans. It's probably too late now. I don't even know how long I've been out."

"Two days," said Cove, he paused for a moment.

"Do they know Leaf rescued me from the cells?" Barren asked.

"No."

"So they think I am dead."

"It is safe to assume that, I think," said Cove. "But they know the rest of us aren't, and we have Devon. Without him, they have hit a dead end. There isn't much they can do beyond Cape Oceaniana."

"Devon?" Barren said quietly, his brows came together. "Devon and....and Em? Are they both here?"

Cove nodded.

After meeting Em in the towers of Estrellas, Barren hadn't been convinced she or Devon would help them. There was something about the bloodstone neither one wanted to revisit, and as much as Barren hated to dig up bad memories, he needed them. Devon and Em were their only starting points for locating the bloodstone, and if they couldn't give him answers, no one else could. Alex had said everyone else was dead.

"Where is he? Where's Devon?"

"I will take you to him."

***

Barren was used to feeling exposed to nature—on the deck of the ship, there was little to shield him from the sun or the sea, but as he walked down the open corridors of the palace of Aurum, he wanted to hide. He had never been to the Elfin isle, mostly because he, being half-Elf, would not be welcome—and the way he was being watched now was only a testament to that truth. He couldn't see them, but he knew Elves hid in the forest beyond, scrutinizing his every move.

Barren tried to focus on his surroundings. The walls of the palace were smooth, as if the entire place had been carved from one massive stone. Earthy tones ran through the walls—grays, browns, greens, and golds. The walls were lined with columns, which reached high toward the ceiling and arched together like naked trees, bowing to each other. And the windows through which he was being watched were large and invited the natural world outside to wander within. Ivy vines wrapped around columns, and clung to the ceiling's branches.

As the corridor ended, a great hall opened up. Golden light poured in from an opening in the ceiling, highlighting a rectangular pond filled with emerald water and white lilies. The water ran from the pool down to a smaller stream, which exited into a reservoir outside. Barren walked up to the windows, pulling back sheer curtains. He found that the emerald pond extended far into a garden, white lilies gleamed brightly in the light, and wild orange and red flowers burst open, filling all the green with color. It was beautiful.

He turned and beheld the rest of the space—like the arches in the hallway, tall columns rose up and meshed with the ceiling like branches of trees in the middle of winter. The sun streaming in through the ceiling caught pieces of the gold embedded within the walls, so everything seemed to shimmer. A wide staircase was nestled in the far corner and led to another wide hallway, full of open windows, greenery, and light. It was at this point Barren realized that Cove was watching him, patiently.

The pirate cleared his throat. "This place is magnificent."

"Yes," he agreed, hands behind his back. "The Elves love nature. The closer they are to it, the better they feel."

Suddenly, tension flooded the room. Barren's eyes returned to the stairs where he saw figures approach. One Barren recognized as Leaf, only he had exchanged his usual dirty gear for more...formal attire. He wore a gray tunic and black leggings. Around his neck, a silver clasp held a flowing black cloak. His straight blond hair looked no different, except that a silver circlet was now tangled within his locks. He looked lordly, like a king.

Beside him was an Elf of equal height. His features were more severe—eyes of ocean blue and a strong, clenched jaw made him seem unpleasant. He was dressed in layers of blue fabric, tailored with fine threads. Long silver-white hair draped his shoulders, and his pointed ears stuck out—the left bearing a strange silver cap. Unlike Leaf's simple circlet, this man bore a heavy diamond-encrusted crown. Barren knew him as Leaf's father, the King of Aurum—Lord Alder.

"Nice of you to finally to join us," said Leaf with a smirk. Barren felt a little relief—at least he hadn't lost his humor. Then Leaf glanced at the Elf beside him. "This is my father, Lord Alder."

While Cove moved into a bow, Barren found that he couldn't—his body merely refused, stiffened from its injuries. Instead he nodded to the king and hoped he wouldn't take offense. By the look on his face, it seemed he didn't care.

"It is good to see you returned to health so soon," said the king. "I trust you will be able to travel soon, though I hate to see my son go."

There it was, and without subtlety. Lord Alder did not want Barren here. It wasn't any surprise, really. Barren did have full intentions of making the lord talk about the Lyrics. No matter how much he wanted them to go away, he couldn't erase the fact that they had once survived. But Barren had a feeling that the root of Lord Alder's dislike was much simpler—Barren was half-Elf: a tainted version of their pure race.

"I apologize for the intrusion," said Barren. "If I had any say in the matter, we would not have disturbed you."

"You were in no state to make decisions," said Lord Alder. "Indeed, you were very close to death when you arrived."

"You can thank Christopher Lee for that—whatever he did to me, well, it felt like death."

"You were poisoned by a hemlock needle," said Leaf. "One prick of the finger and you're pretty much dead. Luckily, you had a skilled healer aboard your ship." The Elf gave a smug smile, though Barren vaguely remembered that Leaf had been frantic when he found him. His fear led to what Barren would have called a rash decision had he not been so close to death. "But I could not keep you from dying. There was only one place I could go where I knew you could be healed."

"Who did it? Who healed me?"

"I did." Lord Alder's voice seemed to resonate all around them. Barren stood, both shocked and grateful.

"And what is a hemlock needle? How did something so small destroy me in an instant?"

"It is a hollow needle laced with hemlock. By itself, it causes little damage, but when strengthened with magic, it can kill."

"And how did Christopher Lee come into possession of such a thing?"

The king shrugged. "I know not the matters of Lord Christopher Lee. At the moment, you should focus on yourself. As you will feel the sting of the poison long after you have awakened from the sleep."

"What do you mean?"

Lord Alder, however, had stopped speaking, and instead, turned his head toward Leaf, leaving his son to explain. Leaf hesitated and then cleared his throat.

"You will be attacked by random bouts of paralysis without warning," he said. "It is an effect of the poison accosting your body."

Barren took a deep breath. So this was what Lee meant when he said the effects would never let go. Was he supposed to feel defeated? Or useless? He looked down at his hands and squeezed them into fists, his joints flexed beneath the skin. Then he let go. Everything worked fine now.

"Let it come when it will," he said. "I will face it then."

Chapter Twenty
STRANGER

The trio watched as Lord Alder departed. Barren kept his eyes on him longer—he felt heat rise to his face and his eyes hurt from staring too hard. He knew the Elfin king could feel Barren watching him—his frame was too tense as he moved back up the steps. Leaf turned to the others, clapping his hands together.

"Well, that was interesting."

"Your father does not trust me," said Barren. "Did you expect it to go differently?"

"Actually, I expected him to ask you to leave immediately," said Leaf. "I guess I underestimated how glad he was at my return."

"I guess that means you already spoke with him about the bloodstone?"

Leaf nodded his head. "He does not deny anything, but says that everything is simple: the Lyrics lived and they died, and the bloodstone is safe where it is."

"Does he want William to possess the stone? Surely he knows that my brother will not extend the same kindness that Eadred or even Cathmor showed him."

"You are lucky he is letting us stay here," Leaf reminded Barren curtly. "It's dangerous to harbor us. William and Christopher are not held to the same treaty as the king. They can harm my people."

Barren quieted at that. He knew that was all-too-true. He felt guilty for bringing danger to these people, though he didn't understand Lord Alder's unwillingness to help...unless he did not trust Barren with the stone. Perhaps he felt that he would become corrupt in the face of such power, especially since he wished to avenge his father.

"This is not the end," Cove reminded him. "Devon is here, and he can hopefully give us some insight into the whereabouts of the stone."

"Cove is right. We did not journey into the tower or Estrellas for nothing," said Leaf.

No, they hadn't, and Barren needed to keep reminding himself of that because the horrors he and Larkin had experienced there were far too great to be for naught.

They headed down a set of wide steps at the back of the great hall, and then continued down another open corridor. Barren noticed parts of the palace were tangled within the forest beyond. Walls of earthy stone peeked out from behind green ivy, and because of this, it was hard to tell exactly how big this place was. His eyes returned to Leaf and Cove who moved before him side-by-side. He wondered how much his crew discussed while he was out. The thought made him a little angry, but they couldn't make decisions without him. He was the captain.

The corridor ended at a courtyard. It was a round space, filled with thick green grass. At its center, a fountain rested, and water rose up from a spout and trickled down tiered pools until it reached a basin filled with white lilies. Willow trees were arranged in four corners of the yard. Near the fountain, a stone terrace extended. There, he saw Alex, who was standing, leaning heavily upon his cane as he conversed with three people seated on a bench before him. He recognized Em, though she looked different from the women he'd met in the tower. Her hair was loose from its braid, and fell down her back. She was dressed in a simple silver gown. Beside her was an older man with stringy salt-and-pepper hair and a short beard to match. His forehead had been bandaged, and Barren noticed that scratches and bruised marred his aging skin, though from this distance, he could not tell if they were old or new. He was dressed in a black tunic, embellished with gold designs. This, he assumed, must be Devon Kennings.

Alex moved back slightly, exposing the last person to Barren fully. She sat on Em's right. The first thing he noticed about her was her hair—it was a lively, fiery red. Then he noticed her green eyes—they seemed to brighten each time she blinked. Her head snapped toward him, and when she noticed Barren, her smile faded. There was something about her that was unlike the other Elves he knew—it was in her gaze. It was almost supernatural and infinite.

When the Elf with red hair ceased talking, the others looked his way. He suddenly felt panicked. They rose from where they sat, and Barren took that as a sign that he should move toward them. He took the steps from the corridor into the courtyard and approached, though he couldn't help feeling he wasn't particularly welcome, judging by the way the red-haired Elf glared at him.

"Barren! Good to see you awake," Alex was the first to speak. The old man moved toward him to clap him on the back. Barren couldn't help feeling guilty—Alex and Mary were the closest things to parents he'd had since his father died. He imagined it wasn't easy for Alex to see him hurt.

"I'm glad I don't hafta give Mary any grim news."

Barren laughed a little. "Me too. She'd never let you out of the house again."

Alex laughed, too, then he gestured to the old man beside Em. "Barren, I'd like you to meet Devon Kennings."

Before Barren could acknowledge him, the red-haired Elf tore away from the group and hurried out of the courtyard. Em looked apologetic. "Excuse me," she said as she hurried after the Elf. Barren watched them retreat, wondering why his presence caused her to react in such a manner.

"Barren Reed," he heard his name slip from an unfamiliar mouth, and his gaze turned to storm-like eyes. Devon Kennings looked tired. Close up, it was easy to tell that his life had been a hard one—from a long scar on the side of his face, to the lines around his eyes and mouth. "Never thought I'd see you again."

Again? Barren wasn't sure he'd ever met this man.

"I don't remember you," was all Barren could say.

Devon didn't seem surprised by that. "You wouldn't remember me. I was not around much. Let's walk," he said, raising his head a little. He eyed the sky as if he mistrusted it.

Barren hesitated for a moment, looking back at Leaf and Cove. They were watching him with curiosity from the shelter of the corridor. Barren couldn't figure out why he felt so awkward around Devon. He had no reason to fear what this man had to say, not if he wanted to figure out if his father was innocent, and not if he wanted to figure out where the bloodstone was.

The two passed before the Elfin palace, and Barren could gauge the size of the kingdom a little better. The main part of the palace was at least six stories—the highest bearing a balcony that Barren imagined overlooked the forest straight to the sea. The rest was a collection of various towers, bridged together by hallways with large open windows. Parts of the structure seemed to grow out of the surrounding forest—vines consumed whole towers, and moss covered the rooftops.

Barren and Devon set out upon one of the many paths twisting into the forest. Trees quickly consumed them. Here the leaves were turning golden-green as autumn descended upon the Orient. Barren watched the sunlight stream in through the canopy in thick rays. Somewhere in the distance, he could hear a river bubbling. It was peaceful out here and beautiful, though Barren knew there was more to this wild wood than meets the eye. It was full of danger—not just because of the Elves who occupied it, but because the plants were just as deceiving. Some were poisonous and some were hallucinogens. It was likely that unwelcome guests wouldn't make it to the palace walls if they challenged the forest.

Barren swallowed hard at that thought and turned to face Devon. The old man had been starting at him, waiting for questions.

"Do you know who took you from your home in Conn?" Barren asked.

"Tetherion's soldiers," said Devon.

"That's impossible. Tetherion knew we were going to Conn to meet you."

"One thing I am most certain about was who took me from my home," and the tone of Devon's voice told Barren not to second-guess the pirate, at least not to his face. But Barren couldn't bring himself to believe that Tetherion had been responsible for Devon's arrest. It didn't make any sense.

"Well what did they do with you in Estrellas then?"

"Interrogated me," Devon said, then he sniffed. "Tortured me. Lot of good it did, though. I don't remember anythin' about the bloodstone, and even if I did, I wouldn't tell them. I don't trust

Tetherion as far as I can throw him."

Several things bothered Barren about what the old man just said. "What do you mean you don't remember anything about the bloodstone?"

The pirate shrugged, as if it were nothing. "I don't remember. Everything before your father's death is just a blur. It's all hazy. As if I was in a fog the first part of my life."

Well, that sounded all too familiar to Barren.

"You don't remember," Barren said quietly.

Devon's eyes narrowed upon him. "Is that what you want, too? The stone?"

Barren focused on Devon for a moment. "You must remember something. There's fear in your words."

"You're too young to say something like that."

"I've had a lot of experience with those who fear."

They stared at each other for a moment, and Barren realized he had to gain this man's trust if he was going to get anywhere with him, and that surprised him. If Devon Kennings had been a member of Jess Reed's crew, why would he mistrust his son?

"What do you want with the bloodstone?" Devon asked.

"I was asked to find it before my brother does."

"Asked by Tetherion?" Devon prodded. Barren noted his disregard for Tetherion's title, his hateful tone—the king must be Devon's hang-up.

"Yes. He asked me to find it and return it to him. He said he would keep it safe."

"Safe," Devon spat. "Let me tell you, boy, that stone is far better off stuck in whatever hole it was placed. It's not the stone you gotta worry about keeping safe, it's the Orient."

"Why do you say that?"

"Do not believe for a second that Tetherion wouldn't use that stone to keep himself invincible from threats. I don't need memories to know what dark magic can do. No matter the virtues of Tetherion—of which I am sure there are none—dark magic would corrupt him so fast he'd never know what hit him."

"Why are you so sure Tetherion has no virtue?"

"No man who would send an assassin to kill his brother is a good man."

Barren only heard that Cathmor had sent assassins, not that Tetherion was involved, too.

"I protected Jess," said Devon. "I protected him from Tetherion and Cathmor's threats. I don't care how often he interfered with their plans. There is no honor in that. It shows that Tetherion would do anything for power."

"So what is your suggestion? Leave it alone?" Barren asked, becoming more and more irritated. "Because my brother is after this stone, and if he does not die getting there, he will be the invincible one, and if you think Tetherion has no honor, my brother actually succeeded in killing my father."

"I know that well," Devon said. "I would not suggest leaving such a thing in existence. I would say destroy it."

"But it cannot be destroyed," Barren said desperately. "It is dark magic!"

"Anything made can be unmade," said Devon. "You just have

to know how to do it."

Barren's shoulders fell, and he felt defeated and tired. After all he'd gone through just to get to this man, he found that he was bitter and rather useless. He'd only succeeded in making him question Tetherion's motives—which made his head swim with more than dizziness.

"If you promise me that stone will be destroyed, I'll help you," Devon's voice was low, but it was sincere, and Barren could finally sense a little bit of sympathy.

"So you do remember?"

"Not exactly," the pirate shook his head. "But after the haze, there is a memory I possess—the strongest one I have of your father." Devon extended his arm. On his forearm, lines of black marked his skin.

It was a drawing, and from Barren's point-of-view, it looked like a tree, engulfing another tree. The bigger one branched into a 'V', and its limbs curled. Nestled at its center, the smaller tree was abstract—a line with curved limbs, and at random, three black dots that mimicked berries. "Your father marked me with this. He called it a map, but I know you won't likely read it easily. I believe it to be a map to Sysara and the other Lyrics. If you can figure out how to read it, I think you'll find the bloodstone."

"But you are not sure?"

"No, but it seems you have few options."

"You remember nothing before my father's death," Barren said, "and neither do I. What happened to our memories?"

"I am afraid your father is responsible for that," a voice came from behind them. Barren and Devon whirled around to face Em. She was pale. The blush of pink that had been upon her cheeks was gone, and there was a sadness to her eyes that carried an overwhelming amount of guilt and grief—very different from her stone-like composure in Estrellas.

"Your memories were taken from you—anything that involved the Lyrics, anything that involved the bloodstone. I was responsible for seeing it through. I gave a draught to Devon, Christopher Lee and to myself. Your father could not destroy the bloodstone, so he thought he would, instead, erase the memory of it. The only problem is that the fix was temporary, and the memories are coming back."

Barren took a moment to register what she'd said, realizing now why she'd shown such pity for him when he'd told her he wanted answers—because she was responsible for the absence of his memories—of everyone's memories.

"You gave it to Christopher Lee? Do you remember why?"

"In his younger years, he was a member of Jess's crew...his involvement with the bloodstone, though, I am unsure of."

That didn't sound right—hadn't Larkin said Christopher Lee fought Jess during the Ore Wars? As admiral of a ship?

"Right, you took the poison." Barren paused, running his fingers through his hair. All this loyalty to his father—it seemed suicidal.

"I am sorry Barren," Em said quietly.

"I know," he replied without looking at either of them. He was piecing information together. Jess gave Devon a map after his memory was already gone. There was a purpose for that, even if Barren didn't understand it at the moment. But what role had Christopher Lee played, and did he even remember it himself?

"Barren, though it may be hard for you to believe, nothing your father did was ever in vain."

At the moment, that *was* very hard to believe.

Chapter Twenty-One
BETRAYAL

Larkin opened her eyes. There were bars all around her, and an ugly yellow light flooded her body. She sat up slightly. Though there was a bench across from her, she woke up on the floor. Strange that all the time she'd been with Barren, she hadn't spent a single minute in the brig. Thunder boomed outside, and she could feel the floor sway as the Orient's anger became more and more apparent.

Her head throbbed with pain and tears immediately spilled down her face. When her father had found her in the cells of Estrellas, she'd been conflicted. After she'd killed Cas, she wanted to feel safe, but knowing that Barren was near made her afraid for his life—and she'd been right to fear. She closed her eyes tightly, trying to push the memories of his torture from her head. Why hadn't they just arrested him? Didn't it make more sense to take him into their custody? To return him to Maris? But they didn't. They'd beat him within an inch of his life and left him for dead, just like all those prisoners in Estrellas. She hoped he was alive. She hoped Leaf had found him and healed him.

Footsteps sounded somewhere in the darkness, and she lay down again, stifling her tears. She tired to remain still and act as if she were asleep. Her heart raced, not wanting to face whoever was coming. The thud of boots crossed the floor toward her, and she heard the groan of her cell door as it opened and closed. Then there was nothing. The silence strained, and Larkin could feel the tension grow thick from the other body occupying her space.

"I know you are awake."

William's voice was different. He had always been awkward and distant, but now he sounded tired and his voice was dead. Larkin opened her eyes and looked up at him. He stood at her head, studying her face. When he saw she had acknowledged him, he headed for the bench. Larkin moved away from him quickly, putting as much distance between them as possible. She shivered under his stare, and suddenly her pain was replaced by fear.

"Where are we?"

"We are on a ship heading for Cape Oceaniana," replied

William. "It is your father's hope that Barren will follow us there."

"He is alive?" The amount of hope in her voice made William's brows knit together and fury ignite his eyes.

"That is what the twins tell me."

"The twins?" Larkin gazed at William in disbelief, trying to find any indication that he was lying.

"What? You mean you didn't know? Oh, they have provided some very beneficial information. Through them, we've been able to track Barren for quite some time, and it proved even more valuable after the king attempted to outsmart my attempts to locate the bloodstone."

Larkin was quiet while William spoke. How could the twins be traitors? They were Barren's cousins. They had joined his crew willingly, and sailed with him for the past few months. Why would they go through the trouble....unless the whole purpose was to trap Barren? Now that she thought about it, the twins were always quiet and reserved. They both sort of just faded into the background. They were also the ones who were always sent as lookouts, right before attacks like the one on the Cliffs. Now the twins were sailing with Barren, and he was ignorant of his cousins' betrayal. She needed to warn him—but how? By the time Barren found her at Cape Oceaniana, it would be too late. And what did this mean for Tetherion? Was he ignorant, too?

"You were with my brother a very short while to be so dedicated to him."

"I can sympathize with his situation," said Larkin. "Though I do not always agree with his decisions."

"So you haven't forgotten his crimes against Maris? Because Barren is a pirate and he deserves death for his deeds." He spoke steadily, and Larkin could feel a lump rise in her throat.

"You are a murderer, but no one calls for your death."

She watched, expecting William's face to change—for his jaw to tighten, his eyes to grow darker, narrower...but he gave no hint of anger, and for some reason, that was even more frightening.

"What happened to you two?" she asked, her voice low—a whisper in the silence of the brig.

William looked away from her, his face turned into the shadow. She couldn't be sure, but she thought he was hiding something—his faltering composure, maybe? She watched the rest of his body, searching for signs of his mood, but he was a master at self-possession.

"There is no affection between us," said William at last. "It ended the day I killed our father. He was the link we shared, the only source of brotherly love. I have no wish to recall what once was."

"What about your mother?"

William's brows rose, but he didn't look at Larkin. His eyes became distant, endless pools of black. "She is like a distant dream," he whispered. "She was beauty, she was power. I thought she would live forever."

"So you remember her?"

"I remember the way I felt when Jess told me she was dead. Barren did not understand. He was...unaffected. Though, why shouldn't he be? He had everything—Jess's affection...Jess's attention. He never did any wrong," he paused. "You see...Barren...Barren only understood my heartache once he lost his father."

"What are you saying?"

"Jess killed *my* mother," said William, his lips barely moved. "You should understand. You of all people—he killed your mother, too!"

Larkin was very quiet as the impact of what William said hit her. "What?"

"I know you've wondered where you came from—who she was. She was a Lyric, just like my mother. She died trying to destroy the bloodstone."

Larkin felt both relieved and empty at the same time. Suddenly her mother had an identity; she was like Barren's mother, she was a sorceress, a powerful but dead being—and Jess Reed had taken her. Larkin cringed at the last thought: it didn't *sound* right and it didn't *feel* right.

"How do you know this?"

"Your father, why else do you think he and Jess became enemies?"

Larkin never knew they had been friends. "What do you mean, *became*?"

"Your father and Jess were once friends, but after Kenna's death, Lee swore he would have his revenge."

"But...that doesn't make any sense, they could not have been friends...."

"One thing has never changed about your father—he has always been a traitor."

Larkin kept her lips pressed tight, but she wondered why Tetherion had not spoken of this before—surely he had known that her father was once on Jess's side.

"Now you have been told the truth, and must understand my wish to kill Barren."

"I do not."

"What?"

"I do not understand your wish to kill Barren." Larkin's eyes were dark with disdain for William's assumptions. "And what you have given me is little evidence in support of your crime."

"What evidence do I need other than your mother's death?" spat William.

"That is not Barren's crime," Larkin glared at William, and her breath came in deliberate drafts.

"You have been brainwashed," William attempted to shake off her comments.

"No!" Larkin's voice was severe. "I have not been brainwashed! I have been free to think, to come to my own conclusions about others! And I do not believe for a second that Barren Reed is deserving of death."

William's jaw was clenched so tightly, Larkin wondered if he was going to speak. "You forget one thing, Larkin Lee—you still have to marry me."

"I will not," her voice rang with promise and silence followed as William processed what she said. He was used to her over speaking, but not about their marriage—it had been arranged by her father, and she never defied him.

"What did you say?"

"I will not marry you," Larkin's voice rose, defiant and strong.

"I see my brother has had more of an effect on you than I thought."

"He has done nothing to sway my opinion of you," Larkin's voice stung the air. "I have always thought unfavorably of you, and even your brother but—"

"But what? What has he done that I have not?"

"He's sorry," she said desperately. Somehow, she knew William would not understand. "I believe his pain, and while I do not agree with his decisions, there is something about him worth holding on to. Worth giving a chance to."

"So you would see to it that a man who did nothing but wreak havoc on the coast of your home, be given more of your favor than me?"

"I gave you a chance, and I was willing to marry you despite the fact that I would never love you, but what I hated about you then, isn't what I hate about you now. I shudder to think what I would have faced had I not been kidnapped!"

"And what, may I ask, makes you think you won't be my wife now that I have you back?"

Larkin glared at William as he moved out of the cell and into the shadow.

"If it is your wish to live in fear of your life, then take me as your bride. It's your gamble."

"I would not be so eager," said William, closing the rusted door to her cell. "But I know whose heart yours has turned to, and before I see you with my brother, I would see you dead."

She listened as William's footsteps thudded over the wood and a door shut somewhere in the distance. She shivered; she felt cold and exhausted, both mentally and physically. She never expected to learn about her mother in such a manner. In fact, she had never expected to learn about her mother at all. Why had her father felt it was necessary to keep such a secret? And why had Tetherion avoided this piece of information? He didn't seem to be on William and Lee's side, but things weren't adding up on Barren's either.

Outside, Larkin heard water and wind crashing against the hull. The massive ship groaned beneath the fury of the Orient. From where she was, she could hear cries erupting on deck; chaos ensued above. Part of her felt that this was revenge, revenge for the pain and the abuse William and Christopher had inflicted— she knew the Orient worked in that way. Or maybe she was angry that they were trespassing on her waters. Barren had said if the Orient did not want them to pass, they would all die.

As Larkin sat there, she pulled her knees to her chest and wrapped her arms around her legs, examining the bruises and the long red marks across her skin—evidence of her fight with Cas. Her heart pulled tight and she withheld the waves of tears threatening her eyes. She did not want to die here, not with William and not with her father.

Another wave crashed into the hull and she fell to the wooden floor, ignoring the pain accosting her. She lay very still, closing her eyes as tears spilled down her flushed cheeks. In this moment, she could only think of one person. One person who had saved her life over and over again, and she wished he were here now.

Chapter Twenty-Two
THE LYRIC

Barren felt silly as he looked in the mirror. The Elves had brought him clothes to change into and now he wore brown leggings and a green tunic. He much preferred his clothes, though they were less than acceptable—caked with blood and mud from Estrellas. They would probably need to be burned.

A knock sounded at the door, and Leaf entered his room, presenting a mug filled with steaming tea.

"Drink this before you head out tonight," he said. "Your limbs won't get sore from standing."

Barren took the drink and put it to his lips. He blew on the hot liquid before taking a sip.

"Cove told me you want to go to Cape Oceaniana in hopes of rescuing Larkin."

Barren did not say anything; instead he turned from the Elf and walked toward the row of windows in his room. He'd forgotten he'd told Cove that. "What if she does not want to come back? Have you prepared yourself for that reality?"

"Yes, Leaf," he said, irritated. "It's not about coming back to me. It's about her freedom."

"Is that what you're telling yourself now?"

"Believe what you want," Barren looked at his friend, and the Elf raised his brows, partly amused, partly as a challenge.

"I didn't think to warn you not to fall in love with your brother's fiancée…that would have been the worst luck, after all."

Barren scowled, but Leaf only smirked and then nodded to the drink still in Barren's hands. "Finish that or you'll regret it."

The Elf retreated then. Barren had half a mind to throw the mug at him, but instead he sipped the hot liquid, knowing full well that Leaf wasn't lying about regretting it later. When he'd finished the mixture, he made sure his knives were concealed. It was probably frowned upon to bring weapons to this gathering, but Barren never liked being unarmed. He left his room. Though the huge windows outside his room would allow anyone inside, he locked his door. He'd felt uncomfortable ever since he woke up this morning.

Tonight, he planned to confront Lord Alder about the bloodstone whenever and wherever he could. It would probably be a mistake, but he knew the King of the Elves would not allow a private audience with him, so Barren was going to have to manage with whatever he could get—even if that meant leaving Aurum tonight, and possibly facing Leaf's disappointment.

Barren headed down the hall. At night, Aurum took on an ethereal feeling. Candles and lanterns illuminated the halls in a way that made them glow, and while it was dark outside, the sky was filled with stars and a full moon, causing silver to blanket everything. Entering the great hall, he was met with the same otherworldly feel. It was well known that the Elves were beautiful, and having so many in one room, all dressed in fine silk and shimmery robes, made him forget for a moment how untrustworthy they could be. Without a doubt, Barren knew every last one of these elegant and willowy creatures was deadly. Sure, their skills varied: some were better with bows, others with swords, but most liked to use their hands because weapons made too much noise. That simple bit of knowledge, which Barren had learned directly from Leaf, always made him feel that the Elves were far more brutal than the world actually knew.

Barren kept close to the windows. Being in tight spaces made him uncomfortable, and the fact that he was half-Elf in a room of full-bloods, didn't make him feel any better. He sifted through the faces in the crowd, seeking members of his crew. He hadn't seen everyone yet—the twins, for instance, had gone to the shore. Barren imagined they'd felt very uncomfortable in the Elvish kingdom considering their mother had been from Aurum and ran away when they were young, giving way to a strained relationship between humans and Elves.

"Who are you looking for?" Cove asked, coming to stand beside him. The Ambassador had also been given a green tunic and brown leggings and was enjoying a glass of wine. As Barren looked at him, Cove swirled the liquid around and took a slow sip.

"I was searching for the twins," Barren said. "I have not seen them since I woke."

"Yes, they were not comfortable coming here," said Cove. "I would not be surprised if they are spending their time on the *Vasa*."

"It is a pity few can enjoy Leaf's homeland," Barren mused quietly.

"Quite," said the Ambassador. "But you know, we are not so different from Lord Alder. He feels threatened. He sees his race waning—a race that once dominated Mariana. He does what he can to protect it, just as we do what we can to protect our freedom."

Of course Cove would defend him. He was the Ambassador of Arcarum. It was his job to understand both sides. It was his job to offer peace.

"He would do well to trust more."

"You think?" Cove raised a brow. "It seems he trusted Eadred enough to offer him aid in the fight for the throne of the Orient, and Eadred betrayed that trust. It is unfortunate, but the race of men has taught Lord Alder how to treat them. If he is to decide to treat us differently, he must be taught that we can be trusted."

"And how would one do that?"

"I do not know," Cove said honestly. "But not having his trust bothers me greatly. Lord Alder...he is a small power, but a great one all the same."

Suddenly, the crowd hushed and bodies turned in the direction of the staircase. Barren could see three figures moving toward them. They were the royal family—Lord Alder, dressed in deep red. His silver-blond hair fell over his shoulders and seemed to glisten as he glided down marble steps. His hand was held aloft and delicate fingers rested in his palm. They belonged to a woman Barren could only assume was Leaf's mother. She was lithe and lovely, her body clad in a thin crimson gown. The brightest blonde hair Barren had ever seen grew from her head and rested in sheer sheets down her back. On her head, she wore an intricate headdress of gold, laced with glass beads and gems. It looked as heavy as the ruby and gold crown upon Lord Alder's head. Suddenly, Barren dreaded to see Leaf in full costume.

His quartermaster was hidden until they came to the end of the steps, and then Lord Alder and his wife stepped apart to reveal their son. He was clad in odd contrast to his parents—his strong form draped with black robes. A silver circlet was tangled in his hair, and his features were severe in his finery. For a moment, Barren couldn't place his own disappointment, but then he understood. He'd always hoped Leaf would look strange in his role as Prince. Instead, he looked every bit a lord.

Barren took a deep breath.

"Tonight, we welcome my son, your prince, Leaf Tinavin to Aurum," Lord Alder's voice carried throughout the room, resonating like a drum, followed by quiet clapping and admiring smiles. "His stay cannot be long, but for now, we celebrate his presence!"

Soon after the announcement, the crowd was ushered into a dining hall located in an outdoor courtyard filled with stars and lanterns. Barren sat at a fine table with white china, silverware, and more food than he could ever imagine spread before him—and these were just snacks. Though he was hungry, he barely touched anything. The noise around him seemed too loud, and made his head pound. Barren had always imagined the Elves as quiet folk—though he wasn't sure why because all he had was Leaf as an example—but here they were laughing and drinking merrily. Barren would have liked to have run away, escape into the darkness of the forest just within his reach. Already, he longed for the comfort of the sea, but he stayed where he was—though not out of respect for Lord Alder. If anything, it was to confront him.

He and his crew sat at a table occupied by the royal family. Lord Alder was at the head of the table. Barren had a feeling they were seated here, not as guests of honor, but so they could be watched.

A line of servers came forth from the palace, each bearing a silver platter clustered with bowls. They filed in behind each individual at the table and placed their food before them. Barren stared down at it—whatever the soup was, it was white and looked unappetizing. Barren picked up a large silver spoon and dipped it into the thick substance, but before he could try it, his eyes focused upon a symbol embroidered upon his napkin—it was a small tree—the same one settled within the 'V' on Devon's tattoo. Barren let his spoon fall into the soup, and he looked directly at Lord Alder.

"Tell me about them," he said suddenly, his voice rose over the murmur of the crowd. Barren could already feel Leaf's eyes on him, bearing into his soul. "Tell me about the Lyrics."

Barren watched as Lord Alder's body grew still and his feature turned frighteningly cold. He narrowed his eyes, and they were like ice. "I know not of what you speak," he replied.

Barren grabbed the napkin. "What's this? Why is this a part of that map my father gave to Devon to protect?"

"Your father was a secretive man, Barren Reed."

"Not very secretive, Lord Alder, if you have made your entire kingdom ignorant!"

"Barren, calm down!" Leaf ordered.

"No!" he cried. "All I have wanted are answers, and all I keep getting are excuses! Tell me to calm down when I have answers!"

Lord Alder stood. "I welcomed you here, healed you, and this is your payment? A demand for what I cannot give?"

"You are fully capable of answers," replied Barren. "What happened to Sysara? Were you so angry by her betrayal, by her love for my father, that you banished her name for eternity? So that when one like me, an orphan, questioned his existence, he would have no one to turn to? Do you not see my pain?"

"Pain, like all things, will heal, Barren."

"You're wrong. You are wrong." Barren turned from the table.

He tried to avoid making eye contact with anyone, though he could feel eyes following him in every direction he turned. It was no different than this morning, except now he felt like a fugitive, fleeing for his life. There was one gaze that made him look however. It was one that burned into him, one he had seen before. Green eyes filled with fury and deep-rooted hatred pierced him like an arrow. The Elf with the red hair stared back at him from a table in the shadows. She was still clad in white layers, and just when Barren was about to rip his eyes from her, she stood and hurried away.

Looking back at the table he had excused himself from, he saw that no one but Lord Alder looked his way. From here, Barren could see the fury in the Elven King's eyes—and they held just as much hatred as the redheaded Elf's. Barren turned away and hurried inside, down the shadowy corridor to his room.

Barren slammed his door and locked it. He was angry and even worse, Leaf hadn't raised a finger to help him. Instead, his best friend had been more concerned with pleasing his father.

Barren walked to his bed and fell onto the rumpled covers. He lay there for a moment, and then rolled over, looking at his bedside table. Another wooden mug filled with steaming tea sat next to Larkin's crimson scarf. He grasped the fabric, ignoring the stiffness in his limbs that he knew the tea could fix, and rolled over. He wrapped the scarf around his hands and rested his head upon it, falling into a deep sleep.

***

When he opened his eyes to the silver laced night, he couldn't figure out what had awakened him. He lay there for a moment before moving, watching the dark, searching for a figure whose presence he felt but could not see.

Getting up from the bed, he moved to the windows and peered outside. A woman sat near the fountain. Her back was to him, and she hummed a very soft, melancholy melody as she trailed her hands in the water. Barren recognized the fiery red hair spilling down her back—it was the lady from the dinner whose eyes had beheld him with such hatred. She seemed so vulnerable now.

He stepped into the courtyard, and felt a weight upon him. He looked about but saw nothing. In his heart, he knew this was power—it was the woman protecting herself. Maybe she feared him. Or maybe she had others to fear. Lord Alder, perhaps?

"Are you her?" Barren asked quietly. "Are you the statue?"

The woman looked up at the statue; she still had not met Barren's eyes. She smiled wistfully.

"She was one of me, but no—I am not her."

"Then who are you?"

"I am a ghost," she replied. "I am light. I am dust."

"You know that tells me nothing of who you are?"

The woman laughed, but Barren thought it an odd laugh—it was not one filled with amusement, nor one made out of scorn. "It says everything of who I am."

Then the woman lifted her hands from the water and as the drops began to fall, they transformed into balls of light. Like fairies, they flew in a circle around her, and then bounded to

Barren. At first he attempted to swat them away, but the woman's laugh caused him to stop.

"They will not harm you. My magic is not evil...not anymore."

Barren paused and stared at them: they seemed harmless enough, just bright light. This was magic. The woman raised her hand and the spheres floated above them, creating a canopy of light.

"You are a Lyric," Barren's eyes widened a little in realization of who stood before him. This was not how he imagined them to be. Within the name Lyric, there was power, so why did this woman appear to have little? She was drained and pale, her figure was lithe and fragile. If Barren was the type to believe in ghosts, he would think she was one. "I thought you were all dead."

"I am dying, but it has been a slow death," she said quietly. "I suppose it is part of my punishment."

"Punishment? You mean...you are referring to your relationship with the mortals?"

She nodded. "It is the fault of the truly powerful to believe we can do anything. To believe the rules do not apply to us. How wrong we were."

Barren hated how she seemed to blame herself. If she felt ashamed of her decisions—for the decisions of the other Lyrics, for his *mother's* decision, then it was as if he were a mistake. As if his existence really wasn't all that necessary. Was that the reason for her looks?

"I do not believe it was a mistake to love a mortal," Barren couldn't keep the edge out of his voice, and the Lyric's head snapped toward him. Her eyes took on that fierce hue of green that had surveyed him with such hatred.

"Of course you don't," she stood then, and rose to her full height, and though she was small, Barren could feel her power increase. His heart beat faster. "You are the son of Sysara, your father was Jess Reed—always the heroine, always the hero. Always so keen to be self-sacrificing. But I—I wed the worst of the lot. The very worst. I brought destruction upon my people, upon myself. That is why I am left to die this way."

"What are you talking about?"

Her eyes narrowed upon him, and he took a step back. "It does not surprise me that you have no memory of me. I am but a rumor on the tongues of many. The man I loved was powerful and he was kind, but the man I *married* was not that man. He was powerful, yes, but severe and thirsty for more. We were warned—mortals cannot keep from acting on their desires. That is why you are here, Barren Reed, whether you realize it or not. You are in Aurum because the man who sent you has never been able to quench his desire for power."

"You do not mean," Barren began. "But you cannot mean…Tetherion?"

As Barren spoke his name, his heart seemed to fill with darkness, and he knew it was a confirmation.

"Tetherion. Yes, it is he. I know you do not wish to believe me, but believe me when I say, that man has deceived you."

"So you are….Illiana," Barren said. "They said you ran away

with a lover of your kind. Y-you were disgraced for leaving your family."

"I do not need to be reminded of the legacy I have left," she said bitterly. "While it is mostly untrue, I could not have stayed beside the man who was responsible for Sysara's death."

Barren's head felt as if it were going to explode.

"I know he would have you believe otherwise—that he loved your father dearly, and that he would protect you, but Tetherion does only for himself. His relationships only exist for his advantage, and once he has what he wishes for, he will destroy you. I have heard he maintains that Jess stole the bloodstone from Cathmor."

Barren only nodded, he couldn't find words to speak.

"Tetherion knows better than anyone that is false, for he was the one who stole it. He brought the gem to Lord Alder, demanding power over dark magic. He threatened the demise of Aurum and its people if Lord Alder did not comply. Alder could not refuse, for the bloodstone would protect Tetherion, and he had too few soldiers to save his land. In essence, he was powerless. He brought the stone to Sysara, threatening the lives of her sons if she did not fulfill Tetherion's request. Sysara went to Jess with the matter, knowing it to be foolish to give Tetherion more power. They concluded that the bloodstone must be destroyed. Sysara did not believe she could destroy it on her own, so she asked for help from another Lyric named Kenna. Together, they thought they could overcome the evil of the bloodstone...but it was not meant to be."

Silence followed. Barren thought he had felt hollowness before, but never like this. It was not like Tetherion had said at all. This made him responsible for his mother's death, and the death of the other Lyric.

"What did you call the other Lyric?"

"Kenna—you might know her name. She was Christopher Lee's wife."

Barren felt sick—he did know that name. It was the name of Larkin's mother. She'd given it when she'd explained that her mother was killed by pirates. That would also explain why Em had to give him the poison. His memory was directly connected to the bloodstone, *to his wife.*

"Christopher sailed with your father," said Illiana. "He helped Jess betray the king in the name of Saoirse...until the death of his wife. He blamed your father, believing that, without his guidance, Sysara and Kenna would have never tried to destroy the bloodstone."

"But it was Tetherion! If his greed hadn't gotten in the way, they would still be alive!"

"It is my belief that Christopher also blames Tetherion. Is he not responsible for helping William overthrow Tetherion? Are they not seeking the bloodstone? Christopher's grief has not allowed him to forgive Jess, though your father did what he could to see that the bloodstone was no longer in anyone's memory...he even attempted to destroy it himself."

"But would that not kill him?"

"He was cursed, yes," said Illiana, her voice colorless.

"Cursed." While he felt overwhelmed, he suddenly understood. That moment when Barren had turned to see William sneaking upon Jess, when he felt as if he should call out to his father—to save him—it would have been for nothing. Jess was prepared to die.

So this was what it was like to have answers—to have the truth.

"And once he realized he could not destroy it, he took our memories," Barren finished.

This bloodstone could not have had a more fitting title, as it seemed to be the reason for so many losses. It was good for nothing other than turning brother against brother, friend against friend. And once Larkin figured out who Christopher blamed for her mother's death, she would surely also hate Barren.

What could he do? He looked down at his scarred hands. He had Reed blood. If he possessed the stone, he would be invincible. He could take revenge against his brother, he could right all wrongs ever committed against him. Why did that hold no luster for him?

"Careful young pirate," warned Illiana, her eyes watchful and narrow. "Power like that, even in your hands, would be more dangerous than your enemies. You are bitter and hurt. You have not let yourself heal."

Barren felt his face burn with a mixture of rage and embarrassment at her insight. Part of him wondered if she was reading his mind.

"How can I destroy something that cannot be destroyed? I

want to end this."

"It can be destroyed, but only if it comes into contact with those who possess the blood of Sysara and Kenna. You see, one good thing came out of their deaths—the stone drained their essence, but can be conquered if you and Larkin are strong enough."

"Will we not die?" he asked her. "I cannot put her in danger, I will not."

"You are dealing with dark magic, Barren Reed. There is always the chance you will die. If you live, you would be betraying your king, and he will see to it that you are made miserable, hunted, and killed. As for the Lady Larkin, let it be her decision to die for this cause."

Barren cringed at those words. If destroying the bloodstone meant losing his life, that was one thing, but he couldn't let Larkin die. He'd worked too hard to keep her alive.

He heard Illiana laugh. His head shot up and he met her gaze. She seemed weaker now, but also darker.

"Your fondness for Larkin will be your undoing. It is not for you to love, Barren Reed. You are far too selfish."

Barren swallowed hard.

"Why should I trust you? You, with all your magic and power, still could not see past Tetherion's evil!"

That made her change, and Barren saw how terrible she could be. Her eyes grew black so that the whites of her eyes were not visible, and the small balls of light that had been floating around their heads suddenly came to her, piling into her hands.

"You would question my aid? After I have given you everything you need to stop this evil?"

The light grew bigger and it barreled toward Barren. All he could do was fall to his knees and cover his head as the light washed over him. It burned his skin, singed his hair...and he knew he was going to die.

***

Barren tore his eyes open and sat up. His body was covered in a cold sweat, and the air blowing in from the windows sent shivers through him. He reached for his weapons, which had lain on his floor beside his bed, but now were gone.

"Where is my sword, my knife?" he demanded of the figure in his room.

"I took them." Lord Alder appeared in the moonlight. Barren looked around for Illiana, but there was no sign of her—had he been dreaming?

"She came to you in your dreams," the Elf-Lord said, as if he were reading Barren's thoughts.

"Where is she now?"

"She is dead," Lord Alder said simply. "She used what remained of her power to appear to you in your sleep."

He spoke of her death so nonchalantly. As if it were payment in exchange for her betrayal to him.

"You bastard! You threatened my mother! You took me away from her!"

Lord Alder's features were like stone—perfectly sculpted and cold. "I see Illiana has done well giving her side of this story, but let me allow you mine." When Lord Alder spoke, it was as if his voice surrounded Barren, commanding his obedience and punishing him for his disrespect.

"There were rules. Rules that dictated exactly how Lyrics were supposed to act. Your mother broke those rules, and because of that she was not allowed family. More importantly, she accepted it because she knew she would put you in danger if you were left with her. You see, of all those who betrayed their blood, perhaps Illiana was the worst. She wanted Tetherion. She believed she was in love with him and did not listen when we warned her of his deceit. I could not refuse their marriage without the threat of war on my doorstep. She wed him, swearing an oath that she would not speak of magic, but she broke that promise and Tetherion came to me soon after with the demand to give him more power. Illiana was ashamed of what she did, and she blamed herself for the deaths of many."

The Elf paused and took a breath. "Your mother's death was a tragedy, but I had nothing to do with her choice to destroy the bloodstone."

"You *threatened* her," Barren hissed.

"I did," he agreed. "But here you are again, faced with your own devastation and not considering the other side. My people were in danger, Barren. A whole race, and my son—what was I supposed to do?"

"You had magic! You could have stopped—"

"It is exactly that thinking that got your uncle where he is today. I will not stop mortals with magic. I will not stoop to such petty thinking. I did what I felt I had to do." Then Lord Alder smirked, and a horrible feeling crept over Barren. "You should feel empowered, Barren Reed—for you have the power. You can have your revenge all in one day if you choose. Destroy the bloodstone, and avenge your family. Would you not like that?"

Barren did not feel empowered. He only felt confused.

"I would feel empowered if I knew where the bloodstone was. If I knew where you had exiled the Lyrics."

"Pity *she* did not tell you."

"Why not just tell me? Why do your best to keep everything from me?"

"If you had lived as long as I, you would learn to mistrust any but your own kind."

"I think you miss being powerful, that's why you keep secrets."

"I keep secrets to keep my people safe!" he hissed. "Do not pretend you understand me, young Barren Reed. How could you know anything of life when you have lived only for revenge?"

Barren set his teeth and the lord turned to leave, but he paused at the door.

"Dark magic is a tricky thing. It is almost alive, for it holds grudges…. and depending on what it wants, it could choose to keep you alive, but if it does, you need to consider what it wants from you. Because it will *want*…and it will *take*—from only you."

With that, the lord left, closing the door behind him. Barren crashed against his pillow, staring at the shadowy ceiling. He hardly felt satisfied. He had so many unanswered questions. Why had Christopher kept Kenna a secret so long? Why had he not pinned Jess as the killer, if he truly believed him to be responsible? Barren knew he would have to tell Larkin, whether it meant having her hatred or not. He knew how horrible it was to be lied to.

Chapter Twenty-Three
THE PAST

"We will not be returning the bloodstone to Tetherion," Barren said. He had made his decision. He expected resistance. He expected to be told he was stupid—and he hadn't even explained the rest of his plan yet.

They stood beneath the skylight in the great hall. Water trickled in the background, making Barren all the more eager to set sail.

"But that will make you an enemy to the king," Datherious said. Barren had wondered how the twins would react. They did not have the same information Barren had, and he would not divulge what he knew about their father. He didn't want to be responsible for delivering the news. Looking at them now, they seemed surprised and defensive, but perhaps they were merely warning him.

"I have always been his enemy. I am a pirate." As much as Barren hated to admit it, he saw that now. "I threatened his throne. No matter our relations, I cannot exist as a pirate and he a king and not be his enemy. It is the law of this world."

"So what will you do instead?" asked Natherious.

"I know enough now to understand that keeping something so powerful, something so potentially evil alive, would be a mistake. No matter who possesses it. I will destroy it."

His crew exchanged glances, and their stances tightened in defense, but Devon and Em bristled with pride and relief.

"Barren, you know the results of that decision," said Leaf. "You will die."

Barren shook his head. "There's a chance I will live, but only if Larkin chooses to help me. We have no choice but to head toward Cape Oceaniana. I need Larkin."

Leaf laughed. "I never thought I'd hear you say that aloud!"

Barren laughed, too, rubbing the back of his neck.

"And how do you propose finding Larkin in Cape Oceaniana?" asked Cove.

Barren smiled. "Is your famous Network not stationed everywhere? I'm sure they would know if Christopher Lee and William Reed graced their shores."

The Ambassador smiled. "I am sure they would."

"All right then," said Sam, rubbing his hands together. "To

Cape Oceaniana."

***

Barren traced Jess's map from Devon's arm, and Leaf studied its outline. They still had no idea where the bloodstone was, and the only clue was the map. Leaf's brows took turns furrowing and smoothing as he tried to figure out what everything meant, but he was at a loss. He had never seen anything like this before, and he turned it in every direction, trying to figure out what it said.

"If you ask me, it's not a map," said Leaf.

"Then what is it?"

"A poorly drawn picture," Leaf handed the map to Barren.

They sat on the deck of the ship, legs crossed, and a basket of bread and water beside them. As soon as the Elf's hands were free, they dove into the basket, pulling out stale bread and dried fruits for him and Barren to eat.

"This is serious, Leaf. I believe Em when she said my father did nothing in vain."

"The map isn't the vain part," said Leaf. "It's feeding everyone poison so they don't remember anything about it."

Barren couldn't argue with that, though he now understood his father's decisions better.

"I want to know if Tetherion's intentions are truly evil," Barren said quietly. He had told Leaf everything that happened the night before. Part of him still wanted to believe Tetherion only wished to keep the bloodstone in the King's vault, and to not use it for power. He wanted to believe that all the trust between them wasn't false. "Perhaps he has changed."

Leaf considered that for a moment. "Perhaps. It is not wrong to hope."

He could tell by the way Leaf had spoken that he shouldn't be too hopeful. Barren stared unseeing, at the space before him, thinking.

"Only weeks ago I thought my brother would be dead at my feet. My behavior seems silly now. I think I pursued revenge so diligently because I believed I was partly responsible for my father's death. That second before William attacked—those moments when I could have cried out, gotten his attention, made him turn. Now I realize it would have been in vain. He was going to die anyway. He'd prepared himself for it. He'd prepared us all for it. I just wish he hadn't taken my memories with him."

"That is when you must remember that Jess never did anything in vain."

"Yes," he said quietly. "I suppose I must."

Barren could feel the Elf's eyes on him as he sat, staring at nothing in particular.

"You seem most unlike yourself, Captain."

Barren laughed a little. "I suppose I am just regretting my mistakes."

"Is this about Larkin?"

Barren shrugged a shoulder. "Among other things," he replied. "I wish I had not been so selfish."

"You are young, Barren, and the young are selfish, but there is a lot about you that is selfless. You would do anything to protect those closest to you—the result of watching the one you love most, perish, perhaps."

Barren looked down at his hands. The way Leaf spoke of him sometimes made him sound overly heroic, and Barren didn't feel he could claim such an attribute.

"Besides, Larkin has been good for you," the Elf mused. "She argues with you, and that's entertaining. And who would have thought Barren Reed would become fond of someone so willing to defy him?"

"I could never be fond of the daughter of a lord and the fiancée of my brother," Barren replied quietly.

"Well, I don't know about that. You've probably spent more time with her than either Christopher or William."

Barren picked up the map and stood, wanting to put an end to this conversation quickly.

"I am the epitome of everything she hates, as she has made quite clear to me time and time again."

"If you truly believed that, why are you so desperate to help her? Never mind that you need her for the bloodstone—you wanted her before you knew that."

Barren's features grew hard. "You're a pirate—what would you know of any of this?"

Leaf smiled, but it was a melancholy smile. "More than you would ever know," he replied distantly, and Barren knew he'd said the wrong thing. The Elf's features were pained—this was the look of real loss. Of never being able to see, much less touch a loved one again. Barren knew that look well.

Leaf moved from his place on the deck and walked like a

ghost toward the front of the ship where the Orient crashed into the hull. Barren followed, unsure of what terrible memory he had unearthed.

"I joke about many things, Barren, and I know you do not always take what I say seriously, but believe me when I say, I have known love and I have known the loss of that love."

"I-I didn't know."

"Not many do," said Leaf, his eyes were set on the sea, and she, as if in reaction to his feelings, grew more restless. "Remember when I told you I spent time in Estrellas?"

"Yes, for the murder of several men."

"I killed them for her."

Barren wasn't sure what to say next. Part of him felt like he should leave the conversation as it was. These feelings Leaf was digging up had been buried in his subconscious for years, and having them rush to the forefront of his mind was not good. On the other hand, Barren felt that he needed to know more.

"What was her name?"

Leaf smiled, and it was as if he was remembering sunlight, sweetness, and the gentleness of spring.

"Her name was Fira. She was brave, beautiful, and she loved me. Me, the rebel Prince of Aurum—she wanted me. I was never so enchanted and never so much in love."

"What happened?"

"She was murdered," said Leaf quietly. "She sailed with me against the wishes of her father. We came to port on an island called Aryndel, in the Octent. We should not have gone, for rarely are Elves of Aurum welcomed in the Octent. We were only staying there for a night—we needed supplies, but a few drunken men at the Inn couldn't keep their eyes off Fira," Leaf laughed bitterly. "They may not like us, but they like the look of our women. I didn't like it, so I felt it best we leave. We just wanted to return to our ship and sail on, but the men had a different idea and followed us. They surrounded us outside the Inn, and took Fira from my side. They didn't know I was armed, and they assumed they could beat me in a confrontation. When I drew my blade, they split up—three attempted to take me and the other four dragged Fira away.

"The men weren't hard to fight, I must admit. They were too drunk to realize they had messed with the wrong person. They mocked me, and I took them down. All the while I could hear Fira screaming for my help somewhere in the distance. I followed her cries, but as soon as the men saw me, they knew their friends were dead. Only one of the men took his revenge—an ugly, greasy man with black hair. He withdrew a knife and drove it through Fira over and over again. He met his death just as violently as Fira...and the others followed."

Leaf was silent for a moment. When he spoke again, his voice was strained.

"She died in my arms, and the soldiers found me soon after. I refused to move until they let me lay her to rest. I sent her body away in flames and then let them take me. At first I did not care what happened to me. I took the torture, and I wanted to die."

"What changed?" Barren's voice was barely a whisper, and as

he spoke, he felt chills rise over his skin.

Leaf smiled. "A dream, a beautiful dream. She came to me as real and warm as she had been before her death. She asked me not to give up, and I would never deny her what she wanted. Since then I have searched for a dream like that one."

"I am sorry, Leaf."

"It is easier to keep her death in the back of my mind and her life at the forefront. My point is, whether from shame or your stubbornness, do not let what you feel for Larkin slip past you so easily. You will never forgive yourself."

"You make it sound...simple."

"Well, I never said it would be easy," said Leaf. "But the fight for Larkin never promised to be easy. You learned that the day you met her."

Barren touched his chest where she'd hit him with the heels of her boots. She'd been so angry...so unexpectedly violent.

"And you have come a long way from that," Leaf continued. "Which is good...I have never been so sick of the Cliffs in all my life."

Barren laughed quietly. "But it should not have happened. She was my prisoner."

"You don't need to care that it happened," said Leaf. "You only need to know that it has, and embrace it...because the rest of us have been taking bets, and I want to win."

Barren slugged Leaf in the arm, but couldn't help laughing. "I should have known something was up. You never offer advice without something in it for yourself."

"Well, there is something in it for you, too," said Leaf. "She has taught you a lot, and she'll continue to teach you a lot. She's not afraid of you, Barren Reed. Never has been, and never will be."

Chapter Twenty-Four
THE CAPE

For hours, Barren stared at the design he traced from the tattoo on Devon's arm. He had tried to take it apart piece by piece to see if any of it morphed into something he recognized, but so far he had gotten nowhere. He looked between the image and the map of the Orient, thinking he could make a comparison, but he felt as if he really had no starting point.

Throwing his pencil down, Barren pulled his sketchbook toward him and turned the page. Larkin stared back at him. He had never finished the drawing. He had planned to tear it to pieces so no one would ever find it, but he hadn't been able to bring himself to do it. Now, he was thankful he hadn't.

Turning the page, he found the invitation to Larkin's engagement party. For a moment, he studied the handwriting, wondering who had taken such care to write them. It seemed so long ago that he had met her—beautiful and ignorant, but so determined. He knew the only thing he could do was hope against hope that these invitations never came into use again. Without another thought, he tore the invitation in two and shoved the pieces in the sketchbook.

He missed her, feared for her. Every night he lay down to sleep, and images of their time in Estrellas passed through his mind. He saw her pain, the anguish, the betrayal she felt as her father refused to listen to her pleas. Suddenly, Barren was filled with a deep, burning rage. He sat for a moment, brooding in the thick air surrounding him, repressing the sudden wish to take revenge for Larkin.

Then the feeling crashed and it was replaced by severe sadness. Everything Barren was at this moment was the opposite of what he should be—the rage, the merciless thoughts of murder—none of that belonged to him. He was a product of what William had done. Larkin had asked him that once, while they stared up at the stars—an ancient pirate's map.

Suddenly, Barren had an idea and his eyes went to the image of the tattoo. He pushed back his chair and began pulling open drawers, emptying their content upon the floor. Papers spilled everywhere, empty inkwells rolled, and metal mapping tools crashed to the ground. One drawer after the other piled before him.

"Come on, Cove!" Barren growled to himself. "I know you've got to have a star map."

Barren pulled open the last drawer, and it was full of rolled scrolls. He picked them all up and laid them out on his desk. He opened them one-by-one, placing the ones he didn't need on the ground. Finally, Barren came to one scroll with silver edging. As he unrolled it, images of the sky's constellations rose before him. He saw them all—Orion Navis (the ship), Pyxis (the mariner's compass), the legendary Kraken, Jack Ketch (the executioner), and finally the constellation Barren was looking for: Circinus, the drafting compass—the constellation from which Barren could navigate in any direction.

The pirate sat the drawing of Devon's tattoo beside the constellation map—the two drawings were essentially the same design: an open-ended triangle. Both were also the same length. It was then Barren remembered something Leaf had said—that the Lyrics were placed on an island to themselves, isolated, forbidden to interact with mortals. Perhaps the island wasn't far from Aurum.

Barren placed the drawing of the tattoo over the map of the Orient, making sure the symbol of Aurum covered the island. Then he placed the image of the constellation over that: it made sense. The island was located at the tip of Circinus. It would lead Barren home. The words of his father fell into his head as everything suddenly came together. *Stars ensure all that is lost is found.*

Barren headed outside, making his way to the helm. He thrust the map of the Orient into Sam's hands, pointing to an empty space in the water where he'd marked the coordinates of the supposed Lyric island. The helmsman looked amused as Barren explained what he thought resided there and how he had discovered it.

"You want to go here?" Sam pointed to the space.

"Yes," said Barren.

"With no proof that this island is actually in existence?"

"Sam, the bloodstone was just a legend at the beginning of all this. Who's to say I am wrong about the whereabouts of this island?

"Have you told the others?"

"One thing at a time, Sam. We have yet to make it to Cape Oceaniana."

The helmsman raised his brows.

"Speaking of Cape Oceaniana," Sam stopped Barren before he could move away from the helm. "Larkin has not been particularly good luck to you since she joined our crew."

"What are you getting at?"

Sam held up his hands as if defending himself. "I'm only asking that you promise you'll come back."

Barren narrowed his eyes a little, then he laughed. "I always come back."

***

"It will be impossible to come to port in this weather," said Barren quietly. He glanced at Albatross who stood next to him, hands behind his back, staring into the thick fog. It was all around them—like a terrible cloud of smoke, choking their vision. Barren had sent Leaf to trade places with Slay in the crow's nest in hopes that the Elf could see through the veil.

"Quite impossible if you cannot even see the island," said Cove. "Though the sun should burn it away by midday. You could stall the ship."

Barren didn't mind stalling the ship, but there was something making him uneasy. He strained his vision as he peered into the fog, wishing he could peel back layer after layer with his eyes.

"If you did stall, we could discuss our plan for entering Cape Oceaniana," said Cove. "I'm unsure if we should even come to port, in case Christopher and William remain ashore."

Barren met the Ambassador's dark gaze and then called quietly for the twins and Seamus. "Drop anchor," he ordered. "And prepare the cannons."

"Cannons?" Datherious asked with a laugh. "It's hardly likely anyone will find us in this mess."

Barren sighed inwardly. "Perhaps you are right, and if no harm comes to us once the fog has lifted, you can ridicule me as much as you wish, but for now, I would prefer to be overly-cautious."

The three nodded and once they dropped anchor, headed down the hatch to prepare the cannons. Barren turned his body toward Cove and Alex came forward. Devon and Em trailed behind.

"The Cape is heavily guarded on a normal basis because they're so close to the Octent," said Cove. "From what I hear, they normally fight Corsairs from the Avalon. The Cape will not take kindly to anyone coming to port who does not bear their flag."

"What are they protecting?" asked Barren.

"Ivory," Devon's voice rasped quietly.

Barren glanced at the old man and then at Cove who nodded in agreement. "If you do want to find out where Larkin is, it is probably best we sneak onto the island. You are a fast swimmer and the walls can be scaled. After that it's just a matter of finding my people."

The Cape was known for its defenses. As Cove had mentioned, they had to be a little overprotective. Corsairs were a different type of pirate—a different order entirely, and the rules they held themselves to were hardly rules at all. If anyone in Mariana could be accused of cruelty, it was the Corsairs.

"You must also assume that Christopher and William are still there," Cove added. "They've few options in their search of the bloodstone."

Yes. Christopher and William would be at a dead end, and their only possible move beyond Cape Oceaniana would be attacking Aurum...and Barren wasn't sure how desperate they were.

Without warning, an explosion sounded, shattering the peaceful quiet that surrounded them. Everyone drew their swords and stared about, and Leaf jumped from the crow's nest and landed next to Barren on deck. They waited for the ship to settle again, and the water to return to stillness. For a moment, Barren was in disbelief, as the cannon had come from his own ship. There was clamoring below deck in the silence that followed. Seamus was the first to climb out, and the twins followed.

"What the hell happened?" Barren demanded.

"It was an accident," Datherious said, his manner far from alarmed or panicked.

"How do you not intend to light a cannon?" asked Cove, his dark eyes were unkind.

The twin glared at the man. "I thought I saw something move about in the mist."

"If I did not see anything, how did you see anything?" asked Leaf.

"Your eyes cannot be everywhere, Elf." Tension flooded the space between them.

"Damn it!" Barren peered into the mist. His hair stood on end. That uneasy feeling had returned tenfold, and anxiety spread through his chest.

In the distance, he saw an orange flash.

"Get down!" he yelled.

Everyone on deck hit the floor. An ear-splitting crack sounded, and the mast groaned as it fell, crashing into the railing of the deck, and hitting the Orient's surface with a splash. In the silence of the aftermath, Barren rose before the rest of his crew. The mist he'd been so mistrustful of before, was slowly curling away to reveal the outline of a warship before them. It held forty cannons at least, and would surely reduce the *Vasa* to toothpicks—that shot had only been a warning.

"I don't think we can fight that thing," said Leaf.

"We have to try," Barren returned. "Prepare for battle."

The deck erupted into fierce defense, and they had to hurry. Seamus and Alex rushed to the swivel guns mounted on the railing of the ship. They worked quickly to load them. The twins, Slay and others from Cove's crew disappeared below deck to set the cannons toward the attacking ship. Barren hurried into his cabin, throwing open his trunk. He tossed the clothes onto the floor. At the bottom were several powder flasks—glass balls filled with gunpowder. Barren pulled them out carefully, grabbing a shirt as he hurried out of his cabin.

"Take these!" he said, handing the powder flasks to Devon and Em. Barren then turned to Leaf. "Your bow," he said and began to tear pieces of his shirt. He took Leaf's quiver of arrows and wrapped each with a piece of cloth while the Elf dipped them in a bowl of oil he'd poured. Hollow produced a piece of flint and a thick piece of steel. Striking them together, sparks fell on the rags and in seconds they were aflame. The Elf aimed the arrow at the sails of the warship—it was only a few feet from them now, lining up nicely with theirs. They watched as the arrow cut the air in an almost unnatural manner, only to pierce the enemy's white sails and set them ablaze.

In retaliation, the ship began to light cannons. The *Vasa* rocked upon the water with every blow, sending debris flying. A second round of firing sounded, and lead pelted the ship like rain—they had to be using grapeshots. The pirates took cover as best they could on the open deck, sheltering their heads with their hands. Barren rushed to the hatch and cried below. "Fire! Fire!"

The *Vasa* groaned as its cannons burst forth from the gundeck. Turning, he faced Leaf as he rose from the deck, and Cove, too. The Ambassador held his arm against him as blood spilled between his fingers—he'd been hit. "Bandage it quickly, Leaf. Stop the bleeding."

Barren turned, watching the enemy ship as his cannons did minimal damage. His heart sank. Then his eyes caught the image of his brother, and standing close, Christopher Lee. Rage consumed him and he bent over the rail, crying out at the men below deck. "Fire you fools! Fire! Devon, Em!" he called as he took one of the powder flasks from them and threw it toward the ship. They exploded in a fierce burst of orange, and men on deck cried out as they fell. It was a small victory for Barren.

As Devon and Em continued to throw what was left of the powder flasks, Barren hurried to Leaf and Cove.

"What's the damage?"

"Nothing that can't be healed," Leaf replied.

"Good."

Cannons rocked their ship again, and the pirates tumbled to the floor. Barren rose with a ringing in his ears. The severe look on Leaf's face caused Barren to follow his gaze. Then he saw them—the men poised on the masts, ready to make their advance on the ship. Just as he saw them, several crunching sounds caught his attention—grappling hooks were now embedded in the rail of the *Vasa*.

"Cut the ropes!" he cried. Drawing his sword, he ran for the ropes. Devon and Em were already there. Some men fell in mid-swing, while others made it to the deck and battle ensued.

"Barren, they have Larkin," Leaf warned.

Alarm rang through him. Instinctively, he found her amid the sailors rushing about the deck of the attacking ship, held tightly by two guards, her mouth gagged. He could think of only one reason they would have her watch this—so that she could see him defeated. Anger made him tighten his grip on his blade, and he cut down his attackers with ferocity. He had one destination—the foremast. It was the only one left standing, and from it, he could board the enemy ship.

"Barren, where are you going?" he heard Leaf call.

"Just make sure you cover me!" the pirate called back.

Barren climbed the mast with some effort—his joints still stiff from his injuries. As he was about to pull himself onto the platform of the mast, an arrow grazed his hand. He faltered, but before he could fall, he reached for one of the ropes holding the sail in place. He turned in time to see the man who had taken a shot at him go down, one of Leaf's arrows in his chest. Barren managed to make it to the platform. He nodded to Leaf. The Elf hurried after him, climbing the foremast with ease—he would follow behind him. It would be easier for the others to board if Leaf could get the ropes secured.

Barren grasped one of the ropes, and ran off the edge of the platform. The wind resisted him as he managed to pull his bodyweight forward and land on the deck, collapsing to his knees. As soon as he landed, he turned, blocking a blow to his head. Leaf landed shortly behind him, quickly stringing an arrow to take down another attacker. The Elf hurried off, set on bringing the battle to their enemies.

While Barren fought, he set his sights on Larkin. The men who held her were dragging her away, and she fought, twisting and jerking within their grasps. Barren withdrew another blade and charged toward her, taking down any who stepped up to fight him. It wasn't until he came face-to-face with Christopher Lee that he stopped. The lord looked so pristine—his coat buttoned and clean. His black cane gleamed in his hand. He was yet unscathed—and Barren raised his bloody weapon.

"Barren," he said, taking his cane in both hands, he pulled it apart to reveal a thin sword. "So good of you to join us."

"It would not pain me to take your life," Barren said through his teeth.

"Think carefully on that, pirate. If you care for my daughter in any sense of the word, you will do well to keep me alive, but if you feel your affection waning, then by all means—hurt me."

The old man opened his arms, waiting for Barren to strike, and then a nasty smirk accosted his lips. "What horrible circumstances I have been given—that my daughter would attract the attention of both of Jess Reed's bastard children."

Barren's eyes blazed, and he moved to strike the lord. Though Christopher Lee was old, he was no less agile. Barren used both of his blades to fight the old man, aiming to take him down quickly, but he couldn't shake Lee's words—if he did harm

Christopher in anyway, Larkin would never forgive him. She worked tirelessly to please her father, and no matter the wrong he committed, she still loved him. She would never want to see him die, and surely if he met his death at the end of Barren's sword, she would be his enemy forever.

This thought caused him to look for Larkin, but the two men had succeeded in getting her below deck. What did they think taking her below would accomplish?

The distraction cost him one of his blades as it went flying from his hand. He gripped his sword with both hands and moved toward Christopher Lee with speed, going for his shoulder. The old man countered the attack, but their swords locked at the hilt.

"I know why you're doing this," Barren gritted out. "You want revenge."

Lee smiled, though he was out of breath. "Then it seems we are not so different from one another."

Lee pushed Barren back and charged at him again. Their blades crashed, and Barren fought harder, ensuring that each strike left both his and Christopher's arms ringing. When he disarmed the old lord and held his blade to the man's throat, Christopher lifted his head, stretching the skin tight for Barren to cut, daring him to kill him.

"On your knees," Barren ordered.

Christopher gritted his teeth, but did as the pirate ordered. Barren took out the rope from his pocket. "Hands on your head." Lee was slow to obey, but did as Barren said. After he was finished tying the old man's wrists, he leaned down.

"Tell me what you did with the men who chose to return to Maris rather than fight me."

Lee raised his brows, and chuckled a little. "Orders are orders, Barren Reed. Those men were to fight you, not come running back to Maris with their tails between their legs. They met the end they thought they would escape."

Barren struck the lord on the head with the hilt of his sword and left him where he lay.

By now, Leaf had succeeded in connecting the ships, and more and more of Barren's crew were making their way to the massive ship, fighting with their attackers. Barren hurried to the hatch where they'd taken Larkin. If luck held with him, they would be able to commandeer this ship—it was now their only hope for getting to the bloodstone.

The hatch door was open, and Barren climbed down, cautious as he descended the dark steps. In this atmosphere, he had only to rely on his hearing for movement, but that was hard considering the commotion on deck. The stairs ended, and he moved into the main hold. There were barrels and beams he managed to navigate around, trying not to make too much noise. He would call out to Larkin, but he knew the guards had gone down with her and hadn't returned.

Then he heard it—a shuffle and the silver sound of a blade. He twisted and his sword clashed with another. He met the wide-eyed gaze of Larkin Lee.

"Barren," she breathed, dropping her arms quickly. She wrapped them around his waist. For a moment, Barren stood there, unsure of what he should do. Just as he was about to place his arms around her, she pulled away. "Are the twins still with you?"

"Yes," he said, confused. "Why?"

She pulled on his arm. "They're traitors, Barren!"

They headed upstairs, but just as they reached the deck, a bell rang out, and the sounds of battle lessened as everyone looked about, confused by the sound. Barren saw it—another ship was approaching. It was massive in its structure, and kingly. The wood was dark and polished, and three masts rose from the deck, bearing bright white sails. It was Tetherion's ship, designated by the red flag of Maris flying at the head of the first sail.

First he heard Larkin struggle, and then his own arms were taken into an iron grasp as guards seized all of Barren's crew.

"Prepare the boarding planks," Lee's voice rang out. He stood with a white handkerchief pressed to his head. "Our king is about to board."

Chapter Twenty-Five
MUTINY

It was the most decorated Barren had ever seen Tetherion. Dressed in all his formal attire—black pants, boots, a velvet red coat embellished with gold, and a cape. He even wore a golden crown, heavy with rubies. As he passed over the boarding plank fluidly, his boots thudded against the grain like an ominous drum. His eyes surveyed the crowd, and then they landed on Barren. The pirate's chest tightened. Those eyes were not the eyes of his uncle. They were not the eyes of the man who had stood in Alex's office at Silver Crest and asked for help. They were not the eyes of the man he trusted.

The king turned his gaze slowly from Barren and looked at

the crowd of pirates. Christopher Lee came forward and bowed, then he took his place beside Tetherion. Barren watched, his jaw tightening. What was going on here? Wasn't Christopher Lee responsible for betraying the king? Did Illiana not say that Tetherion was responsible for Kenna's death? How could Christopher Lee bow to the man who'd killed her?

There was movement in the crowd as William struggled to free himself from his captors. "I demand you let me go!" he roared.

The king and Christopher looked passive.

"I believe they have orders to restrain you," said Christopher Lee. "Since you raised a revolt against your king, you are guilty of treason."

William's eyes went wide with disbelief. "How dare you accuse *me* of treason!"

Tetherion laughed and the sound filled the air, sending chills up Barren's arm. "It is not for you to deny. Lord Lee has told me everything—that you wished to use Lady Larkin as a pawn in order to begin a revolt thinking you could snatch my throne from me...and when you realized you could not hold up against me, you decided to seek the bloodstone."

William hesitated, not finding the words to speak. "He—but he!"

"He...what? Encouraged you?" Tetherion finished with a wicked smile. "You didn't have to take the bait. You could have refused...though, I dare say, it would have been far harder for me to kill you and your brother."

To hear of Tetherion's evil from others was one thing, but to have it confirmed was devastating. Barren felt angry and sick. He hated that he had trusted this man so completely. Not only was this a ploy to reclaim the gem he'd lost out of greed, but he'd intended to see both his nephews dead. This was about power, and Tetherion's fear of losing it again.

"Don't look so pitiful," Christopher chided William. "I am not the only traitor here."

"Come forth," Tetherion ordered with a jerk of his head.

Barren's heart squeezed once he saw the twins walk toward their father. What Larkin had told him before they'd been captured ran through his head—*the twins, they're traitors.*

He watched their exchange—the twins bowed gracefully and then Datherious produced Barren's sketchbook. The king took it in his hands and opened it, brows rising as he observed the pictures. After a moment, he plucked a piece of folded paper from between the leaves, handing the book back to Datherious. He opened the note. Barren didn't need to look at it to know what it was—the coordinates to the Lyric island.

Barren tried to fight, but his captors held him tight, twisting his arm and stomping on his leg. Barren gave out a cry, which drew Tetherion's attention and the twins'.

"Come now," said Datherious with a gaze that made Barren cringe. "Did you really think two princes would give up their life of status and wealth to sail the Orient with a wanted man? We only did what our father asked."

"You sent them as spies!" Barren roared.

Tetherion raised a brow, as if it had been obvious. "I needed someone to keep tabs on you. Who better than my sons? Your cousins. You were so gullible, believing every word they spoke, so long as it included your precious Saoirse."

"Why?" Barren demanded. "What have I ever done to you?"

"You exist," Tetherion replied.

The twins had been paramount to everything Tetherion and Christopher were able to do. It was how the privateers had found Silver Crest, how William had known to go to Conn to search for Devon, even how they'd known to search for Estrellas. They had played Barren's and William's hatred of each other against them in order to destroy them. Barren's fists curled, and he resisted the bitter urge to fight, fearing the guards might break his legs.

"You see, all of this was to end in Estrellas," said Tetherion. "It was the perfect place for your demise. You would attempt to rescue Devon and fail. William and Christopher would arrive, and Christopher would see to it that William met the same fate as you. We would have the location of the bloodstone…there would be no blood on my hands, just your own folly to blame…and everyone would have been happy. But…things did not go as planned."

Tetherion's eyes focused on Em, and they narrowed. He took a step toward her, but Barren stopped him.

"So this is how you would ease your people's fear?" Barren called angrily, recalling the question Tetherion had posed to him after his people rioted. "Bring them my head?"

Tetherion chuckled. "Yes. What did you think? That we could live in peace together? For a pirate, you are far too trusting."

"But you're family!"

"I will blame your age for thinking blood had anything to do with my kindness to you. It was merely manipulation."

"Why go through all of this? Why not just capture us and kill us when you had the chance? You had favor with us, you could have drawn us to you at any moment."

"Because I needed the bloodstone, and as I am sure you have already discovered, these people do not trust me," Tetherion glared at Devon and Em. "But you, the son of Jess Reed, they'd trust you enough."

"Illiana was right," Barren spat. "You are nothing but evil—you only want power and revenge."

Tetherion's eyes blazed for a moment, and Barren knew he'd struck a chord. The king stepped toward him, breaking the barrier he and his sons had created before their prisoners.

"Where did you see her?" he whispered.

"In Aurum," he said. "She told me everything. I guess some things never change."

Barren clenched his jaw so tight it hurt.

Tetherion tilted his head to the side, smirking as he observed Barren. "So much anger built up over time will not aid you."

He went to turn, but Barren wasn't finished. "Do you even care what happened to her?" Barren's eyes bore into Tetherion's soul, and he swore he could see the evil of this man there. "She's dead." Barren's voice was low and deadly, and then he said breathlessly, "She died."

Tetherion was very still for a long moment. He pushed his cloak away from his arm and stepped toward Barren, striking him across the face. Then he grabbed the pirate by the neck and squeezed, lifting him into the air.

"I sent you on this journey to ensure your death, and I will have my wish. You will ride back to Maris to face the noose, but not until you have delivered the bloodstone to me."

Tetherion released Barren and he collapsed to the floor, gasping for breath. He glared at Tetherion and then at Christopher whose eyes were blank.

"And you!" Barren sucked in a breath. "What about Kenna? Aren't you doing all this for her? You loved her!"

Lee's features were like stone, and without so much as a blink, the lord spoke. "Kenna was merely a means of accomplishing a task, nothing more."

Tetherion smirked. Before he left the ship, he spoke to his sons. "You will sail by the coordinates Barren has deciphered. Bring them all back to me...alive."

***

They were led below deck. It was musty and dank, and the lanterns that hung above them cast sick yellow light upon everything. They were not placed behind bars, though that was an option—the entire corner of the brig was nothing but barred cells. The twins, however, had instructed that they all be separately chained—they knew better than to trust free hands.

Now everyone was captured—Leaf and Slay, Alex, Em and Devon, Cove and Hollow and the rest of his crew. Barren stared at them, attempting to decipher their masked features. He hoped this would not mean their end, even if it did mean his.

"Well, this was unexpected." Slay stretched out his feet and settled against the wall. "Gonna be here for a while, might as well get comfortable."

"What do we do now?" asked Larkin.

Barren rested his head against the wall. "I'm not sure yet," he said. "But I have about three days to devise a plan. What we have going for us is the fact that they only have a map to the island, as far as what is there, we still don't know."

"They'll have one hell of a time beating that storm," said Devon.

"What storm?" asked Cove. The rest of the crew watched Devon closely—no one had talked about a storm before.

"Well, there is magic in that water, dark magic. It messes with the elements, causes the Orient to stir and the clouds to sink."

"So what you're saying is, we'll be lucky to make it there alive," said Hollow.

"It's the Orient," said Alex. "You'll make it if she wants ya to."

"It sounds like even if we make it, our ship might be in shambles," said Barren. "And if the twins are navigating, that's even more of a possibility. They don't know anything about manning the helm."

"Well," said Cove, though he kept his eyes on the floor when he spoke, "I suppose if we are marooned on an island with our enemies, no one will have an escape route. We can end it all there."

"You all began this quest with 'opes of destroyin' the bloodstone," said Alex. "Not with the 'opes of livin'. Remember our purpose."

Though it had been a possibility from the beginning, no one had expected to die on this quest. Barren lived every day knowing it could be his last, but he had never imagined his last days would be spent in the custody of his enemies. If anything, that only made him furious and more determined to come out of this alive.

Barren could feel William's eyes on him, and while his mind kept telling him to keep his gaze away, he looked up, and met his brother's stare. For the first time in years, the hate that had been ever-present in William's eyes was replaced by sorrow and confusion.

"Everything he told me, all the lies he fed me—"

Barren didn't feel like sympathizing with William. Though he had been deceived, there was one truth that remained—William resented Jess and he'd still killed him. In the end, all Barren could say was, "You always tried to fight father on everything."

William cast his eyes down, and his voice rose from that muffled position. "It won't change anything, but I will help you out of this. I'll make sure you do not suffer."

Barren shook his head. "It is too late to ease my suffering, William." And in that moment, Barren felt very tired. "And you are only saying that because you want revenge. You should know it is not sweet, and there will be no reward for you after, only bitterness and loneliness."

William cast his eyes away from Barren, and his shoulder slumped.

"However," Barren added. "It is never too late to change, and you have always had another life to turn to rather than the one you chose."

It was true. William had spent fifteen years as a pirate. He'd only chosen the life of a politician to be as different from his father as possible.

***

The ship groaned, chains rattled, and the ugly yellow lights above them swayed. Various snores and soft breathing told Larkin many people were asleep. It wasn't a surprise to her—everyone was exhausted. She, for one, had never been this drained, which, given her life up until a few weeks ago, wasn't all that surprising. For all her exhaustion, she could not rest. Her head raced with all sorts of questions.

Mostly, Larkin felt confused. She knew her father did not hate her, and she believed her father had also loved Kenna. It was she who kept him up at night, she who still had all his attention. It was her memory—or the lack of it—that Larkin competed with for Christopher's attention, and all the while, she'd been oblivious to it. Then there was Barren who had entered her life and muddled up her future. Granted, a life chained to William's side wasn't anything she was excited about, but returning to Maris would be so different. She would never be the same. She'd always remember the time she had with the pirate.

Larkin looked at Barren, studying his features. His eyes were closed and he appeared to be sleeping like everyone else, his chest gently rising and falling. Sometimes it was easy to forget how young Barren actually was—he had the youthful appearance of an Elf, but the soul of an elder. She leaned closer to him, breathing in the smell of salt.

"Do you think we have a chance?" she whispered, hoping he hadn't drifted into too deep of a sleep.

Barren opened his eyes and turned his gaze to her. Larkin had reason to worry. She had never been in a situation where everyone who could save them was captured. Barren smiled slightly, and with some difficultly, he managed to pull from his pocket a piece of crimson cloth—her scarf. He handed it to her, and she held it tightly. It had managed to resurface each time she believed it to be lost.

"We always have a chance," said Barren. "This seems a little hopeless, but really, it is nothing compared to Estrellas."

She shuddered. That was a place she never wanted to revisit. She noticed how Barren grimaced, and knew he hated recalling the details, too. Then he asked something she did not expect.

"Why did you risk your life to save me?"

She hesitated, not wanting to answer him. She'd saved him because she had to. Because she needed to. "Because…you are worth saving."

Barren's brows came together immediately and the look on his face was indiscernible—perhaps he hadn't expected her to say that, but it was true.

"I-I know it wasn't easy to kill him," he said at last.

"I was warned," she said, releasing her gaze from his, and looking down at her hands. She had killed Cas in self-defense. As long as she kept telling herself that, she believed she could live, knowing she had murdered someone.

"That changes nothing about what you experienced," Barren said quickly.

"I would have saved myself a lot of pain had I listened, and yet I would never have witnessed the maliciousness of my father. I would never have known my mother was a Lyric."

Barren lifted his brows.

"How did you find out about her?"

"William," she replied quietly. "My father…has yet to speak of her to me." She couldn't figure out why—was it because he really saw Kenna as a means to an end? Or was the memory too painful? Or maybe he didn't want to have to explain everything else—the friendship with Jess Reed, the treason.

Barren frowned.

"I never would have guessed our lives were so similar."

Larkin laughed humorlessly. "Neither would I. I tried for a long time to see all the differences in us—I only found more similarities."

Barren smiled, but only for a moment, and then his lips turned down. Larkin's frown matched his.

"Whether it began that way or not, I do not believe you were the product of a plan to deceive your mother," said Barren at last. "I am not sure what your father is planning, but it doesn't seem right that he would side with Tetherion."

Larkin's heart felt a little lighter. "I don't understand why he has hidden so much from me. Would it not have helped me to understand him?"

"He never needed you to understand him. You never questioned him until you met me, and even then you were dedicated to what your father wanted." He glanced at William.

"I...I just want to know why he could not be satisfied with what he had." For years they had lived as father and daughter with the knowledge that her mother was just gone. Sometimes she was sad about not having a mother, but never grievous. With all this new knowledge, she realized Lee had always been grieving. He had never stopped, and she really had never been enough.

"You remind him of the revenge he craves," Barren said softly. "And until he can let it go, he will be consumed by nothing else. Here I sit across from the one I wished death upon for so long, and he lives, and even I cannot ignite the hate that burned in me before now. It is gone, replaced."

"Replaced with what?"

Barren smirked. "A very stubborn girl who challenged the wrongs I committed, and asked questions I never wanted to ask myself." He turned his gaze to her. "Because for so long I fought any voice of reason, and wanted nothing other than to cause pain, because I never realized that pain cannot be eased by pain."

The warmest smile spread across Larkin's face, and then she giggled. "Barren Reed, do you like me?"

Barren hesitated for a moment, and then tried to move his gaze from her face, but Larkin would not have him averting his eyes. She reached for him so he would look at her again, and brushed his hair from his face. She was reminded of their time in the Cliffs. She'd watched him brush his hair behind his ear and she shivered as she mimicked the intimate gesture.

There was no thought to what she did next. She pulled him to her, her lips crashing against his clumsily. He tasted of sea salt, which left her craving more of him. He was everything she'd never had—dry lips, rough face, callous hands, but he was passionate and somehow gentle as his fingers laced with her hair. And then the kiss became his, as he nudged her lips open, his tongue seeking hers. Her hands moved through his tangled hair, grasping the strands as if they were the last link to her sanity. She'd never experienced this feeling before, a fire in the pit of her stomach—it erupted and spread to her mouth, fueling her kiss, and making her brave. Larkin shivered as a low growl escaped Barren's lips, and she found that her heart raced with the excitement of hearing it again.

When her hands came to rest on either side of his face, Barren's hands found them, and suddenly he pulled away, looking at her questioningly.

"Weren't you shackled to the wall just like me?"

Larkin laughed.

"When I was young, I was locked in my room as a punishment by my father. In a defiant move, I sat at the lock until I figured out how to pick it, and I have carried this little spec of metal with me ever since." She withdrew a thin piece of iron.

"And there is our little bit of hope," he said. Reaching forward, he pressed his lips against her forehead.

Chapter Twenty-Six
STORM

Natherious stared at Barren's sketchbook, examining every picture.

"I never knew Barren paid attention to anyone but William." He paused. "Oh, and Larkin Lee."

Datherious went from pacing before the desk to peering over Nath's shoulder at the drawing of Larkin. He chuckled. "Such a lovely woman. Too bad her reputation will be ruined after this. She could have been my wife."

"I'm not certain Christopher would have approved."

Dath scoffed. "We are the king's sons, we do not ask, we take."

Datherious's eyes moved back to the portrait of Larkin. "It would be such a waste to see her reduced to the status of a working woman for her involvement with Barren Reed. Perhaps I will take pity on her."

"She will not want *your* pity," replied Natherious. "Even if you do kill Barren Reed."

"Father planned his death in Estrellas," said Dath. "Cas was to take care of him, but pretty Larkin got in the way of that, and ruined our plans."

"Well, the hemlock was still administered," Nath pointed out. "A partial success, because even Alder couldn't cure him completely."

Datherious rolled his eyes, but said nothing to his brother. He didn't understand—the point was that Barren should have died a long time ago, and now Tetherion wanted him brought back to Maris alive. There was something about having to bring Barren all the way back to Maris that Datherious didn't like. Rumors would spread fast across the Orient that Barren had been captured; it could make the trek back home rather difficult. It would be better if he died on this unnamed island.

"Do you think it was strange that our mother did not approach us while we were in Aurum?" Nath ventured to ask.

"Were you even aware of her?"

"No, but—"

"Then why does it matter?"

Nath shrugged. "She was our mother."

"She was a means of accomplishing a task," said Dath. "Her

purpose went no further. Tetherion was an adequate parent."

Nath said nothing. They both knew they were in this situation to betray Barren. It had been their job to maintain their location, and give it away when needed. Nath had not fallen into the task easily, and he really had no reason to—he would never be king, being the youngest twin.

The door to the cabin opened and shut and the thud of boots crossed the floor. Now and then, the click of his cane against the wood sounded between the shuffling of his feet. Tension immediately filled the room as Christopher Lee made his way toward the twins. The three did not get along, and they didn't pretend to. Most of their time was spent ignoring one another. Christopher stopped before the desk and glared at Datherious.

"Lord Lee," Datherious acknowledged the old man with a nod. "Shouldn't you be manning the helm?"

"Do you really think leaving the pirates below deck to plan their escape is a good idea?"

Datherious chuckled darkly. "What are they going to do? We stripped them of their weapons and shackled their hands."

"You are making a mistake—not all pirates work together, but they do. They are probably devising a plan as we speak."

"I am not doubting their plans," said Datherious. "I am doubting their ability to do anything in their present state. If you are so concerned, Lord, then why don't you sit with them?"

Christopher scowled. "So what will you do when we arrive? Who will stay with them? And who will search the island?"

"You are mistaken if you think my brother and I will stay

behind. We have a duty to our father—really, I am not sure why you are here."

"Why *are* you here?" asked Natherious, lowering Barren's sketchbook and staring at the lord.

Christopher narrowed his eyes. "You are both childish. You know nothing about what your father and I have done to get this far, and here you are, taking the weight of what you are about to encounter without consideration, without care."

"I think you are afraid," said Datherious. He dropped his hand from his chin, and then took slow steps toward the old man. "I'm not sure why you have been around here so long. The bloodstone is obviously of no use to you, and you've never been here for our father, have you? You *hate* him."

Christopher's eyes were pale, and he didn't look at the young twin.

"See," Dath said lightly, backing away. "I think when your wife died, you swore revenge. I think that's why you are still here. It could have all been prevented, you know—had *Kenna* listened to father."

"She would have died either way," said Christopher slowly, almost sadly.

"What care would you have had, had you not loved her?" the twin paused and rubbed his whiskered chin. "What good came of it anyway? Your daughter is a disloyal brat. Her reputation is ruined, tainted. She will never be anything in Maris now."

Christopher raised his head slowly to meet Datherious's gaze. He was still smiling, mocking the lord, waiting for him to snap.

The dark twin was succeeding—he could see the old man's eyes burn with rage.

"Unless…."

"We do not bargain with my daughter, Datherious Reed."

"No?" the prince furrowed his brows. "Did you not bargain with William? Murder Jess Reed in exchange for her hand in marriage?"

"A marriage I knew would not last."

"It will not last now—her affection has turned to Barren. I suppose girls make mistakes. She has merely fallen into the trap Barren has led her into. He does not love her, she will see. Once he is dead."

Christopher gnashed his teeth together, glaring at the prince. "Barren may die, but my daughter will not see a future with you."

Datherious shrugged. "Then she will die, too."

"You wouldn't dare."

The twin raised his hands in defense. "If she is not my wife, she is nothing to me."

Christopher moved his cane into both hands—it was his instinct, but as he did, a dangerous smirk spread across Datherious's face.

"Careful, Lord. I am a prince, and the definition of treason can include raising arms against royalty."

"I gave your king my *life*," said Christopher through his teeth. "I will not give you my daughter, too."

"You really think she'll come back to you after this? She has a choice now—she has always had a choice, you just kept her sheltered, immobile. Not teaching her how to swim…that was a good trick. It kept her away from pirates for seventeen years, but I am afraid Barren has done what you would not."

Christopher turned from the twin and headed for the door. "What are you going to do? Go get her? She is my prisoner—a fugitive until I say otherwise."

The old man stood rigid, angry, but just as he was about to turn and face Datherious again, a knock sounded at the door and one of the privateers appeared.

"Your majesties, Lord," he bowed. "Better come take a look at this."

The three men filed out of the captain's quarters. They didn't need to go far to see what the privateer had been talking about— it was right before them. It was night, and all around was darkness, except for the horizon, where light ripped through the sky, illuminating it. The clouds were like billows of smoke piled upon one another. It was both frightening and deadly, and none of the men onboard wanted to go near it.

"There's no way we'll make it through that storm. Our mast will be the first thing to fall," said the privateer.

"Were you asked for your opinion?" Datherious's dark voice cut the air. The man shrunk away, and Datherious's blue-gray eyes turned to Christopher Lee.

"Can you navigate us through that?"

The old man scoffed. "You sailed with Barren Reed and cannot navigate a ship through a storm?"

"*I asked you.*"

"Of course I can't—all that I remembered from those days are gone."

Datherious looked at his brother, and the brother shook his head. "Not me, but there is one who could do it."

The twin waited.

"Barren."

"I will not bring him to this helm. He will kill us all for vengeance!"

Natherious shrugged. "He has a vested interested in reaching that island just as you do."

The twin thought for a moment, running his finger across his bottom lip. "Hmm. Bring me Barren Reed!"

***

Larkin traced the scars that bubbled across Barren's skin. He watched her do it for a long moment, thinking it strange that she felt so comfortable touching them. Each scar had a story, and they were mostly all well-deserved. Some were small and unthreatening, some were long and frightening.

She started on the path of one scar that ran from his thumb and disappeared beneath the sleeve of his shirt. It had been a deep cut, severing muscles in his shoulder. Leaf worked long and tirelessly to save his arm, and he came out fine in the end.

"My skin is a map of scars," Barren said quietly. "None have been good. Those that look the best were mostly Leaf's handiwork. I have him to thank for my survival."

"He is a good man."

Barren smirked. "He is an Elf."

Larkin stopped tracing his scars for a moment and looked at Barren.

"Was Estrellas the first place you thought you might die?"

"Hardly the first where it was possible, but I have never thought of death in those situations."

Larkin's fingers moved to trace his palm, causing an electric sensation to run from his stomach, through his chest and flush his cheeks.

"If we do make it to the bloodstone, have you decided what you will do with it?" asked Larkin.

This was the question Barren was dreading. He would have to tell her—the only way they could destroy it was together, with their blood, but that could mean their deaths, and Barren would not ask her to pledge to that uncertainty. "Barren?" she shifted to look at him, seeing worry pull at his features. "What is it?"

He rubbed his face before speaking, as if trying to erase what he knew was clearly written in his features. "Destroying the bloodstone is a harder decision than it seems, Larkin."

"How? There must be a way! You cannot hand it over to Tetherion."

"It can be destroyed," Barren said evenly. "But dark magic is tricky and there is no way to tell what will happen after it's destroyed. If it were only my life in question, I would destroy the stone without a second thought, but that is not the case."

Larkin narrowed her eyes, and Barren could tell she had already guessed what he was going to say, but she asked anyway. "What do you mean?"

Barren stared at her for a long moment, taking in her fierce gaze.

"The bloodstone can only be destroyed if it comes into contact with the blood of Sysara and Kenna—our blood."

"And that means we may die?"

Barren nodded.

"Then we have to take that chance, Barren."

"*You* should not have to lose your life for this. This isn't...this wasn't your doing."

"And it wasn't yours, either," Larkin reminded. "But what Tetherion does affects both of us, and if we don't at least try to end this thing...he will defeat us and everyone we care about."

Barren swallowed hard. "It's not so simple. It's the magic—that's what determines my life or death—your life or death. Lord Alder said that if it chooses to let us live, it's expecting something in return. I can't imagine what's worse, dying or being a slave to such a terrible thing."

"Well, it doesn't sound like there's a choice," Larkin argued. "Barren, I know you feel you need to protect me because of the code, but I hardly think that applies now that we're held hostage by my father and the twins."

"It's not about the code, Larkin," Barren said and then he bit his bottom lip, as if trying to stop the words from coming out of his mouth. "I don't want you to die. I mean...it matters to me that you live."

It wasn't about the code anymore. It hadn't been for a long time. He watched Larkin as she leaned in toward him, and he was sure she would kiss him again, but in the darkness beyond the yellow lanterns, a loud boom escaped into the air, and two men came forward, their eyes set on Barren. They jerked Barren from the floor and unlocked his shackles.

"His majesty wants to see you," one said, his voice rasped.

"What are you doing? Leave him alone!" Larkin cried. She reached for one of the guards, but he slapped her away. "Better not defend him, Lady. You're in enough trouble."

They dragged Barren away, and all his crew could do was watch and wonder what the twins needed with him.

Barren entered the hostile night. The wind picked up and gusted over the ship. The sky pulsed with fire, just waiting to explode in pounding thunder. Barren recalled Devon's words, and knew this storm was not good—they'd be lucky to survive it, and their only hope lay in the fact that this ship was built for battle.

The guards kicked Barren in the back of his knees so he fell before the twins.

"What do you want?"

"So much anger," Datherious chided. "You must learn to control your temper; you are speaking to your superior."

"Traitors can never be superiors."

"Oh, but you are a pirate—everyone surpasses you."

"You already forgot so much of your past."

"I was only following orders from my father; I was never loyal to you."

As Barren sat on his knees, large drops of rain began to fall. They were like ice as they hit him, increasing as the seconds passed.

"So why pay so much attention to me now?" he asked.

"We need you to sail this ship to the coordinates you provided."

"No," said Barren evenly.

"You want everyone on board to die?"

"If the Orient wants you to pass, you will."

"This is not the Orient's war—it is your mother's."

"If I am at the helm, there is no guarantee we will make it," said Barren.

"Then I suppose we will meet our end."

The guards jerked Barren to his feet and hauled him to the helm. Barren placed his hands on the wet spindles, but the guards weren't finished with him yet. They wrapped rope around his wrists and tied them to the wheel.

Barren glared at Datherious. "You know—just in case you try anything."

"Like jumping off this ship in a raging storm?"

Datherious shrugged. "You never know."

Barren watched as the twins disappeared from view, preferring to stay warm and safe in their cabin. Even as captain, Barren never left his crew alone on deck in a storm, but he expected no such loyalty from the twins. He set his sights ahead, having the coordinates memorized by heart, and challenged the storm.

"Tie down your cannons! Anything of use to you!" Barren called. "And when you have nothing left to save, save yourselves!" From experience, Barren knew just how merciless nature could be.

The first harsh wave rocked the vessel, and water rushed into the night sky, flooding the deck. The privateers were all frightened, and held onto anything they could for dear life. Never had they seen a storm like this.

The rain came down in thick sheets, coating Barren's vision. All he could do was keep his arms strong and resist the oceans push and pull. Wave after wave rose to crash upon them. Barren lost his footing and fell to the ground, his wrists straining against the ropes tied to the wheel.

Steadying himself, he focused on the battle again. Before him, he watched a mirage of light converge. He knew somehow that this was the end. If he didn't get through this, he would have failed, and the Orient would leave them in limbo, lost in the breadth of darkness. As the ship was consumed in light and water, Barren was also—he and all on board. His only consciousness was silence—stark, deafening.

Chapter Twenty-Seven
GRAVEYARD

Barren lay there for a moment, his body weak and sore. As he opened his eyes and tried to move, he was overcome with pain. He waited for the spasms to pass before he moved again and made it to his feet, stretching his back. Somehow in all the madness of the storm, he had broken free from the helm, and now red marks surfaced on his wrists. He looked around, and could do nothing but stare.

Before him were hundreds of wrecked ships, jutting out from the Orient and into thick fog. It was a graveyard of wood, sails, and debris. A few of the ships' masts still rose from the water, tattered flags rippling in the air. Barren shuddered—he remembered this, though it had only been in his nightmares. It unnerved him to see that this was real, and he wondered how many had died in these waters. As he observed the scene, he swore he heard a low, haunting melody. As if ghosts were roaming about him. He didn't like it.

"Why aren't we moving?" Datherious demanded, coming out of his cabin. "Where the hell are we?"

Datherious grew quiet as he saw what was around him—there was something silencing about the graveyard—perhaps it was the realization that they could have joined the throngs of sailors resting beneath them.

"This is where we're supposed to be," said Barren. "The island must be ahead of us."

Datherious's dark eyes fell upon Barren. "Then make this ship move."

Barren wasn't even sure if it could. From the looks of it, they had lost most of the crew. Only a few haggard men, Christopher Lee and the twins were on board.

There was barely a breeze, but the few men who were left, freed the sails. They were off to a slow start, which was probably best, as Barren had to cut through a maze of wrecked ships and their ancient debris—it was good he had spent so much time among the Cliffs of Maris. As they crept along, Barren had the haunting feeling that his father had done this very thing.

No one spoke as they passed the graveyard, even Datherious and Natherious remained on deck, staring out at the destruction. The only person who didn't seem affected was Christopher Lee, and Barren wondered if he was slowly remembering what had taken place all those years ago. He seemed troubled and pained.

Barren peered through the mist as it swirled around them like smoke, looking for any sign of land. It was no use, however. All he could see was a wall of gray.

"Must've been fate that got us through the storm," said Natherious.

"Yes, but for who?" questioned Lee.

Datherious smirked. "I think you used up your turn when you got here the first time. It's someone else's turn now."

"Do you even know what you are looking for? Or the significance of such an object?"

"A stone composed of dark magic that will give our line invincibility—pretty significant."

"You think Tetherion wants you to rule?" Christopher laughed. "Tetherion will let no one but himself come into possession of the stone. He has no wish to share power with *you*."

Datherious' eyes turned dark—it was a very calm anger, eating away at his irises.

"The stone only makes my father invincible. It does not make him immortal," Datherious replied curtly.

Shrouded in thick fog, the graveyard seemed to last for an eternity. Barren soon noticed that the amount of debris was lessening, and that the fog was dissipating. The first thing he could make out in the distance was the tall peak of a mountain, then a thick curtain of greenery, and last a white strip of beach. The fog slipped away, and in this state, the island exuded peace and serenity, but Barren had a bad feeling about what lay beyond that shore. As he stared, flashes of his nightmares reeled through his mind. He remembered standing on the sandy beach, staring wide-eyed at the graveyard, and watching his father and William fight.

As Barren and the rest of the twins' crew prepared to dock, he noticed Datherious growing tense. Now it had come to it—the race. Who would stay and who would go? There were three people on this ship who needed the bloodstone, and all with different intentions.

Barren began moving toward the rail of the ship when a harsh voice cut through the air.

"Where do you think you're going?"

Datherious had turned and stood with his sword drawn. "You don't get to leave this ship, and neither do you." He looked at Christopher Lee. "My brother and I are the only two who are going."

"And how are you even going to find what you're looking for?" asked Barren.

"It can't be too hard—it's a small island, and I will not risk the loss of such a powerful weapon to my enemies," Datherious said through his teeth. "Get him!"

In response to Datherious's command, the door of the hatch flew open, and Barren's crew pushed through. The sounds of battle ensued. Larkin ran for Barren, tossing him his sword. He set his gaze on the twins and lifted his blade. They were already pushing toward the rail of the ship, but before they could make it to the edge, Leaf landed lightly before them, an arrow drawn back on his bow.

Natherious swung at the Elf, and he jumped from his place, landing behind the twins. He used his bow to strike Datherious on the back of the knees. The twin fell and Leaf stood back, drawing his sword. Barren hurried to help.

"Bastard son of an Elf!" Datherious spat, standing on his wobbly legs. "I'll see to it that your people suffer!"

Datherious charged at Barren, and Natherious at Leaf. Barren attacked fiercely—going for the shoulders, the neck, and the hip—each blow Datherious deflected with a fierce counter. If Barren could keep up the strength, he would do this all day, if only to keep Datherious from coming into possession of the bloodstone. Because if that happened, there was no way they could win.

Over the twin's shoulder, he saw Larkin jump to the rail. She glanced back at Barren before she dove into the Orient. Barren paid for that distraction as he took a hit to his shoulder. Datherious pushed him back and Barren stumbled and fell. Finally free, Datherious took off for the sea. Barren reached for the twin's ankle, causing him to fall on his hands and knees. Datherious rolled over, giving out a harsh growl. He swung his blade at Barren, and he was forced to let go of Datherious's ankle in order avoid the blow.

The twin rose to his feet and brought his sword down upon Barren. At the last minute, he rolled away, and found that Datherious's blade crash with another. When he got to his feet, he found Hollow standing in his place, sword interlocked with Datherious's.

"Barren, go!" he commanded as he entered into a fight with the dark twin, a challenging smirk on his face. Barren obeyed and hurried to follow Larkin.

When he hit the water, he felt that he couldn't swim fast enough. His arms were weak from fighting Datherious so hard, and his body was still stiff from injuries sustained in Estrellas—it had been a couple of days since he'd drunk one of Leaf's draughts. He was regretting that now.

When he reached shore, he dragged his feet in the sand and paused for a moment, looking about. He'd been here before, but only in his nightmares. William and Jess fought upon this island. This is where William had told him how different they were. Even if all of that had been a nightmare, he knew his father had walked on this shore before, and so had his mother. His eyes shifted to the encroaching forest, and he was overwhelmed with a feeling of loss.

"Barren!" Larkin's voice snapped him back into reality. "We must hurry!"

He nodded, and together they disappeared into the tall forest.

***

As soon as they were among the trees, everything outside seemed to disappear, and it was as if this forest wasn't even a part of the peaceful island they had beheld. It was dark; mist floated between the trees—some massive and old, others scraggly and crooked. The ground was uneven; at the very mouth of the forest they could tell it was going to be a tough run. Part of the wood seemed to rise up like a hill, and moss covered rocks dotted the landscape.

Barren drew his sword and began cutting at the long stringy vines that hung down from the dense canopy above; Larkin followed suit. There had to be millions of them, tangled within the thick mass of leaves above. Not only that, but tall stems with thorns grew up from the ground and wrapped themselves around anything within their reach.

"There has to be an easier way through this," Larkin said, as she shoved vines aside while stepping on a thorn bush. They had managed to make their way up the hill, and now it was steadily declining into a valley—the bottom filled with a dense fog.

Barren shook his head. "We have only to be mindful of our target. The mountain consumes most of this island." Larkin looked ahead and saw nothing—the lack of visibility made her feel like they'd be stuck here forever. Maybe that was the point of this forest. If one did manage to past the threatening storm, they would get lost here and die. She shivered, wrapping her arms around herself.

Before diving down into the valley, Larkin looked over her shoulder, fearful that the twins would appear out of nowhere. As she faced forward, she felt the silk of a spider's web on her face and screamed. Brushing the threads away from her face with fury, she dropped her blade. Barren stared at her for a moment, and then chuckled.

"Really? After everything you've gone through—a spider web

unravels you?"

"Hush! Look at this place, can you imagine how big the spiders are?" she hissed. Picking up her sword, she continued forward, brushing more invisible webs from her body. She could still hear Barren laughing at her. "You know, you have to be afraid of something. Pirate's aren't fearless."

Barren's response was only laughter as they continued down the hill. Larkin watched her feet as she moved over the ground. The trees above were deep green, but foliage from years before still littered the forest floor, decaying where it lay, glistening as if it had just rained.

Walking with her head down for the moment, she was unaware that Barren had stopped. He put his hand out, and she came to a halt, looking up slowly. The first thing she noticed was that they had made it to the bottom of the valley, and the mist rose above them like a halo of clouds. It was beautiful and ominous. Next, she noticed a figure before them, and her eyes grew wide.

There, her father appeared—like her and Barren, he was wet, and he held his sword aloft. His stare was cold, and she knew by the way he stood, he would not leave them without a fight. Larkin just wasn't sure who he wanted at the end of his blade.

"After everything I taught you, this is what you choose? A good for nothing murderer? You disgrace me!"

"You made him a murderer!" Larkin could feel her skin burn and her eyes blaze with anger. It was he who was responsible for creating the monster inside Barren—it had been him all along.

"You took his father away—"

"And I would do it all over again!" the old man snarled.

"What? Kill the wrong man for your own gain? A man who trusted you as his loyal friend? Remind me again of your motive—revenge, right? Against the man who did not murder *my* mother!"

"Don't pretend you understand!"

"You never gave me a chance. What did you think? That I would question your wrongs?"

"You questioned nothing until you met him! And suddenly I am your enemy!"

"You are my father!" Larkin said through her teeth. "But you do not know me, and I cannot trust you. If I am a disgrace to you, then it is a disgrace to be your daughter. You preyed on an innocent child, took advantage of his insecurities! Do you not realize the damage you have done?"

"Do not blame this pirate's actions on me!" Christopher pointed his long, bony finger at Barren, who stood quietly by while Larkin engaged her father. His sword was still drawn, however, and he was ready to fight the second Christopher attempted to move.

"At least this pirate knows what he is fighting for! What has motivated you all this time? Was it power? How could you use my mother's memory in such a way?"

"You are both children, completely unaware of what you have stumbled into. This is much bigger than your petty crush, and you will only learn that with his death."

Just as Christopher raised his sword however, both Barren and Larkin's eyes grew wide with fear. Barren stuck his arm out and pushed Larkin back a little.

"Don't move," he ordered Christopher.

The lord laughed. "Are you afraid?"

"No, I am not afraid of you, but I am afraid of snakes."

Christopher Lee chuckled. "A pirate, afraid of a snake? Where is it?"

Just as he asked, a terrifying hiss escaped from behind him. It was almost thunderous as it echoed in the quiet clearing. Christopher turned slowly and was met with the beady black eyes of a huge snake; its body was the size of a large tree trunk. It came out of the mist, suspended from one of the branches above, causing the limb to moan as it leveled itself with Christopher, ready to strike.

"Get down!" Barren snarled, and Christopher collapsed, just as the snake snapped. The old man rolled to his hands and knees and hurried away as fast as he could. The snake didn't go after him. It moved forward, toward Barren and Larkin, its scale-encrusted body slithering over the branch. It was brown in color, but at the top of its head and gliding all the way down his back, were black diamonds. By the size of it, Larkin guessed it could eat all three of them and still be unsatisfied.

"H-how did your father ever get through this forest?" she managed to whisper.

"I'm not sure," he replied slowly. "But on the count of three, take a step back. One, two, three…"

But as Barren began to move, the snake opened its wide, fanged mouth. Barren pushed Larkin out of the way and slid to the side as the snake struck, but the creature was prepared, and twisted, following the pirate as he went. Barren lashed out at the snake and missed as it raised itself above his head, hissing again. Barren jumped out of the way, hitting the trunk of a tree as he fell.

As he tried to compose himself from the fall, the snake dove after him. Just as its huge jaw was about to capture Barren within its mouth, the beast was distracted as a large rock ricocheted off its head and landed near Barren. The snake turned, now occupied with Larkin, who just seemed to realize what she had done. A hiss escaped its mouth as its slimy belly brushed over the tree's bark. The snake was fast, and opened its jaws wide, ready to engulf the girl without a second thought. Larkin drew her sword and braced herself for whatever would follow.

Without warning, Christopher jumped between them. Wielding his sword, he swung, cutting off one of the snake's fangs. The reptile convulsed for a moment and an unnatural shriek filled the air. Its thick mass fell from the tree and piled upon itself.

It wasn't the end. As it recovered from the pain and shock, it rose again, leveling with both Larkin and her father. Blood dripped from one side of the snake's mouth, landing on the ground before them and splashing their clothes. Suddenly, the snake jerked and let out a gurgling cry—Barren pushed his blade through its slimy belly. While it was distracted, Christopher grabbed his daughter's wrist and pulled her away from the scene, through the thick fog and up a steady hill. Larkin tried to pull free from her father's grip. "Let me go! Barren is back there with that monster!"

"And if he dies, it will be of little consequence to me!"

"Everything you have ever done is of little consequence to you! What about me?" Larkin ripped her arm free from his grasp.

"You obviously don't know what's best for you!"

"And why do you think you have a better idea?" asked a voice from behind Christopher. The lord whirled around to face Barren. He stood with his sword raised.

"You! You have been nothing but a burden to my existence since you were born! It ends today!"

Christopher brandished his sword, and charged at the pirate. Barren spread his feet apart and prepared for the attack, but the sound of rustling leaves and bending branches caused their attention to be diverted. They paused, watching the thick air around them, waiting for the snake to attack, but all went silent again.

The group relaxed a little and then the snake exploded from the trees, wrapped its massive body around Christopher and slithered away, taking the screaming man with it.

For a moment, there was complete silence as the reality of what took place settled upon them. Larkin's body trembled. Would that be the end of her father? Was his final breath to be one of venom and blood?

"Larkin, we must go!" Barren called. She snapped her head in his direction as if coming out of a trance. Without a second thought, she ran toward him and together they disappeared into the woods, cutting their way through the tangle of forest as fast as they could before the snake came after them—or worse, before the twins caught up to them. By the time they stopped, they were both out of breath and unsure of where they were.

"I can't wait to be out of this place," said Barren as he looked around for a direction to go—they didn't seem to be getting any closer to the mountain. Everything around them was dense forest, and it seemed to have gotten darker somehow. Hadn't Barren said the mountain took up most of the island? Then why did it seem that this forest went on forever? But as Larkin looked up, she spotted something through the curtain of vines—a castle. She parted the curtain of vines and stepped through, disappearing immediate from sight.

***

"Larkin!" Barren hurried after her, but as he stepped through the vines, he stood beside her at the base of a mountain. His eyes traveled up the structure before him, in awe of its grandeur. The face of a castle stared back at him, carved out of the side of the rock. It was both massive and beautiful. Tall pinnacles reached into the sky with the rest of the mountain, and dark windows peered like evil eyes into the forest behind him. He felt an overwhelming sense of pressure all around—as if the power and magic contained within wished to explode upon the entire island. A crumbled and steep staircase led to a large arched doorway. Gargoyles guarded the entrance with razor teeth and dead eyes.

The forest, over years, had begun to consume the castle. Ivy and moss covered portions of the stone, eating away at the exterior. Barren swallowed hard. He wasn't sure he was prepared for this, and even if he entered the castle, how would he know in which direction to go?

Shouts escaped from behind them and Larkin's hand squeezed around Barren's. "We have to go!"

They hurried up the crumbled steps and into the darkness of the castle. Rot and decay met them on the inside, and the only light was from the windows, creating a dim path to follow. For a moment, Barren just stood in the entryway, staring at what was once his mother's home. It was ghostly, and he *sensed* the familiarity, but knew he had never been here.

A wide corridor extended to their left and right, and windows overlooked the forest they'd come from. Darkened chandeliers with crystal drops decorated the ceiling and every now and then the sun would catch the tears and cast rainbows on the walls. The floor was covered with dust and bugs. Barren ran his foot over it and white marble peered up at him from underneath. A wide staircase rose before him, which was also covered in dust.

As he stood here, he felt something familiar, but it wasn't in his surroundings. It was something invisible—a force. It was power. The same power he'd felt in the presence of Illiana, only this was stronger and more frightening.

"Barren, we don't have time! Do something," Larkin begged, she was looking behind her, out the entrance.

"I—" he hesitated and then focused more on the power he felt from within the castle. While it seemed to curl around him, as if drawn to him, he could tell it was centralized. "This way!"

He headed for the staircase and with each step, a cloud of dust rose around him. As they ascended, the light in the castle dimmed—they were moving away from the windows, losing the light of the day. When he came to the end of the stairs, he stood in the heavy atmosphere, unable to tell in which direction he should go.

A long and dark hall extended on either side of him. Before him were two large doors—they were closed, and they seemed to produce the coldest feeling Barren had ever felt—it was worse than ice—it was like the emptiness of death. He fought to feel the centralized power he'd noticed at the base of the stairs. At the moment, all he could feel was the power wrapping around him, constricting his movements and suffocating him. Then he realized *it* was trying to confuse him. *It* didn't want to be found. *It* didn't want to die.

Barren opened his eyes. Of course the bloodstone would feel like emptiness—because that's what it was: a soulless gem that had stolen the very essence of his mother's life.

He moved toward the doors just as Datherious's voice sounded at the base of the steps. "Follow them now!"

Barren and Larkin hurried inside the room and shut the doors tightly behind them. When they turned, they were faced with a large throne room. Columns lined both sides of the room, and light streamed in from narrow windows. Aged flags hung bearing the symbol of a tree—the same tree on Devon's arm, the symbol of Aurum. At the far end of the room, there was a single throne—the strangest throne Barren had ever seen. It looked to be composed of clear sea glass, polished to a shine and made to look like water. Barren moved toward the throne and stopped. He could feel both the emptiness and the power strengthen from the corner of the room. There, he noticed an open door.

Barren's heart raced in his chest. He couldn't risk discovering the bloodstone with the twins so close in tow. He would have to wait until they couldn't follow.

"What are we going to do?" Larkin asked.

Barren turned to face her and withdrew his sword. "We fight them here," he said. "We can't risk getting any closer to the bloodstone."

Larkin nodded and raised her blade. They stood apart from one another and waited.

It wasn't long before the doors moved, groaning as they opened for the traitorous twins. Datherious entered first, his features twisted in anger until he saw Barren and Larkin waiting for him, at which point he seemed to relax. His cold laugh filled the space between them, and Barren ground his teeth together. He hated that he'd been unable to see through them. Most of their success had to do with their quiet disposition, a characteristic Barren was discovering, Datherious didn't actually possess. He strode into the room, head held high, basking in his triumph as his father had done after boarding the ship. He seemed to think he'd won.

"Oh, this is quite entertaining—didn't you two fight so hard to be enemies?" Datherious stopped only a few feet from them. Natherious lingered behind him, weapon drawn. "Perhaps if you had not been so...aware of each other, you might have noticed our antics sooner."

"It was my trust in you that blinded me," Barren said evenly.

Datherious barked laughter. "It was your naivety—how could you really think your *royal* family would stoop to the level of piracy? *Despicable*."

Barren found himself smiling. "It wasn't all that surprising considering my father was a *prince*."

"Oh yes, he was a prince—but a traitorous bastard, nevertheless!" Datherious hissed. "Your father is a disgrace to the Reed line, and you've followed in his footsteps just the same!"

Barren gripped his sword tighter. "At least my father didn't need magic to be strong!"

Datherious's eyes narrowed and he drew his sword slowly. The ring was steady in Barren's ears. "And look at where it got him—dead!"

Barren struck, and their swords slid against each other. His eyes worked fast, seeing openings where he could cut at Datherious's body and disable him quickly. When he heard another set of swords join him, he knew Natherious had engaged Larkin, and while he wanted to look away from Datherious, the angry gleam in his eyes told Barren not to.

Datherious moved in to strike at Barren, but the pirate jumped back, and the tip of the Datherious's blade nicked his arm. Barren had never fought with either twin, and he had a feeling they'd never actually fought to their full potential until now. Datherious kept his moves tight and calculated. Barren struck hard and fast, moving forward slowly, forcing Datherious away from the power that pulsed behind him. As Barren went in for another strike, Datherious slipped out of the way and Barren was forced to twist, meeting Datherious's blade before it lodged itself in his shoulder. He couldn't afford to make those kinds of mistakes.

Their blades slid from one another and they stared, gauging the other's next move.

"Why are you fighting your father's battles?" Barren took in a ragged breath.

"My father is king. He does not fight his own battles."

"He is a coward! He seeks magic to ensure he keeps his throne when practicing as a just and kind king would solidify his reign all the same!"

"A just and kind king cannot survive in a world like this," Datherious wiped his mouth with the back of his hand and then lifted his blade. "You strive to separate yourself from us, Barren, but you have been just as ruthless."

Datherious attacked, and Barren knew instantly that the twin was trying to pin him against one of the columns—he could feel the growing pressure of something behind him. Datherious struck, aiming for Barren's shoulder, but he moved in time so the blade hit the stone. Barren jumped back, putting space between them, and Datherious laughed.

"Do you feel threatened?"

Datherious didn't wait for Barren to respond. He advanced upon him, using his blade with full force, trying to disarm him quickly, but doing so left him vulnerable to injury. Barren's blade slashed his shoulder as soon as it was open. His cousin fell back, but Barren couldn't allow him to recover. He advanced, following him, fighting him fast and hard until his back was pinned against the column. Then, gripping his sword with all his strength, he struck it against Datherious's, drawing his dagger from its sheath at his waist. He ran the knife along Datherious's knees. The twin started to buckle to the floor, but Barren held him against the stone column, sword pushed into his neck.

"No!" he commanded. "You will stand until I say otherwise!" Then he stabbed his smaller blade through Datherious's shoulder. The twin cried out in pain, and his sword clattered to the ground.

Barren bound Datherious's wrists together with the rope he kept in his pocket, then he moved to Larkin who stood with her sword at Natherious's throat. The screams of his brother had been enough to distract him so that Larkin ended up with the upper hand.

"Give me your scarf," Barren said.

Larkin untied it from her waist and handed it to him. He used it to bind Natherious's wrists together and then dragged him to his brother's side. He searched both twins for weapons and tossed what he found out the window to be eaten by the wild forest. Before he left them, he pulled his blade from Datherious's shoulder, satisfied when a gritty cry escaped is lips.

And now it was time. Barren moved toward the door at the back of the room. It was nestled in the corner—an escape for the one who occupied that throne. In his heart, he knew his mother had sat there. He hadn't thought of whether or not she was seen as a ruler—but she'd been the strongest. She was the one they'd looked up to. She had died to protect the Orient from Tetherion.

The last thought made him grip the hilt of his sword tighter.

There was nothing special about the door, except that the air that met his face as he approached was cold. While it did not ease the sweat on his brow, it did make his hair stand on ends. He entered the room, Larkin following behind him. They moved down a short hallway. It was dark, and everything seemed to be tinged with red. He couldn't figure out where the light was coming from until the hall ended and they came to a circular room.

The red light spilled forth from lanterns that were hung from chains about the room at different levels. It cast everything in a muted blood-red color, which Barren found turned his stomach once he saw what occupied the space. A large gold and ruby tomb rested upon a raised pyre. Snaking their way around the base of the tomb were lilies and ivy and they seemed as fresh as the day they had been picked.

Somehow he knew it was his mother who rested in that tomb. It was the feeling about him—the caress of the power that heated his face. Mixing with that power was the coldness of the bloodstone and he hated that he had to feel both things together.

Barren swallowed hard and he glanced at Larkin.

"Go," she said quietly.

"Can you feel it?" he asked.

She nodded, but she didn't look at him. Her eyes were transfixed upon the strange altar before them.

It took Barren a moment to move forward. He was going to have to look down upon his mother—a woman he'd never seen in the flesh before. He felt the acid in his stomach churn violently and he wanted to vomit.

He moved up onto the platform where his mother's tomb rested and noticed glass covered its length. His breath caught as his eyes beheld what lay beneath: a woman barely aged in life much less in death. She was by far the fairest creature he had ever seen and her features radiated power. Her face was sculpted— high cheekbones, full lips. Her hair was golden and rested in waves over her shoulders. She was dressed in white, and her hands lay over her immobile stomach. At the center of her chest, an ornate compass rested at the end of a length of chain.

Barren wasn't sure why, but he wanted it—it made something in his memory spark; as a child he would grasp the pendant while his father held him. That was it. It had belonged to his father.

Placing his hands on the glass, he pushed, shifting the fragile sheet and pulling it from atop the coffin.

"Barren, what are you doing?"

He ignored Larkin as he managed to lean the glass against the base of the coffin. He reached for the compass without much thought. The object was *cold* to the touch, almost painful, but still so beautiful. The face of the compass displayed the Elvish tree, the directions were inlaid with ruby, and the whole thing was encased in gold. Barren ran his finger over the glass front and shivered: this was a piece of his childhood.

Turning over the compass, he found a raw, red gem lodged in the back of the device. Its edges were jagged and ugly, and it was almost as if the thing pulsed. Suddenly, a shock raced through him and he knew that this was the bloodstone.

His eyes shifted, and his mother's body came into focus—the frightening image of a dusty corpse. Hollow eyes, fleshless face, and interlaced bony fingers. Barren staggered back, and fell, dropping the compass as he landed. It clinked against the stone floor, bouncing away from him. Barren reached for it, but he froze when a sword jammed itself between his fingers. Shaking with adrenaline, Barren looked up into his brother's eyes.

"William," he breathed. His brother was pale, and his shirt was stained with blood.

"What are you doing?"

Larkin drew her sword, but William looked over at her. "This is not your fight."

"He's right, Larkin," Barren said, and he moved to his feet slowly, drawing his sword. "Can I ask why?" Barren had resigned himself to letting his brother live. He thought he would change, and believed he could. Obviously that was not the case.

"Because I cannot let you live," he said. "Not with her."

His mouth quivered and Barren glanced back at Larkin. She stood on edge, her features tight with anger. "This should not be the end for you, William."

"You never know...maybe I'll win."

"She'll hate you...she will never love you."

"But she will not love you either."

"Death does not end affection, William."

William shivered noticeably, and Barren couldn't tell if it was from his words or the air.

"All I ever wanted was for him to love me like he loved you. And he couldn't. He saw me as a passionate, angry child. Now, after five years, I have to face the same thing again, only my fiancée finds you a better match than me. I cannot watch it again, I won't. I—It should have been you all those years ago. Why didn't I see that it should have been you?"

Again, Barren was reminded of the dream—when William fought Jess with anger and hate—the same hate that took Jess's life. William never changed, and his wish for acceptance, for power, for greatness, had led him to this.

"I am sorry, William."

That only seemed to trigger William's anger, and he attacked—and though this is what Barren had been waiting for since his father's death. He had none of the exhilaration that he had expected to feel as he fought for revenge. He knew this was wrong in every sense, and it took all his concentration to keep fighting. He watched William as he fought, angry and determined; wanting the fight to end as quickly as it had begun, but the brothers were evenly matched, and strangely in tune with each other's movements.

"I don't want to do this," Barren said as William's blade

clashed against his. He pushed his brother away.

"You spent your entire life preparing for this moment!" said William. "You can fight me this one time. You may never get this chance again."

For all the hatred Barren had built up, he couldn't find that anger now. Their blades met and retreated—it was like the ocean and the ship, one fighting to survive against the other's natural anger. Barren's sword glided across William's, and he latched onto the hilt, but just as Barren was about to rip the sword from William's hands, numbness overtook him and pain slid down his arm. He jerked, dropping his sword. For a moment, he didn't understand what was happening, and then he recalled Christopher Lee's words as he stuck him with the hemlock needle, "*The effects will be slow, but once they take hold, they will never let go.*"

Barren slid to the floor; he couldn't hold himself up anymore. On his knees, he was thrown back against the floor with a harsh kick to his chest. He lay on his back, the cold marble burrowing deep, and he felt like this might be his end. The only image above him was that of his brother holding the sword to his neck.

"This is a very dishonorable way to kill you," said William. "But I lost all dignity when Christopher betrayed me."

"What happened, William?" asked Barren slowly. "What made you hate our father?"

William ground his teeth and pointed at Sysara's coffin. "It was for her. His death was to avenge her."

"But it wasn't," Barren's voice was a hoarse whisper. "You

were jealous."

"I didn't want to kill him," William said quietly, and his mouth quivered. "I didn't. Did you see me? I was frightened by what I had done. I thought he would fight me. He would have won, Barren! He would have won!"

"He was cursed, William, and you approached him, wishing to fight out of hatred. Father warned you about that."

William pushed on the blade harder; his breath was harsh and shallow, as if he were suddenly possessed.

"Why are you doing this to me?"

Barren's eyes turned dark.

"Because I want you to understand how easily you disregarded my father for a man who only tortured you. Did you think you would find acceptance once Jess was gone? Did you find it in the false father who took you under his wing? Promised you a wife who does not love you? Did you?"

"You know nothing!"

William reared back, and Barren prepared himself for the blow—he expected this moment to go differently, but he had prepared for both possibilities. He would accept death. As he closed his eyes, he imagined his father before him, smiling, arms open. He was the image of Barren, only older. Barren felt young again as his father embraced him—a child of five, wrapping his arms around his father's neck and snuggling against his shoulder. This had been his comfort as a child.

A gasp escaped into the air and Barren ripped his eyes open, his pain reached a crescendo, and he could feel again as the numbness seeped out of him. Before him, silver erupted from William's stomach and disappeared with a jerk. William fell to his knees and then onto his face. Larkin stood wide-eyed behind him, her hands shook from the realization of what she had done. Barren moved quickly, pushing his brother onto his back. William stared back at him, his pupils swelled with the image of death.

"I—I—am sorry," William huffed, and tears streamed down his face. He took a final fearful breath, his eyes went blank, and his hands became cold in Barren's. The pirate sat for a moment, still and unsure, staring at his brother. Yes, he had imagined this moment much differently. If there was one thing he had learned, it was that revenge was not sweet, and right now the most dreadful feeling consumed him. His family—his mother, father and brother were gone. His uncle and cousins were traitors. Though he knew he wasn't alone, he couldn't shake that very feeling. Barren pressed his brother's eyes shut, and then he gently placed William's hand on his stomach.

He stood and turned to Larkin, tears streaked her face. They were quiet and sad.

"I...I..." she tried to speak but she couldn't find the words. She dropped her sword and her hands went to her mouth. "I couldn't let him kill you."

Barren understood her shock more than she knew. She'd only killed one person before, and that was out of self-defense. Now, after weeks of feeling torn at the idea of either of their deaths, Larkin had been the one to commit the deed.

Barren bent to pick up the compass. Securing his fingers around the bloodstone, he pulled it from its snug place. The stone sat in his hand, vibrating with life. Closing his fingers around it, he looked at Larkin again. She started to back away from him, fear clutched her, but he reached for her, taking her wrist, and pulling her into him, embracing her tightly. He kissed her forehead. "Do not apologize for saving my life, Larkin."

He released her, and bent, pulling a knife from his boot. "We have to end this. Larkin, I cannot promise we will live after. I don't know anything about what we're dealing with...but I know that if we are able to destroy this thing so that Tetherion never has its power, even if we die...it will all be worth it in the end. But I cannot ask you to die with me. All I need are a few drops of your blood...you can run away...run far away."

Larkin stared up at him for a moment, regarding his desperate expression. She reached carefully, pressing her hand to the side of his face. "We're in this together, Barren, and if I have learned anything about dark magic, it's that it won't matter how you use my blood to defeat this thing—either way, it can end my life."

He nodded, pressing his lips to her palm. Then he turned her hand over and slid his knife across her soft skin. She watched as the blood pooled there. Barren ran the blade along his own hand.

Cupping Larkin's hand in his, he dropped the bloodstone in the center of her palm. Instantly, the stone absorbed the blood.

"Larkin," said Barren, and as she looked up, his lips captured hers. He covered the bloodstone with his hand—and just as it had done in Larkin's hand, the stone absorbed the blood. Light burst forth from between their fingers, consuming them completely, pure and bright. The stone became like a hot coal in their hands, and it was as if it were sucking more and more blood from their bodies, for they weakened quickly.

As the pain grew, Barren held their lips tight. The edges of the stone pierced their skin as it began to crack, pulsing with life. The light grew brighter, and the stone hotter—it fueled the passion of their lips, the heat of their skin, until they could no longer stand. They crashed to the ground, barely conscious, hands still tightly intertwined. Though the light was blinding, they managed to open their eyes and glimpse each other—it was the most vulnerable either of them had been, the weakest they had felt...but the most redeeming decision they had made. And then everything went dark.

Chapter Twenty-Eight
TRUCE

Barren had a feeling he had been here before—it was a bright courtyard. All around them was greenery and in the distance he could hear water bubbling—he recognized this place as Aurum. Sitting on a stone bench were two very opposite looking people. One was a woman dressed in a white gown. Upon her head was an intricate headdress of silver and glass beads. Her hair was golden, streaked with near-white strands; it fell in layers down her back. Her skin was milky white against that of the bronzed man she smiled at. He was dressed in brown tones and wore muddy black boots. A leather hat covered oily blond hair, but his smile was just as bright as hers.

He knew them. They were his mother and father. They were images of perfection and they were bright and happy and...in love. Barren wasn't sure why, but his heart swelled at the idea—he knew this was real.

Just as easily as Barren saw their images, they were gone and his body was being shaken. He opened his eyes, and the blurry image of Cove Rowell was over him.

"Barren! Barren! I swear to Saoirse if you don't wake up, I'll kill you!"

"Leave it to him to be sleeping on the job," he heard Leaf add.

Barren pushed Cove's hands away. "I'm awake!" he growled, but his hands felt rough and hot and his head hurt. He sat there for a moment, recalling what had happened before he fell unconscious. All he could remember was blood and fire...and then the clear image of his parents.

Suddenly he looked around for the compass. "Where is it?"

"Where is what?" asked Cove. He stood up straight, his arms folded over his chest.

Barren was on his hands and knees. A few feet before him, he saw the compass. He reached, grasping the long gold chain in his hand and he turned it over quickly. Ash blackened where the raw red stone had been. Relief flooded him—they had succeeded, but just as suddenly as he felt relief, it was replaced by dread. They had succeeded, they had lived...so what oath had dark magic bound them to?

Barren turned the compass over and stared at its face. The needle bounded back and forth. It was broken. He placed the chain around his neck and hid the pendant under his shirt.

He looked up at Cove whose brow was raised in question, but he said nothing as he extended his hand to the pirate and helped him to his feet.

"What happened?" asked Barren, looking around.

The room looked nothing like he remembered. Before it had been dark and cold, and now it was alight with the day—all the windows were uncovered, and streaming rays illuminated dusty particles in the air. Parts of the wall were blackened, and smoke still rose from the marks, as if something had scorched them. The raised pyre was still there, only it had been concealed by a velvet cover, so that the body resting inside had peace.

"You tell us," said Cove. "We found you and Larkin sprawled on the ground, and thought you were dead. You both had pieces of glass stuck in your skin. If you look at the walls you can see where the hot shards burned into the stone."

Barren started to touch his face, but Leaf slapped his hand away.

"You'll irritate the burns," he said. "It could have been worse. The shards could have been bigger, pierced your eye or your heart."

Barren rubbed the back of his neck.

"You sure you're all right?" asked Cove.

"Yeah, I am fine," Barren said lightly. "Where are the twins?"

"The twins and Christopher are being watched by Alex and Devon."

"Christopher? He's all right?" Barren was sure he wouldn't see

Christopher again, not after that snake carried him off.

"Yes, as far as we could tell. We came upon him in the forest, chopping a giant snake to pieces. I think he was scared out of his wits, because he let us take him hostage. He didn't demand that we let him go. He only asked for Larkin."

Barren's heart picked up pace. "Where is Larkin?"

"She is in the courtyard below. She found it earlier and hasn't left since."

Barren was about to move past Cove when the Ambassador stopped him and nodded toward William's body. "Did you?"

"No," Barren shook his head, and gave his brother a remorseful stare. "No, I didn't."

Cove nodded his head once in understanding and let Barren leave the throne room.

It took Barren some time to find the courtyard Cove had spoken of. He'd ambled down the halls of the Lyric castle, watching as the dust danced in the air, and the sunlight tarnished the walls. He could no longer feel the intense pull of the bloodstone calling to him, but there was still magic here. He almost hated that he could feel it.

At last, he came to the end of a hall that opened onto a wide terrace. Here, Barren stood before magnificence. Mountains rose in tall peaks and the clouds seemed to be only a few feet from him; their backdrop was a bright blue sky. The courtyard that rested before him was filled with yellowed grass. Images of what it had once been were still visible—tall stone arches made a walkway into the yard, and pieces of the same stone fashioned ruined monuments. One of those monuments, a woman with her hands over her heart, peered back at Barren from the entryway.

He stepped outside into the sunlight, and was overcome with a variety of smells—that of crisp, cold air, and decay. As he moved along, examining every inch of what used to be his mother's home, he wondered what it had looked like before it fell to ruin.

At last he found the figure he was searching for. In the distance, he saw Larkin's back. She was hunched before a piece of stone, her legs drawn up and her chin resting on her knees. He approached her carefully, watching as her hair twisted in the wind. He stood beside her; his shadow crossed a gravestone marked with her mother's name. Larkin didn't look up at him, and he knew why—he could hear her quiet sobs as she tried desperately to wipe her tears away.

Barren bent to his knees and sat beside her, pulling her into his arms and soothing her uncontrollable tears.

"I'm sorry," she choked. "I have never cried over her before."

"I understand."

Barren held her until the sun dimmed, and the clouds above grew a little darker. She pulled away, wiping more tears from her puffy eyes. He could see the marks on her face where the shards of the gem had burned her skin. He wanted to reach up and touch them, brush them away and forget that he had dragged her into this life...but without her, none of this—this triumph, this heartache, this hope—would be possible.

"I found her," she said, gesturing toward the stone. "I didn't think she was here. I'm so glad she is."

Barren nodded. "Me too."

They both looked at the stone. "I'm sorry about your brother," she said at last. "I couldn't let him kill you. It's ironic that I would be the one to deal the deadly blow when I protested his death so feverishly."

"It was not your fault, Larkin, and for all that it's worth, I am glad you were there to save my life," he paused for a moment and chuckled. "I think we're two for two now."

She smiled faintly, still fighting tears.

"Will you stay with me?" Barren asked so suddenly, the question surprising him, too.

"What?" she asked. He studied her face—her lips parted, and her hair stuck to her wet cheeks, but her tears paused for a moment.

"Will you stay with me? Will you sail the Orient with me?" he began to clarify. "I know a pirate's life isn't glamorous, and I cannot always offer you the best protection, but you can take care of yourself, and..." his voice faltered as he began to ramble and he exhaled sharply. "Please stay."

Larkin laughed, and then rubbed her face. "Yes," she nodded her head. "Yes, of course I'll stay. Oh!"

She threw her arms around him, and they tumbled into the yellow grass. Barren wrapped his arms around her, grateful that they had survived everything. Grateful that, after this long and arduous road, he still managed to have Larkin by his side, even if she had been the most difficult female he had ever encountered.

***

William's body rested in the dinghy comfortably, though the look on his face was not one of peace. The more Barren observed his dead brother, the more he wished he had spent the last few years doing something other than seeking revenge for his father's murder. If only he had known then what he knew now—that this would not bring peace, only heartache and a deep wish that nothing had ever come between them.

He felt a hand on his shoulder and he turned to see Leaf.

"Do not burden yourself with the way things could have been," he said. "He's in the otherworld now. That is the ultimate form of Saoirse."

Of all people, Leaf knew that best. Barren nodded and then moved to the head of the boat. Together, he and Cove pushed the dinghy into the Orient's waters. She rushed forward and grasped the ship with all her strength and propelled him along.

Leaf stood with his bow and arrow. Alex dabbed a few drops of oil onto a piece of cloth and tied it to the Elf's arrow while Hollow sparked flint against a stone. The flaming arrow was released into the air and landed with ease in the bed of hay where William rested. Flames erupted and consumed William's body. The pirates stared as the boat was taken away over the horizon. William would sleep eternally where he belonged—with the sea.

***

Barren walked the length of the deck, watching as his crew worked—Slay labored up the tall mast, heading for the crow's nest, Seamus inspected cannons and ammunition, Sam took the helm, and Leaf checked the sails. Cove, Hollow and his crew had taken on the duties of the twins, who remained below deck with Christopher, chained to the wall. Alex had pulled himself up on a barrel and removed the wooden peg from the end of his leg all while reminiscing with Devon and Em.

Barren came to the back of the ship, his eyes taking in the waning image of the island they had labored to reach. He almost felt that he was leaving a piece of himself behind. It was strange to have felt the power of the bloodstone call out to him, strange to feel it pulse in his hands—and now all that had faded, and what it left behind was a surprising emptiness.

"The name is D'Avana," Devon's voice rasped.

Barren turned to face the old man. Em was at his side. They were both watching the last bit of mountain disappear at the horizon.

"D'Avana?" asked Barren.

"The island of light and dust," said Em.

Light and dust. Barren had heard that before—from Illiana. She'd said she was of light and dust.

"Do you remember everything?"

Devon shook his head. "No, but I will let time give me back my memory—I am not too eager to remember the folly of my past."

"How many were there? How many Elves were like my mother?"

Devon shrugged. "I do not know, but if I were an Elf with the power that the Lyrics possessed, I would not tell a soul. It comes with too many responsibilities, too many expectations."

Em smiled at Barren, then she and Devon moved away from him. He turned his gaze to the horizon again. He hadn't thought about the prospect of there being more than three Lyrics. If no one knew exactly how many there were, how could anyone truly know if they were all dead? They'd already been wrong once. The thought bothered him more than he liked, and he pushed it away quickly.

Larkin approached and filled the space beside him. She didn't speak, but Barren could feel the tension rise between them and knew she had something to say.

"What's wrong?" he asked.

She didn't respond immediately. Instead, she leaned over the rail as if to get a better look at the Orient. At first Barren thought she would express more grief about William's death, but the conversation took a different turn.

"I saw my mother," she said.

"I saw my parents, too."

"You know what was strange?" she asked, staring at him. "I saw my father, too. It was an image of them together. They were happy. They loved each other, Barren."

Barren understood—Tetherion's words had been that they had used the Lyrics to gain what they wanted, disregarding all attachment easily.

"My father is going along with a lie and I don't know why."

"Perhaps he fears losing his title. Without his status, he has only one option: to become the thing he hates most in the world—a pirate."

"He did not mind that once," she said quietly.

"Then I'm not sure." Barren couldn't give her any more excuses for her father. "You can ask him."

She shook her head. "He will tell me nothing. In his eyes, I have chosen a side."

"Haven't you?"

She smiled, but it was a wistful smile. "I hope we are not always divided by sides," she said. "But, yes, I suppose for now I have chosen Saoirse."

***

The sun was fading, casting orange rays of light over the stone courtyard. The rumor was that Barren Reed had been captured, and he, with his crew, were en route to Maris to face their deaths. Tetherion had received Datherious's correspondence over a week ago informing him of their victory against Barren and their prompt return to Maris. Now, the courtyard was packed with people from all over Maris—the nobility crowded the balcony, while the peasants stood against each other, clustering around the gallows. Many were here because they did not believe the son of Jess Reed could be caught; they needed proof.

Tetherion knew his people were watching him closely. When he'd returned to Maris to find them revolting, he'd promised them justice, and now he was bringing it—as soon as Barren handed him the bloodstone. Tetherion clenched his fists in anticipation of the exchange. He would be the most powerful man in the Orient—no one could oppose him: not his people, not the Elves and their *magic*, and certainly not the despicable spawn of his brother, Jess Reed.

Trumpets sounded in the courtyard, and two lines of soldiers led a group of prisoners with hoods over their heads. The crowd roared with excitement, throwing vegetables, dirt, and rocks at the men who marched to their deaths. As the soldiers managed to make a path through the unruly throng, the prisoners stumbled along with difficulty, tripping over the chains that held them together. When one fell, the others would tumble down with them, lost in the darkness of their masks. It was almost impossible for the soldiers to get them to their feet again, as the crowd began to attack them—kicking, hitting or beating the prisoners with whatever was in their hands.

The captives were led to the gallows, and the chain that linked them removed. The hangman placed each man beneath his respective noose, and then stood back as Tetherion got to his feet.

"My people! Today you will witness justice! The tyrant Barren Reed has been captured and he will finally answer for his deeds!" There was a mixture of cheers and boos, and at Tetherion's words, the prisoners began to wriggle in their bonds, their muffled screams filling the air. Tetherion smiled. "But before we hang these selfish men, you should be allowed to look upon the faces of these murderers. Witness the man who killed your loved ones, take revenge upon him in death! Remove their hoods!"

The order came with a steady drumbeat as the guards returned to remove the hoods. The drumbeat ended and the masks were removed.

"Get them out of those nooses!" Tetherion roared. "Barren Reed! Find Barren Reed!"

The princes, Datherious and Natherious, stood with nooses around their necks, and their mouths gagged with cloth. Christopher Lee stood beside them, a scarlet scarf tied around his mouth.

Tetherion's rage stirred fear into the crowd and chaos ensued as the soldiers who led the prisoners into the courtyard rushed toward the exit, intent on finding the ship they had come from.

Tetherion turned toward one of his guards who had come from the ports. "Who delivered the prisoners?" he snarled.

"Why, Ambassador Cove Rowell of Arcarum, m'lord. Looks like Barren Reed fooled even him."

Tetherion's eyes blazed and he tore through his guards, intent on heading for the port himself. A sudden explosion caused everyone to fall to their knees—but just as suddenly as fright had shocked their hearts, awe replaced it as colors of blue, yellow, green, and red burst into the sky—fireworks littered the inky night, meant as a celebration of Barren's death.

***

From their ship some distance from Maris, Barren and Larkin stood on deck, watching shimmering explosions of light in the sky—it was beautiful—it meant freedom, but it was also a signal to run.

"Guess that means Tetherion knows," said Larkin quietly as they watched various golds and reds illuminating the sky off the coast of the island she once called home. Barren grasped her hand and drew her close. She rested her head against his chest, comforted by the sound of his heartbeat.

"Are you sad?"

"No," she said. "Though I never thought I would have to run for my life."

"It's really not so bad."

"Says the man who has been a fugitive since birth!"

"True, you are the only one who is new to that title, Lady Larkin," he mused.

"I cannot very well be a lady and a fugitive at the same time, can I?"

She pulled away from him, and Barren placed a finger against his cheek as he thought. "Well, you can be my lady and a fugitive to the government all the same."

"What do you intend to do now?"

Larkin didn't finish the sentence, but Barren knew what should come next...*now* *that William is dead. Now that your vengeance is realized.* That still made Barren's stomach turn. The thing he'd waited five years for was bitter and tasteless.

"You may disagree with my decision."

"And why would that be a surprise?" she asked, a smile turning the corners of her mouth, and Barren's matched hers briefly before his eyes became somber.

"I am waging my own war against the crown. I will do as my father did and impede the king's efforts for power, slavery, or anything I find in conflict with Saoirse."

"So where will you begin?"

"With the impostors, the privateers," said Barren. "I've no desire to see them taint what I stand for any longer."

"Will you kill these men?"

"I do not know," Barren said honestly. "If either I or my crew is threatened, I will not hesitate to end a life."

Larkin regarded Barren in silence.

"If you come with me, you may see things you never wished to see. Things that might make you wish you had never agreed to accompany me."

"Perhaps those things will be true," Larkin said, taking one step closer to Barren. "Or perhaps you will be ever-vigilant in reminding me why I chose the life of a pirate."

He smiled at her and then kissed her. It was a little simpler now, a little easier, and yet there was still something so new about her mouth against his—something that caused his stomach to flutter and his chest to pull tight with anxiety. Heat flooded his face, and soon his entire body felt like a hot spring. He pulled away, staring into Larkin's eyes, glazed with passion.

"I will remind you," he said, brushing his thumb over her lip. "Once I told you my heart was the only thing I was loyal to as a pirate." He grasped her hand and pressing her fingers to his lips, whispered, "And after all of this, it has finally chosen you."

ACKNOWLEDGEMENTS

CUTLASS is a book I've been with for almost nine years. I've been writing for ten of those. This book has seen many versions and many edits. What it is now is, I think, exactly what CUTLASS was meant to be. And while I am happy to move on to something else (like the second book in the Trilogy), I am also a little sad.

I have so many people to thank. The first is my Dad and Mom. I remember when I was young, I asked my Dad if Elves existed because I really wanted them to exist and he told me yes. He might not remember that, but I do. My parents fueled my imagination, and they completely and utterly believe I can be whatever I want, no matter how hard. I cannot thank them enough for believing in me, and reminding me everyday that I'm going to be a New York Times Bestselling Author.

Next, I have to thank my boyfriend, Armand. He, like my parents, has always been supportive of my dream and has helped me with that dream by learning Photoshop, formatting, and whatever else he needed to do to ensure my book had its best chance. I could have never asked for a more gifted and awesome person to be by my side during this process. I love you!

Next, my second family: Shryl, Allan, Shelby, and Strider. It all began with Shelby, who is such an awesome brother, he has saved nearly EVERYTHING I have ever written (which is also embarrassing), and then Shryl and Allan just adopted me. You guys are so amazing and so supportive.

To Mrs. Applegate - I cannot thank you enough for everything you've ever done to encourage me. I will always owe the greater part of my success to you. Thank you for reading my work from the beginning, for giving me a chance, and talking to me all those days at lunch about writing. As your former student and friend, I can say that, without a doubt, you are a prime example of what all teachers should be.

To my best friend Emily - Thank you for all your encouragement and reminding me of my purpose in life. You have talked me through the bad, and made this journey so much easier. Thank you for making sure I didn't settle and for listening to me complain a lot. In your own words, you are a B.A.M.F!

To my best friend Crystal - You've supported my dream since the beginning with small but important things like asking for my autograph. Thank you for your encouragement, and always believing in me. Thank you for reminding me that the decisions I make are never bad ones.

To Barbara - All your feedback and support has been amazing, and I'm not sure I would be without you! I know you always say I would be exactly where I am now, but I don't believe that. You are why CUTLASS is in this form! Thank you for all your suggestions, your resources, and your friendship! I love you and I love your books!

To Anne - Thank you for letting me share my story with you and sharing yours with me.

To Jason, Capri, and Elijah—Thanks for being my first #1 fans. You guys are awesome!

Thank you to my editor, Jena O'Connor! I'm so grateful I found you and that you were able to help me offer up the best version of Cutlass! You are wonderful and fast and sweet!

Thank you to all my friends, family, and fans who have supported me forever. You all know who you are. I love you.

©Ashli Amador Photography

ABOUT THE AUTHOR

Ashley was born and raised in Oklahoma, where the wind really does sweep down the plains, and horses and carriages aren't used as much as she'd like. When she's not writing, she's hard at work on her Master's degree in Library Science and Information Technology, working out, or pretending she's Sherlock Holmes. Her obsession with writing began after reading the Lord of the Rings in the eighth grade. Since then, she's loved everything Fantasy--resulting in an unhealthy obsession with the 'geek' tab on Pinterest, where all things awesome go.

www.ashley-nixon.com

www.ingramcontent.com/pod-product-compliance
Lightning Source LLC
Chambersburg PA
CBHW031413240626
47154CB00001B/23

* 9 7 8 0 9 9 1 1 3 2 3 0 0 *